# Wings of Friendship

Also by Ned Rorem

*The Paris Diary*
*Music from Inside Out*
*The New York Diary*
*Music and People*
*Critical Affairs*
*Pure Contraption*
*The Later Diaries*
*Paul's Blues*
*An Absolute Gift*
*The Nantucket Diary*
*Setting the Tone*
*Settling the Score*
*Knowing When to Stop*
*Dear Paul Dear Ned*
*Other Entertainment*
*Lies*
*A Ned Rorem Reader*

# Wings of
# Friendship

Selected Letters, 1944–2003

## Ned Rorem

Shoemaker Hoard

Copyright © 2005 by Ned Rorem

All photographs are courtesy of the author.

Library of Congress Cataloging-in-Publication Data
Rorem, Ned, 1923-
Wings of friendship : Selected Letters, 1944–2003
p. cm.
Includes bibliographical references and index.
ISBN 1-59376-035-3 (alk. paper)
1. Rorem, Ned, 1923-—Correspondence.
2. Composers—United States—Correspondence.  I. Title.
ML410.R693A4 2005
780'.92—dc22      2005003763

Text design by David Bullen
Printed in the United States of America

Shoemaker Hoard
An Imprint of Avalon Publishing Group, Inc.
Distributed by Publishers Group West

10 9 8 7 6 5 4 3 2 1

# Contents

# Preface

*"Les lettres sont des ailes de l'amitié."*
Madame de Sévigné (1626–1696)

Do people still write letters? Do the young still mail hand-penned *billets doux* on scented stationery that will be stored in cedar chests and wistfully reread decades later? Or are love-notes (and hate-notes) more often sent by e-mail, then forgotten? I, in any case, like most of my generation born in the 1920s—and like all literate folk before that for a thousand years—still send handwritten messages in stamped envelopes. These messages will arrive days—as opposed to seconds—later; other messages, typed on an old Olivetti, are preserved by carbon copy.

But although I've always kept letters from friends and lovers and relatives, it was not until around thirty years ago that I began making copies of my letters to them. Meanwhile, much of my correspondence, to & fro, now lies in the Library of Congress, and is hard to get to.

In 1930 Cocteau wrote *The Human Voice,* a rambling one-sided phone "conversation" between a woman and her unfaithful lover. We never hear the lover's replies, but it would be revealing, if perhaps less theatrical, to get his side of the story. Similarly with a book of letters. Though nine-tenths of such books (e.g., Nancy Mitford, James Agee, Paul Bowles) are one-sided, those that aren't are usually between just two people.

When Trish Hoard and Jack Shoemaker asked for a collection of letters, we agreed this would be solely my letters to others, not others to me, since others-to-me would involve endless permissions, refusals, payments, long waits. (If legally the paper belongs to the receiver, the ink belongs to the sender.)

About four hundred letters are now at the Library, with the understanding that I'll annually augment the store from the thousands still in the home file. From the home file, dating generally from after 1970, the present book is formed. A few earlier letters (to Virgil Thomson, my parents, Frank O'Hara, etc.) are included here, thanks to various libraries and to heirs of the recipients.

With Shoemaker & Hoard we also agreed that nothing in French be included (Gide, Cocteau, Marie-Laure de Noailles, etc.), and that the inclusions be chronological; thus various personalities crisscross over the decades. The only letter chronologically out of place is the first one, to the *Times Literary Supplement* in London, which is a review of Prokofiev's letters, a review that explicates my notions about the genre.

How different I seem from year to year, from receiver to receiver, yet not really so different. How I would love to have you know how the other half reacted, a half that might seem my superior literarily and emotionally; or to have you eavesdrop on conversations with, say, Jerome Robbins or Carl Van Vechten. That may be for next time. For now, a word on various recipients.

Claude Lebon, a musical dentist, broke my heart in 1956. The letter excerpted here, originally in French, never sent, is a long, long *cri du coeur.* Forty years later, he killed himself in Paris. . . . Daron Hagen was among my first composition pupils at the Curtis Institute. . . . Leontyne Price is America's greatest soprano, while Reynolds Price is Carolina's foremost prosifier. . . . Norman Podhoretz, whom I knew first at Yaddo, and who solicited two articles from me for his magazine *Commentary,* was a left-winger who turned far right.

Alfred Kinsey, whom I met through mezzo-soprano Nell Tangeman in 1948, interviewed me as well as both my parents. He was planning a book on the sexuality of artists, and after the formal interview, I gave him some off-the-cuff lowdown on who "was" and who "wasn't" in the music world. A year later, while living in Morocco and France, I wrote him to *stop the presses!:* sexual behavior outside the U.S. is something quite else.

John Simon too had preconceived misconceptions on homosexuality, as is suggested in one long letter here.

Frank O'Hara I met in 1952 at John Latouche's on a brief trip back to New York from Paris. Immediately we began corresponding and, indeed, collaborating. His aperçus on what an American opera should be are so much more lucid and concerned than mine. His death by a beach taxi, while visiting Morris Golde on Fire Island in 1966, stunned us all. He was the first of the so-called New York Poets (with Schuyler, Koch, Ashbery) to vanish. I set to music all of them extensively, but their close relation to the sonic art is never, but never, mentioned by critics and biographers. In America the arts do not interconnect.

Gloria Vanderbilt has been a precious friend since first, with many highs and lows, we were introduced in 1962 by her fiancé Wyatt Cooper. Likewise Glenway Wescott (a pioneer novelist) since around 1959.

Gunther Schuller is a staunch colleague with whom I sometimes disagree.

. . . John Cage, who always seemed more a zany theoretician than a composer, forced me once to say: "What a fake! Yes, but a fake what?"

Gary Graffman, in the sixty years of our acquaintance, has become the world's grandest keyboard virtuoso, for whom I composed a Left-Hand Concerto. . . . James Salter and Romulus Linney are my favorite fiction writers, except for Edmund White and John Cheever. Gary Schmidgall and Andrew Porter are my favorite nonfiction writers, except for Edward Albee and James Hamilton-Paterson.

Rosalyn Tureck, who played Bach on the piano, persisted in crippling the melodic line with mordants and trills, which were originally used to simulate a sustained tone on the nonsustaining harpsichord, but are unneeded for the pedal-piano, which Bach never knew. That was our chief bone of contention.

Virgil Thomson was my first and only boss when in 1944 I worked as his copyist in exchange for orchestration lessons. I learned more in six months than in my six years at Northwestern, Curtis, and Juilliard. . . . Through Virgil I met Lou Harrison, who also taught me a lot in just six hours. . . . During that time I lived with Morris Golde at 123 West 11th Street.

Except for Myrna Loy (and in France, Jean Marais), Angela Lansbury is my only movie star. Also connected with movies was director Jim Bridges, Jack Larson's partner when I first knew them in 1962. . . . Stephen Sondheim: another staunch colleague. Likewise Lenny Bernstein, whom I met in 1943, just before his overnight burst into the stars.

Howard Moss and Charles Henri Ford couldn't be less alike as poets, one being the "formalist" poetry editor of *The New Yorker,* the other a self-styled surrealist and founder of *View* magazine during the war. Both supplied verse to be musicalized by my pen.

Paul Bowles was the first professional composer I ever met. I was seventeen and in Mexico with my father (who nobody thought was my father). Jane Bowles was there, too, contagiously appealing, "bohemian" in contrast to Paul's "propriety." They both remained my staunch acquaintances for the rest of their lives.

We changed each other's lives, Judy Collins and I, beginning in 1975. Her artistic world, like that of Bobby Short, ran parallel to mine without overlapping. Then by another turn of the screw they overlapped. André Previn too is of two worlds.

Eugene Istomin was my classmate at Curtis in 1943. Russell Platt was my student at Curtis in the 1980s. Claus von Bülow, Carl Van Vechten, and David Diamond are old friends from the 1950s. So are James Purdy, James Lord, and Gore Vidal.

Jack Larson (Jim Bridges's friend) was my collaborator, as was Kenneth Koch. Dolores Fredrickson, the midwestern pedagogue, wrote an article on my piano music. Cynthia Ozick and John Ashbery are the day and night of my "inspiration." David Del Tredici is an affectionate ally.

Have I forgotten anyone, or are there just forty-nine? On another day, in another book, there could be forty-nine quite different mortals. And my voice would sound quite different. Though that's not for me to say. Only to write.

*Ned Rorem*
*January 2005*

# Wings of

# Friendship

Selected Letters, 1944–2003

# By way of introduction:

To WILL EAVES

*Times Literary Supplement*
*August 1998*

Dear Mr. Eaves—
Here's the review of Prokofiev's letters.

It is idle but fun to ponder the rapport between artists' lives and their work. Idle, because nothing can be proved about the resulting value of the work (a good man may produce bad pieces, a bad man masterpieces); fun, because everything counts in an artist and all angles intermesh. But how? Does Dora Maar resemble her portrait by Picasso? Does the portrait resemble Dora? Does she resemble her own self-portrait? Does Dora resemble herself? When it comes to letter writing, do artists resemble their letters? Yes, except when they don't. Each case defines itself. By definition an artist resembles his letters because he wrote them. With professional authors this assertion is most tangible, since letters, like their books, are made from words.

"Letters," said Madame de Sévigné, who wrote the best ones of her century, "are the wings of friendship." The metaphor describes a mode of communication that endured for millenniums, until around 1950. (No one writes letters much anymore.) If Madame de Sévigné's sole literary oeuvre lay in her well-paced, revelatory billets-doux, prolific novelists and poets, like Henry James and Frank O'Hara, spent countless hours on scattered missives about recipes and philosophy and the heart laid bare, all penned in the same colors as their professional output. Yet letters by other great authors are of the terse "to confirm Tuesday at five" type: they are loath to squander style on mere correspondence, even to loved ones.

With composers the rapport is tougher to locate, since music—at least non-sung music—can't be proved to mean anything. (Mendelssohn: "It is not that music is too vague for words, it's too precise for words.") Dozens of composers are skilled prosifiers—Schumann, Berlioz, Debussy, Stravinsky, Thomson—but their subject is invariably their craft or autobiography. True, some write their own librettos (Wagner, Blitzstein, Menotti, Floyd, Tippett), but who besides Paul Bowles leads two independent careers, as musician and fiction writer? (Unless you include Noël Coward.) Bowles's music is always *vraie naïve*, heart-on-sleeve, vaguely inexpert and cheerful. His letters, cool and adult, resemble his morbid fiction, though dare one claim he's schizoid? Meanwhile, the letters of the musically suave Mozart and Ravel and Britten could have been scribbled by ten-year-olds.

Sergei Prokofiev, who died in 1953 at sixty-two, lived into the final epistolary generation. What "kind" of composer was he?

In Chicago during the late 1930s I and a couple of other fledgling composers were educating ourselves not on the classics but on the music of our day. The genres were broad, but quality ruled. Stravinsky was on a par with Cole Porter, as was Milhaud with Duke Ellington, and Ravel with Gershwin, who both died in 1937 leaving us bereft and feeling near to them. Many passed through Chicago, and we experienced (without judging) them in the flesh. Rachmaninoff was the performer who also composed, Prokofiev the composer who also performed. No one was "better than," though some lingered longer in the air. If we sensed that Shostakovich at his best was deeper than Prokofiev at his best, Prokofiev at his worst was more fun than Shostakovich at his worst. Prokofiev's "best" lay in the two Violin Concertos, his own recording of the Third Piano Concerto, Ashton's campy ballet called *Gala Performance* based on scores never intended for dance, and the scary sonic background for *Alexander Nevsky*. We longed to learn whether he, and which other of the mysterious Russians, were homosexual, but Romola Nijinsky's biography of her husband was not forthcoming despite the scandalous comments on Diaghilev. We weren't sure yet whether music could betray the sexuality of its maker, but Prokofiev's sound seemed muscular (as distinct from Poulenc's), formally flawless (thanks to his fabled mentors, Glière and Glazunov), esthetically "barbaric" (meaning Slavic), with memorably solid and defiantly chromatic tunes (hadn't his young son revealed that "Father writes out the score, then adds the wrong notes"?).

In the intervening six decades my take on Prokofiev has probably not changed (I still admire him uncritically), though I think about him less. Now here comes his *Selected Letters*, bringing back the good old days.

Harlow Robinson, who teaches Modern Languages at Northeastern University, translates from the Russian with far more grace than the much-touted Richard Pevear and Larissa Volokhonsky, whose current renditions of Dostoevsky are unreadable. Robinson, a Prokofiev specialist, has now assembled ten chapters of correspondence, devoted to ten recipients plus two or three random others, all of them Russians, and a few responses for continuity. Each chapter is preceded by remarks as instructive and interesting as the letters themselves.

Jascha Heifetz (hyped on the jacket) is granted five innocuous lines, in contrast to III pages devoted to Prokofiev's lifelong colleague, the symphonist Nikolai Miaskovsky (not on jacket). The other addressees, four female and seven male, including Diaghilev and Eisenstein the filmmaker, share around forty pages each. If his salutations to Olga Koussevitsky and Eleanora Damskaya seem a touch coy ("I kiss your little white hands"), how about for Miaskovsky ("I kiss you on the lips," and later: "Aslanov is so in love with you it's disgusting")? These are innocent Russianisms; he wrote much the same, in style and content, to all his pals. The tone of these several hundred missives hardly swerves from recipient to recipient. The "Russianisms" do not extend to being mad or morose, philosophical or fantastic, haunted or just drunk. As a man he was apparently *terre à terre*, a practical joker, optimistic.

Books are not mentioned except as they obtain to his operatic settings *(War and Peace, The Gambler)*, and even then the authors are not examined with the insight he presumably reserves for his musical approach to them. There is not talk of food, nor of love, nor of sex, much less gay sex. The only hint is in reference to Nicolas Nabokov in 1927: "... his music is rather light; the attraction seems to lie in the spiciness of the Nabokov-Diaghilev combination," to which Robinson in one of his 900-plus footnotes explains: "Prokofiev is referring to the romantic attraction between the two men." But the much-married Nabokov is the one member of the dramatis personae that I myself knew, and he was straight as a die.

There is little talk of health, his own or anyone's, which made him impatient. He believed in Christian Science, of which he often spoke. There is little talk of death, and when there is, it seems a mere prelude to more urgent matters. To Meyerhold in 1929: "First of all, let me express my deepest sympathy at the loss of your daughter. Although I didn't know her, now that I'm a father myself I can fully sympathize with your sorrow. You probably received my postcard from Brussels, where I want to start rehearsals for *The Gambler.* . . ." As for being a father, there is little talk of that, or of his wife, except in passing. ("Lina sends love.") Even his touching paragraph on Diaghilev's demise evinces mainly concern for his own career.

There is little talk of politics, even during the Revolution of 1919, and no talk of religion. And despite wide travels when most of these letters are sent, there is little talk of the look of a place (with the exception of Cuba and Cleveland), nor indeed of any visual art. Finally, though there is continual reference to his work, there is little talk of *method,* nor of when and where he labors, nor of the grief or joy it provokes.

What remains? Business chat mostly—contracts, engagements, ticket prices—and the rest is gossip. The business chat is stunning to a composer in our philistine aftermath. Virtually every ballet and concerto and symphony and opera he composed was in rehearsal in every port of the globe every week of the year. Their publication in print seemed to materialize from nowhere, as did commissions and requests for his engagement as a pianist and conductor in forty cities in six months. When did he find time to travel from Cairo to Omaha, to sire a family (presumably a faithful husband), to write a dozen letters a day, to arrange for readings by major orchestras of all his friends' music, much less to compose his own huge catalogue of concert fare and movies?

The gossip? Well, all literature can be conceived as gossip on some level. Prokofiev's letters are never literature (nor have they the finesse of even his slightest musical étude), but they are deliciously readable, and contain a critique—mostly dismissive—of all that was new in music during our first half-century. "Ravel's Concerto is rather dry, but still superbly written." "Roussel is not a first-rate composer." "Medtner performed his new sonata . . . dreadfully boring and unnecessary." He was not cowed by his seniors. "Rachmaninoff performed with the proper ordinariness." And later: "He played a most atrocious program excellently. Ever since he had his hemorrhoids surgically removed, he has become noticeably more cheerful." He was contemptuous of the United States and Les Six. "That son of a bitch Koussevitsky . . . also served up a symphonic piece by the American Copland —I nearly died of boredom." "The Tailleferre is nonsense, the *Promenades* of Poulenc are also rather bad." He continually chided his beloved Vernon Duke for selling out to New York with his "tra-la-la" music. Prokofiev despised jazz.

In his messages to Miaskovsky in 1913 we read a report on all the ballet novelties. The assessment of *Petruchka* could have been written today, so cannily does he accept the "modernism" and the use of "fillers": ". . . And even if we agree that Stravinsky is trying to open a new door, then he is opening it with the tiny, very sharp knife of the quotidian, and not with the big axe that might earn him the status of a titan." Three years after he changes his tune. "Stravinsky and I have become good friends. We get along very well both as individuals and as composers. His new *Pribaoutki* with orchestra is just remarkable." But Ravel's *Daphnis* "is boring and amorphous—it makes you sleepy when it's being poetic and makes you laugh when there's drama and movement . . . [while] Florent Schmitt with his *Tragédie de Salomé* is just vulgar." Et cetera.

He was a paradox. Prokofiev cared deeply about music while remaining always somehow aloof. To his friends (all of them musicians) he was generous with time, money, and connections, yet showed streaks of schoolboy meanness. Was he perhaps more of a friend in letters than in person?

And was he saying the same thing in music as in words? I wouldn't know. If the arts could express each other, we'd only need one art.

## Part One

# 1940s & 1950s

## To Virgil Thomson

*123 West 11th Street**
*New York 11, N.Y.*
*August 23, 1944*

Dear Virgil,

I've finished copying the "Meditation" (as per directions) & now have the parts to do.

Father was in town last night and I had another long and slightly harrowing talk with him, the final result being: that I can study here (with individual private teachers, as you and I had planned) with the provision that I continue working 4 hours a day for you (which would give me the $20 a week which I told him was the amount necessary for my education), and he will give me $20 a week to live on. If I manage to get lessons for less, I can keep the difference.

This will all start around October 1st or before, and since you won't be in New York before then, can you give me the names and addresses of the people I'll need to look up so that I can arrange with them fairly soon the matters of time, price, etc.?

Hope you're having a nice healthy time.

Affectionately,
Ned

## To Virgil Thomson

*6-17-46*

Dear Virgil—

Meant to tell you in my other letter that I recently bought a copy of your *Stabat Mater*, which I had never heard (or even seen) before, and while playing it through on the piano I found it so natural and perfect in prosody, so beautifully simple, and so un-ornately religious, that when I reached the last page where the strings have their two little finishing measures, I was moved to the point of weeping.

Affectionately,
Ned

---

*The return addresses, here and elsewhere, are those of Ned Rorem.

### To Virgil Thomson

*9 May 49*

Dear Virgil—

I do hope you'll be able to come to a going-away party I'm giving for myself this Saturday (the 14th) from 5 to about 8—because we never see each other anymore (it's been nearly a year), and I *want* to.

But if you *can't* come, maybe we could get together before I leave for France on the 25th.

And I'd like to play you some new stuff; I'm *so* much better than I used to be. Or you could hear it, if you're interested, when Leon Kirchner and I are having a forum May 19th at Macmillan Theater.

Much affection

Ned R.

### To Virgil Thomson

*c/o Dr. Guy Ferrand*
*Hôpital Indigène*
*Fès, Morocco, N. Africa*
*9 September 49*

Dear Virgil—

The night of Nell Tangeman's party (after my Columbia Concert May 19), you mentioned that when I returned from Europe in the Fall you could give me a few lessons in *form*—as you felt you knew exactly where my weak points were. . . . Did you *mean* it?! Because I really feel in need of such aid. If you were really serious, here's my situation:

I have a boat ticket back to America for Dec. 9 which would get me there in order to start lessons just after Christmas. But I want awfully much to stay on over here, and will probably cancel my sailing if you think I shouldn't have the lessons (though they're *very* important). . . . I doubtless *couldn't* pay you in cash unless I got a Guggenheim (for which I've just mailed my application with your name as reference), but could copy music as before. So will you let me know?

I've been living in Morocco now about 2 months, 300 miles south of Tangier where I spent last weekend with Paul & Jane Bowles. I'm very much in love for the first time in years—the country's bewitchingly beautiful, and I'm working hard and living quietly. Here's a little snapshot of me. Going back to Paris around the middle of October.

(Oh!—I might *have* to come back to join the Army—but I hope *not!* Also to do a play. I hope *so.* And then I could pay you.)

All my best—

Ned R.

## To Alfred Kinsey

> *Hotel Cocard*
> *Fez, Morocco*
> *(Af. du Nord)*
> *Dec. 1949*

Dear Dr. Kinsey—

This has been my home now for 7 months; a paradise where I've never composed so well or been so happy, and where certainly you would find a fruitful and different source of information for your work. . . . In three weeks I go to Italy to do concerts of American music with Nell Tangeman. . . . A very good and productive New Year to you.

Sincerely—

Ned Rorem

## To Virgil Thomson

> *53 Rue de la Harpe*
> *Paris*
> *15 April 50*

Dear Virgil—

Morris Golde wrote to my parents (who in turn wrote me) that you had told him that I had just received the Lili Boulanger award. But I have had no direct news about this, and Nadia B. isn't in town at the moment.

I'd appreciate it very much if you'd let me know something more about it—some details—when I'll get the money, etc. I'm certainly excited by it all —but vague too.

Paris is warm, glowing, and beautiful this Spring, though I find I miss the security I had in Morocco. I shall return there in June.

Working well.

Much affection—

Ned Rorem

To Virgil Thomson

*66 Rue des Saints-Pères*
*Paris*
*27 March 51*

Dear Virgil—

Being aggressive enough to send you this picture which you might be able to use sometime (not having an agent I suppose I might as well send it to you myself, don't you think?).

I miss you very much but I'm never coming back.

A Symphony of mine's being played in Vienna tomorrow. Can't go— train strikes—and naturally that depresses me. So maybe I'll leave Paris again, perhaps for Morocco. For it's hard to know if a city, like this so very sentimental one, is good to a composer who wants to work. I've been being kept by a woman named Marie-Laure de Noailles who drove me nearly to suicide, and though she's quite influential no one takes her friends very seriously.

Would like very much to see you but don't suppose I will.

Much affection anyway.

Ned (Rorem)

To Alfred Kinsey

*11 Place des États-Unis*
*Paris XVI*
*23 July 53*

Dear Dr. Kinsey—

Thank you so much for your good letter which touched me all the more, realizing how very busy you must be. . . . I do hope that one day you'll be able to do some research in Europe. After nearly five years I have realized that the sexual psychology of the European (the Latin—*not* the Scandinavian) is quite different from that of the American. This is because he is Catholic—whereas even the American Catholic is essentially Protestant (Puritan) by nature of being conditioned in a Protestant country. I can't even mention Morocco—where I lived for two years—it is so very far from what we Americans have been taught to think.

I've been working very well since I went away and have had a good many performances all over Europe, as well as giving concerts of my own music. I see Nell Tangeman from time to time when she comes to sing at the festival in Aix-en-Provence. . . . I still have my bad habits: I drink too much (but all I do is excessive); though I feel myself happier than the average man—and I love my work.

When will your new book on Sexual Behavior of the Human Female be published (in France)? All of my friends (especially women) are anxious to see it.

All my best wishes for your work, which I admire.

Very truly yours—

Ned Rorem

## To Frank O'Hara

*11 Place des États-Unis*
*Paris*
*3 Novembre 53*

Cher Frank—

*Finally* I've finished making a song from one of your poems: "Let's take a walk you. . . ."

And of course I want to send you a copy but am not at all sure of your address. Could you send it to me *quick* (& also some more good poems maybe)?

Tell me how you are—you and our friends; New York's so far away!

Winter's come and I'm going on tour in Germany.

I think of you tenderly—

Ned Rorem

## To Frank O'Hara

*11 Place des États-Unis*
*Paris*
*24 Nov 53*

Cher Frank—

You've probably already received the song. I've received the new poems and *like* them.

Bobby [Gold] and Arthur [Fizdale] are here and I've seen them several times. Tonight's their recital.

And we have an idea:

I want to write them a piece in 3 or 4 movements for 2 voices (baritone and soprano) and 2 pianos. . . . Perhaps contralto & tenor—but only *two* voices with 2 pianos in a regular 4-movement sonata form of 12 or 15 minutes. Could *you* write us the verses for it? It seems that Jimmy Schuyler has done something similar with Paul Bowles. *Our* piece could conveniently be performed on the same program with theirs. . . . I'm enthusiastic, having always wanted to do something for Arthur and Bobby, but never having the proper incentive, the human voice being my strong point. How about writing four love conversations?—a page each—with repetitions and very much in verse: a marriage, a quarrel, a making up, a divorce. . . . No, all that would be bad. At the moment I'm using lots of Dryden and find it ideal. . . . Something serious, romantic, with duets, sadness, a gay waltz, perhaps a blues song, no dirty words, maybe in strict sonata form—not too short.

Think it over, and let me know soon. The lyrical parts of *A City Winter* are good, only not in sonnet form or too "profound" or complex (in ideas) if sung.

We all send much love and want your news.

Ned Rorem

## To Frank O'Hara

*Munich*

*24 März 54*

Dear Ank, Frobby, Barthur:

For the past two months I've been here in Germany doing the enclosed program all over. It's a weird and different country from what I've been used to, but I'm beginning to kind of like it and to fall in love, et cetera. Public performance is a good experience for my introverted soul, and Teutonic influence healthy for all my Frenchiness; but I haven't had a moment for any composition and I'm beginning to miss terribly the *silence of creation!* Especially since the 4-movement piece I was doing for you was ⅔ finished when I left Paris—and then I had to stop. . . . Now—if I go to Rome for 2 weeks next month I won't be back in Paris until about April 20, plus 10 days to finish the writing, 12 days to copy, 4 days to photostat, and 10 days of ocean travel—which means the piece won't reach you till about June 1st. Is that O.K.? How do Arthur and Bobby like Frank's poem? And *what* can we use as a simple title? Also I'd like to know in detail how Paul B.'s piece was and went.

I spoke to Dr. Karl Amadeus Hartmann about you. He heads "Musica

Viva" here and is the most important man in Germany for contemporary music—but he *hates* (and is quite ignorant of) Americans. I told him all about you and persuaded him that you must see this country, etc.

So how are you? What are your plans? When'll I see you? Write me in Paris and send me gentle kisses, which I need. How was the Copland opera?

My piece is for 2 pianos, tenor, and mezzo (Nell Tangeman and David Lloyd). The story's a little like [Leonard Bernstein's opera] *Trouble in Tahiti*, don't you think? About 15 minutes.

All love—
Ned


### To Alfred Kinsey

*Rome*
*21.2.55*

Dear Doctor Kinsey—

How glad I was to receive your note of the eighth and learn again (through our bi-annual correspondence) that you're interested in following my progress from afar just as I follow yours in silence and respect.

Before I left Paris two months ago I saw Bill Miller who spoke of you with great warmth and friendliness. . . . Also Nell Tangeman is coming here in the Spring and we're to give some orchestra concerts together in Germany.

I've spent the winter in Rome which has been almost too sensual for my Puritanism! In about five weeks I'll return to Paris where I feel much more at home.

I was very moved that you thought of writing me again. Will we meet one day once more?

All best wishes
Ned Rorem


### To Frank O'Hara

*Florence*
*25-2-55*

Dear Frank—

Well, the first performance of our dialogs went pretty well. The next night we recorded them for the radio and they went even better with diction perfect and all your words coming out elegant. I'll try to get a copy of the transcription for us. . . . Enclosed is a copy of the program and also the *speech* I read aloud before the performance.

On May 9 my opera *A Childhood Miracle* (libretto by Elliott Stein) is having the first of five presentations in N.Y. by the Punch Opera, Inc. at Carl Fischer's. Will you get all your friends to go? It's just possible I might return for it. Otherwise I hope you'll send me a program, and I'll see you next fall.

Love—

Ned R.

## To Frank O'Hara

*Rome*
*12 March 55*

Very Dear Frank—

Perhaps you'll be pleased to know that finally the first performance of our four dialogues for 2 voices & 2 pianos will take place here on the Rome Radio March 24th. We're trying it out first at a private concert at the Contessa Pecci-Blunt's (ask Bobby). The performers are all Americans: Victor Delafosse, tenor; Nina de Courson, soprano; pianos: myself and a boy named John Moriarty. The piece takes 17 minutes and the execution will be just so-so (from the *ensemble* standpoint, it's hard to get it up in so short a time), but I'll try to get a recording of it for you which I'll send either via Bill Weaver or will bring myself next fall.

How are *you*, dear angel? My life's been sort of a nightmare the past six months, but is beginning to calm down a bit.

I'm returning to Paris on the 25th of this month. . . .

All love—

Ned (Rorem)

## To Frank O'Hara

*Paris*
*19 May 55*

Très Cher Frank—

Your detailed letter about my first opera was an instructive masterpiece. I'm going to propose our *Dialogues* for Punch's next season as an "operattina" to be used as a divertissement without action. . . . Since I didn't see my

*Miracle,* I can only suppose that all you said about it was just: I'd already shared certain of your reactions to the libretto. But then why don't *you* write the needed American libretto? Bill Weaver (is he back yet? tell him to write me, the bastard) is presumably doing one for me this summer and I *count* on it.

I just received the recordings of my *Symphony* and also my *Design* for orchestra is being premiered in Louisville next week: another U.S. performance I'm obliged to miss! But I'm definitely planning an extended visit to New York next Fall and then we'll see each other every day and I'll read all your writing.

Meanwhile my projects are undecided: I'm still in love with Italy, but cannot *practically* return there for the moment.... Have just finished a huge work, *The Poets' Requiem* (chorus and orchestra) and now feel "désoeuvré" —at loose ends.

Sam Barber came through here on his way to Greece. And Aaron Copland's here now; I adore seeing him again though he criticizes me like a *very knowing* father.

Dear Frank, Goodbye....

Maybe we'll see each other sooner than we think.

Love—

Ned R.


To the family, New York to Philadelphia

*30 January 56*

Dear Mama and Papa, Rosemary and Olga—

Just a quick note to say that the concert last night went wonderfully well: I played gorgeously and Mattiwilda sang divinely (as you'll hear on the records when I come home). You've probably seen the reviews in the *Times* and *Tribune;* there was also one in the *Journal-American;* but the best was in the *Post,* which I'm sending along with the *Telegram.* There was a big negro audience with a lot of old friends like Sally Simmons (who was in ecstasy) and Margaret Bonds; also Carl Van Vechten (now a photographer) who wants to take my picture! Dorothy came backstage to see me, looking stunning in a very fancy egret hat.

. . . We must now begin to think about publicity in the Philadelphia papers! . . . I'm not sure if I can get to Philly for the weekend: I have *so* much to do here. But I'll plan to come and stay from Wednesday the 8th. Morris

Golde wants to come down for the *Miracle*. Also perhaps Frank O'Hara. Are my *Dialogues* still scheduled for the 13th at the Art Alliance?

I had a million phone calls today, including one from Virginia Fleming, who wants me to accompany her Town Hall recital in April. I'm going to see her about it tomorrow; if she pays me enough I'll do it. The maximum price (including rehearsals) for an accompanist is $150; I'm going to ask $500. . . .

That's all for now—
all tender love—
Ned

## To Carl Van Vechten

*2 February 56*

Dear Mr. Van Vechten—

The other night backstage after Mattiwilda Dobbs's concert, you were kind enough to suggest you might like to take some pictures of me; then a hundred people came between us and we were unable to finish our conversation. I hope, then, that you didn't think I was disinterested: on the contrary, I was flattered, and would be glad to oblige at your convenience.

I've already seen some of your photos of Tom Keogh and Marie-Laure de Noailles. For the past three years I've been living at the home of the latter, and it was there I read your books—and with great pleasure.

Hope we might get together soon.
Sincerely yours,
Ned Rorem

## To Frank O'Hara

*15 February 56*

Dearest Frank—

What awful weather!

Thanks for your sweet note. I'm sick that you couldn't come to Philly (Elliott didn't come either).

Our *Dialogues* were done the other night in a performance not fit for man nor beast. It just wasn't any good; and the audience was idiotic. But Marc Blitzstein's sister got up and defended your words (as did I) at the top of her lungs. People just didn't *get* it.

Nevertheless it was reviewed, which is rare for this kind of program. They're enclosed here.

I do hope the Boston version will be better! When is it? March 6th? Should I come up?

When will you be here again? Call me the minute you arrive. . . .

I'm not at all in good health, but haven't time to see a doctor.

All love —

Ned

## To Carl Van Vechten

*March 56*

Cher Ami —

. . . and thanks so much also for the very gorgeous enlargement which just arrived today.

Perhaps soon we'll see each other once again more than through just the eyes of a photograph.

Your —

Ned Rorem

## To Carl Van Vechten

*Easter Day*
*1956*

Dear Carl Van Vechten —

The pictures *are* beautiful.

And there's a great deal of *you* in them too. *C'est-à-dire*, there is a sort of combination of the two of us which wouldn't have existed if I'd been in the same clothes on the same day at someone else's house.

I'm thrilled when I look at them. And so is everyone else who's seen them! Thank you.

I've been told you have a book called *The Tattooed Countess* which might make a good opera libretto. What do you think? Could you tell me how I might get hold of it? . . . I've always thought the *end* of *Nigger Heaven* would make a good opera situation too, but not the whole thing.

Your envelope was almost as beautiful as the photos (like Genet's jardinier *"plus beau que ses roses"!*)

All best —

Ned Rorem

## To Virgil Thomson

*24 April 56*

Très cher Virgil—

I can't tell you how very moved I was by your opera *[The Mother of Us All]* Monday night: everything about it. It seemed to me so *right* in all ways: beautiful music and touching words (so generously prosodized), particularly the part about Quakers—since I am one—and a troubling atmosphere that purified. Thanks, then, for writing it—already a classic. I'd like to talk of [Susan B. Anthony] more at length.

But it's not easy to find you on the telephone, and, since I'm staying on in America it seems, I'd wanted to speak to you of this and that. Do you think we could get together soon? You know it's intimidating for me to call great opera writers too often.

Your affectionate—
Ned

## To Frank O'Hara

*435 West 23*
*New York City 11*
*24 April 56*

Dear Frank—

Am sick not to have seen more of you at the party where I was too drunk to remember if I spoke to you of the following:

I've recently given all my mss. to my publishers Boosey & Hawkes who will act as agents for my unpublished works and who now need to "clear" all my vocal music written to words not yet in "public domain" so that they can pass out complimentary photostat copies for promotional purposes without being sued by the writers of the words in case the songs get sung. When they deem it profitable they'll publish the things I've done with you at which time you'll receive a contract or set fee or percentage of my royalties of the *Dialogues* (written in collaboration) and a set fee (probably no more than $15; you never make money on art songs anyway) for *Let's Take a Walk*. If it's all right with you, could you therefore write me a letter (signing your full name) in which you agree to liberate these two works for promotional purposes until the question of publication comes up? And would you do it soon?

Freezing cold and I'm sick. . . . I'm so tired. Wish I were elsewhere!
When will you return?

Your—

Ned

## To Carl Van Vechten

*Paris*
*9 November 56*

Dear Carl—

The other evening I went over to visit Alice Toklas. It's because I'd set
a little poem of G. Stein's to music: *I Am Rose,* and wanted to know who
gives permission of copyright before I give it to my publishers. She told me
to get in touch with you. Well, all I need is a letter giving my publishers
(Boosey & Hawkes) permission to distribute as many manuscript copies as
they wish for promotional reasons—and, in the eventuality of publication
of the song, the Stein estate will receive a set sum (probably no more than
$15) or else a percentage of sales (which would amount to even less). Could
you accord me this authorization?

I'm returning to New York in exactly a month, at which time I'll give
you much more news than appears in this letter. The world over here is in a
sad and depressed state of tension and panic, and I'm sick at heart at the
errors and repetitions of errors all about. . . . But that's not why I'm coming
back; it's because of an important 1st performance of my *Poets' Requiem* by
Margaret Hillis in February.

All my best regards to Sol, and to our other friends.

Affectionate greetings.

Ned Rorem

## To Carl Van Vechten

*215 East 60*
*New York City 22*
*29 March 57*

Cher Ami—

We don't see each other enough! and I'm sorry. Because I've thought
of you many times since the morning six weeks ago when you so moved me
by your telephone call in which you showed you'd understood my *Poets'
Requiem.*

Since then I've had a rather desperate season: I lost the faith of the person on earth most dear to me, and after such a shock of moral sinking I can only hope to rise again. But this can only happen with an antidote of a singular nature—and I don't know where to look. . . . Could you help me? you, who know everybody?

If I don't get a Guggenheim I'll probably stay on in America. At any rate I'll be here for at least five more weeks. During this time could we get together—or perhaps talk on the phone?

All my faithful best

Ned

### To Claude Lebon

*New York and Paris*
*March–May 1957*

Cher Claude,

You've come and gone.

I write to you now in my journal because I no longer dare speak. You've imposed a straitjacket, though if I could get out I'd be more useless than before: suffering only seems unreasonable to those who cause it. Yet haven't I in these very pages exclaimed that hysteria (as in Ionesco's theater) is the nervous disease that most galls me?

And I'm writing in French, because when I think of you it's in that language, and I think of you always. To hear it now hurts the heart. I've tried to rid my room of your traces, but go into the city only to find you there again in fifty souvenirs. I can't stop shaking. Every morning at the mailbox, knowing there'll be no letter, fearing what you might or might not write. All composers, like dentists, become, through the years and unbeknownst to themselves, sadistic, by dint of doing a job that obliges people to shy away. I reread new meanings into everything, from your first impotence of last October to your indifference of last month. Was it that in having, you no longer wanted? You said you'd loved me in secret four years before we met, for *my* indifference, but wasn't the result more conquest than affection? It's harder to investigate the shadows of one's own soul than of someone else's, but we've got to try, or we'll never know each other (though must people know each other?). You criticized me too much for me not to suspect a lack also *chez toi.* How many times a day you'd ask: "What are you thinking about?" You must contribute too a bit toward something you've half-invented. . . .

Once you wrote that I belonged to you. That meant ownership, not affection. To be jilted unexpectedly is rough. It's crazy what two people will do bad to each other, as though the world weren't going to anyway. Flay each other without anesthetic. I've never been left before. Yes, my vanity's touched: why not? Happiness is made mostly of pride. But I'm saddened by what will have been errors in judgment, in having selected someone unable to get over the shock of clay feet, the vague conception of what virility is supposed to be in anyone. Thank God I'll have learned it soon enough to be able to find a taste for life again—though not soon enough to have had heart bruised or ideas altered about what used to be called human relations. Now you lower your eyes before the deluge you've provoked. . . .

You used to miss me when I went to the bathroom. I'd based my life on such myths of charm. Now it's sickening to watch weeks go by without the relief of change. A month ago I stopped living. One word from you (which will never come) and I'd start all over. It's not your fault if you no longer love: it's the one thing we don't regulate. . . .

After strong pain could one end up loving again the person who caused it? *Réchauffer la soupe?* Before seeing that person one plays the martyr through inventions of memory. Suffering of which we ourselves are the cause is harder to conceive; conversely, inflicted on us, it becomes all we know. What's pathetic is that the end of unbalanced love (what love's balanced?) is the sole situation we can't control. Less than war. When I think of all the hearts I've hurt! Yet now have nothing more to look forward to— anticipation being the very nourishment of life. Oh God Claude, Oh God Claude, *je m'étouffe!* . . .

Thanks to David Diamond, who had introduced us a week ago at the Scala restaurant, last night I visited Mitropoulos. Arriving at his bachelor quarters in the Great Northern at nine, a bundle of scores humbly under my arm, instantly I sensed his goodness, his open warmth, his resignation. We sat down to tea and honey. Ten minutes later I could no longer control the formalities and broke into tears. Mitropoulos closed the music he was examining, and asked me (why?) if I were being blackmailed. I began the story which flowed out like time and the river. He said look, let's forget the music for tonight and I'll take you to supper at the Blue Ribbon. Two hours later he said, as we sat over our empty cups of kirsch, looking straight at me, at the state I was in: "How I envy you! How I'd love to crawl, on the floor, in the mud, at the feet of one I loved. If you're strong you can rise from it all reborn, a new man with solider values. But I'm too old now!" And we walked back to his hotel through the warm March wind as he told me stories of his youth. Those words, his more than gentle force and beauty, were like an icy balm for the moment at midnight. But all melted again this morning. . . .

It's the first morning of spring and I wish I were dead. . . . Sexual tension's been horrible: there may be pleasure with others, but they don't exist when I think of what I liked from you, and you in me, and I catch fire and can't put it out. Are any two people alike? Your New York humiliation was beyond control: far from your milieu you functioned only as my friend. . . .

Yes, in New York I knew everyone, you knew only me and the need to get used to dozens of new circumstances in so short a time. I mustn't defend myself too much or we'll never be on equal terms. To be able to say: music must always come first! But I read and reread your letters, between the lines, a thousand new meanings. To have been so blind! and today clearly see those many moments you tried to escape at intermissions. How I understand your impatience to quit the bad dream of New York where you smothered like a kitten beneath a sow. Now it's I smothering, but don't need to kill myself. You've done it. . . .

Should I admit what I did? Two years ago I met a baker named Marcel on the Avenue Friedland. He specializes in pastries to my delight, then to my disgust explained how filthy his work was: peach pies covered by smoke and saliva. Anyway, we got better acquainted in a hallway, and saw each other maybe twice later, and then I stood him up, and that was that. Well, two weeks ago in fierce loneliness I sent a letter, a love letter, to *Marcel le pâtissier* with no last name on the street without numbers where he lived. The letter was returned: Address Unknown. . . . In *Other Voices, Other Rooms* there's a character in love who no longer knows where his lover is. He writes the world over, care of General delivery—to Oran, Frisco, Shanghai, Frankfurt, in vain. He hadn't got it through his head that the incident was one-sided, that it was finished, that his friend no longer cared. Today I'm that character, nor do I know where you are, nor have I got it through my head that you don't care, but continue to hope against hope and pray on my knees for all soon to be better between us. The worst moment of a life is when you look in the mirror and say (knowing it to be true): "No one wants you anymore."

. . . You dropped a bomb without turning to see the explosion, leaving me to limp through the ruins. But maybe he who's left is the more powerful—he held on. But the cause, the causes! You tell me that the mass of contradictions are contradictions only to me. Well, sure! And so?

I won't rest until they're swept up. Was it conflict of careers or a jealous disdain of my hamminess that got on your nerves? But I don't want your slavery—except to my body from time to time. . . .

Today's your birthday. Is it possible to dwell on you more intensely than I've done for the third of a year? Not a minute goes without wondering where you are and who you're seeing. It's classic—the banal fixations of leftover people. But one mustn't, at such moments, expect consideration from anywhere. Nor is there consolation in thinking back to our frequent conversations which remain my most valuable possessions. Your image persists like my love, my love and dreams vomit up a thousand pardons from which I awake each day with a face drenched in tears.

You left America a month ago, and since then there's been not one gentle word from you. If you could have foreseen the aftermath, would you have tempered your revenge? No. By accusing me of irony do you clear a bad conscience? But letting me destroy myself is a sin. Was I too weak or too strong for you? Could you tolerate such fishwifely questions? You make me dance to a whip of icicles yet won't listen to the musical shrieks I can no longer notate, notation which no longer makes a difference, the difference in your future loves will be lukewarm, but at least you'll never be the same again.

The weather's still marvelous this morning, sweet and silvery, bringing a terrific urge to make love, not done (or hardly, or badly) since you went away. With whom? The bizarre mixture of my talent and physique loathed or envied has never brought much more than sadness. Everyone thinks my narcissism is unequaled. *C'est faux.* I'm less sure than most, but openly admit what others hide like gangrene, and it's a fact I've been more loved than I've loved. To love is to put on the spot, whereas I take what I see and make it mine. . . .

I love you. Because you don't see as I see, you miss everything. But if you saw as I saw I wouldn't love you, for I need only mysteries. Music is a mystery. To *understand* music is to love it less. (I love it less and less.) Nor do you know much about me. It's better that way. I want to be *the* person for you, meaning the one thing beyond your work you need. Thus I could spend years away from you. Yet alone my successes would be empty: they need to be shared.

You simulate all emotions—which gives your face a stingy beauty. If my principal quality (quality, not virtue) is frankness, yours is concentration; you never lose a minute. Thus all your minutes are lost. Though maybe nothing's lost. Or gained. No love is happy. Art is happy, though life is drab. An only son is a child in a tower who, when he becomes a man, holds onto his independence as to his mother, that is, to something inexistent. . . . A free man? Free of what? For solitude does not exist either.

I show my foliage too much, heart, ruses, I shouldn't: I'm the mountain who goes to Mohammed. But no one changes anyone. Since no one has anyone, how do other people pass the time? Love is impossible. But when it becomes possible it's no longer love.

As I think incessantly on you, you infiltrate yourself like a jiggly flame between myself and the music staves. At heart I'm a good person; one's never credulous enough—not the French. My passivity is active.

To a point of sickness you're obsessed with freedom. But, I repeat, freedom from what? Liberty's just an easier path, and you'll find out one day too late. Love's a specific renunciation you ignore—a race in a labyrinth, and only young love lasts. One must descend, descend to the chest's roots, a hard trip for two. . . . I observe my errors. Don't you prefer someone soft whom you can, without complication, dominate? Are you "my type"? What's a type? Did you take for vanity what was enthusiasm? Do you have my number? Speak my language? Dig my camp? No. You don't realize that, like you, I'm French, and though the French might wittily be true to speech, they never, like Americans, boringly speak the truth. To speak the truth is to speak one-dimensionally.

I'll keep these sinister gifts in my red red heart until they mix with my blood through the dissolution of sweet events in a future as uncertain as your feelings for me, but no, no, what's the use, I give up, give in, surrender. Thrown to the ground I'd paw it, but no longer have the strength to say *au revoir* or *adieu,* because I can't stand anything anymore. A venture on which two beings mutually embark—if it must end, must end mutually. But that's easier said than done. Let me now take my will in two hands and rebecome myself without you. . . .

You're indefatigable because you economize the efforts of your heart. You will say: "What a beautiful picture," but not that Mary Magdalene was *amoureuse.* You appreciate a *chef-d'oeuvre* more than the heart that made it. That strength is in lack of reaction; those who don't react are dead. People passionate about the arts are heartless: green oils and high strings come before "real life." Yes, you do react, but it's so rare that the glow in your eyes is that of an unknown planet which I catch and freeze and hide away in a private treasure chest. Perhaps only artists (so-called) can afford the luxury of love or madness which empties and fills them, a lonely luxury by definition. I only like what I can't understand. But all masterpieces are a bit boring; it's hard to catch on quickly to new rhythms.

I have been too much loved, which has led me too much to drink. Truth to tell I'm shy with people. And animals. I drink only for the hangover from which emerges the moment of truth, the *coup de grâce,* the involuntary detail, the All of engrossment underlining laughter of human hyena females on a subway. Trees, porpoises, don't bother to laugh—or are they always? It's not that they don't give a damn: they don't *not* give a damn. There's a demon in sobriety causing wars that could be avoided if the sober realized they're really lushes who don't know it. Unfortunately most people aren't drunk most of the time. It helps in meeting people, a hangover, by its power for concentration: concentration toward a spot on the ceiling which eventually moves (it always *did,* but we never waited long enough in bed). When our ears ring do we listen? When the larks flap before our very eyes who sees them? . . . Hangovers make you receptive, hot and hungry. A stupor of illness permits focus on a thumbtack generating light of its own, a luminous jewel and our sole gift to the unknown. There's a fourth dimension to the hungover world through which we perceive the fifth-dimensional one of sobriety. Another is sobriety's prisoner with only three auras.

How *do* people meet? There is a look of possible love exchanged by strangers (at a party, on a bus) who, through shyness or duty, never speak—

and spend their remaining lives regretting the fact. Sometimes I feel the most faithful union is that sealed by a glance from a passing train to a boy in a pear tree.

Your systematic and somewhat inhuman way of seeing everything could end up exasperating me, making me so ill with jealousy I'd roll in your old sheets, bury my head in that drawer of soiled clothes like a bee in gray roses, eager to retrieve your crotch and underarms, needing to possess your yesterday's sweat. . . .

Always injure the perfect in a flash, then choke on your own sweet time, the virtues of idleness. (Play hard to get in haste, repent in leisure.) . . .

What an ugly sunset!

Yes, we act according to our dreams. Let's act according to our real needs and not have wars. Dreamer, I built from something real (our meeting) something unreal (your devotion), but since public opinion sways you, you strangle me at the very moment I cry out: *je t'aime!* Happiness is the perfect balance between work and love. But balance is stupid, and happiness should be aimed at only secondarily. Can you dream, you? Have you recognized yourself in any of these words? You bastard? . . .

For myself I dream of being tied down. But can any self-made oath truly help us change? How can we keep from being invaded by a sort of hazy sorrow at the futility of any try at loving? Finally love becomes only a frail scabrous game; and if, proudly, you show your tactics too much, you've lost before you've started. I don't know why you suggest that out of bed I may show no real interest in you, but you're not the first to say this. That bed, that wound, and I recall my long years of lying there inert and alive with a hangover late into the warm wet spring afternoons of darkness with curtains slightly blowing, and from the outside world came the far sound of separated children laughing or hammering, or the ting-a-ling of a Good Humor cart. You were then not yet in my life, and today I am no longer in yours though not two months ago you came over a toy sky to find me. And I'd even thought of suicide to clean up the mess. But one can see. Suicides which work, fail: having your cake and not eating, or something. So I try to be persuaded that music must always come first (will always be the one faithful love), and that creation is the genius of inevitable choice and elimination and seeing things as they are not. Thus seen, they become, since all exists. Literally I'm dressed in the skins of former love. And a lover is the worst rival since there is another ego to feed.

Nobody, even if he's fed up, has the right to do to another what you've done, in changing without warning, condemning without trial. Yet haven't I done it myself so many times? You claim you're the least complex of beings, and it's true for you who've never tried to know yourself as I have tried to know you. At such moments we find reproval or seek consolation in any breeze, and I came across a Whitman verse of unrequited love and set it last night to notes. . . . The headsman locks the dungeon and goes off forever calmly. Put an ocean between you and the prisoner and you've no more worries. Unless the prisoner escapes.

Love is mutual respect; I'd forgotten that you existed too. And love is always a game. And an invention. And what we learned in the last affair trains us what to unlearn in the next; yet when the next's over we realize that what we now refrained from was just what should have been done.

You helped me look into myself, so I love you, to know how to live this little life, and also, curiously because you didn't encourage me to love you. I love you for what you are not, with a constructive ego, the best way: one can't healthily love without faith in oneself; and though I haven't it any-more, it will come back.

April 1st. *Poisson d'avril!* Have lost nearly all the false narcissism which was nevertheless a refuge for one who lacked a base of self-assurance in spite of appearances. If I could replace it with faith! Only we know such good resolutions aren't easily realized. These kind warm days of early Spring I perceive through a fog seeping down my throat that makes me cough up dumb old things to be thrown at new ears.

Today if by chance you were to come across these pages you'd hate me in not finding yourself because you don't see yourself as I do yet you think you see yourself entirely. Never again will I believe what were nevertheless the dearest words I've ever heard—those murmured by you in discovering yourself *grâce à moi*. Pray God that if ever I'm granted another love it'll be on another plan or plane, because one can't ripen by always following (as one evening we longly followed your Canal Saint Martin) experience after experience in exactly the same fashion, unassured and possessive epoch after epoch. But this future love: could it be again with you? Even though you've withdrawn and taken back all you gave? Even though you've cultivated my soul while deriding my family? Even though we're new children about to inscribe on the erased blackboard? Even if I've started again to drink like a fish in former routines? Even when you deny old desires while the whole autumn through you struggled with me against an innate laziness (even to the point of wanting to do a libretto), and regretted only that you weren't the first of my loves (although you *were*—and I can't stop harboring that)? Even if you knew that now I stuff myself with sleeping pills (which used to appall me) in order to forget you a few hours a day? And even if you knew that I roam around each night looking for just anyone to fill the wounded bed which seems all the same to stay empty, empty, empty, empty? As long as you're sure of me this will be impossible. But the neurotic me *(le moi nevrosé)* of whom you once were sure, he exists no more. How I loathe you.

How I love you. Face growing gaunt and lips tight. Handsome does as handsome is. This is brought home so strongly now when entering a bar, and no head turns. Does a tiger consider the antelope's pain? or an Iroquois administer anesthetic before scalping? Suddenly today I am standing apart to see the young among themselves, their arms frailer than spider strands and voices like spider breath failing. But what unrehearsed voices! what strong, strong arms! Old songs, their skin, the tears, the expressionless, the isolating, the young among themselves. I used to think that being conscious of your own youth was a first sign of age. Nevertheless, the young, with all their teasy ways, *do* have smoother skin and see their whole lives before them. Or minutes. But minutes are life, and what can I look forward to but years? ...

For me there are no more first times. But at least the Lovelies of our cinema have more in common with me than Poppea—or even Lillian Russell—for the simple reason that we're all living now. And whether or not the Lovelies like it, they and I will forever breathe parallel lives. That's one consolation. Except for me, can the naughty old world pretend to give a damn (since it does give terrible damns), spinning, trapping, recoiling, conspiring, leading them to misfire? How *not* be consoled in knowing they'll finally die? Dear one, everything dies, even our children, even the sun.

Today I received this letter:

> Dear Mr. Rorem,
> Your frankness, and urge for outburst and exhibit of your distress is exactly the most important element a creator, a composer must have besides his knowledge. That is why your music spoke to my feelings and that is why I programmed it for the evening of 12 October 57. That is for your information, and as a kind of antidote against your actual poisoned condition. May thus, the power of a spiritual sperma annihilate the power of another wasted one!!
> With many friendly feelings,
> Dimitri Mitropoulos

Do you recall, in that Amsterdam hotel, the plump Negro girl whose window gave onto our courtyard, and on whom we spied at midnight as she, naked, fingered a silent keyboard with two dictionaries on her head? ... But where is a homeland when you've stayed away as long as I? America always seems home while away and a return is as inviting as the renewal of an old love affair. But being here, I haven't really *seen* New York, not knowing where I am now, nor how to take hold, nor the way to truly love myself, which would help me learn to love you. These many French pages indicate this, for I criticize you for being incapable of an "errand into the maze" and speak of the wounded bed as though it were a title. But have we a right to accuse others of failing at things we ourselves don't dare? Today is gray and hot with a lacy rain, and we're well into April.

How little nations understand each other, or try. That's said from the impotent placement of a poet who's spent a good part of his life liking an earth he's not understood. In Paris, an uprooted American, he was held secure by the balance imposed on a false shelter by two powers like winds battling. And learned never to expect anything from anyone except himself. Now he feels the start of a wavering. Which way? When, if ever, we see each other again, we'll be the same actors but in a new play.

After midnight. Weather's turned cold. Back from the movies, the movies where you always liked most to look at me—in profile with glasses. How I adored being alone with you! Never take a Frenchman literally: promises are no more than exercises in style. It's not for you I say it: you with a chest frozen before the prospects of a marriage which would have comprised so many readjustments. So you returned to a rich solitude. Where now are you going? who frequenting? what indeed was your former way? . . . Was I perhaps less capable than you of holding the reins of that heart-shaped horse, but don't realize it since you in detesting me make me want you all the more? . . .

To live is to make souvenirs, both in romance-memories and those left through solitary production. To love is to desire to live *with*, and is more than only life. Without it there is no reason, though reasons *for* it have no definition. Sterile today and tomorrow I'm making no memories. Have I an unrequited love for myself? . . .

There can be he who kills himself at the death of a loved one *not* so as to retrieve the lover in heaven, but so the two can be in the same position in relation to the world. . . .

To say: I love you. Look. A perfectly lovely sentiment. . . . Of course thoughts sound louder than words even if, alas, we only grow old above the waist. To think: just two days ago I was always the youngest at parties.

Well, that's how love is—don't we agree? Clenched heart, a parade of good-byes, then the long good-bye, a long postscript, an expedition of waiting. I remember the muse of love growing larger as she walked away with no cure for our sentiment trailing like a sick rat on a leash. But the impossibility makes love love, whose only clinching vow (we all agree) is dying. The desire fulfilled to be indispensable turns out duller than the disciplines of art. Oh, that dumb need to share. . . . Here lie I, caressing my thigh, and calmly file and clip and trim and smooth the ends of my chewed hands, lying demurely with lowered eyes in the midst of our vertiginous galaxy, for comfort offering order to the sky that doesn't know that it doesn't know. What goes wrong with chaos that we must classify? Must invent also a trap for the heart (I, for one, always fall in), hoping permanence squashes solitude. *Such* a habit! Yet try to retrieve it and find that now old lovers have new lives too (or has anyone anyone but himself?): that mysterious surprise makes us love them all the more. Absence, it's agreed, stimulates fancy. Wait, wait, and wait—kill, kill, and kill. Oh, I love you. . . . But when the door's finally knocked, *how* to react? Open-armed?

*Depuis que vous avez quitté New York* . . . since you left New York you've not unhappily left me but settled like lead even when I come home late on purpose from hollow exploits, torso gnarled as a cauliflower and nape bruised by strangers' teeth. You, though, crushed the heart into gelatin unable to harden toward new adventures as I stagger blinded among grimaces. The *cafard* is insistent, ever present, like a sentimental poison numbing. I feel I've no longer any power over anyone. Your letters which envied the joy I may have known previous to knowing you, which promised relief, now burn these fingers which begin to find a joy owed to nothing but self-inquest. I'm destined to live with myself so must get used to it. Later's too late, and you were too strong. Happiness may exist only in sharing and lovers have a marvelous solitude *à deux*. But it's also a selfishness *à deux*. How boring are loving couples to their friends! bereft of elegance or dignity! Whenever a friend gets married we lose him. How stupid the happy lover! and how stupid the rejected one! Fickle as fairies who break each other's hearts more easily than peasants twist geese necks. . . . You must never learn how indispensable, irreplaceable you've become, how I seek you in nightmares, and by day pitifully in the features of others, in wet places, bars somber and stuffed, or rainy streets or public baths, bottles of gin, or slimy mouths offered risibly. You resent what I've been able to keep of you in me, the you of yesterday who is no more and whom you've forgotten.

The sad thing is that we were both so weak, so dumbly weak after such wasted investments. Anyone's capable of 90 percent more than he does, but only inertia keeps us going. This evening I'm so depressed in remembering all the failures of my demi-life, in knowing suicide solves nothing since we won't hear the aftermaths. With all my heart I wanted this to work. It's the disappointment of a life.

. . . Love is a fantasy and no one's fantastic anymore. Shall I invent a fantasy for you? Listen. Since Youth is Body, that's what initially attracts. One step beyond creates a really physical romance. If the outside delights us, how much more gorgeous is the interior's clockwork of artery and purple nerves, its maze of muscle and yellow organs! Let's take a doctor as hero, since he (not a dentist or Jack the Ripper) normally explores the corridors around our bones; he, and only he, sees past the silly beauty of a face, can slash open his mistress's belly confronting all color, construction, and patient evolutionary threads. When alone he longs for the sight of his lady's lungs, the touch of her real heart, her cold odor of blood through a honeycomb-skeleton. He hears her veins and would lick her spine. . . . It began when an unprepossessing woman entered the office of my surgeon, who ignored her face and chest and tiresome complaints, but the instant of incision smashed heaven's doors: never has he known such a velvet liver whose cancer flows golden. With unbounded affection he weeps into her wound. . . . But she heals and goes off. He grows lonely, sentimental for that distant orderly inner room. Can his nostalgia prepare a trap into which she'll tumble and break her stitches, bringing her back exposed to his arms which will caress again the long pink warmth of her intestines?

Mitropoulos is right: remarkable health can result from abject dejection, and from rejection wherein one is nothing, nothing. Yet what's the use of being healthy in a sick society? I miss you as one of my own members which however I myself tore off in trying to understand, like children ripping open their dolls. To penetrate and receive in giving and taking through these two acts (which are really one) is to love. Each note of music is written for you, whether you will or no, so strong is the need to give, to give; and I need you because I love you, though I don't love you because I need you. I hope. Why not marry? You can't live amongst the willows and wasps as though they were your neighbors: man, dreadful as he is, is all we've got. Don't keep yourself from it.

I really liked being in your company. With P. in the old days I always felt: "Go away, so that I can see us in some relief." With you it's: "Come back, because I can no longer stand to think." But you're far off, and will stay far off. That first evening, you said: "The sad thing is that Americans must eventually go away." Later we concocted a love without identity.

During the past two months and for perhaps two months more I'll have gone from shock to paralysis to astonishment to rage to despair to *l'anéantissement* to uncertainty to resignation to selfishness to indifference to remembrance to forgetfulness. I don't wish you to be my life, but to be part of it, to help me again to hear the sounds of nature. These ears have grown numb in trying to become your equal. When we first met the days were growing shorter, colder. Now they're lengthening into springtime and it's possible that soon I'll return to Paris. To be acquainted with all the seasons in you so as to better analyze the source of this failure, to better feel Ives's music named "The Unanswered Question."

For weeks in the middle of the night I've burdened the saintly Morris Golde, wept and pleaded for advice as for a drug. With endless patience, he calms, suggests, tolerates, comprehends, lends his time as I crumble, and aids genuinely. Next day another shot is required. But I'll be forever grateful.

We failed thanks to the twentieth century. Because one flies over seas. Because one's in a hurry. Because so many of us see love as being loved (and we're right) that few are left over. Because of the difference between falling and staying in love, because we confuse relief-from-loneliness with infatuation. Loneliness is hard work, infatuation is laziness. Not just anyone can be unhappy—*n'est pas solitaire qui veut*. Laziness takes us away from the *practice* of love, like practice of music or dentistry. We're certain of only the past and death. *Et encore!* We're ashamed of love though it's the cheapest remedy for solitude. Or is love evil because it destroys the necessity of aloneness? Art's a substitute for love, but paradoxically on a higher plane. . . .

It's very late at night and I'm back from the Tourel recital with Jean Stein. Over the weekend I was drunk to obliteration, which somehow cleansed me nevertheless, awakening early in the headache haze to look closely and in a single dimension at my blanket of red and orange which became *childhood colors seen again for the first time*. Only a hangover can reproduce such a focus.

Have always felt a little guilty at liking what pleases me. From that comes excitation for music, pastries, and for certain acts of love. And from that comes the sadistic fear, alcoholic.

The courage of upset starts to evaporate thank God and I don't much want happiness but vital activity. A dentist plays God by fabricating a true part of a human body which his customers will carry around until death and long after. A composer can't say as much. Not to be able to love doesn't necessarily imply not to be able to love Ned Rorem—though you'd never believe it after all this. Nevertheless, disenchanted, you couldn't prepare me for the downfall. In *The Robbers* I have the Novice say: "There is a difference between the planning and the act." Can false love (oh my) be so fast substituted for true, as you maintain, without infection having germinated from the start? We never calmly asked where are we going? Have we tried to keep first impressions which are finally all that count?

Failed thanks to the century. . . . The French fright of being caught by feelings. Everything's now more hurried than basics, we've no longer time for anything. Americans are cured through excess, the French through ridicule. Modern life, alas, is no longer adapted to the Tragic. To perfumed wounds. Ridicule? An American's ridicule would be to go back to Paris and find you once again involved with a phantom. *Mais il faut être capable de tout.*

Am I going mad? Unfortunately not. Insanity means being unaware of insanity. . . .

You'll never be at ease in love for the simple reason that you seek an ideal. Now your ideal, being unique, by definition can't be found in another. All dies and passes: plans, youth, genius, love, combats, worries, works, and simple hearts. All passes and dies: young people with gorgeous genitals in decay, day and night and life and death die. A ship can sink at daybreak. What we've waited for all our life can come and go away without our recognition. Deceptions, disappointments disappear and die as well. . . . And my ultimate reaction is of great disappointment. Then, too, I'm a little scared of you. You, you, you! *Oh, toi!!* Otototototototototoi!!!

Easter Sunday. Awful hangover. Awful cold. Awful aches and pains from yesterday's excesses on 28th Street, awful heat. Finally will be the approach of an end to something, when you no longer need worry about where your next screw is coming from. "And why? Have I been too much loved," I wrote in June of '52. "I think I have been too much loved, and a little success is the same as a lot."

. . . The end of love is like the *Boléro* played backward. . . .
Rejected—*plaqué*—atrocious word. Admittedly of course I rationalize, ball you out, sing your praises while looking, looking for an urgent alley of explication, while the plain truth is that I miss you insanely. Tomorrow therefore, and wrongly, I'll buy a ticket to Paris, where I'll pretend to be indifferent. You see? . . . I'm less deceived by your attitudes about love than by your ignorance of friendship, your blind good conscience, by the risks you run without running risks. For instance, our last morning in Holland you said: "Well, tonight we go back. The pain if you said what a nice outing, and now *adieu!*" Tables turn. You speak in formulas as you act. I'd not understood, that night in Pigalle, when you said a *voyage à deux* would be

determining, for usually others tired of you in a fortnight; I'd not understood that "others" meant yourself. Not understood that, like 90 percent,
you existed through habit by surrounding with halos all passing excite-
ments. But to have humiliated me! I've thought too much about you lately
to have anything left to say when next we're face to face.

Why did you come to America if you knew from the start you hated
me? A demolishing Columbus needs funds. It's curious, even amusing, how
two beings tonight are intimate as twin embryos and tomorrow as distant
icebergs. You were the first to say *je t'aime* and the first *à rompre.* Show your
photo to another person and risk losing a bit of yourself; show a whole
scrapbook and you'll lose the other person as well. Happily life starts (or
starts up again) when love starts up again (or starts), and it's unimportant
*(et tant mieux)* that these actions reflect themselves infinitely. I've said I love
you to I don't know how many, each time was the first, and each sincere. For
the "always" of lovers is a Time set apart and out of daily usage. One has
time for everything if one wants: being busy's a pallid excuse. You'll see
when you grow up. When I grow up I'll have lost curiosity. Anger begins to
replace languor, it's health, are you glad or not? There remains simply the
question of faith. . . .

In Bernard Rogers's opera, Delilah blinds Samson with white-hot pok-
ers, then asks: And how do things look now? In *The Big Sleep* Humphrey
Bogart says: They knock your teeth out, then accuse you of stammering!
How's your quiet conscience? All around I see the same drastic mistakes
re-procreating themselves as if adults never had time to learn from their
children. In just two weeks I take a plane for Orly despite awaiting perils.
I'm afraid of nothing. But rumors of war thrill me less than the thought of
seeing you. (We'll know the answer in three minutes.) You dissimulate your
game so well! Not a game? Yes it is: silence is already a game. I lied from the
start. The result sickened and cured me. We've never been friends. Just
lovers a little, never friends.

Quite sick and full of codeine. The smell of your sleep awakened me.
Hysteria's turned to disgust. Kissing is a waste of time. My strength is
stronger than myself. I've a terror of being forgotten, from which comes the

strength, stronger than me, preventing fear of being forgotten, etc. The Nordic says love me or I'll kill myself. The Latin says love me or I'll kill you. . . . Love commences with shock and continues through habit. Six years ago I wrote: I'm the image of love, not the thing itself, and can't be slept with more than statues, though one takes statues to bed with faces impassive and shoulders stony. Which is why I weep, stones weep, because I was granted all, not part, and all can't be shared. Only the incomplete can enjoy love. . . .

Still sick as a dog, sinus infection, high fever, wandering about watching the quick flame of spring fertilize Manhattan, which bursts each moment into hot emeralds, all suddenly more close and precious, as always, now that I'm so soon leaving. The great heats, jonquil orgies on Park Avenue, and Central Park's again a cathedral of green lace over croaking kids and whining frogs in crocuses which strike at the heart like rattlesnakes, and the sky has a cloudless yellow smile as I've grown fond of someone who aches at my leaving and will maybe be glad when I return next fall.

Instantly there I am fortuitously precipitated into a monster gulf, a void, scabs ripped from the wound. Gradually the gulf fills up, with our own blood, blood of dizzy forgetfulness, a bit melancholy. Such are the ways of nature. A public cherub. With that face of yours *on te donnerait le bon Dieu sans confession*. But let's recall Marie-Laure's first word at your photo. *Sadique!* . . . I remark, seeing someone in the street, *je serais bien dans ses bras.* You remark, *ça serait bien dans mes bras.* So who's a mirror? And you're quickly discouraged. I've never been in so many beds as during these last ten weeks. You never especially pleased me physically, love seldom can. I'm quite another person from the one you last saw. A week from this afternoon the plane leaves for France. Lou Harrison has always seemed to me America's most *inspired* composer. Paris will disintoxicate these blue thoughts. We're all just customers to you.

Tomorrow I go to Paris. With a camera's accuracy I recall mirthlessly every minute we spent together. Am feeling little friendship for you now, letting myself be so guided by the heart, but was it really to the detriment of work?

*Paris, chez Marie-Laure*
Well!! We've met again. Last evening. *Nous avons même fait l'amour.* And though it didn't work too brilliantly (as you say) it was not so much

from my shyness as your casualness. Yet I think we both were moved, that you were even lonely and would start up again (on quite another foot, of course—we're no longer the same people, etc.). Maybe I'm wrong. You know, I rather despised you later? All the same, in the taxi home there was sorrow caused by the strange-familiar streets of your far part of town, your slaughterhouses of La Villette, the heavenly prison of blue Paris again. I'd sworn never to confront you with injustices, nor will I (*d'ailleurs* you'd shield yourself French-style) since vengeance is not a strong point. But neither will I ever tell you my true feelings. But will tell you this because you want to know: yes, I still love you (what a dull word now) but with a love denuded of gentleness, one doesn't feel gentle toward the heel of a shoe. So much was, and will remain, unsaid. No doubt best. I only ask to see you amicably, painlessly from time to time. But yes, I detest you somewhat. So take it easy for God's sake, you are a careful surgeon after all, and your hand's too magic on the flesh—don't step in those screwy corners of my lungs.

I'm not sorry you didn't suffer, Claude; I'm only surprised you think you're incapable of suffering. But you don't give yourself time. Try. Less masochist than a sleepwalker. (Though I've seen you suffer.) Anyway *I* have, and can't begin again as though nothing had happened. Do my ears deceive me! You speak of trips to Rome, joint excursions to the *fête à la* Place de la Nation or the Château de Vincennes! Remember my memory and wait a while. . . . Yes, I was tempted to write you. But you never answered my last (the one that began with the passion of Hungary), and besides, what's the use? On the other hand I wrote all those slobbery pages with the half-veiled notion that one day you'd look. And you will, maybe not right away, maybe with a little embarrassment and a lot of boredom because you won't find yourself but you'll find me and understand the privilege of contradictions uttered in self-defense to keep me breathing.

Do you know what touched me most last night? When you said: "No one phones unless they've got a toothache." Know that I'm here, like you, am glad to see you, have some things that belong to you.

I've no more time to lose with those who don't pay me court. It was myself who made me suffer, not you; myself who was able to endure the purge, not you. Anyone else could have been an indirect cause. Not you.

June 1st. Eight years ago today I first came to France. I miss your conversation and your arms. Close up the worst and give of yourself, everyone. It's only innocent people who feel the need to justify themselves.

Oh, this wonderful hot weather! Beauties come out now on the street, *débraillées,* and Paris light stays until nearly ten in the evening (and dawn is at three) with a lemonade glow, and the streets seething with the nervous and happy. The season changes, bringing the past like a flashlight into the Chicago parks where, as an adolescent, I lay (ignorant of danger: hence safe) in the arms of adults smelling of sun and gasoline and strength, the spring human smell of the *débraillé.* . . . When was it? Where have they gone? Today we have lunch in the garden. I go to the movies, one cannot be an amateur of both theater and cinema: I choose the movies.

For nineteen years I have been making love. Eva Gauthier used to tell her male singing students: "Just be glad you're not a soprano obliged to give a recital in spite of her 'period' when with every high note she feels blood rushing downward and prays that the audience be unaware of the red puddle forming on the floor." . . . These steaming spring evenings what else can we think of? Love and sex along the river bridges. I'm different in summer than in winter, different in Paris than New York. And I see the arms around that little boy grow tighter, smaller, more distant, and somehow I'm no longer jealous of my childhood.

The heart—his heart—will shrink in its safety fault; I can't begrudge that unconsciousness, any more than the little bitch of *The Bad Seed,* the final revenge for my indifferent innocence. The *petit bourgeois* of the 19th Arrondissement, hobnobbing with artists and playing Don Juan, can now go stew in his own juice. Because we see each other as monsters, each unfair to the other. Kick me in the mouth like Bogart. I've too much heart, and you: none. (But am your equal in bad manners.) One doesn't torture another almost to death only to be later merely vexed that the "victim" misunderstood. You pushed to the utmost limits, cat and mouse, exasperated. From self-protection here's the definitive break. I've had you again and am not interested. Therefore I dump you—*je te plaque.* As conquest I cost you plenty. It's always a mistake to show one's love too much. You bastard.

These are the calmest, the least mean words with which to end this letter addressed to a misunderstanding. How changed a person I've become only someone else will tell. But I would rather have as remembrance the smell of those arms in a Chicago park tighten sharp around me nineteen years ago again tonight in the heat of France. *Salaud! Espèce do maquereau!* you pig, you real pig! you bad damn son-of-a-bitch, you prick. You shit!

To Virgil Thomson

*12 II 58*

Very dear Virgil—

Only *you* could be always so thoughtful as to send me those gorgeous glasses for wine. Come and drink from them as *soon* as you return.

Thanks also for your October letter which just arrived.

I'll call you Sunday.

Your faithful—

Ned

To Virgil Thomson

*247 West 13*
*New York 14*
*29.VI.58*

Good Virgil—

Last night we all went to see *The Goddess* which, as I suppose you know, has finally opened here with immense critical and popular success (the lines in front of the theater are a mile long, and the reviews have been raves). Your music—which is always certainly very *you*—gives a dimension which I've never felt in movies up till now: its sprightliness comes out with a sordid effect, and its calm makes one nervous. It is always very present (at least for me), and without it the film would be much more endurable—which of course it shouldn't be. So bravo! You're still a pioneer.

Paul Bowles is in town and I went to ask him what he thought about Jane's play as an opera. . . . He says he can neither play nor sing, so I had to read through his whole opera *Yerma* with him over my shoulder. It's very beautiful in part and is full of ⁶/₈ choruses and fast Spanish dances (like "The Wind Remains"), but is full of misspellings and hard to read so I only got an overall idea. . . . Paul looks good, older—I hadn't seen him for 8 years —but Jane seems quite depressed.

The weather is growing into summer and you are sorely missed. Morris will, I suppose, give you any urgent gossip you might be wanting. Meanwhile I'll be staying on in Manhattan throughout the summer and have no plans except to assist at the birth of my sister's fifth baby at the end of this week.

Do let me know when you return, and please give my love to our mutual friends in France.

Your faithful—
Ned

## To Virgil Thomson

*247 West 13*
*New York 14*
*17 July 58*

Dear Virgil—

Thanks for your nice answer to my letter about *The Goddess*. . . . There's a damp heat wave on and we're all dying here. . . . I rehearse frequently with Nell Tangeman on a tentative Fall recital (half me, and half Scarlatti and Stravinsky); she sounds better. Your picture is in *Life* this week in connection with Mademoiselle Boulanger; should I send it? or can you find it there? . . . I may do an opera on *Mamba's Daughters* with Jimmy Baldwin (negro novelist) and am seeing Audrey Wood about it tomorrow. Meanwhile *Garden District* [plays of Tennessee Williams for which NR wrote the background music] is closed, so I hope I can get unemployment insurance because I'm broke again and my family (though all angels) is no longer free to help me. I must get a cheaper apt. and a job with a steady income; maybe you'll have some ideas on your return. Incidentally, my pupil also is looking for a job as copyist; can you use him? . . . May go to MacDowell [Colony] in September—but now I'm attending A.A. meetings which I need and which are helpful. . . . Did I tell you that Lenny's doing my new Symphony next season? . . . Have you seen Marie-Laure? . . . I miss Paris deeply, and we miss you here. *I liked* the *Carmélites* [Francis Poulenc's opera *Les dialogues des Carmélites*], but only the set numbers (Ave Maria, etc.), which had nothing to do with the exposition. . . . When are you coming back?

Best to Wendel and affection to you
Ned

To Carl Van Vechten

*247 West 13*
*New York 14*
*25 VII 58*

Caro Carlo—

Thought you might be interested in knowing that I've *finally* found my ideal libretto for a full-length opera: [Dubose Heyward's] *Mamba's Daughters!* And James Baldwin will do the adaptation. . . . What do you think? Have you any ideas on who could sing Hagar—perhaps Carol Brice?

I hope that if you're ever in contact with either Audrey Wood or Mrs. Heyward you'll put in a good word for me. Because I'm trying to convince them to let me have the rights to the script.

I also hope that we might get together again soon if you're going to be in town for the summer. I'm stuck in the city and hate to think of all this time going by without our seeing each other at least once a year!

Your faithful
Ned

To Frank O'Hara

*MacDowell Colony*
*Peterborough, New Hampshire*
*11 IX 58*

Cherished Frank—

Already for weeks I'd been pondering about using your title "In Memory of My Feelings" as an overall name for a huge series of pieces (big and little, orchestral and chamber, vocal and instrumental, *but* to be played consecutively *as one work*), so I was not surprised when Hindemith used almost your same phrase on pps. 38–40 of *The Composer's World*. Because it's what music *is*. Look at it. And then, when you can (soon, if possible), do send me your poem from which this comes—because I won't be back in New York City until October 1st and am anxious to organize my thoughts with (as has happened before) your help.

How I long to have you relate the foreign trip and know your reactions to the Europe I miss.

Life here is too perfect: quite sexless and voraciously industrious in an atmosphere of unshared beauty. The leaves are already red (here are 3 for Joe [LeSueur]) and the nights cold.

Please write—and love to you both—

from Ned

### To the family, New York to Philadelphia

*30 XII 58*

Just a quick note to end the year!

Enclosed is a photo of me with the unpleasant baritone for whom I orchestrated the Chopin songs. . . . Also an announcement of a modern music series on which I'm featured.

Tonight is my opera *The Robbers* at the Manhattan school and I'll have to give an impromptu speech!

I loved, as always, the holidays at home. So did Joe LeSueur, who thinks you are *wonderful people!* Tell Rosemary the cookies are a huge hit.

More later. Love, and happy New Year

Ned

### To Virgil Thomson

*Yaddo*

*28.VI.59*

Good Virgil—

Although I haven't written, I've nevertheless been *close* to you these last days—because I've been re-reading some of your books. The main reason for this (other than the joy I always have from your articles) is that I've finally accepted the Buffalo offer and the burden of it will involve giving lectures, something I've never done before. So I'm looking around for themes to steal, and you provide one of the best sources. The "dessert" at my lectures will be live concerts which I will organize, having as many as 20 musicians. And I would love to do *Socrate* [by Erik Satie]. Could you tell me if it's possible in America to procure the orchestra parts for this work? (Though I like it on the piano almost as well.) Also is it kosher to use more than one singer in any one of the three sections? Like most music schools this one probably has a lot of good voices around, and it would be nice to use as many as possible. . . . I'm a little nervous about the job, not only because of its new opportunities but also because I'll probably have a bit of theater work in New York (as well as our communal vocal concert) which will involve a lot of commuting. Perhaps you'd like to come up and give a lecture?

I feel nostalgic about your being in Paris! Have you seen my lost youth around?! Have you seen maybe Marie-Laure and other of our mutual friends? A note of gossip and impressions would always be welcome—and a bit of advice about the Satie of infinite help.

My address until September will be the one below.

Your affectionate and faithful

Ned

## To Edward Albee

*Philadelphia*
*3 July 59*

Wise Edward—

As I had anticipated your amendments to the script of *[The Death of] Bessie Smith* improve it—and as a play now it dazzles with terror: we know where *we* are and who *they* are, and the theatrical *trouvailles* seem original and should work.

I'm in a state of hysteria about Buffalo because my forthcoming duties there seem so vague I don't quite know what to prepare for, yet hate to arrive empty-handed and mute. I could wish it were all behind me!

... I'll doubtless be back in New York around the 20th and will call you on arrival.

Meanwhile, bravo and love—and thanks again for the flattering dedication which deeply honors me.

Ned

## To Virgil Thomson

*Buffalo*
*November 59*

Dear Virgil—

*Happy Birthday!!* I've nearly finished your book, so I know *all* about you! (I could *add* a few things, but in general it's very good & readable—even touching.)

How do you feel about our concert? I was disappointed! Considering how professional and distinguished it was—there should have been a better reception. But I want to do more still. I *loved* your songs and will repeat them here with Regina [Sarfaty] on December 3rd.

Impossible to procure more copies of *Socrate*. Ricordi's never heard of them! What'll I do?

See you over Christmas, I hope.

All affection,

Ned

Part Two

# 1960s

*27 April 60*

Good Virgil:

Where, oh where does the Gauthier Society procure its singers?! I wasn't at the concert, naturally, but heard various catastrophic reports. Now John Gruen writes me about the next recital. Dorothy Renzi is intelligent, catholic, and musicianly, but her voice is nothing special; I've never heard Pritchett, but I have my doubts; I *have* heard Fr. Fuller and he's frightful from every standpoint. I've the impression that these people are John Edmunds' personal friends—and the whole thing looks much too friendly. It's exactly the kind of amateurish mediocrity that Bill [Flanagan] and I've been trying to avoid by making song *professional* again. Well, anyway John Cage was around here last night and gave a rather boring concert. He intends to attend your *Requiem* in Potsdam next month. How I *do* wish I could (they very kindly sent me an invitation). But I doubt it: I have rehearsals all that week for the first performance of my own piece which will also be with you, and I do hope we can see each other before you go off. I'll be back in New York for about two weeks from around 28 May, and would like you to come to my house and drink cold white wine, either alone or with poets. On June 15th I'll go to Yaddo for two months and will probably sublet. Incidentally, what happens to your place at the Chelsea when you're in Europe? Any possibility of my staying there an occasional weekend during the summer, and perhaps during the fall after school resumes? . . . Spring is here.

Affection
Ned

*Yaddo*
*Saratoga Springs*
*New York*
*30 July 60*

Dear Virgil—

A heavy and interminable rain today, so thick it looks like a forest. Rather pleasant. And so I said: why not write Virgil? No other motive to this note (unless it's nostalgia for Paris and you—provoked by the monotone routine and company here—and hope for a little gossip from there).

Also I finally decided to finish Thomas Mann's *Dr. Faustus* on page 401 of which, big as life, is your name—which startled me! . . . I've been here seven weeks and will return to New York in mid-August before going back to Buffalo until around February 1st. Meanwhile I've completed a *Trio* (flute, cello, piano), some short choral pieces, and a *play* in the form of a dramatic-burlesque for one actress! . . . Yaddo life (for me) eschews both carnality and alcohol which are replaced by early mornings and rich meals; also a great deal of reading. Otherwise there's little news to send you. Bill Flanagan is going to England this month to accompany Edward's tryout of a new play there. Morris's brother had a throat operation while the former was in Europe where you may have seen him. You also saw there, I'm told, David Posner, nervous poet from Buffalo. Miss Toklas said she loved your *Requiem*. So did I. . . . And Yvonne, Sauguet, Marie-Laure? I plan to go back to France toward mid-April; will I see you here or there before? . . . Everyone seems to be in love—which is sort of the new trend, now that abstract expression (in music as in pictures) is a thing of the fifties. Except me: I'm not in love, *hélas*—but then of course I was never an abstract expressionist. . . . What are your news? what are you writing? how does Paris look and feel? and who do you see that you like? . . . Know that we miss you, and send the pleasantest of affectionate thoughts.

Ned

### To Virgil Thomson

*247 West 13*
*New York 11*
*28 February 61*

Dear Virgil—

Thanks for your nice words about my speeches and play. I've now two more of the latter for you to read someday. . . . How I envy you your voyage into the exotic countries. But I envy myself too now that I'm finally coming back to Paris. . . . Which brings up your apartment: it is perfect, tasteful, well-situated, independent, and *ideal* for me, *BUT*—now that I won't be staying at Marie-Laure's (which I'd vaguely been planning on), thrift is utmost! Having no income, the European sojourn will be sustained only by my recent earnings, and I want to make it last. $125 per month is really too much, plus light-gas-femme-phone. If you could possibly see your way to reducing it to 75 or 80 dollars a month for May & June, I'd definitely take it (paying the extras myself, of course)—and be a reliable tenant. Do let me know soon: it would be a boon for which I'd be extremely grateful—but if you prefer not, I'll certainly understand.

How'd the *Requiem* go at Champs-Elysées? Who's important musically these days in France? Anyone I ought to make a point of seeing? Contacts (even interest, a bit) are nearly lost, and it means starting from scratch.... Not sure how long I'll stay abroad; maybe a year—maybe just a long summer—to return around the same time as you.

Let's keep in touch—

All affection—

Ned

## To Virgil Thomson

*10 March 61*

Dear Virgil—

Thanks so much for bringing the price down. The two months will therefore come to $150 rent. In your first letter you said to pay Madame Desailly; in your second, the French-Amer. Banking Corp.... Which? ... I don't think I'd want a *femme-de-ménage* more than twice a week. Possible? ... In any case I'll write both Mesdames Langlade et Desailly about ten days before arrival.... So would you now tell those ladies it'll be somewhere between the end of April and about May 2nd? Can't tell you how conveniently delighted I am by our arrangement; I love your apt. and am sick of hotels. In the long run it's probably a disguised blessing that I *don't* stay chez Marie-Laure; there's no point in pretending to be the same person in Paris after such long absence.

... Also, if & when I *do* return by *boat* (though unlikely) will of course bring your belongings.

... Have been creatively sterile and somewhat at loose ends since returning from Buffalo (where apparently David D. is applying himself with sobriety) and *do* feel the need for a change. Will probably rent an upright for the first six weeks in France. O.K.?

Edward Albee has literally become the most famous playwright in America. As for Bill, he likens himself to Job! ... Morris is in Las Vegas recuperating from gout. My sister's in her sixth pregnancy. And the weather is rather perfect.

Love—

Ned

To Virgil Thomson

*Friday*

*5 May 61*

Dear Virgil—

What a heavenly apartment: the first *chez moi* in Paris ever! Arrived Monday; saw Langlade; arranged with Annie H. to come thrice a week; have invited Koons for this afternoon; rented an upright Gaveau to be placed in front of *cheminée;* have seen Marie-Laure *(déchainée),* and countless others already, in spite of lousy weather, and all speak tenderly of you. Meanwhile, whenever I hear steps in the courtyard I peek through the curtains like a concierge; did *you* ever conquer that temptation? . . . Haven't yet got the "feel" of Paris: the expected shocking thrill-of-return was somewhat lessened by a week in London, and also of course I'm no longer the same person—but *they* still are!

. . . Should I plan to stay on in France, what are the chances of my taking over again when the Morisettes leave? I'd like to.

News of the Far East would be more than welcome. How *do* they behave? and how is the congress going? How long will you stay there?

. . . Three of my Buffalo speeches accepted by *London Magazine.* Morris arrives in a month. . . .

Do write soon—and tender regards from us all—

Ned

To Virgil Thomson

*Paris*

*5 June 61*

Cher Virgil—

Francis Poulenc (who was unable to attend the rather vast "coqueteyle" I threw two weeks ago without breaking one glass, and who thought you were still in Paris) requested that I place *une bise respectueuse sur ton crane.* Which I do.

Meanwhile thanks for your last note. The Isaacs had already given me your news in person. . . .

Saw [Manuel] Rosenthal who raved about your *Requiem* (which however I didn't know was to be broadcast the 18th, *hélas*). He's doing Nabokov's *Rasputin* here in 2 weeks, which was apparently a shocking flop in Cologne.

Saw Barzin also as you suggested and we got along fine, but not so fine as with Noël Coward who picked me up (I was sober) at the Elysée-

Matignon where I was dining with Philippe Erlanger last week. Details later. . . .

. . . Little musical gossip because the city's not only icy and black but un-aural. [Georges] Auric has made another million on his literal transcription of Brahms for the new Sagan movie, and resultantly has a guilty conscience and very bad temper. . . . You are very famous in the *quartier*. . . .

Your paperbacks are a joy. . . . I work reasonably well (song cycle, [Howard] Moss poems) but long for quiet and love and heat . . . Marie-Laure is quite *adoucie*. . . . John Ashbery not without influence in the painting world.

Let me know your plans.

Love—

Ned

## To Paul Bowles

*Saint Bernard*
*Hyères (Var)*
*France*
*16 July 61*

Dear Paul—

. . . Did I tell you in my other letter that I took mescaline again—about two months ago right in Manhattan. Horrible! Details when I see you. Because it looks as though I *will* come to Morocco on August 1st by plane from Nice or Marseille. Could you find me some sort of pleasant but non-expensive hotel room? or will you already be in Marrakech? I've been told that Bob Faulkner has an apartment he'd like to rent, but I don't know quite how to go about doing that. . . . Yesterday we had a dreadful massacre at noon right in the Place de la Rade of Hyères: an Arab went berserk and killed some people (who were waiting for a bus) and disemboweled a dog. I pray that this won't happen to me in Tangier, because I just had a tetanus shot (for a smashed thumb) which nearly killed me. Anyway I may be spending most of my time in Rabat chez Guy Ferrand who has a good Steinway I can work at for a month. . . . How do I get in touch with anyone when I arrive?—do you all have phones? . . . Oh, how awful I feel with my sore throat! . . . Marie-Laure de Noailles at whose house I now am is a fan of yours and would love to know you but I suppose that's forever impossible since she won't budge. . . . Yes, I've written two one-act plays which I'll show you; also will bring a lot of records. . . . Heard Alice Esty sing your songs—

beautiful—although nuance of style and beauty of tone are scarcely her strong points.

Do give my best to everyone, and hope to hear from (and see) you soon. All very best—
Ned


## To Paul Bowles

*c/o Ferrand*
*Ministère de la Santé*
*Rabat, Maroc*
*22 August 61*

Dear Jane and dear Paul—

You were so very pleasant to me in Tangier that I'm embarrassed to have left as souvenir only those two weird plays [*The Pastry Shop* and *The Young Among Themselves*, written in 1959 but not produced until 1970]. Perhaps I can make up for it soon; because I'll be passing through again at the end of the month en route for Spain. Will arrive Thursday the 31st for 48 hours and will call you from whatever hotel I'm staying, hoping we can meet either that night or Friday. Perhaps this time we can arrange a *séance de disques,* Paul, because I'm really anxious to hear *your* music. . . . Saw a picture of you looking quite plump in the Yaddo album last summer. Going to Marrakech tomorrow and love the heat. Am vaguely involved with North Africa's tennis champion, Lahcen Chadli by name, who's also the trainer of the Sultan in whose palace he lives with his wife and child—but will doubtless return anyway to America in October and rent an apartment in Tangier until next March. What do you think?

More soon—
Ned


## To Paul Bowles

*136 West 13*
*New York City 11*
*10 January 62*

Dear Paul—

Happy New Year, and thanks for nice letter. My sister Rosemary gave me your *Yallah* (which she obtained in Philadelphia's Wanamaker sale) for Christmas, and it's in every way gorgeous.

How sorry I am that Jane's not feeling well. Since I've been back I've seen no friends of hers (like Libby) except Stella Adler who sends her touching regards. Her daughter, Ellen (very beautiful), is the image of Jane. . . . I just reread Jane's play for maybe the seventh time with an eye to its libretto qualities; but it probably wouldn't work. I have to write a full-length opera for the City Center and need a text desperately since my previous project fell through—thank God! *You* wouldn't want to write (or adapt one of your stories) a text, would you? in a month? if you got paid?! If so let me know *quick!* It would be quite a *coup* . . .

That pleasant Dragadze girl has written me several letters since last we met in Tangier. Since then America has provided nothing but a nest of competition, orderly chaos, and flops that announce themselves as masterpieces. I'd been thinking of Morocco as the sole refuge, but what you announced about the descent of beatniks has dampened my nostalgia.

Give my regards to H[arold] Norse and tell him his friend Dick has gained weight—judging by his nightly appearances at the San Remo. . . . Regards, as well, of course, to Christopher and Jane. Perhaps we'll all meet soon.

Sincerely—

Ned

Virgil's 65th birthday was celebrated with official pomp in Town Hall with a program of his music (not his best) performed by distinguished executants, speeches by [Gian Carlo] Menotti and the Mayor's assistant, a telegram from President Kennedy, etc. Virgil was very pleased. . . . Aaron's about to tour the world as conductor. . . . Who else? Oh, well, I'll tell you in the next letter.

### To Paul Bowles

*283 West 12th St.*
*New York 14, N.Y.*
*18/III/63*

Dear Paul,

Ages ago I think I wrote you about maybe your doing an original libretto: perhaps an adaptation of one of your books. The opera I was commissioned by Ford [Foundation] to do for City Center was composed—but now I don't like it. So I'm desperately seeking a new "property." If a satisfactory payment were made to you, *could* such an idea appeal to you? In which case I might come to Tangier for awhile in late Spring. It's just a suggestion —but do let me know soon.

I still toy with the idea of Jane's *Summer House*—but can't know if it would work sung.

### To Frank Anzalone, a young playwright

*14 July 63*

Dear Frank—

Thank you for your complimentary and moving letter. It recalled somewhat one I wrote Paul Bowles years ago: he influenced my youth in a manner he never knew. . . . I'm not sure I deserve the *kindness* of your words (I feel myself to be quite self-involved). And, if it's true I've "experienced life," that's mostly because I've lived longer than you! What you are suffering is partly due to your age (I don't mean to be condescending), but you are lucky beyond belief in knowing what you want of the future, and in your perseverance in how to achieve it. . . . But I've never thought of myself as "happy" either (it's not a state of mind I seek: it's more urgent to be *alive*, which in itself contradicts happiness), nor certainly peaceful: that last comes in dying.

I leave for Saratoga next month. If you'd like to have a talk before then, nothing could be easier. But I doubt if any advice could help much: one does, after all, what one wants to do, and hears only what one opens one's ears to. No two lives are the same and emulation, though normal, is risky. The most important thing in your case is to be talented, and if you are, that will be your chief force. No one can give that to you. Though when the time comes I'll be more than pleased to put you in contact with key people who might be useful. The outside world you allude to—and which you're approaching—is no joke, but I'm afraid it's the only one we have.

Thanks so much for the pictures which are successful, and which I shall value.

*Appelle-moi lorsque le coeur te dit*
All best—
Ned

## To Frank O'Hara

*16 VII 63*

D.F.

This $50 is really from Alice [Esty] for your poem which she loves —
but she asked me to pay you so as not to set a precedent with poets in this
particular project — to keep it confidential.

L.

N.

## To Paul Bowles

*10/IX/63*

Dear Paul—

. . . Ten days ago I shattered an ankle in a gratuitous bicycle smash-up.
At the emergency ward I was given crutches, a cast, and a heavy dose of
codeine. Back at Yaddo I fell into a long stupid sleep of bad dreams. Groggy
and drugged the next morning I was awakened by the delivery of your
mescalinian thesis, and in this perfect state I read it.

It's really a sort of masterpiece. Henry James' *The Great Good Place* is
the closest positive version of your dimension. I "identified" with each horrible sentence, and recalled alertly my last such experience a year ago with
psilocybin while very drunk: you can imagine the results. In my diary I've
written up my three trials, but they read like Little Lord Fauntleroy next to
your letter. Maybe it all should be published — though I don't know that
anyone's interested any longer in such actions per se without conclusions.
Were you the only one to have taken it? Will you ever again? For myself I
may someday try a double-dose with a doctor, though finally it's too discouraging, and now unsure as to what more it can show *new*.

Is Alfred Chester in Tangier? I don't know him but have read three of
his stories with admiration. I also read one of yours here lately (about a
Swiss instructress *dans le bled* at Christmas) which was extremely moving.

I'm certainly at an impasse with all thought of operas. For the moment
I'm writing two big "tone poems" called *Lions* and *Whales* to pass the time.
Also the background music to Purdy's *Color of Darkness* (five short adapta-
tions) which opens off-Broadway on the 30th. If my crippled state permits
I'll probably hobble back to New York then and stay there till Spring, at
which time I may return to Europe, or possibly Morocco if I could find a
place to live. (Guy Ferrand has been *muté* to Algiers.)

The City Center now seems dubious about my changing librettos in
midstream, and I feel hopeless & embarrassed. Opera, at worst, is silly—
and it's ridiculous to compose one without iron-clad guarantees; at best it's
time-consuming and expensive. Yet ideally I'd like to collaborate with you.
I don't know how you'll take this; but it's so difficult doing these things with
an ocean in between. Please let me hear from you soon again.

. . . I hope Jane is well; it would be nice to have news of her. . . . Have the
Beatniks all gone?

All very best—

Ned

## To the family, New York to Philadelphia

*16 X 63*

As you see from the front page, the *Village Voice* has made my article the
main feature this week, and I'm glad—because I was really upset about old
Cocteau: France is another country without him. . . . As with Poulenc I
tried to be comprehensive rather than flattering in the appraisal: I hope I'm
not sued for libel! The *Voice* doesn't seem to have *italics* so the numerous
French phrases are indistinguishable from the English—but that's my only
complaint. The little drawing he made as a cover for a song I wrote to
Elizabeth Bishop's poem about Ezra Pound.

Spent last evening with Tallulah Bankhead, who's to be the star of the
Broadway revival in December of Tennessee Williams's *The Milk Train
Doesn't Stop Here Anymore,* for which I'm doing the music (for a flat fee of
$1000). She's indeed a character, a star, a legend, etc. but after 20 minutes
she's a bore since she never ceases her drunken deep-voice palaver; she's a
big unreal child. Tony Richardson, the English director, on the other hand
is (for the moment) easy to work with.

. . . Thanks, father, for your letter of two weeks ago, and for the various
opera suggestions therein. The latest is that I may do a version of Maxwell
Anderson's *The Wingless Victory.* Read it and see if you don't think it's perfect in every way, operatically. . . . Could you perhaps photostat the Cocteau
article as you did the Poulenc? (I seem to be the chief obituaryist for the
*Village Voice!*) . . . It was wonderful seeing Mother and [Aunt] Pearl here.
They came to a little party chez moi and really gave it a *tone.* Everyone was
impressed with them. . . .

More soon—

Love—

To Glenway Wescott

*22.XI.63*

Very Dear Glenway—

I'm writing this only a few minutes after the official announcement of Kennedy's assassination. It's shaken me. Less, perhaps, than Roosevelt, because I'm older; but the reaction (like probably everyone's) is: What's going to happen to *me?!* Gee, nobody's invulnerable—not even Balder or Achilles—and the worst thing is that JFK was so sexual, so sexy, and guided the country (for better or worse) accordingly. Madame Kennedy could now become the Marie-Laure of America; viewed from a distance she's a Greek queen: her prince and king both died in the same year—and her college thesis was on Baudelaire, Diaghileff, and Wilde (you knew that, didn't you?)! Well, anyway. Your life and mine, and that of a few of our friends, are minuscule, but the only solid threads in this tawdry drama, and will hold the fabric together long after vice presidents have collapsed into limbo. (My intentions are as talented as the image is shabby.) . . . After you left I *did* continue drinking, then put on dark glasses (my face was swelling from Antabuse, but I didn't want to tell you), went to the party, awakened next day with a remorseful hangover. Since then Harold B[rodkey] has been a boon—egocentric and difficult—but a boon. . . . Sorry, very sorry, not to have seen you Tuesday, but that wouldn't have been the right way with the diaries anyway. I shall let you borrow all the journals to keep as long as you see fit. And I'd very much like your advice about legacies and things. Your eyes, they tell me, are in less serious condition than you may have feared— and I'm relieved. Please let me know as soon as you want us to get together. It's always a pleasure (and more than a pleasure) to see you.

All very best—

N

To Glenway Wescott

*21.V.64*

Dear Glenway—

Finally I *have* made out a will, and I did include you and Robert Phelps as two who might look after my "private papers" etc. & perhaps give them to Indiana or a publisher or someone. Is that all right? (But I trust we won't have to worry for years!)

Life is dreary and sad at the moment. Are any revelations left? Probably

I stay on here through the summer. Invite us for a little weekend & I'll bake you a gorgeous cake.

Think of me.

Love

Ned


To GLENWAY WESCOTT

*3.I.65*

Cher Glenway—

You *are* hard to reach!

Could you come for supper this Wednesday the sixth at 7:30 with Gavin Lambert?

I hope so.

Let me know.

Tenderness—

Ned


To GLENWAY WESCOTT

*29.XI.65*

Dearest Glenway—

In a month I'm off to Utah where for six months I will teach and work quietly and return abstemiously—unless, of course, they lynch me for those recent remarks, or for the appearance of the diary (in March) which Braziller now seems to want to launch most scandalously. Which makes me extremely apprehensive. I may be desperately needing all the friends I can hold onto. Anyway, they seem to want "jacket statements" from the great— explaining who I am. Hopefully they'll eventually want you to review it for the *Tribune* or somewhere. Meanwhile, would you be willing to commit yourself in a brief statement they could use on the cover & in advertising?

The opera reactions have somewhat discouraged me, but mostly I feel misrepresented—even sabotaged: what I had conceived did not take place. Thank God, though, I have three other large-scale pieces commissioned which I must finish before next summer.

. . . I'd be so happy if you came again to dine before I leave.

Mille tendresses—

Ned

To Virgil Thomson

*The University of Utah*
*College of Fine Arts*
*Department of Music*
*Salt Lake City*
*14.II.66*

Very Dear Virgil—

This will be mostly about books! I made off with two of yours (Mellers & Myers) but please don't worry: you'll have them back soon. I trust Joe returned the various others I borrowed? . . . Braziller informs me that you might be pleased to write a blurb (or, hopefully, even a review in the *New York Review of Books*) of my forthcoming diary. I could ask for nothing more! . . . How is *your* book coming? . . . And who is Nick Rossi—who writes me from Los Angeles on your behalf about a book *he's* planning?

Dear Joe [Adamiak, NR's lover at the time] seems to be languishing so I'm glad you're being good to him. I'll be back in about three weeks for about three weeks and will try to set things right. Meanwhile, Utah, in many respects, is not to be regretted. I've been in all respects abstinent since my arrival, and resultantly have completed not only a whole Mass (unison chorus & organ for Catholics in English) but an extended cycle on Kenneth Koch poems, two of which you used too. Hope you don't mind. Aaron was here for a week, bringing a touch of sophistication with him: that's something this town hasn't; eventually one wearies of the necessary limits beyond which one can't go. The housewives are of maximum cordiality though, and the theater department does excellent productions of Ionesco and Albee. Now the Christian Scientists have asked me what I'd charge to set Mrs. Eddy to music! What would *you* charge? . . . After five weeks of paradisical weather, terrific blizzards have finally arrived. Mostly I stay home & work & read, society being only (seemingly) plausible with the Abravanels— though he, despite an overdose of good cheer, is very very defensive. She is French. Jewish. . . . I do look forward to seeing you soon, and trust you are well and working as usual.

Much affection—

Ned

## To Paul Bowles

*The University of Utah*
*Salt Lake City*
*84112*
*U.S.A.*
*22 April 66*

Dear Paul—

On June 15th my first book will be published. It's called (*en toute simplicité*) *The Paris Diary of Ned Rorem*, being extracts from the 1951–55 volume of a quite self-involved journal. Braziller is putting it out. And you're mentioned in it too (nicely, of course! God knows how many French friends I'll lose!). The advance reviews have been "favorable," though they make me out as a freak. Anyway Braziller & Co. would like to send you a copy in a couple weeks with the hope that you'll make a "statement" they can use. Naturally I'd like you to have it anyway—so should we mail it to Tangier? or where might you be? . . . I'm in Utah teaching for two quarters, but I'll *never* do it again for any salary! America is strange and Mormons are stranger and I do miss normal countries like Morocco. . . . Isolated though I am, I finally procured a copy of *your* book which I swallowed in admiration and terror as I have everything you've done. . . . Do you see Jane often? Please give her my very best regards. . . .

My best, dear Paul—
Ned

## To Paul Bowles

*27 June 67*

Dear Paul—

In September a new book of mine—a continuation of the Diary—is to be published by Braziller. In it I describe detailedly the session we had with mescaline at John Goodwin's in 1958, and I mention you by name. I can't imagine that you might find this objectionable, but one never knows, and the editor's lawyer asked me to check with you. If necessary, I can send you a copy of the "offending" reference; or if you'd prefer I'd use initials, that's possible too.

Boy, I'm sick of New York! Am longing to go someplace wilder, perhaps Morocco, or tamer, maybe Denmark. But when and how? How is it there?

All most pleasant and gentle regards to you and Jane.
Ned

To Paul Bowles

*3 July 67*

Dear Paul—

... Impossible to tell you how wearily shocked I'm getting with New York. I nevertheless just had a big premiere for my *Sun* for voice & orchestra by the Philharmonic; that was nice, of course. But next week I'm retiring to Yaddo for the rest of the summer where hopefully the non-"orgy" ambiance will inspire some reflective work. Probably at the end of the year I'll cross the ocean again.

What you say about Morocco no longer being off-limits sounds promising; though God knows where any place will stand six months from now! I'm sorely tempted to return there, or maybe Greece (never been), or anywhere but here. Have you, then, been able to see Jane again?

Next week I'm having lunch with George Braziller and shall certainly highly recommend *Love with a Few Hairs.* . . . Meanwhile James Purdy's new novel is a sort of masterpiece, and I've just begun Alfred Chester's wild one. Is he there? . . . One smokes too much.

Affection—

Ned

To Paul Bowles

*24 July 67*

Dear Paul

Your book finally reached me here in Yaddo. I've read it, and will forward it to Edwin Seaver—unless he tells me he's already got it from Peter Owen . . . I finished it in two fell swoops and loved it. Amazing how both your and [Mohammed] Mrabet's personalities come through as completely independent entities. Yet obviously dependent. The story has real appeal, gentleness. I hope Braziller takes it. *Life* seems to like your collected stories, so I shouldn't think you'd have much trouble with publishers here.

*Love with a Few Hairs* was, for me, most evocative of Tangier. It's been eighteen summers since you first showed me the beaches there, one weekend when I came up from Fez. I want to come back. And perhaps I will around, say, early March, but that depends. Ages ago I suggested our doing an opera together (that is: *you* doing a libretto). Now I'm all out of commissions and at loose ends and sick of America and want to do something big & vocal & theatrical. Did you ever actually make notes, or have you still an idea, or are you still interested? In which case I'd love to come and work with you for 2 or 3 months in Morocco. Let me know, and I'll start making plans. Eventually I'll want to go on to Tunisia and Greece, neither of which I've ever seen. But I'll decide that later.

... Rain, rain, nothing but. Do you ever write music anymore?

What was actually the matter with Jane? Perhaps I should visit her on my way to Africa. Glad she's better. How do you get from Tangier—I mean *New York* to Tangier, anyway?

Ned

<br>

TO THE FAMILY, YADDO TO NEW YORK

*14 VIII 67*

Dear Mama & Papa—

A few days ago I phoned Olga (and talked to her ½ hour) to find out where you were. Then this morning came your lovely and well-typed letter from Iowa. You've been wonderfully active: I rather envy you all that travel. It will be a pleasure to see relatives in New York though: Kathryn, whom I've not seen in twenty odd years, and Hutch whom I've never met.

By this time you should be at Rosemary's in Philadelphia. Do tell me how the *tone* of the neighborhood seems. After reading about the race riots all over I was sort of concerned for the Marshalls. But there ain't no hiding place down here; and sometimes outside impressions are more spectacular. When I was in Morocco I wasn't even aware of the revolution that was going on.

Saratoga, by contrast, is extremely calm—at least Yaddo is. The town-proper is now seething with awful people here for the racing season. But we're out of it all. My life is uneventful and healthy, but for the first time in years I rather miss New York, and will be anxious to return on September 1st. During September I *may* go visit Shirley [Gabis] in Truro; more likely I'll spend the weekend with Tom Prentiss on Fire Island.

... In the July 28 issue of *Commonweal* (an intelligent Catholic magazine), there's a long review of my *Music from Inside Out*. I guess I already sent you a card announcing the imminent publication of *The New York Diary*. I suggest that you do *not* read it. It will be followed in a year by *The Final Diary*, and the three diaries together will represent Hell, Purgatory, and Paradise. They should be read progressively and collectively. . . . Meanwhile, as I think I told you, I'm doing another music book for Braziller to be published in around ten months.

Right now I'm laboring over a long review of a Poulenc recording. It (the review) will appear in November's *High Fidelity* magazine ($100). Also I've been asked to write a preface ($200) to a book on music by, of all people, Ezra Pound.

Congratulations on your 47th anniversary! . . .

Love—

Ned

## To Virgil Thomson

*Yaddo*

*20 August 67*

Dear Virgil—

I've been asked to write the introduction to a reprint of Ezra Pound's *Antheil and a Treatise on Harmony* which I've just re-read with bemusement. I was wondering just how much formal music education Pound had, and also if you possessed a score to his opera *Villon?* Did you ever see that opera? Also, how would you personally assess Antheil's music today? (Pound seemed to worship him!) If you help me out on these things I'll naturally quote you nicely (and with your approval), as I always do!

Also I'm doing another Music Book for Braziller. One section will be based on interviews with friends on Where Music Is Going. Perhaps you'd be willing to grant one such interview? Anyway, I'll be back in New York on September 1st—and not a moment too soon: I'm dying of boredom, and feel the need of cheese, Chateau d'Yquem, unlimited sex, some good air pollution, and a bit of conversation. Perhaps you'd like to come over for some *homemade carrot cake* on Sunday the 3rd? Or will you be back from Rhode Island?

Fondly—

Ned

## To the family, Yaddo to New York

*August 22, 1967*

Dear Ones—

*The New York Review of Books* has asked me to do a rather extended essay on the Beatles. I'm extremely pleased, since that magazine is the most cultured in America today, and the Beatles make the music I like best . . . I got stung on the knee by a bee. Hortense Calisher treated it with her special salve. She and Curt Harnack are here, and send you their love, as do I.

Ned

To Glenway Wescott

*31 August 67*

Dear Glenway—

Tomorrow I leave for a month in the needed tranquility of Yaddo: I have 2 hours of music to compose and orchestrate by Christmas, and the very prospect chills me. Hence I won't be able to attend your celebration for the *Pilgrim Hawk*—but it will remain one of my seven favorite stories!

Thanks for your dear letter, and its concerns about my book. In Paris I was never really a part—so much as an observer—of society; here, inasmuch as society is "high," I'm not even an observer. Nor could I ever care to be in the same sense that, say, Truman C. is. Strangers always love us for what we've accomplished, ignoring the fact that, by definition, that very accomplishment no longer touches us. For instance, when my phone rings at 3 a.m. and some anonymous fairy tells me he's just finished my book and, O dear, how he *identified* with all that fancy melancholy existence and would adore to meet me, I sigh with fatigue and say, well maybe sometime. . . . I've just finished a marvelously boring book on *music* (the word "I" doesn't occur once!) which Braziller will print in February; and now I'm working on a big voice-&-orchestra cycle called *Sun* for Jane Marsh to sing with the Philharmonic next June.

I'm dying to see you, to ask you your ideas on my next diary (which you hint at), to extract from what I suspect was a *renseignement lubrique* on the part of our Lou, but mostly to hear and gaze at your intelligent voice and handsome face.

Fondly—

Ned

To Paul Bowles

*April Fool's Day—1968*

Dear Paul—

It is satisfying to own the copy of *Love with a Few Hairs* which Edwin Seaver gave me last week. I was pleased to get your letter then too. . . . And *Lemon?* Is that by you & Mrabet, or by you alone? . . . Your stories—most of them—had a great effect on me, especially those (few) I'd never read before, like "If I Should Open My Mouth." . . . I too've just finished another book—mostly about musical things—which will come out next fall. . . . Yes, Virgil had the grippe, but is flourishing again now up in Hartford, getting deafer by the minute, but still so bright while somewhat *adouci.* . . .

Despondent to hear about Jane again, and don't know what to say. But tell her, please, how I admire and like her, and hope to visit her there eventually.

I'd half expected to see you here last fall as you'd announced. Do come soon, to California. After Lyndon Johnson's announcement last night things should change drastically, and hopefully for the better. You'd make such a good teacher; do you like that sort of thing?

I still have not given up the idea of a libretto from you. Your interest though seemed dampened when last you wrote of it. Probably I won't change continents soon, as I'd planned. Reasons of the heart. But at loose ends in work. Next December, though, there will be Town Hall concert of just my songs—celebrating the 25th (!) anniversary of my first public performance. I knew you long before that. You see!

Fondly

Ned

Spent January in Mexico. It was hardly the same.


## To Paul Bowles

*26 April 68*

Dear Paul—

. . . John Goodman did write me (not with fury, but coolly) about *The New York Diary*, claiming, with a certain justification, that I had misquoted him concerning description of mescalinian reaction. I would have answered him cordially—and still would—if I had some sort of reliable address for him; have you one?

My new book, *Music and People*, comes out chez Braziller in October. I think you're mentioned therein three or four times (always very nicely!), including as one of the few good song composers of the forties. That last is in the reprint of my Beatles essay for *The New York Review of Books*. Did you ever see it? In December I'm giving a very grand all-Rorem song recital in Town Hall. Or did I tell you? That will be your Christmas vacation. . . .

Virgil's opera's *[Lord Byron]* more or less done, very Virgil, swell libretto by Jack Larson. Maurice [Grosser] on his way to see you. Am distressed, as is everyone who knows, about Jane's continuing problems; and do hope she'll come with you to America.

I am not living alone again.

Fondly—

Ned

To Paul Bowles

*27/IV/68*

Dear Paul—

Postscript to yesterday. . . .

I sought and found John Goodwin's letter, dated Nov. 14, 1967. The stationery was of The Ahwahnee Hotel (in Yosemite, California), and he said he'd found my book in the bottom drawer of his room there. The gist of what followed was mostly that after so many years he was sorry my "trip" was so ferocious despite what sounded like beautiful impressions induced; but then, he adds, probably our values are opposed since so much of what I wrote was verbatim quoted from himself. "However," he ends, "it surely did not reveal the *absolute* truth of perfect reality to you as the Cresco house was no mansion nor was Eryx a mongrel. . . . May you sell better than you ever have before."

No doubt, if I were to read about myself in someone else's diary as he read about himself in mine, I'd be annoyed (though I wouldn't write a letter, sarcastic or otherwise). So I'm upset, sort of, that John took it so hard (as, according to you, he did). But if I understand his emotional reaction, I find his literary reaction literal and indicative of the un-artist I've always felt him to be. If authors gave credit to everyone they quote, or misquote, their books would be endless. We all steal, but artists take the stolen goods and make them their own. Not that my diary is necessarily that of an artist, as far as John's concerned. And I'm willing to apologize to him, if it would do any good. Anyway, if you write him, tell him I took your words about his words about my words to heart. . . .

Best—

Ned

To Glenway Wescott

*15 December 68*

Glenway most cherished, whom I never see:

Your dear note arrived just before my concert and agreeably increased my nervousness. It was satisfying to know you were there, even though we didn't meet after (I'd have liked you to come to a party; Robert [Phelps], though, said you were ailing). . . . Have you a poem—of yours, or a favorite of someone's—you'd like me to set? I want to write a song for you.

Merry Christmas meanwhile—

Ned

To Virgil Thomson

*2 April 69*

Dear Virgil—

Your *Praises & Prayers* are all of them successful and touching, among the most satisfying of your pieces that I know, and certainly the high point of Miss [Betty] Allen's already fairly high program. Thank you for them.

Thank you also for the perfect cuisine last Friday. I liked it and you and all those ladies better than the guest of honor. Boulez is really quite a shop-talking pedant, who nevertheless (no less than I, and possibly more) has made it as much on charm as talent. *Nous n'étions pas faits pour nous entendre*, and after twenty years he no longer intimidates me. So he rather bores me —though he's gorgeous.

Jim Holmes, despite sharing my bout with the flu, has been practicing your "Panga Lingua," and is wondering about some of your metronome indications therein. They're not all clear to me either. Maybe we can all look at it together sometime.

I wish that I could be with Maurice before he leaves. Anyway I'll call him. [Maurice Grosser was Thomson's closest lifelong friend.]

Love to Jim and Jack, and especially to you . . .

Ned

To Paul Bowles

*18 West 70*<br>*NYC 10023*<br>*28 June 1969*

Dear Paul—

Do you heave a sigh whenever people are told to look you up? I used to sigh a lot during the years in Paris: every June huge rafts of colorless Americans arrived with letters of recommendation from colorless acquaintances and I'd pretend I was leaving the next day. . . . Anyway, you are the only person in Africa, and I've taken the liberty of asking some people to call you at 178-83 (is that still your number?). . . . They are the Meyer Levins: he wrote *The Old Bunch* and *Compulsion,* and she's French and writes diaries. I don't know them very well. . . . Also the Fred Plauts, who are in their early sixties: he's a skilled A&R man for Columbia Records and a good photographer (he's done a book on India), and she's Franco-Polish, Rose Dercourt, a Poulenc expert and rumored to have sung Mélisande in Algiers in her teens (c. 1917) and very very sweet. I know them well. . . .

They'll all be there (but not together) soon.... I'm staying in New York for the summer, as is Virgil. His opera—the Jack Larson *Byron*—was turned down by the Metropolitan, so he's a bit at loose ends. I'm coming to France and London for three weeks in October, first time in five years, but won't get to Tangier, though I'd love to see you and Jane. Is she the same?... We never got a chance to talk about California; was it instructive?... Don't feel constrained to welcome the abovementioned people if you've better to do. I hope you're writing another book of either stories or non-fiction, and that you're writing music too.

Fondly—

Ned

To Paul Bowles

*Assumption Day*<br>*1969*

Dear Paul—

I was appalled by your description of Tangier: the guns, arrests, torment of the Hippies, Jack Larson's detention. It seems to be occurring all over the world, and the "new permissiveness" in America's already a thing of the past. Do you think this is the beginning of the end? or the end, *tout court?* I hope, though, that Jack got some feeling for Morocco other than his frisking. If he's still there please give him love.

... Brion [Gysin]'s book was reviewed incomprehensibly in the *Village Voice* by Burroughs whom I've always found uninterestingly illogical, a trait, even if valid on its own terms, [that] is certainly inappropriate for criticizing a book which itself would seem to be, well, unusual. I'm not especially anxious to read it.

Your new book, on the other hand, sounds marvelous, and important. It's time someone else did a book *about* you too, since you can hardly explain that you're America's least appreciated first-class composer, but you are.

I'm finishing a song cycle for [Gérard] Souzay, a Piano Concerto, and two books for next year—one on music, the other a Final Diary.... Have you received from Boosey & Hawkes my *Letters from Paris,* a choral piece on words of Janet Flanner?

Virgil's let his hair grow long. Result: still shiny on top, but quite curly behind: he resembles Dali's portrait of Sade. He's seriously deaf and testy. He now has much more of an eye than an ear for music (I think he always

did), and makes horrendous misjudgments and pontifical blanket statements, false, and unsubstantiated by example. He's not easy to be with, as
you may gather. The refusal of his opera by the Met understandably disap-
points him (he doesn't talk about it), and now he's writing Etudes for Band.

I hope you're composing also. Are you? . . .

Fond wishes to Maurice and to Jane—

Ned

# Part Three

# 1970s

*18 West 70*
*NYC 10023*
*22 November 1970*

Dear Paul—

One Ronald Patterson has been writing me about you from Buffalo. Certainly you're an artist as deserving of a book as any I can think of; but the kind of questions Patterson asks are best answered by you, i.e., might *Let It Come Down* be "viewed in terms of counterpoint, but how valid is this application of musical terminology to a literary text." Etc. I wrote him that when one starts misapplying the technical terms of one art to another, one gets into hot water. As when Gide calls *Les Faux monnayeurs* a fugue, which it isn't, since its various themes are quite differentiated. Anyway, I told Patterson I'd help him, if I could, about you yourself as I know you, but not about your work which, as the saying goes, speaks for itself. Is all this serious? and would you like me to pursue it? He seems pedantic but thorough.

Aaron Copland (who, on his weekly broadcasts, just did a program on you) has had his 70th birthday celebrations with flair all over America. The party last Saturday at Essex House was big and expensive and as nostalgic as such things can be: testimonies by everyone, 250 guests, tears and champagne, gifts, Claire Reis, and finally Aaron and Lenny (quite drunk) performing at two pianos the *Danzón Cubano* about as well as 8-year-old sight readers, this for national television. . . .

Would love to have your news. The last was last May. Did my *Critical Affairs* reach you? End of March I'll go to Paris to see again those few friends there who are still alive. Then to Greece (have you ever been?) with Ellen Adler. My new Piano Concerto to be premiered next week. It sounds like you. Queda el viento.

Fond wishes—
Ned

## To Virgil Thomson

*Good Friday 1971*

Dear Virgil—

Sorry we couldn't meet when last you were around. But during that 2-week period I composed, orchestrated, copied, and conducted the synchronized taping of 40 minutes of music for the film *The Panic in Needle Park,* and during that period there was a good deal of non-musical bickering with directors, agents, producers, lawyers, and publishers.

Now it's all in the past, I'm pleased with the score (fee $7000), and feeling rather smug. When next we meet I'll be breathing easier.

I'm here now (except for the brief sorties to Cleveland and Illinois) until late July. Most of my time I now spend either reading you or reading about you in newspapers, always with pleasure.

Tenderly—

Ned

### To Lou Harrison

*18 West 70th Street*
*New York, N.Y. 10023*
*6 November 1971*

Golden Lou—

I've been invited (and have accepted) to write the entry on you, for the next edition of Grove's Dictionary. Nothing could be more agreeable, since I've always loved both you and your music. I know pretty much the tone and content I'll use. But could you provide me with (or tell me where I might procure) a fairly complete list of your works, in all categories, published and unpublished? Also suggest a biography which you approve of?

It's, as you know, Virgil's 75th year, and all Manhattan has been mobilized to celebrate this week. Would that you were here! Virgil deserves every drop of it, and is thriving from adulation.

What are your news (as the French say)? and what especially are you composing? I sent you a telegram at the time of your new opera a couple of months ago, but I wonder if it arrived, with the strike and all.

I love you.

And Bill too.

And also Jim.

Ned

### To Kenneth Koch

*18 West 70, NYC*
*24 August 72*

Dear Kenneth—

I'm sorry you're unhappy about the opera not being in your collection. Since Boosey & Hawkes, which represents my work, is a music publisher, and since Random House, which represents yours, is a book publisher, it becomes contradictory for Random House to publish (at whatever price) the complete musical score before Boosey & Hawkes does.

Boosey & Hawkes has spent energy and money preparing the opera for printing, and will spend still more for promotion. They are willing to grant Random House a representative portion of the music for your book to illustrate any point you wish to prove. But for them to cede the engraver's plates (or my manuscript) of the whole piece is defeating to their (our) interests. . . . Would Random House allow another publisher to publish the mss. of other works they had invested in or acquired rights to?

The play *Bertha* is yours, Kenneth, with all its deserved fame. But the opera as an entity pertains to my *oeuvre* (although you will share in publicity given the music and its eventual performance). Don't forget that I gave you $750 for rights to set the play, and that Boosey & Hawkes gave you a contract to your specifications.

It now amounts to the fact that you are asking for 100% rights to the opera in spite of the B&H contract and the fact that as an opera, and therefore a piece of music, it is a more major item in my catalogue than it is in yours in the role of libretto.

I believe in you and respect your rights, and would like you to respect mine.

All best—
Ned


To Kenneth Koch

*28 July 1973*

Dear Kenneth—

The published copy of *Bertha* will finally be out, chez Boosey & Hawkes, in about three weeks—with a red white and blue cover. The first public performance [K. Koch was to act as narrator in this performance] will take place on November 25 and 26, at Alice Tully Hall, at two concerts of my recent chamber music. Jim Holmes will direct mezzo-soprano Beverly Wolff and a dozen young singers in an unstaged version of the piece, with me at the piano. (Please put this down in your date book. Also, I'll see that you get as many copies as you want of the printed score.)

As for *Hearing*, I'll be accompanying a good singer in this next month in Vancouver. And it's being done here in New York on October 2.

I was very touched to receive your note. I've always loved using your words, have hated the thought of a misunderstanding, and have missed you. After returning from Marlboro in around ten days I'll be probably visiting out near you (at Ruth Kligman's or the Gruens') and will most certainly call you.

Fondly,
Ned

### To the family

*Thursday*
*2 August 73*

Dear Ones—

After the first day of difficult acclimation I feel quite at home in Marlboro. Everyone treats me deferentially, and Mr. Serkin is quite affectionate —though I hardly know him. The place is geared to performers more than to composers, so I'm not getting much work done. But it's a very advantageous and attractive place to spend a week. The Hendricks's house looks the same (after 38 years) but the surrounding landscape is now covered with white dormitories and practice rooms. The "tone" is professional, German, young, and ambitious.

Last night: a nice half-program of my music.

Serkin sends you his regards, as does Sol Schoenback, a Philadelphia bassoonist.

Casals is an arrogant old fart looking much younger than his 97 years, with an elegant lovely wife.

I return Monday.

Love & miss you.
Ned

### To Lou Harrison

*October 73*

Thanks for the "Lines to Ned Rorem" on my birthday:

> Dear Ned,
> These Sapphic stanzas are to send you love—
> to wish you every pleasure of your coming
> fiftieth year—a year that I found finest
>       yet of all I'd lived,

the year in which we know we've likeliest not
another half to live, & thus impatient,
prod to live at last most as we want to, &
       slough off false duty.

Your beauty is lengthier than other men's
& all who see you know this, all who hear your
melodies in concert halls delight to seize
       your music's nature.

As only a few years older, & not more
wise at all, still joyous & still most lusty,
We send together from our later Eden
to you in your city of towers & thunder
       much much joy—


## To Virgil Thomson

*13 October 73*

Dear Virgil—

Donald [Gramm] and I have enjoyed working on your songs, and they make a very good opening group. We'll be repeating the program next Friday in Atlanta.

We're all concerned about you in Israel, and hope you'll return safe & sound.

Fondly—
Ned


## To Paul Bowles

*15 March 1974*

Dear Paul—

Not having heard from you makes me apprehensive about your reaction to my book. (Or perhaps the book never came?) Virgil, they say, was not pleased about "his" chapter, nor has he communicated with me for eighteen months.... I would, though, be pleased to hear from you. My next book—*The Final Diary*—comes out in October. But somehow now the whole Book Business seems vain and hopeless. The publishing and critical scene is far more commercial and second-rate with literature than with music, and when finally a book does appear nobody cares, or even knows, unless it's Vonnegut or Barthelme or some other simplistic heterosexual popularizer which the *New York Times* deems to be Where It's At. . . . Meanwhile I've just reviewed, for *Saturday Review,* Tennessee's new little volume of short stories which comes out late next month. Which means that I reread all of his old fiction, to counterbalance my viewpoint. And my! how very very solid and inspired and unusual those first stories were! better even than I'd remembered. The new ones are disappointing, i.e. weaker imitations of the past, but still genuine enough to indicate that if he'd stop writing those pot-boiler plays he could become America's very best short-story writer. Present company excluded. . . . Katharine Hepburn recently played his *Glass Menagerie* on the television, and the music (by England's John Barry) was a pale imitation of yours. . . .

Is it true that Gavin Lambert's living in Tangier now? Would you give him my warm best? I wonder if that's the place to be? America is shaking itself now almost to a cracking point, which makes everyone nervous and polluted and broke. Africa thus seems inviting. But then, I'm thinking of the Africa of my past, already distant, in 1949. Old friends there, except for you, have all left. Guy Ferrand's in Laos. Robert Levesque in provincial France. . . . Jennie Tourel is dead. Lenny Bernstein is interested now in only his own (pseudo-Catholic big-statement) music, and conducts nobody else except Mahler—and that only for TV cameras—when he's not giving brainy lectures on the relation of Chomskian syntax theory to musical composition. I'm not kidding.

My father (do you recall him from Taxco?) is about to be 80, and my mother 76. We meet weekly.

More news, when you send me yours. Yours always interests me far more than maybe you guess.

Toujours

N.

## To Eugene Istomin

*9 April 74*

Dear Eugene—

In the long run a performer, once he takes a given piece into his repertory, spends more time with that piece than its composer ever did. Which doesn't mean his understanding of the piece is more intense than the composer's; on the contrary, it's more relaxed. Thus the performer might find it normal to fool around, to question, to rearrange, and to make variations. This was standard procedure before the twentieth century. In my experience with my own music, for example: the only music of mine which I really "know" is that which I perform (as accompanist) in public, and on which I must therefore practice. I practice it as though someone else had composed it, and find the same technical problems in it that any "outside" performer finds. Sometimes, years after, I'm tempted to make a change or two—but I seldom do. I hesitate to improve upon the *souffle* of the earlier Ned whose first impulse, for better or worse, is what made the piece. (We'll go into this another time.)

All this is by way, as you've guessed, of saying that I've been relooking at [Debussy's] *Reflets dans l'eau,* and really, I must take the side of papa. Admitting that I'm preconditioned (as aren't we all) by my first hearings of this ([Leopold] Godowsky on Brunswick, twelve times a day for a year), the sight of it on paper also convinces me. Certainly you're right in feeling that what you call symmetry (what you really mean is literal repetition: symmetry means mirror image—or inkblot) is Debussy's weakest and most annoying (and most frequent) mannerism. But to use the fact of this mannerism to substantiate your need to repeat those right-hand roulades is risky. Precisely what makes Debussy Debussy (in matters formal) is his slight cracking of symmetry when you least expect it. . . .

I beg you, dear friend, to play what's written, so far as that makes sense to the eye. It's not a question of going back to the manuscript for verification. . . .

Never have I penned such a pedantic letter to a friend. This will reach you where you're quite literally reflecting on the water, if your scheduled boat trip came about. Give my love to your talented colleagues, and ask their advice, but just remember *I'm* right.

. . . Whatever you decide, I'll be awfully anxious to hear your renditions and *they* will be right. . . . Doubtless you've read my series of Reflections of Debussy. Whether you agree or not, you realize what he means to me. I'm thinking of doing the same for Ravel next year. Do you realize it will be his hundredth anniversary?

*Je t'embrasse*
Ned

To Howard Moss

*2 May 74*

Dear Howard—

You'll be interested in knowing that *King Midas* is to be recorded. It's about time, after nearly fifteen years! Yet it's more and more difficult for any contemporary music to reach disks, and virtually impossible with big companies now. At least for me. Anyway, this will be on *Desto* label. The singers will be John Stewart (who sang at Bill [Flanagan]'s memorial, perhaps you remember) and Sandra Walker (a supple mezzo). Probably I'll play the piano, *faute de mieux,* though I'd rather have a real pianist—that is not a composer and not a so-called accompanist. This will be in early August. We'd love you to do program notes, if you're so inclined.

Thanks so much for having your new book sent, and also for the Gotham invitations. Maybe see you there. Jim Holmes and I have rented a house in Nantucket for the summer (except for the first week in August, of course). What are you going to do? It would be nice to see you.

Warm regards—

N

*May 1974*

HAPPY MOTHERS' DAY
DEAR MOTHER

Perhaps you might want to go to the enclosed concert. I don't think I will, however. Let me know when you get back from Philly. I go to Normal, Illinois, from Thursday the 13th through Sunday the 16th.

Love
Ned

To Leonard Bernstein

*17 May 74*

O Lenny—

It's your most persuasive music yet. Inventive, controlled, honest, scary, full of chances which come off, and full of contrasts between different kinds of slow meters. I wasn't bored from start to finish.

Love always—

N

The orchestra, by the way, sounded marvelous. So did the orchestrations, for the most part. The biggest compliment I can give you is: I don't at all know how you found some of those sounds.

(I wonder if, in the Concert Suite, you'll decide to do away with the voices. Any way is good though.)

To John Simon

Re. "Homosexuals in Life and the Arts"

In *The New Leader,* 28 October 1974

*27 October 74*

Dear John—

Nice to see you and Sharon last night, as always.

Thanks for the *New Leader* piece. You asked for a reaction, and following will be just that—not a review.

Because you know I'm your fan, and the fact of your abilities is among my permanent convictions, allow me to consider this essay as not your most reasonable. (Maybe it's a wee bit old-fashioned too: the "problem" doesn't make much difference anymore. But that's another article.) A few examples and questions:

Why balance the "sickness" of homosexuality with the "neuroses" of "so-called healthy heterosexuals"? Anyway, what on earth could be the value of a "cured" homosexual artist?

To "wonder whether such practices [in the past] did not take their toll on wives and the status of women" is pure chauvinism; it (incorrectly) implies you're writing only about male homosexuals. Even so, we all know that the *least* toll on women past and present is due to male homosexuality. Conversely, imagine the toll on the poor families of old Sappho, Saint Joan, Clara Schumann, Bella Abzug!

Parenthood is just too bourgeois a concept for you (are you a father, by the way?) to bring up, especially in an article mostly about the arts. Heterosexual artists can be, often inadvertently, terribly damaging parents (Mann, Isadora, O'Neill), while frankly homosexual artists (Goodman, Vita Sackville-West) have spawned—not adopted—perfectly decent offspring.

If you are uncomfortably right about those aging types (am I one?) glimpsed at intermissions, how about other milieus—professional locker rooms, trigonometry classrooms, the pastures of Kentucky—where Narcissus has not imposed his traits on the more rustic features of quite active inverts? Meanwhile, isn't there a strong androgynous look to Alban Berg, Frank Lloyd Wright, Rockwell Kent (all above reproach), or to every Englishman over 50—not just Bertrand Russell?

As to middle-aged homosexuals having better *bodies* than their straight brothers, that's a question not of carnal penchant but of nationality. Take, for instance, even so undifferentiated a gang as the Latins. All French males, straight or gay, are slobs after 35, preferring food to figure. All Italian males, gay or straight, are svelte after 35, preferring clothes to food (and the well-known Roman narcissism is unrelated to homosexuality). Rich Arabs (all bisexual) are all fat after 35. Poor Arabs (ditto) are slim. Incidentally, John, your body looks in awfully good shape. *Méfiez-vous.*

To claim that homosexuals go only as far as their replica is no more meaningful than to state that members of given classes marry each other. Actually homosexuals (viz *Bloody Sunday* by your own observation) seek physical opposites. But what of that? To declare "that difference is the most precious thing mankind possesses" is to make up the rules *en train*, rules which would be sentimental were they not so hard-hearted.

". . . a question of (as some people are indelicately wont to put it) what you stick your thing into." Who are some people? You, since you wrote it? Other people like to get things stuck into them. For everyone who buggers, someone gets buggered, and turnabout is seldom fair play in such games.

Homosexuals, as you've noticed chez moi, are no more disposed to "copulate on the dining room table" than are your heterosexual hosts and hostesses. I, for one, find any lengthy display boring: endless close-ups of gooey balls are no less tiresome than those of pink clits. Let's have more story line! . . . If, though, there is enough repugnance between the sexes (hard to prove) it does not apply to cultivated people. Unlike a woman or a black, a homosexual in principle is only that while *being* that—not while looking into microscopes or watering plants or discussing non-sexual subjects—such as Elliott Carter—with John Simon.

You mention "the Albertine strategy," yet isn't Proust, finally, the greatest novelist of our century? You suggest that camp is violence in check, yet isn't that like calling minor the sad side of major? Why have any categories? Personally I don't believe camp intends to be hostile. But if homosexual wit (which you propose as those artists' one sizeable contribution) does exist *sans* camp, give me one, just one, example.

All this may sound defensive. But your article does take the offensive to a degree that, knowing you, I feel to be too strong.

In the long run the only interesting side to all this is not whether there is a homosexual art per se, and if so whether such an art is "any good," but whether there is homosexual art above and beyond subject matter. Would Marlowe or Michelangelo have been worse, better, different, or used other source material, had they been straight? In music, especially non-vocal music, the question is still thornier, since music has no tangible "plot," no subject. Would the music of Bach or Chopin, Tchaikovsky or Ravel, Bernstein or Copland or Schuman or Carter have been of a different "kind" (not to mention quality) had their sexual proclivities been other? The always fascinating question of the relation of an artist's life to his work is even more fascinating in music, because music is not "about" anything. The experience of my own existence sheds no light, since my life and music have always gone hand in hand: how can I conceive of my music as coming from other than myself? And who is myself?

The older I grow the more honestly I feel that sex has nothing to do with art or artists. Perhaps that's my androgyny setting in? Perhaps, though, the best art is androgynous; and inasmuch as an art like the theater deals with concrete matters and its perpetrators come to have more identifiably wizened faces than the faces of, say, abstract painters, that art is low class.

Enclosed is a Xerox of The Horse Entry from *The Paris Diary*, 1951. You can answer this letter by stating in your review of *Equus* that it comes too close for comfort to my immortal prose.

Warm greetings, also from Jim,
Ned

## To Paul Bowles

*6 January 75*

Dear Paul,

Thanks for liking the Diary. I told James Purdy what you wrote about his thoughtfulness, and he was pleased, especially since he admires you so much. Coincidentally, both his and my new books have been almost totally ignored by the press, as well as by our respective publishers, and we feel paranoid; your words thus come as a balm.

The balm of your words is supposed also to have flowed through *Rolling Stone* recently. Everyone (from Francine Gray to Morris Golde through *Rolling Stone* staff members) has promised to get me a copy, but so far no luck. . . . Don't you find that prose interferes terribly with your music? Did you ever make any concrete decisions about the conflict? Because the audience for words is so much larger than a composer's audience I find it hard to say no to magazines that want articles, etc., and then resent them for filching my "creative" time. Both vocations get frightfully more difficult with the years, and I'd gladly give up both for sunshine and apple pies, if it weren't for narcissism and also money. (Have to pay for the house in Nantucket. Did I tell you that I bought one there? Nantucket reminds me of Tangier more than any other place. I'm serious. The hills and gardens and crooked streets right in the town itself. Of course, the people are different, but maybe not much. Very right wing.)

Surely I told you I was asked to write your entry for the new Groves—an updating of Peggy Bate's from twenty years ago. A nice thorough job, but they cut it. (Yes, of course I told you—you sent me lists. Thanks.)

. . . I'm writing two big pieces for the Bicentennial, for the Cincinnati and North Carolina symphonies. . . . Never see Virgil, I'm sorry to say. Perhaps this year. May it be a happy one for us all. However, in America everyone is very scared about the Arabs, especially Jews who feel quite genuinely that they'll be wiped out within the next ten years.

Fondly,
Ned

## To ANDREW PORTER

*21 February 75*

Dear Andrew—

Your intelligent essay on Barber's opera contained an arguable clause about a subject close to my heart:

> . . . the publisher, who, in the blunt modern manner, has tied together the tails of eighth and shorter notes, as if voices were no more than wordless instruments. This procedure regularly prompts singers toward metrical delivery rather than an eloquent utterance.
>
> . . .

Assuming that singers learn by note rather than rote, i.e. by themselves rather than with coaches, and that even when a phrase is memorized and "in the voice" they'll retain that phrase (as many good musicians do) through the mind's eye rather than as a series of sounds, you'd still be hard put to prove that their interpretation depends on how that phrase first looked on the page. Do we never hear metrical delivery from one who learns from old unbeamed "vocal" editions, or eloquent utterance from another who learns the same music from an updated "instrumental" edition?

Can a mere listener know that the "home" note value of, say, a Chopin scherzo is a quarter, rather than the psychologically faster eighth or sixteenth? Can he know that the "home" note of a Haydn largo is actually a sixteenth rather than the psychologically slower quarter or half? Sure, the appearance of the music necessarily affects the performer's learning, but the public ear can't vouch for it. At least my ear can't. After a lifetime of pondering the pros and cons of notation (first as a student, then as a paid copyist, finally as composer), and of hearing new music and later studying the scores of that music I am continually excited at how different the notes can look from how they sounded. Especially notes for vocal music.

Vocal music in growing more complex has tended to be written instrumentally, beginning with Berg and early Messiaen. Today, with the notable exception of Britten and of certain elderly conservatives, all composers beam rather than syllabify their vocal lines (or they'll use both methods, like Boulez in *Le marteau*), although much of the time there's no choice since vocal lines now are so often melismatic rather than recitative. (But when they *are* recitative, a metrical delivery would seem implicit, not because of the looks of the notes, but because of the sense of the words.)

Publishers, at least in America, are of two minds about all this. Singers themselves don't seem to care ... they don't even think much about it. What singers (arguably) lose at first sight in word sense, they gain in rhythmic clarity. But anyway, as we all know, singers (including the most intelligent ones) more than any other performers tend, no matter what the "school" of music they're singing, to veer from the score once they've learned it. Which is why I'd love you to show me just one singer who, due to a publication "in the blunt modern manner," is regularly prompted to metrical delivery when metrical delivery is not called for by the composer.

Warmly
Ned

## To Virgil Thomson

*30 April 75*

Dear Virgil—

To say I wasn't bored would be a compliment, since most things—even the very best—bore me. To add that I felt constant joy is the highest praise I know. Your new settings are the only "serious" pieces I've ever heard (not excepting Mozart's) whose humor works—whose humor is part of the music rather than foreground to the music, and so American. Yet, despite the literary point of it all, foreigners too should enjoy these pieces: the antiphony of solo and chorus, the high variety produced by the smallest shifts in piano rhythm, the clean wedding of tune with poem, all this was pleasure, pleasure, pleasure. Lear's your best partner since Stein.

Your prose lately has also been a pleasure. The article on Stravinsky's operas, and the interview about Natalie Barney.

And it's a pleasure to write you these words.

Soon after June first I leave for a solid summer of work in Nantucket (during which JH will be commuting off and on). Before that, perhaps we can meet again. I'd like to give a tea party in a fortnight, and will let you know. Will you be around?

Warmly always—

Ned

(Phyllis Curtin and I are giving a fundraising recital for and at Yaddo next summer, and had planned to do me and you and Aaron. Perhaps your group should now be a big Lear solo, if Phyllis can learn it in time. Anyway, I'll be anxious to own the score when Schirmers . . . .)

## To James Salter

*Nantucket*

*23 July 75*

Dear James—

What a sad and luxurious saga.

That you should think to send it to me was both kind and cruel. In its concern for time passing, for the lavish richness of living which so often seems useless, useless, and for death, your book hits the nail on the head too closely for the comfort of someone like me in whom decay and boredom (especially now at my age) are daily gruel. And I'm sick with jealousy, professional, that you can state so cleanly and so originally what from me sounds like slovenly bromides.

It's the real thing, and I like you for it. The title could have been Marguérite Duras's; *Des journées entières passées sous les arbres*. Such languor. You do for the intelligent American non-creative well-off bourgeoisie what Proust did for the French non-creative upper-class. I love you and thanks....

Ned

It was not, of course, *Henri* de Toulouse-Lautrec who compiled the recipe book (as might be implied from your page 227) but his (I think) niece, Mapie.

To Paul Bowles

*28 West Chester*
*Nantucket, Mass.*
*02554*
*24 July 75*

Dear Paul—

Did you realize that over the past twenty-six years you've sent me more than forty-five letters? I've just mailed Xeroxes of these to Jeffrey Miller in California. It's an unusual but perfectly legitimate idea for a man to supervise the publication of his own mail (Glenway Wescott's doing it too), and I, for one, will devour your book.

Rereading your letters was like reading a saga filled with unanswered questions and/or unquestioned answers. It flows smoothly enough, and always literarily, but sometimes (as with all one-sided collections) I wonder about the other end of the matter, even when the other end is myself.... Have you by chance kept some or all of my letters to you? If so, would you permit me to have copies? or explain how I might go about procuring them? They would make a nice complement (at least for me) to your own set. Now, with advancing years, I'm getting a sense of order which I'm sure you comprehend; yet I never started keeping carbons of even business letters until five years ago.

What are you writing and what are your plans? Might you come to Nantucket where I now spend five months of the year? I'm writing a lot of music, but no words at all....

Write me your thoughts and a bit of gossip....

Fondly—

Ned

### To Virgil Thomson

*28 West Chester*
*Nantucket*
*Labor Day 1975*

Dear Virgil—

Phyllis Curtin and I will be doing three groups—by you, me, and Copland—at Yaddo on the 24th. We won't be able to rehearse together until a day or two before. Meanwhile, much of my music is still in New York (where I return on the 18th).

Your group consists of the Frank O'Hara poem, and the long Lear solo. Two questions:

What is the title of the O'Hara song?

On the last page of "Bongly Bo," first measure, right hand, second beat, is the half-note truly a B-flat as written, or might it be an A? I'm using the faded Xerox you sent, and have penciled in many "corrections," but this B-flat is the only real uncertainty (because the cross-harmony seems not in keeping with the rest of the piece). The song is very rewarding, but the piano part is hard, especially the l.h., because it's so exposed, and because the triadic formations are seldom twice the same. I'll be interested to hear Phyllis at it.

Nantucket's been ideal all summer. Lots of work and no sociability. I received an anonymous fan letter from someone in Vermont who sent a picture but no name or address and who said that, thirty years ago, you and Maurice had, by your contact, revolutionized his life.

Jim is perfect, and sends his warm greetings. Hope you're thriving and fruitful.

Fondly—
Ned

### To Howard Moss

*28 West Chester*
*Nantucket*
*11 September 75*

Dear Howard—

This was the summer when, after various tries during the past four decades, I read Proust *d'un bout à l'autre,* and it's natural that you're the first person I'd want to notify of my change of life. What an experience to complete him at 51 rather than—like so many people—at 21. (Has anybody ever read him at 36?) I used both the *texte* and the Moncrieff-Blossom about whose lives I'd like to know more. And now about Proust himself I suddenly feel uninformed, and have so many questions to ask you. Jim Holmes was supposed to bring your *Magic Lantern* back from New York, but looked high & low and couldn't find it. I realize now that I never did have it, but thought I did and was putting off reading it until I'd read MP himself. How do I obtain it?

In a week I go to Yaddo to raise money with Phyllis Curtin. In mid-October to North Carolina for a premiere of a big new orchestra piece. Otherwise I'm here (since last May, and maybe into November) which I've loved. How was *your* first summer in *your* new house? We must compare notes, not only on Proust but on weeding. And also on the recording of *King Midas* which is presumably out by now.

Have you been fruitful? Jim sends his love as do I.

Ned

## To Morris Golde

*Nantucket*
*Friday 26 Sept. 75*

Dear Old Morris—

Despite a raging thunder storm and acute attack of hay fever, Phyllis and I, night before last, raised six thousand dollars for Yaddo by offering that least remunerative of commodities: an all-American song recital. The local swells gave us a standing ovation, and Phyllis has never sounded better, like a 20-year-old. We did three of Virgil's, of which the "Bongly Bo" was the hit of the evening. We worked very hard on it and I'm sorry he couldn't have heard it. But tell him Phyllis plans to do this same program for the next twelve months, beginning next Saturday.

Despite the acute attack of hay fever and a still raging thunder shower the plane last night made it from Albany to Nantucket, and here in the radiant sunshine I now am. Jim left this morning for New York but returns next week. Last night we went over his Thomson-Bach program, which he'll play on October 26. How elegant and original it is! Organists usually couple their Bach with Messiaen, when they want to be up-to-date, but JH's combination is far fresher and so theatrical.

The newest local horror is that the Unitarian Church has repaired their campanile. You will recall the disgusting "concert" that emerged twice daily last summer from the Congregational tower (the soupily amplified recordings of smarmy hymns)? Well, add to this now the thrice daily playing of 52 strokes from the Unitarian tower (to call sailors to work at seven, to dinner at noon, and to bed at nine), plus the hourly time-telling chimes, and you have 212 peals each 24 hours. I bitterly resent this, particularly since editorials in the paper here say that 99% of the islanders love it and the remaining one percent should seek haven elsewhere. This makes me bitter.

On the sweet side are my blackberry bushes, still bearing, with perfect purple fruits the size of golf balls, ideal for deep-dish pies. This afternoon I shall go swimming, I think.

Thanks for your two messages. As of now I've still received no invitation in any shape or form from the North Carolina Symphony to attend the premiere of *Assembly and Fall*. (Oh, various minor secretaries, who write for publicity photos and program notes, etc. and how I'll be lionized, etc. But I can hardly be lionized if I pay my own way.) Another orchestra would long since have booked my passage and reserved hotel rooms. (Ormandy himself invited me to his performance of my *Eagles* last week, which, incidentally, was called "a masterpiece" by the Philadelphia *Inquirer*.) But N.C. conductor John Gosling, far from having told me he likes the piece, hasn't even given me a rehearsal schedule, much less asked my advice about the tone of it all. Considering it's the hardest thing I've ever written—a single movement 25 minutes long—I'd think, wouldn't you?, that he'd like a word of advice about how to hold it together dramatically.

As you see, I'm in a huff. Doubtless at the last moment they'll invite me. If not, my duty to myself (not to mention my curiosity) will probably take me there incognito. In any case, I wish you'd plan to go. By coincidence, Phyllis sings on the same program!

I've nearly completed my *Eight Etudes* for piano, for Emanuel Ax. Now for Akron I must write a 15-minute piece for mezzo soprano with two strings and piano. Any ideas about texts? I'm thinking of either 18th-century love poems, or maybe Jimmy Schuyler and/or Adrienne Rich.

They say the Erick Hawkins show was lamentable. Well.

Wallace [the cat] thrives, now out of the hospital. And Mother is better, I saw her—them—twice last week. I stay here now until at least October 9th. Call or write. Hope you're well. Love to all. New address: Box 764.

Ned

To Lou Harrison

*18 West 70th Street*
*New York, NY*
*29 December 75*

Beloved Lou—

On January 10–13 the San Francisco Symphony is playing my *Air Music,* a long suite in ten movements, premiered only last month by [Thomas] Schippers in Cincinnati most beautifully. It turns out to be a quite difficult piece, more so than I'd planned, so the SF performance might be cut and/or rough-edged. I wouldn't presume to ask you to go, but could you possibly send me any (if any) reviews, bad though they may be? The west coast (which means you, since I value you most of those there) seems ever farther off, especially now that, with James Holmes, I've bought a house in Nantucket. We go there for long summers, and even for occasional icy winter weeks. I'm working quite a bit—though a lot of my *need* (not to mention my breath control) for musical composition has weakened. Virgil, who's having something of a (deserved) comeback, and I are on good terms again, thank God, and life is full mostly of books and desserts. Sugar means a lot to me now that I don't drink or smoke or swear anymore. I pray that handsome Bill Colvig thrives, and that you'll both give me news of yourselves (and of that which emerges *from* yourselves) soon. Meanwhile, warm wishes for this and every new year.

Ned

To Judy Collins

*1 February 76*

Very dear Judy—

After we spoke I *did* come down with flu, felt monstrous, but am picking up gradually.

Meanwhile five kilos of Collinsiana were delivered to the door.

The autobiography in the *Songbook* rings very true. (We've been lounging in our respective sick beds reading each other's confessions.) You write as you sing, with a clear, honest, unvibrating, restricted but nonetheless full, voice.

As for the records, I've not begun to be able to hear them all. Let me say just for the moment that your French is most comprehensible, and that the understatement of the "Pirate Jenny" song is most convincing. (I saw Marc

Blitzstein often while he was doing the *Threepenny* translations. He's one of the few composers in the world who could sing his own material—who could put it over—yet he had absolutely no voice. Take it as a compliment if I say that you remind me of *Marc with equipment*.)

By now you'll have gone to and returned from Chicago. See you Saturday. Jules [Feiffer] and Susan [Crile] will be here too, and my dear friend Jim Holmes. . . . On page 195 of *The Final Diary* I must add your name to that arbitrary list of J.C.'s.

Fondly forever—
Ned

## To Leontyne Price

*13 May 76*

For a musician a song exists in the abstract.

For the public a song is what a singer makes of it.

For Ned there is only Leontyne.

The two greatest thrills of my life occurred the same week: winning the Pulitzer, and hearing you sing my music.

Forever Yours,
Ned

## To Judy Collins

*29 May 76*

Dearest Judy—

Tried to call you back.

Tomorrow (Sunday), all crumpled and anxious, I leave for the whole summer in Nantucket where my address will be as below.

Where will you be?

It's beginning to rain. And the thrill, the childlike thrill, of a new vacation season about to begin, is superseded by the anxiety, the adult anxiety, of one less season just chalked off in life.

I believe in you.

Faithfully—
Ned

To Paul Bowles

*Nantucket*
*4 June 76*

Dear Paul—

I've just won the 1976 *Pulitzer Prize*. It's for a 10-movement orchestra piece called *Air Music*, commissioned and premiered by Thomas Schippers and the Cincinnati Symphony. The Pulitzer's something I've always wanted (and felt I deserved) but assumed I'd never get because of my wicked ways. Perhaps it's natural that I'd want you to know: you're the first real composer (after Leo Sowerby) to whom I ever showed my little pieces—in Taxco in 1941, if you recall—and now we've all grown up, more or less. Please tell Gavin, if you see him.

Am in Nantucket again now, for the summer, and in all my smug glory I feel a bit impotent, as though every note or word I write henceforth has to be "good." Well, anyway, in a recent interview, when asked who the *one* composer in America I felt musically closest to was, I replied without hesitation, Paul Bowles.

A fortnight ago at a party John Hammond was wondering about you, and so I gave him your address. All right? Please let me know about [Edouard] Roditi's health. Virgil's in the hospital with a bad foot, but otherwise thriving and very performed.

Alice Esty's retired, paints nice pictures, and subsidizes a chamber music series.... Ellen Adler divorced, also painting.... Not much good art around, and standards lowering everywhere. For example, I just returned from Ohio where a new piece was premiered. (A piece for singer, two strings, and piano.) In addition, Akron University gave a concert of all my music, I gave a speech also to the Fine Arts Dept., and later at Kent State gave a reading to the University at large. Each of these four well-publicized events was in a hall seating 300. Each pulled a crowd of maybe 36 people— which did not include the music faculties who were (in the case of Akron) at a rock concert in the amphitheater next door. The Kent State trustees have meanwhile cut the entire $15,000 budget for the Artists-Lecture-Series, but granted a million dollars to the athletic program. I should think that Morocco or Sweden or even Paraguay are no more abject than this.

Affection—
Ned

## To Cynthia Ozick

*10 November 76*

Very dear Cynthia—

I loved your book. You have a great deal to say and you have your own voice. The position from which you view things (though not necessarily your "viewpoint") and the things you choose to view and then to write about, are so removed from my own that they strike me as brand new. And your way is that of the real writer: insanely precise. Which gives all the stories a dream quality. Above all you have a good ear—a better ear than, say, Paul Goodman. (Which doesn't mean you're better than he, but that, more than he, you have a gift of gab.) My favorite is "Virility." It begins like a daft mixture of [Henry James's] *Four Meetings* and Auden's libretto, *Elegy for Young Lovers* —only the theme, that is—and then turns into pure Ozick. Someday we'll talk about your writing from inside a man's skin. (As Paul Bowles once narrated from inside a woman.) A slippery but thrilling business.

Thanks also for your letter. When you write that you are "badly disorganized" you mean, of course, that you're badly *organized*. Surely, then, when you state that passion plays "historically accomplished instigation of pogrom, massacre," etc., I can take that with a grain of salt. Christian uprightness (which stems right from Jewish uprightness) may well be the cause of much bloody history. But the Passion Play itself, no more than *Oedipus* or *The Golem* or *Hamlet* or Bach's *Saint Matthew Passion,* never made anything happen, but only reported on what *had* happened. No genre is in itself invalid. As for Judas, did you know that within the Church he is considered "the greatest sufferer" insofar as he was forced to execute, against his logical will, what was prewritten? And then, despite this act, was denied sanctity, though he performed God's will?

I agree with you about the junkiness and opportunism of *Superstar* and [Bernstein's] *Mass.* And maybe we agree about the possibility of James's life as an opera. Anyway I can't do it for a long time.

In music I've never been able to "insert" my birthright religious textually into sound, because the Society of Friends has no musical history. I've set to music tons of the Old Testament, and the New, both Protestant and Catholic. But now finally I've written a long non-vocal piece for organ solo, called *A Quaker Reader.* It's being premiered on February second in Alice Tully Hall by organized Leonard Raver. Will you consider putting that on your list?

Let's be friends, and meet again during the coming winter.
Warmly—
Ned


## To Paul Bowles

*17 April 77*

Dear Paul,

A pleasure, as always, to receive your letter, especially quite out of the blue. I'm glad you saw the *Music Journal* reference, which I meant with all my heart. It was not I, incidentally, who titled that years-old review, "Come Back, Paul Bowles," it was *The New Republic*. Would I write such a piece today? I know that in the case of Virgil I'd never re-do what I did to his Lord Byron. Artists, good or bad, do what they must do, and won't veer just because some reviewer tells them to. If that reviewer happens to be a friend, there's a real moral problem involved (you surely felt it yourself in the *Tribune* days). I now think it's *wrong* to criticize publicly the work of friends, especially now that I've reassessed VT's music and have different slants. Have I changed about you? Certainly I don't like your music less, but do probably like your prose more—especially the extraordinary books with Mrabet, and many of the stories from all your "periods." Many weeks ago I gave Millicent Dillon a printed essay-plus-notes about "Song in America." Did New World Records (probably not) send you the record which this essay adorns? Donald Gramm sings, beautifully, two of your songs. Let me know if you don't have this. You're the best thing (except for [Theodore] Chanler) on the disc. As for Dillon, she struck me as earnest and capable, and surely Jane deserves a book. Jane's play *A Quarreling Pair* is on the regular bill of "The Little Players" (puppeteers) with prelude and interlude— very evocative—by you, from (I think) *Music for a Farce.* . . . Of mutual friends I've recently spent time with Aaron (very very famous, and happy, but a wee bit *oblieux*); Lenny (maritally separated and rigorous champion for Gay Lib—at this late date!); and Virgil, very deaf, but very appreciated by press and performers everywhere. . . . Would love to have more news of you. Is Morocco pollen free? Hay fever destroys me, and I'd love an excuse to return to Africa for a while.

Fondly—
Ned

## To Paul Bowles

*25 May 77*

Dear Paul—

The only thing about your news of Lenny Bernstein (his having in no way altered except physically in twenty years) that surprises me is that he was to meet Felicia in Paris. Last year they very publicly split up, and Lenny very publicly "came out" (as they say here), and yes, he doesn't get less overbearing as the years flow by. . . . Last night the Everard Baths burned to the ground, killing a dozen customers and severely maiming a hundred others. That's the top headline nationally this morning, and disconcerting. . . . I'd hoped to see Jane's play before writing you again, but have been feeling punk (allergies) and can't go out. People love it. When I lived in Europe people always assumed I received all reviews but I never did. So I'm sending you the enclosed, though maybe you've already got seven copies. . . . I've finished a book called *An Absolute Gift* which Simon & Schuster will publish next March. My eighth. But I can't begin to write "fiction" as you so thrillingly do. . . . If only I could see Morocco again, especially because you are still there. Maybe next fall. But the older I get the less need I feel to spread wings. . . . Will write again soon. Best to all, especially Gavin [Lambert] and Edouard [Roditi].

Have you another book soon?

Ned

## To John Cheever

*16 June 77*

Oh John,

Your souvenir of Elizabeth [Ames] was very very touching. The last time I saw her was with you. I hate to think of Yaddo without her. (Or without Polly [Hanson].) Will you be at the memorial tomorrow? I won't, alas, but I *will* be at Yaddo during most of August. Otherwise the summer will be spent in Nantucket (where I now have a house) and in California, and in the heat of New York.

Meanwhile, I've just read *Falconer* and loved it. I would never (as Virgil Thomson's mother, age 90, declared after hearing her first John Cage concert of music for "prepared" pianos) have thought of doing it myself. Your cast, every member of it, is remote from me. Yet your portrayals are so compassionate and true, and your writing so elusively easy and so necessary, that

I almost felt comfortable in your prison. What a gift you have! If I didn't love you, I'd envy you.

I wish we met oftener. Below is my phone if you ever come to town. (Has this been sent to the correct address?)

Fondly ever—

Ned


### To Paul Bowles

*7 August 77*

Dear Paul—

Yesterday I stopped by the Gotham Book Mart and saw, bought, brought home, and read *Things Gone and Things Still Here* and *Next to Nothing*. You haven't lost the touch. The stories all have your signature, energy, and pathos. (Would you consider again using an American setting, as you've occasionally done in the past? Your particular strangeness in a familiar setting—familiar at least to an American—could seem still stranger.) . . . The long poem is the real thing: a poem, not versified prose. It is likeable, believable, and even moving. (It is not optimistic.)

Have just returned from a fortnight in San Rafael where I was composer-in-residence at a music festival. It's been eleven years since I set foot in that very foreign state of California. The drought there is sad to behold. More disconcerting, of course, is the human fauna: golden WASPS behaving like Mexicans. Everyone is blond and muscular and Irish, but with a mañana tone of placid vagueness about Art and Life. They think a lot about health foods as though the ensuing strength would protect them from the imminent earthquake. New York by contrast is befouled and vicious, but has a vitality and a conscience.

Just talked to Virgil, speaking of vitality. He's having a big season, and deserves it. He's just back from Yaddo where tomorrow I go for three weeks in order to start a largish orchestra piece called *Stages of a Saint* and another piece for guitar and flute to be named *Romeo and Juliet*.

Do you remember Jim Holmes? You dined here with him nine years ago. Anyway, for the past many months he's been going through a very very very trying period which reminds me a bit of Jane's (that is, of what little I saw of her woes, and would presume to allude to), and sometimes, vainly perhaps, I wish you were here to give me advice. Patience, sympathy, and logic seem unavailing. But perhaps patience and sympathy and logic aren't what's needed, or aren't what they appear to be for the person preferring them.

I never answered your last nice letter about your rereading my books. I have still another one due out next spring, to be titled *An Absolute Gift*. If Simon & Schuster sent you an advance galley would you consider writing a blurb? It would be a real honor.

Do you publish your work now with Black Sparrow by preference? The editions are indeed beautiful, and the paper stock is better than that of larger houses. But it would be pleasant if you had a bigger distribution. Not that larger houses are a guarantee of a bigger distribution.

Fondly
Ned


To John Ashbery

*Nantucket*
*23 October 77*

My only John—

I've already read your marvelous *Houseboat Days* and realize, as Viking's ad in today's *Times* warns, that I'll never "look at the world or at words the same way again." Indeed, I'm afraid now of exploring [Lawrence] Durrell's *Sicilian Carousel,* since the same ad tells me that "no person, place, or thing can ever quite remain the same" after this experience. The same as what? as before reading John's book? or as after reading John's book? I wouldn't want to be changed from what your book changed me into. Anyway, Nantucket, where I'm all alone trying to get some work done for a fortnight (and today's my birthday) is unbearably clear and cold and bright. Wish you were here. Will you come sometime? Meanwhile, I return on November fourth. November twentieth, a Sunday afternoon, would you like to come hear five 19th-century English poems, as musicalized by me, at the Guggenheim Museum? If not, perhaps you and David [Kermani] would come for that overdue meal chez JH and me.

I'll phone you around the 8th.

Fondly—
Ned

## To Judy Collins

*23 October 77*

Dearest Judy—

By the time you read this you'll have put the operation into the past. Let me know as soon as you feel like it how you feel. If you want to feel worse, read Norman Podhoretz's despicable article, hawkish and bigoted, in the current *Harper's*. If you want to feel better, come to Nantucket: it's cold and unpolluted and bright yellow all over the island today, and in the back yard are four fat pheasants, gold and crimson and dowdy, like the queen of England. If you can't come now, then plan on Thanksgiving. I return to New York on Nov. 4th. Then Jim and I will come back here on November 21st, a Monday. You and Jerry might plan to come on Tuesday or Wednesday, but arrange it now with either Air New England, or with Northwest and the Boston shuttle. . . . Jim tells me I'm crassly wrong to make critical comments to you about the construction of your record albums, and to presume to suggest program-making improvements. I suppose he's right, since you've never asked for comments, and never criticized me along the same lines. But I can't help it. Bear with me. Tender thoughts ever. (Today is my birthday.)

Ned

## To Norman Podhoretz

*23 October 77*

Dear Norman,

With alarm I've read your pieces in *TV Guide* and *Harper's*. As a professional thinker you will now be heeded by the mobs who see these magazines. But in your heart can you truly defend your dangerous contentions? You put forth opinions as absolutes, then draw conclusions as laws.

Who, beyond yourself, detects the ghostly presence of Vietnam behind our treatment of "other events"; and why, if it does exist, is that presence wrong? Do no wise people consider our withdrawal from Vietnam other than "defeat and humiliation"? Is preparedness the only lesson to be learned?

You say "pacifist" as though all shared your contempt; yet pacifist Quakers (among whom I am birthright member) are not generally despised—indeed, they received a Nobel Prize. You say "war seems to be regarded as the greatest of all imaginable evils" as though the regard were daft; yet what is more evil? You say there is a "revulsion against America itself" as though the country we live in did not belong to us all—except to traitors who doubt the morality of the arms race. Their treachery you link with homosexuality, as though homosexuals had fared better than Jews or Gypsies at the hand of Hitler.

You speak as though there were no alternative to war, whereas today there is no alternative to peace: isn't it obvious that equality of strength no longer pertains to who can wipe who off the globe? It should seem childish to need to point out—to you, a logician and a "mind"—that method, if not madness, has changed since Germany, even since Vietnam.

Many a sober American (and, who knows? maybe even an occasional gay who loves his homeland dearly) now works staunchly toward international understanding—or at least toward reined-in misunderstanding—through solutions other than the eternal folly of fighting.

Sadly,
Your friend—
Ned

## To Virgil Thomson

*14 Nov 77*

Dear Virgil—

*Four Saints* is the one work which can withstand both good and bad performances because it has no faults. I liked being present at it last week. As for *Socrate* (as near to my heart as to yours, perhaps) we'll talk of that when next we meet, which I hope is soon. . . .

Missing you.
Fondly,
Ned

## To Gore Vidal

*16 November 77*

Dear Gore—

In a week or two Simon & Schuster will send you bound galleys of *An Absolute Gift—A New Diary*. This is a terrible imposition, I know. But a blurb from you on a book by me might just change (for the better) the face of American letters. In any case, I'd be grateful for your reaction.

The book's quite formal for the diary it purports to be, and is mainly about music, queerness, death, and the "esthetics" of being an artist today.

I wish we saw each other oftener than quadri-annually. Would you phone sometime when you're in America? (I just may be in France next May—first time in six years.)

Please give my fond regards to Howard.

Warmly ever—

Ned


To Norman Podhoretz

*Nantucket*

*22 November 77*

Dear Norman—

I'd have acknowledged your letter ages ago but for the fact that I only just got it. Commuting as I do between Nantucket and New York, mail accumulates at each end.

We shall always remain friends, and that relieves me, though we shall never never agree about crucial points, and that saddens me. My whole life has, in its instruction, been diametrically opposed to your theses, and surely I'm not about to change. Perhaps someday we can talk about these things *à vive voix*. If we live that long.

Just one more little thing: You say in your letter that homosexuals in their literature express contempt for ordinary life. But whose literature, pray, extols ordinary life? Not Dostoevsky's surely, nor Faulkner's, nor Jane Austen's nor even George Sand's, nor Philip Roth's, nor your own (learning from Leavis, or hobnobbing with Huntington Hartford, or editing *Commentary*, or, indeed, writing books, is not ordinary life). Of course, I don't know how you define contempt, much less ordinary life. If by ordinary life you mean middle-class heterosexuality, I, for one, think that's swell. Why not read Donald Windham (a hundred percent homosexual)'s new novel, *Tanaquil*, which is one of the most beautiful and crystalline apologies ever penned in defense of young heterosexual productive love. It's risky, I feel, for heterosexuals (and homosexuals too) to be too quick at assuming that gay artists are equipped to express only what's shakily named a gay sensibility, rather than, simply, a sensibility of human artists.

Anyway. Please give my greetings to Midge. Tell her she's in my new book, *An Absolute Gift*. . . . (It's my eighth book, which is incredible, seeing as how I'm not even a writer.)

Best always—

Ned

## To Judy Collins

*27 April 78*

My only Judy—

Your *cri du coeur* reached my own heart and I'm sympathetic to all you're going through, now and for the next weeks.

Jim (who has ups and downs) and I leave Sunday—standby—for London, from whence we return, wiser and older, on May 13. We'll write you from there. Later we'll try to find an apposite meeting.

Read and think.

With more than love,

Ned

## To Morris Golde

*Nantucket*

*18 June 78*

Thanks, dear Morris, for sending the *Nation* review. It's open and fair, don't you agree, and with the points well taken? Of course, like everyone else, [Ben] Sonnenberg (who is he?) wants me to remain what I can no longer be—a precocious brat. And when he ends the piece by stating that he's sure I'll know what he means, I feel like giving Gide's reply: Don't be too quick to understand me!

Lenore Ross sent a note plus Alvin [Ross]'s brochure, which plunged me into the sad and thrilling past, and how long we've all known each other, cutting through so many textures. Alvin's pictures seem now absolutely gorgeous. I can't call them "uncompromising" simply because there was never a question of compromise; he did what he wanted rather than (like a whore) what was required by abstract-expressionist dictates of the time.

Thanks also for lending Mina Curtiss's *Bizet*. (It turns out I already had a paperback of it, so I'll return your first edition when next we meet in New York.) It's a big and interesting help to my *Carmen* essay. I'm also reading her *Other People's Letters*. My God, she's perspicacious and admirable. But there's something about her I don't like, a sort of ungrateful pushiness with all those Parisians who went to some lengths to help her research. I realize that others criticize in me what I criticize in her (an easy narcissism, a biter of the hand that feeds); but I never feel an added touch of vulnerability, of sweetness, chez elle. Do you know her? The Bizet book's dedicated to Marc [Blitzstein], and I do remember him talking about her. I'm stunned to discover how many people mentioned in the *Letters* book I actually knew, if only peripherally, people who by their very inclusion were friends of Proust. Curtiss was in Paris in 1947–48, that is, during the whole year before I arrived. But by 1949 it seemed largely "cured" of what she complains of: bad heating, food shortages, etc. Or was I still young enough to find that romantic?

Nantucket meanwhile is identical to itself. The weather's been idyllic and we've been raking lots of grass and making pies. Am not working at all, but reading vastly and combing the cat. JH is in the city for the weekend (his church, etc.), and I'm expecting a (female) reporter from *People Magazine* who's coming—a perfect stranger—to spend several days. (She'll stay at the Folger House.) I have mixed feelings about all this, the vulgar media it's called. Yet as I look around at, say, Susan Sontag or Pierre Boulez, doing exactly the same thing, despite their so-called high integrity, I realize that the only way to get heard is through the fat channels that are now part of our culture, even though the hearing is made up mostly of misquotations. And now Felicia [Bernstein] too is dead.

It would be pleasant if you want to come for a few days. Mother & Father will be here for a week as of July 14. I'll be in NY for a week as of July 20. Also August 20. But call, and we'll fix up something maybe.

I love you always.

Ned

### To Judy Collins

*Nantucket*
*7 August 78*

Ah yes, Judy—

Are we to meet on the 18th with Louis? Jim won't be able to make it, but I'll look forward to it.

Meanwhile, keep this in mind:

I go to Yaddo on the 20th and will stay there until the 27th.

On Friday the 25th Ormandy will rehearse my new piece, *Sunday Morning*, at 10 a.m. and then the world premiere will be performed that evening on a mixed program that includes Emanuel Ax playing the Chopin Concerto for which he'll get a standing ovation, while I am left out in the cold, since audiences don't know what ever to do with live composers. As you see, I'm nervous. Your presence, if you still think you might like to come, would give me moral support. We could go together to both the morning rehearsal and the evening performance, and you could come up late Thursday night. Let me know how you feel about it.

The Saratoga people phoned this morning to say that the 25th is also Nelson Rockefeller's 70th birthday, and since he'll be there, and has given millions to the Center, would I dedicate my piece to him. Jim said it was okay, so I said okay, despite mixed feelings about Rockefeller, who, nevertheless, *has* been more helpful toward the arts than many a liberal.

If you want to come to Nantucket this coming weekend, you'd be welcome. I'll be here alone. . . . Otherwise, September.

Love ever, ever—
Ned


## To Gore Vidal

*16 September 78*

Dear Gore—

I am a slow reader, but last week in one sitting I finished *Kalki* and haven't been the same since, dazzled and depressed.

People (I've done so myself) sometimes refer to aloofness as your Achilles heel. But if one doesn't contemplate one's navel (I've done so myself!), one's fellow Americans get suspicious. Whatever your outward reactions to individuals, surely *Kalki* shows you as terribly concerned about the planet.

Bravo and love—
Ned


## To Leontyne Price

*9 October 78*

Oh Leontyne—

I heard (saw) your program here in Nantucket, as did my sister in Philadelphia, and my parents in New York.

You've never sounded more meltingly strong and gorgeous. And you looked like a teenager.

I was especially moved at sharing the bill with my beloved Margaret Bonds. Did you know that she was my first piano teacher? In Chicago.

Love to you, Leontyne. You deserve showers of silver from heaven.
Ned

To Charles-Henri Ford

*Nantucket*
*Thanksgiving 78*

Very dear Charles-Henri—

The reason I've not yet sent a contribution to your *Blues* is because twice you stipulated that you were hoping for something "scandalous." Now, I have no notion of what that word could possibly mean to you in this day and age (surely nothing sexual, nor political, nor experimental). My suspicions are, however, that you would be bored with the only kind of prose I'm capable of: a sensible and responsible reaction to the morality and the art in the world around me, as diagrammed in my usual précis-style diary. Thus, unless you want to use this letter, you most forgo my formal expressivities, while knowing that you have my sincerest wishes for the success of your magazine. May it be endlessly outrageous according to your manner.

Love forever—
Ned

To John Cheever

*Nantucket*
*28 November 78*

Dear John—

When next we meet (that won't be too far away, will it?) I'll tell you how I feel about your book of stories, two copies of which were given me on my birthday last month. Meanwhile, though I've only, and with great pleasure, read half of them, I'm compelled to point out a couple proofreader's errors:

586, third line, the Italian is incorrect (as also on last line of 593)

*ce* should be the reflexive *se*, i.e. *"La moglie se ne va"*

On the same page (and on 586), you refer to Bach's two-part variations,

though surely you mean two-part Inventions.

673 *Cri du Coeur* and *cri du ventre* NOT *de*
Other misprints are more personal—very personal—
Wherever one looks one sees you.
It's only because I'm jealous that I send this *cri du ventre*.
*Je t'aime*
Ned

### To Leonard Bernstein

*4 January 79*
*Thursday*

Dear Lenny—

Could I show you a 20-minute suite called *Sunday Morning* for large orchestra, which I'd like you to consider doing the New York premiere of?

In any case it's time for our bi-annual confabulation. You've been very much on my mind these past months.

Love
Ned

### To Andrew Porter

*6 January 79*

Dear Andrew:

It is axiomatic that our favorite critics (among whom you rank high on my list) not only inspire us with many a "How true," but also with vital exasperation and sometimes even with perplexity, especially when they propose a grand notion and then leave it dangling. On this last count I must wonder—since your current essay implies that great composers are great (or "active") insofar as "each new work of theirs breaks new ground"—what you mean by new ground. Surely the criterion is modernistic, inapplicable to anyone before Beethoven (and even *he* might have missed your point). Meanwhile, the ploughing of unexplored but arid fields has for a century been par for the course of dilettantes, while various great composers (Chopin for example, or Ravel) never broke new ground, either within their epochs or within the progress of their own lives—in the sense that they "advanced" from one "period" to another.

Now specifically with Carter, as opposed to Messiaen whom you disqualify on these terms, what new ground was broken between, say, his settings of Elizabeth Bishop's poems and those of John Ashbery? Is the ground a group of instruments? or the use of a subliminal Greek voice? or a harmonic vocabulary? By such tokens could not Messiaen's promised opera be called new ground? But how does this ground make either of them great?

I can't dispute here your choice of "perhaps six established very important composers." Still, your definition for their very importance is also very important, yet seems too vague for the comfort of some readers.

I loved seeing you recently for tea, and wish we met too oftener.
Yours in friendship for the new year ...
Ned


### To Judy Collins

*27 January 79*

Chère grande amie:

Your letter shook me, pleasantly.

I'd been wanting to call you soon anyway—partly because I feel (in the sadness of life passing irretrievably) the need of a "Meeting" or two.

I bumped into Jules [Feiffer] yesterday on 12th Street. It was his fiftieth birthday. Congratulate him: it's really an accomplishment for anyone. ...

I'll be in Philadelphia when you return, but come back on Tuesday. Let's meet soon thereafter.

Love ever—

Ned

I'm of mixed feelings about Anita Ellis's Feb. 4th recital. If she doesn't sing me I don't want to go. Is that wrong?


### To Paul Bowles

*26 February 79*

Dear Paul,

It's been too long. I'm penning this from Nantucket where I've been for the past week, trying to write songs. Had planned to fly back to New York this afternoon, but the island's fog-bound and heavy rain has been falling for three days. Planes grounded. So along with the songs I'll write you.

My friend Moira Hodgson—she of the ivorine skin and hair like ginger ale, youngish and beautiful and almost albino—says she visited you last year (do you recall) and that you "held court" each day in your apartment. Moira, meanwhile, had a malignant tumor deep behind her left retina and the whole eye was removed in September in London. Now she wears a black patch, while awaiting the manufacture of an artificial eye.

What news can I give, that you don't have already? All of our mutual friends are identical to when I last wrote, though older. Aaron is dismayingly forgetful: he can't remember what he said or did from any ten-minute period to the next, yet paradoxically this does not interfere with his lucrative conducting career: apparently a piece of music, existing in its own time slot, carries him along. . . . Virgil, though hopelessly deaf, is anything from senile, and receiving a great deal of musical attention. . . . Lenny, after spending months in bed after Felicia died, is now very public, very theatrical, smokes incessantly, and has a boyfriend whom he makes no pretense at "hiding." . . . Elliott Carter has been canonized as America's official Great Composer, now that he's seventy, and a slew of (to me) uninteresting others —like [George] Rochberg and [Jacob] Druckman—are also "almost great." . . . Your songs appear on song programs oftener than you might think, and two of them are "required" for contestants of the upcoming vastly publicized Rockefeller singer contest. . . . And Jane's name appears frequently on the gratuitous "list of five favorite authors" proffered by young writers, who never knew her, on their qualification exams.

Remembrance of Jane is part of what brings me to write. My friend Jim Holmes (you met once, in 1968) has for two years lived in a depressed, dark, persecuting cloud, and doesn't seem to be able to make things fit together. Therapy's been unavailing, and so has hard-core perseverance. We talk and talk and talk. And sometimes when we talk, I remember your talking with Jane (and your talking about talking with her), especially when you were at Libby [Holman]'s in 1959. You seemed so patient, sitting up night after night with her, and she seemed sometimes to get better, then fall back. It's dumb, and maybe wrong, of me to bring this up now, especially since JH is emerging from the Long Night of the Soul. But what did you *tell* Jane? What can one tell anyone? Can anything help? Are there answers to these awful questions? It could be us next time.

I think of you always with pleasure.

Ned


To Edmund White

*Nantucket*

*27 Feb 79*

Edmund, Edmund—

The island's quite fogged in and the rain won't stop (who'd have thought the old sky had so much blood in't!) so flights have been cancelled. Thus I'll send you a note instead of phoning, as I'd planned, tomorrow.

Your diary—or is it a poem? a book of puns? a dream notated?—is unique, almost, and terribly you. It's neatly from the same pen as the author of *Forgetting Elena* and *The Joy of Gay Sex*. As I've already told you, the "speaker"—although surely not yourself—with all his folly and artistry and fancy, is a cool thinker, austere, responsible to no one but himself. (Perhaps sometime if you wrote in the third person you would paradoxically become more personal; though why should you? except as an exercise.) The nocturnes are rich and heady, and few writers could get away, as you do, with such opulent Huysmanesquéries. If Djuna has laid a shadow here and there (*Nightwood*'s final line resembles yours), the only other "voice" I hear is my own. I'd be interested for you to read the "Letter to Claude" in my *New York Diary*, and then tell me what you think. But of course all great works are without counterpart. . . .

I love your work, and believe in it, and am glad to know you.

Fond greetings to Chris.

Ned

In the next edition you might want to explain what "triplets of dotted eighths" are. Also *Für Elise* is not a song.

### To Paul Bowles

*16 March 79*

Dear Paul,

As soon as your letter came I phoned New World Records. They will send you the disk titled "But Yesterday Is Not Today" (after your words) which includes two songs by you, "Once a Lady Was Here" and "Song of the Old Woman" (nicely sung by Donald Gramm), and songs by Barber, Duke, Copland, Chanler, Citkowitz, Helps, & Sessions. Also a long essay (plus special commentary on the composers) by me called "The American Art Song from 1930 to 1960." I also called Simon & Schuster to send you immediately *An Absolute Gift*. Your generous blurb came too late for the jacket, but was used on an advance brochure. (There was, however, no advertising, needless to say.) I'll be interested in your reaction to both, and do hope they get past customs. . . . Might you have *Antaeus* and the Collected Stories sent my way, when the time comes?

Thanks for your words about Jane. (And I just reread *La Chambre*. I'd forgotten how very excellent those early Sartre stories are.) The illness of others is difficult to cope with, not from lack of compassion obviously, but from sheer impotence—impotence of doctors, mainly, and for formula-ridden shrinks.

Sam Barber is very ill. Cancer of the marrow. It's possible he could go on a long time, and he's not in dire pain apparently. But it makes one sad.

I've been elected to the Institute of Arts & Letters, which means, that after the induction dinner on April 4th, I may have a mass of *potins* to send you.

Fondly,
Ned

## To James Bridges

*12 April 79*

Beloved Jim—

Finally saw your *China Syndrome* and was stunned with pleasure and with (good) pain. Every frame is stamped by your power and charm, and the whole thing is stronger—rather than weaker—in the horrid light of the 3-Mile-Island calamity. It's my favorite of your four movies, and Jack Lemmon and Jane Fonda are quite perfect. (I was uncomfortable with the man who played the photographer: he's too influenced by your own social style to have an identity, but perhaps this won't bother people who don't know you.) Nothing is too long, nothing is too close or too far, nothing is superfluous (except the loud dumb music), nothing is irrelevant to the mounting horror, nothing cheats, and there's no breach of tact or of taste (except maybe some dirty words). I congratulate you with respect and love. If only the [Christopher] Isherwood–[Don] Bachardy play, which is marvelous, had done half so well. Please keep ever in touch, and come to Nantucket whenever you want. May three tons of rubies be yours, and a barrel of kisses to Jack.

Ned

## To Paul Bowles

*25 June 79*

Dear Paul,

Here I am alone in the middle of the house in the middle of the island in the middle of the ocean, with sunbeams rolling like giggly peach-colored sapphires across the carpet, though it's already eight in the evening and Quaker ghosts have started to stare in at the windows. Hardly a noise, no neighbors, no distant transistors, just the pheasants cooing on the lawn, and on the stove a simmering vegetable stew. (I never eat meat when by myself.)

The afternoon was squandered in concocting a cantaloupe sherbet which I'll have for dessert, along with store-bought chocolate-chip cookies, while meditating on Madame Porte's pastry shop in Tangier. Does she still exist? Nantucket, although having a fair share of zonked-out swingers, is still puritan enough to think in terms of salt instead of sugar. But since I no longer drink or smoke or fornicate my one indulgence is sweets. Now, during the half hour before adjourning to the porch, there to spread a yellow linen in my lap, leaning forward to read the propped-up book (Spender's wartime essays, better than I'd thought, or hoped—indeed the terse pages on *Poetry and Revolution* are the clearest statements I've ever seen on that subject) while dining, I thought it would be proper to type you my semi-annual letter.

Little new news (and no catastrophes) re mutual friends since last we wrote. Aaron ever forgetful but very feted. Sam Barber "in remission" and in Italy. Morris Golde thinly tawny and often in Mexico. (While writing that, it occurs to me: wasn't it just thirty-seven years ago that we met in Taxco? Chez Magda and Gilberte? Remember? I was with my father, whom no one believed was my father, and Gilberte made a cake, yellow, with fudge frosting.) In April Phyllis Curtin and I performed a small recital of Virgil's songs in honor of Virgil at Yale where, as you doubtless know, he "gave" his papers in exchange for *one hundred thousand dollars*. I'm not even jealous. Anything a composer can glean in this bleak society becomes grist for the mill. Is that the right expression?

America would nonetheless seem anxious for culture, but aims low. New York in particular feels the need to canonize artists, but always on extra-artistic terms: for being Jewish or queer or female or—worst of all—new. The three saints currently in highest place are Elizabeth Hardwick, Steve Sondheim, and Woody Allen.

Hardwick's thin tome *[Sleepless Nights]* (have you read it?) is good, but not *that* good, and adds up to less than the sum of its parts. Excerpts strewn about during recent years, in prose and the NYR etc., read exquisitely alone, but sewn together they don't mesh. They seem, hmm, well, feminine —yet not feminine in any urgent way, like Jane's writing. For example, "Is it true," asks Miss Hardwick, "that a bad artist suffers as much as a good one?" More, wouldn't you think? A bad artist has no true appreciation, while a good artist (even if he later commits suicide), during those moments when he's working, can purge himself, can "get it out," and does know real love.

However, the personal suffering of artists, good or bad, makes no difference to anyone, much less to art. That it does make a difference to Hardwick places her on about the level of Anaïs Nin.

Sondheim's *Sweeney Todd* (have you heard it?) is okay, but not *that* okay, and is being bruited as the breakthrough for opera. In any context but Broadway his complex tunes would sound puerile, if not flatly derivative of his betters (mainly Weill and Bernstein), and the music's appeal lies in the lush orchestration—by Jonathan Tunick. The plot of Sweeney, what's more, is irredeemably ugly. *Your* operas are more novel and likeable ( just as your comprehension of Lorca is more telling than George Crumb's. But that's another tale).

Woody Allen's movies (have you seen any?) are smart enough, but not *that* smart, and they try too hard. I've never been a comics buff, putting Groucho above Garbo, and I sit through Woody's movies like the black fairy who never cracks a smile. Ironically, he hasn't much sense of humor. New Yorkers root for him because he's a professional Jew whose style, like the style of twenty years ago, is to deride the chic of the moment while being himself the chic of the moment. His latest, *Manhattan,* I saw here on Nantucket only last night, and although the audience of Bostonian WASP warts were primed like a laugh track, they didn't know what they were laughing at. The film does contain the likeable adolescent, Mariel Hemingway, portraying what is presumably a nymphet, although everyone feels she acts like a virgin. Whatever that means—since certain worldly types, like Marie-Laure or Theda Bara or even myself, when you get to know us, turn out to be quite sexually innocent.

Well, America longs for genius and is willing to pay. But America, not the genius, makes the rules, so you can't win. If you're scratching your head at all this fine writing ("giggling sunbeams," indeed), know simply that time passes slowly now that I've given up being An Artist, and you across the Atlantic are my outlet. For me to assume you don't know what's up over here is to forget I lived in Morocco for three years myself; but that *was* in another era, and now the wench is dead. Did the book and record, supposedly sent months ago, ever arrive?

Hey, my stew is boiling over. Write quick.

Love,

Ned

## To Judy Collins

*Nantucket*

*12 July 79*

Dearest Judy—

Your phone call warmed the far corners of my heart. I had a week of depression, crying for no especial reason (except that life seemed pointless, and so did death, and body all achin' and racked with pain), and unable to concentrate on anything except the France of yore to which it's impossible to return. Now I feel better, and am reading *Pride & Prejudice* again, the model antidote for self-indulgence. Jim feels I should see more people. So I invited Rosalyn Tureck over twice (I'm sure you remember *her*). Her endless pedagogical talk of fingerings, and Bach editions, and lambasting of other 18th-century experts, takes my mind off myself and has a lulling purgative effect. Also we talked about performance of Debussy (which I'm practicing at the moment, in preparation for that Washington recital), and it's healthy to get suggestions—which I'll nevertheless not follow—about French impressionism from a Bach expert.

After we hung up I felt a bit overbearing about asking when you'd sing my songs. You'll do it when you do it, and the songs themselves should speak louder than my insistence. Please don't think I'm coercing you: probably nothing of mine is actually suitable. . . . As for composing something special, that's a possibility. James Dickey is dying for me to set some of his poetry, though it's a bit longish and dense. He might be interested in writing something special for us. Do you know his work? Or Adrienne Rich? What about poems (or prose?) by friends of yours? Or Christina Rossetti? Violence and simplicity. Of course that's what those old ballads are.

I've been making some canny and beautiful translations of Verlaine and Mallarmé. Maybe I could versify in English some of those French pop songs we talked about. For you. Meanwhile, why don't you look into Marc Blitzstein's madly clever translations of Offenbach's songs, which Jennie Tourel used to do.

Let's keep August 6th open. . . . When are your public dates in September? Let's also make a time for me to go with you to one of them.

Love forever.

Ned

## To Paul Bowles

*Nantucket*

*26 September 1979*

Dear Paul—

I'd have answered your last letter sooner, but was waiting to read, as you requested, your story in *Antaeus*. Waiting in vain, as it turns out. Since *Antaeus* is not readily available on Nantucket newsstands I wrote Daniel Halpern (also asking for a subscription) for it. He didn't answer. Nor when I was in New York a fortnight ago was he available by phone. Perhaps he was avoiding me, since I had also asked if he'd be interested in my submitting a rather extended piece (around 8000 words) called "Being Alone." I do feel editors, however, owe former contributors the courtesy of a yes or a no. Maybe you as co-founder could put in a word. Meanwhile I never did find the magazine (at least not the issue with your story) while in New York. I did, however, meet Stephen Koch, when he stopped by here for a visit from Martha's Vineyard, at which time he was reviewing, for the *Washington Post*, your new collection (which I haven't seen either), and he was enthusiastic. I've since reread some of your old stories, and am dazzled anew at your construction—at what used to be called technique.

Saw Virgil for an evening while in New York. Probably you have his news regularly, so I'll say only that he's vibrating with life, is very *appreciated* and sure of himself, and is traveling all over. The musical scene otherwise is sheer dreariness. The New York Philharmonic is turned back thirty years with the conservatism of the present conductor Mehta. The Metropolitan Opera under Levine announces such upcoming novelties as Meyerbeer's *Le Prophète*. Of the very few song recitals announced for the coming season, not one features a singer (even an American singer) who plans to program anything in English.

Worst of all is the City Opera, now starting its first season under Beverly Sills. Have you heard of her—the erstwhile diva, the hick's notion of glamour? Irony surely lurks behind the *Times*'s claim that "Sills seems to be on good terms with almost everyone . . ." as if to attack her is to desecrate the flag or put down the Muppets. This could be true of opera buffs who are more concerned with singing than with what is sung, or of TV viewers who are able to relate to a star when she's just folks. But among first-rate composers—who are, after all, the spine of all music always—few take her seriously, precisely because she doesn't take them seriously, when she takes them at all. Even with Menotti (whose latest opera Sills starred in, as a swan song), her attitude, judging by press interviews, is one less of respect than of contempt. Her projected repertory is not so much stupid as mindless (Bel Canto, Sondheim, Lehar). So much for all of us.

Just finished [William] Styron's big novel *[Sophie's Choice]*. Despised the first 200 pages, which seemed show-offy and verbose and macho and anxious to be a masterpiece (masterpiece to Americans necessarily means big), but was moved finally by the whole. I think [V. S.] Naipaul is quite good, do you?, if a wee bit lacking in energy. Your acquaintance, Truman C., has another mean vignette, this one on Marc Blitzstein, in *The New Yorker*.

I proposed you, as well as Lucia Dlugoszewski, as a recipient for an Arts & Letters award. In both categories—music & literature. Is that okay?

Love,
Ned

## To Angela Lansbury

*20 October 79*

Dearest Angela—

Your brilliant bouquet has finally drooped and disappeared, but I continually gaze at the place where it stood, and am reminded of how the flowers of friendship never fade.

After mid-November can we meet again?

Tender thoughts forever to you and to Peter.

Ned

## To James Bridges

*17 November 79*

Very Dear Jim—

Forgive the burden of the enclosed galleys, but if you read them you'll understand.

Christopher Davis is a friend. More important, he is also a unique American voice, nothing if not serious, and very (as we used to say) "socially conscious" both in his fiction and in his documentaries. An example of the latter category is *Waiting for It*. To write this book Christopher Davis spent many a brave month in the ambience of a Georgian death row. The result, gleaming with the coarse elegance of a born author, brings new truths about the tremulous value of human life and the inexcusable cruelty of regimented death.

Twenty years ago Jane Fonda made her stage debut in *There Was a Little Girl,* an adaptation of Christopher's first novel, *Lost Summer.* That play (the tale of a raped girl who is finally rejected by even her family—and by even the rapist himself) was surely no closer to Jane Fonda's sympathies than the present book. Christopher mentioned that a blurb from Fonda would prove valuable, not only to the book itself but to the "cause," but that he had quite lost track of her, and now she's "unapproachable." I told him that you might be willing to: (a) pass the book along to her; (b) divulge her address so that the publisher could write her directly; (c) read it yourself and see what you think. The pages are painfully urgent, well worth the time, and, who knows?, they might suggest a movie script.

Not incidentally, Christopher Davis is the nephew of Marc Blitzstein from whom he inherited the knack of being able to melt random horror into formal art.

When are you coming to New York? I love and miss you, as I do Jack.
Ned

# Part Four

# 1980s

## To Judy Collins

*Nantucket*
*New Year's Day*
*1980*

Fond Judy—

Well, I don't have a hangover, do you?

I spent New Year's Eve quite alone on this island, reading an old volume of Debussy letters and polishing one of my new songs, on a poem of Witter Bynner.

A flaming sun today.

Will return on Thursday.

Did you note on your calendar to come to dine at seven on Jan. 14th, a Monday? Angela Lansbury and Peter Shaw will be there—here—too.

Love for this year

and for all the others

Ned


## To Paul Bowles

*8 January 80*

Dear Paul—

Are you all right?

One hears that these days Americans in Moslem sites might not be all that welcome, even such distinguished fixtures as you, and so I've been a bit concerned. It would be interesting to hear how the Moroccans—so geographically remote from Persia—view the current crises.

No news, beyond the usual *good* news of one's famous friends. Aaron and Tennessee (along with Martha Graham, Henry Fonda, and Ella Fitzgerald) were very grandly, and dignifiedly, celebrated by White House endorsement on national television on New Year's Day. Good choices, don't you agree? in light of the usual praise of junk. Lenny B. gave a tasteful speech and conducted with flair. He, by the way, after a slump during which he looked like a corpse for eight months, is extremely rejuvenated and extremely "public" about what over here is known as Gay Liberation.

I suggested to Raymond Smith, who with his wife, Joyce Carol Oates, edits the *Ontario Review,* that you might contribute. Is that o.k.? He'll write you. (Her write-up of your book was pretty good, I thought.)

I'm going to Paris for three weeks on April 13. First time in seven years. I have a free apartment, otherwise the prices would be prohibitive. It would be tempting to dip down into North Africa, but my round-trip requires I return via France. No chance of your being there?

Am reviewing books occasionally for *Washington Post Book World.* *Misia,* by Fizdale & Gold, is gushy but quite informative and has beautiful pictures. *States of Desire* proves again that Edmund White is a real writer.

Fond wishes ever . . .

Ned


To the *New York Times*

Re. a review of Edmund White's *States of Desire*

*9 Mar 1980*

To the Editor:

Nothing is easier than the negative inventory—the list of omissions at the price of inclusions. Taking the subtitle of *States of Desire* (Feb. 3), *"Travels in Gay America,"* literally, Paul Cowan, laying down rules as he goes along, tells us that this is no travel book—not at least as a Theroux or a Hoagland might have conceived it—and thus the author, Edmund White, is "an inadequate guide."

As one who has also reviewed *States of Desire* (the *Washington Post Book World,* Jan. 27) and has read it perhaps no less carefully than Mr. Cowan, I am interested in our verging reactions. Can Mr. Cowan have so missed the point as to waste every word—*every word*—on explaining what the book is not: not a Baedeker or a moral treatise, not a work on liberation or "command of structure and language"? Well, I'm from across the tracks, and view Mr. White with a more docile eye, less documentor than diarist, less the magnanimous case worker than the prejudiced microscope, less the "unskilled interviewer" than the "wonderful writer" admired by Vladimir Nabokov. In short, I view him as an artist.

And it is with his artist's voice, personal and undogmatic, that Mr. White presents the American homosexual male: not, for once, as tragedian or victim, but as *l'homme moyen sensual.* Whether this is the "right" presentation, Paul Cowan is in no position to say, since he is presumably not homosexual.

Now, although it is probably unfair to feel that only insiders should throw stones, I do feel that the *New York Times,* always quick to assign blacks to blacks and women to women, should think twice, when dealing with the still sensitive homosexual issue, before assigning such an author to a heterosexual who mistakes a work of literature for a guidebook.

Ned Rorem
New York City

To Paul Bowles

*6 August 80*

Dear Paul—

How long was it—ten years? twenty?—that we corresponded briefly about the possibility of your writing a libretto? Could the notion still intrigue you? I have reasons to think I *might* get a decent commission for an opera within the next six months, so I'm casting about for ideas. On the face of it you would seem to be ideal, having written an opera yourself, and knowing (as a man of letters) what a librettist should *not* do, such as solving the composer's problems for him by writing "musical" words and scenes. Also, I'm personally attracted to your style, and to your visual (and, in the sense that it's often mysterious as well as human, theatrical subject matter). However, the obvious doesn't always pan out, and also you might not be pleased with the process. . . . But think it over. Should anything come of it, we should talk about meeting, if need be, and also about money. . . .

Ten years ago I might have wanted to do a *tragic* opera, or a violent melodrama. The tendency's still there, although today I'm more attracted to something abstracter (like *Four Saints* or the poems of Kenneth Koch), which would be an excuse for music to pour out as airs and trios and quintets, while remaining physical enough to attract a director. Write me your reaction.

Recently in Santa Fe one Peter Garland gave me his thesis on you. Thorough and complimentary (deservedly) and an honor, I suppose. Yet I never feel that these people hit the nail on the head. *Can* a thesis-writer hit the nail on the head, when dealing with an artist, unless he himself's an artist, in which case he doesn't need to hit someone else's nail on the head, but his own? Or something? After seven years absence, I went to Paris last May, and found it wanting. But I did see Brion Gysin (after *twenty* years' absence) and found him tensely cheerful and extremely touching.

Fond wishes forever,
Ned

### To Paul Bowles

Dear Paul—

The day of your letter, another came from Joyce Carol Oates asking if I'd second her nomination of you to the American Institute of Arts & Letters. Since two seconders are needed, I forwarded the citation to Susan Sontag, thinking of her as a logical supporter, and reminding her that you were also a composer. (Oates's 50-word précis, otherwise serious and thorough, speaks of you only as an author.)

Also I've lately been singing—or should I say whistling?—your "In the Woods" to myself, that song having just reappeared in an *Art Song Album* along with thirty others by Americans of the 1940s published by Associated. I still hear Janet Fairbank whistling it in a recital in 1946. Very touching.

. . . I appreciate your words about librettos. You tell me what you don't want to do, and I know what I don't want. A good beginning. But I won't restrict myself to plotlessness, nor would I reject *a priori* a "Moroccan opera." I would never, however, make the mistake of composing an Arabic pastiche, any more than I'd use Old English instruments were I setting Shakespeare. But there must be something about—love, death, food, hate. And I like the idea of starting right out (no overture, no nothing) with a set number in full gear, an aria, say, or a duet.

Of course, I don't have any commission yet, and all this is still singing in the dark. But stranger things have happened than writing an opera by correspondence. (Copland and Graham apparently never saw each other during the making of *Appalachian Spring*. Yes, but that's not an opera.)

I sympathize with your hopeless feelings about thesis writers. Parasites all. And even when they get facts straight, it never makes much difference.

Love

Ned

### To Leonard Bernstein

*Sunday Morning*
*8 Feb. 81*

Dear Lenny—

Your faith in me takes my breath away.

You more than anyone know that nothing is so important for a composer as the right reading of the right piece. Thus, I owe you my life.

Love,
Ned

### To Howard Moss

*20 February 81*

Very Dear Howard—

I was dismayed to learn (from Ed White) about your heart attack.
Please say when I can come for a visit. Jim sends his fond regards. Thinking
of you with affection.

Ned

### To Rosalyn Tureck

*20 March 81*

Dear Rosalyn—

The future will take care of itself. I'm not really concerned on what
instruments my music is performed. (But I do hope it will be performed.)

I feel, however, that recordings and tapes, made today, will indicate to
future generations the viewpoint—the earpoint!—of our renditions and
sonorities, something which is radically different from our viewpoint about
the past.

Do I detect a vague anxiety in your questionnaire? I don't think the
future can be judged by the past. I don't really believe in authenticity, whatever that means. (We know everything about the nuances of Bach performance today except the most important thing: How did people of that time
react to music, and what was their thought about the purpose of music?
We'll never know. Because we are comparatively non-believers.) Nor do I
believe in the feuds between harpsichordists and pianists. The harpsichord
today is a *modern instrument*.

See you soon, at Joe Machlis's, and probably at the Library.

I do wish you'd consider coming to my recital at the YMHA on Thursday, April 2. My new songs are rare and beautiful, Phyllis Bryn-Julson is an important singer. And our collaboration is the most significant since Poulenc played with [Pierre] Bernac.

Fondly—

Ned

## To Claus von Bülow

*3 April 81*

Dear Claus—

I regret if what I may have said has been used to wound you. This was far from the intention of any remarks.

With best wishes always,

Ned

## To Dolores Fredrickson

*Nantucket*

*3 July 81*

Dear Dolores—

I very much appreciate your intentions in telling me that Emanuel Ax likes my *Études*, but that his management says audiences aren't ready for them. However, he is lying—or, at the very least, employing euphemisms. He's passing the buck to managers by pretending that they are passing the buck back to the public. Ax is in a position to play anything he wishes; if he believed in my music he could play it whenever he chooses. The implication that management too believes in it is specious: management means that the audience isn't ready to PAY for new music. (What audience is really ready for anything? what does ready mean? who's ready for Beethoven? or Machaut? or Schoenberg, which Ax plays regularly?) Management is interested exclusively in money. What they don't realize is that a star brings in money on his name, not on his program, and that the public will listen to whatever they're given. This state of affairs is one I know intimately, since, like all other composers, I live with it daily.

The truth is: though Ax may indeed like my *Études,* the few times he's played them, reviewers have spent more time on them than on him. (Critics generally are, and should be, as interested in premieres as in who plays them.) Obviously, Ax is annoyed by this. Maybe not. But whatever the reason he gives, his methods in regard to myself are specious. I'm all the more annoyed that he can play my music as beautifully as it will ever be played— but he doesn't play it. Paradox.

Now that's off my chest. Please let me know how your concert goes. I look forward to seeing you when the time comes. Between now and then only a calm clear mind (which I do not have) can prevent my going crazy at the mountain of deadlines that must be met.

Warmly ever—

Ned

### To James Lord

*26 September 81*

Fond James—

Eugene Istomin, who as you know is one of this world's greatest pianists, has a good collection of art in his Washington apartment including several drawings by Giacometti, whom he adores. He has also read your writings, especially the little portrait of A.G., and would be pleased to visit with you when he's next in Paris, probably in February. If you're there then, he'll phone you, unless you prefer that I not give him your number. . . . Eugene is a lifelong friend. He's also married (happily married) to the beautiful widow of Casals, and they live in our nation's capital where Marta is head of the artistic branch of the Kennedy Center.

I'm glad to have this excuse to write you. It was a bittersweet occasion, seeing you all too briefly seventeen months ago. Will I ever get to Paris again? I do wish you'd come see me when you're in New York. I see Henry McIlhenny from time to time, since I'm now teaching part-time at Curtis, right across the square from him, and he gave an ample but morose dinner on the night of Sam Barber's funeral. . . . Would you send me news of France, and especially of yourself therein?

Best always—

Ned

## To Eugene Istomin

*27 September 81*

Fond Eugene—

I read and was moved by James Lord's *Giacometti*. I'd like an excuse for writing to him anyway, so if you're serious about wanting to meet him, let me know when you'll be in Paris, and I'll announce your coming. He's *very* canny and sensitive about painting. . . .

Talked to Chuck Turner (one of Sam Barber's heirs) about the possibility of a Barber book. He thought Fizdale & Gold might be a good idea, and so do I. They loved and often played Sam's music, and they write good prose, viz. *Misia* and their current book on Balanchine. Also they're well known. . . . You might think about Phillip Ramey too, who's done many smaller essays on Barber.

The weather's turning dark and cold even as I sit here typing, but the thought of you brings light and warmth.

Love—

Ned

## To Paul Bowles

*Nantucket*

*15 October 81*

Dear Paul—

You may be pleased to know that there is a shelf of Bowlesiana in each of the two Nantucket bookstores, and from thence I bought your recent *Midnight Mass* and have read it *d'un seul souffle*. You've not lost the touch. I liked especially "Here to Learn," and would wish to see you write more stories (I've told you this before?) with American backdrops.

Two weeks ago in New York, Robert Craft conducted *L'Histoire d'un Soldat* with Aaron Copland as Narrator, Virgil Thomson as Devil, and Roger Sessions as the Soldier. In English. Madness. Virgil, stone deaf though spirited, came in wrong often; Aaron, deeply forgetful in life (to put it mildly), was accurate and "expressive" on stage; and Sessions was meek and distant. They're all full of spunk in their eighties, which gives one hope.

Now I'm back in Nantucket for three long weeks, before resuming my classes at Curtis, and am finishing an organ piece, and beginning another work for voice and oboe and strings. Reading Doctorow's *Loon Lake* with displeasure—it's all self-admiring machoism without much to say—and rereading *Les Faux-monnayeurs* for the fourth time in forty years, with always-increasing admiration.

At the Stravinsky performance, by the way, was Morris Golde with Millicent Dillon under his arm. The latter seems immensely pleased with what seems to be the success of her book about Jane, and she has every right to be. I recently reviewed Auden's biography (Humphrey Carpenter) for the *Chicago Tribune*, declaring it wonderfully readable though less touching than Dillon's book, precisely because, unlike Jane Bowles whose vulnerability was her earmark and thus her literary appeal, Auden kept his wounds at bay, and thus we don't feel sorry for him. Well. . . .

This is just to say that I liked *Midnight Mass.*

Let's keep writing. . . .

Fondly—

Ned

### To Lou Harrison

*18 West 70*
*The Ides of March*
*1982*

Lou, Lou, Lou . . .

As doubtless you know, the new Groves emerged a year or two ago, with your entry whittled down as here enclosed. Now they're planning an American edition, and they want updating.

Could you be a jewel and return the enclosed, with a revised work list? And could you add a few succinct sentences on your convictions about non-tempered tunings?

It was a pleasure to judge with you last January. I wish I was with you in California. Love to Bill, and from Jim.

Always your faithful—

Ned

### To Edward Albee

*18 West 70*
*15 March 82*

Dear Edward—

Eleven years ago, when the new Grove Dictionary was in the process of renewing itself, I contributed the entry on Bill [Flanagan] which—when the book came out two summers ago—appeared in the whittled-down version herewith enclosed.

Grove now proposes an American edition, and has asked that I revise and update my various entries. They're especially interested in the works list. You're the only person I can turn to about that. If you've any idea about how the list could be more complete, or more representative, I'd appreciate it. As for the body of the article, they'll probably not change anything, but I could try.

In 1979 I attempted to contact you about the possibility of assembling a memorial concert for Bill, it being a decade, but it was hard to get people together. But the times seem to change so rapidly, as well as the nature of the musical heart. Frequently I find myself (as you doubtless do) in college centers, and people ask: What was Bill Flanagan really like? Young composers, flailing away at songs once again, seem interested in him. Maybe we could do something formal about it someday.

I do wish we saw each other oftener—or differently. Perhaps God doesn't wish it. Though we will certainly be in Miami at the same time next June.

Warmly—
Ned


## To John Cheever

*15 April 82*

Very dear John—
Congratulations on your recent and various glittering prizes.
I think of you tenderly every day, and so does Jim.
Love,
Ned


## To Edmund White

*May First 1982*

Even if, my fond Edmund, I'd been in New York and received your note in time, I would not have attended the series. Lukas Foss is a dear and old friend, but I disapprove of Reich & Glass not only esthetically but morally. They may have a mild and obvious theatricality, but musically they run counter to everything I believe in. Thus I would not wish to seem to endorse their mudpies with my august presence.

I commend you on your direction of the Institute [New York Institute for the Humanities at NYU], and pray that the Gallatin Lectures will, in the future, stress quality over vogue.

May we meet before summer?

Best—

Ned

To Bill Whitehead,

Edmund White's editor at Dutton

*Nantucket*

*31 May 82*

Dear Bill Whitehead—

If I don't exactly know what to make of Edmund White's book, I mean this positively. Like any real artist, Ed gets away with murder, and the murder is good; he can go too far and still come back. A writer's course is always dangerous, and in *A Boy's Own Story* the danger is especially thorny, being that potentially dullest of themes—childhood and self-discovery. Since the novel (you can call it a novel, but is it?) is fragmented, and since each fragment is a recycling of the same merrily bittersweet anxiety, Ed almost but not quite falls from his tightrope. What saves him here is the unique "murder" that grandly bespatters all his work: his way with words, so gorgeously rococo, which no one else dares.

I've always felt that Edmund White's overall subject is the avoidance of Christian responsibility. In *Forgetting Elena* the leading man shuns duty toward wife and world by cloaking himself in amnesia; in *Nocturnes* the author kills off his lover even before the curtain goes up, and so is faithful to a "mere" memory; *The Joy of Gay Sex* focuses solely on carnality, not on True Love; and True Love is hardly what the narrator of *States of Desire* seeks, or at any rate finds, to document. In the latest book a sense of comradeliness is impressionistically rather than profoundly depicted. This stress on avoidance of responsibility recalls, in a less cruel and melancholy manner, the movies of Antonioni. Indeed, Edmund White is the optimist's Antonioni.

Well, anyway, I adore this book, as I adore each of his books. They're all of a piece (coldly friendly), yet each so different from the others. And I adore the way he deals with the smell of sex more than with the touch of it. One can even say that he deals with the *sound* of sex, since more than any American today Edmund White has his own voice.

Best—

Ned

(On pps. 141–42 of the galleys there's a passage disconcertingly close to an entry in my *Final Diary* about erotic statues.)

## To Mary Cheever

*19 June 82*

Dear Mary Cheever—

How much my heart is with you today.

Your husband was an old friend of mine (as of so many others) from Yaddo and I loved him with aggravating tenderness.

Please accept my condolences and extend them to your children.

Warmly,

Ned Rorem

## To Andrew Porter

*31 Aug. 82*

Dear Andrew:

To your presumably rhetorical question, "Is there any bad Elliott Carter?" the answer is Yes—namely two recent vocal works, *Syringa* on John Ashbery's words, and *A Mirror on Which to Dwell* on Elizabeth Bishop's, both failures because they neither heighten, add new dimension to, or even illustrate the verse.

Never mind that, to my certain knowledge, at least one of the poets despaired of the music, or at least one of the singers despised the voice line. Songs, after all, no longer belong to their composers, much less to their poets, once they are finished; and a performer's opinion finally has little to do with how convincingly, or even correctly, he performs those songs. No, the Bishop cycle fails because the vocal arch, being continually disjunct, grows undifferentiated from song to song; because the orchestration, being superfluous ("all those cluttered instruments"), grows merely fussy where a clean piano would have sufficed; and mostly because what is sung never represents what is read. *Insomnia,* for instance, never seeks the bluesy lilt, and thus the acrid humor, of the stanzas, while the setting of *O Breath* descends to the amateurish duplication of words or syllables which the poet felt the need to state only once. As for the Ashbery rendition, it fails for the same reasons, and because the composer, lacking the courage of his

American poet's convictions, dazzles and distracts us with a substructure in Greek.

Although I agree with the contention in your very next sentence that "Rochberg writes music whose appeal is to closed, unadventurous minds ... and could become fodder for the New Right: Down with progressive thought!", your implication that Carter can do no wrong strikes me as irresponsible—indeed, as fodder for the Old Left—for surely you'll agree that there is even bad Beethoven.

I say this, who have elsewhere and often written of the unique power and grandeur of Elliott Carter's instrumental masterpieces.

Fondly,

Ned

### To David Diamond

> *Nantucket*
> *Nov. 82*

Very dear David—

The Aspen performances were, on the whole, marvelous. Dufallo did my big *Sun* (1966) for voice & orch, with Kristine Ciesinski, maximally rehearsed, and Edo de Waart did *Remembering Tommy* (the Double Concerto) a week earlier. Also there were a half-dozen chamber pieces, and a whole evening of songs. I felt touched and desired and nearly cried. Santa Fe, however, was a bit more professional. (It will all, presumably, be on TV next January, so you can see for yourself.) The Chamber Music Festival really cares about American music, and you should be on their list now as a guest-composer. . . .

In Miami in June I had another big premiere, this one sung by Kristine's older mezzo sister, Katherine Ciesinski. It's called *After Long Silence,* a suite for voice, oboe, and string orchestra. The orchestra was the Camerata Bariloche of Argentina. . . .

Edward [Albee's] play? It's titled *The Man Who Had Three Arms,* and I despised every word. It does—as you request—have a beginning, middle, and end, but it's mean-minded and small and vulgar and tired. I so seldom see him, that at the party given for all us visitors I tried my best to "communicate," but Edward's never very forthcoming, at least with me. Needless to say, he didn't attend my performance. . . . I did, however, see Robert Ward's new opera, which I am afraid lacks all distinction. But it's not as disgusting (because not as pretentious) as the Rochberg opera which I attended in Santa Fe a month later. David, you must *not* propose Rochberg for the Academy. *He has nothing to say.*

...I gave the commencement address (and got another doctorate) last May at Curtis, and will resume teaching there—with my three students— next month.... Meanwhile, my parents, now in their late eighties, are anxious. They're considering seriously going to a Retirement Home, and next week I'll come back from Nantucket for 36 hours in order, with Jim, to drive them down to visit Cadbury, a "home" near Philadelphia. What's your reaction to this? Father's wonderfully handsome and hale, but mother— although physically healthy—is not quite herself. The situation haunts me. What is right, what is right? Is it wrong to grow old? You'd think so, in this land—there seem to be no provisions, no recourses.... My sister, Rosemary, has migrated temporarily to Maine....

We've been reading Lana Turner's book with pleasure. Am also deep into Igor Markevitch's autobiography, *Être et avoir été.* ...

Dear David, I love you.... Life goes on....

Ned


To David Diamond

*13 December 82*

Yes, yes, dear David. I suppose you're right: there is no redeeming feature to growing old. My parents are less serene than you might suppose. For the past two years Mother's been living more and more in a world of her own. And for the past six months she's been suffering from undiagnosed seizures, a sort of *petit mal* every week or two. At first it was hideous to behold: once for a whole hour she shuddered and shook and couldn't speak; now the seizures last just a minute or two. (Wallace, our cat, has a similar condition since five years ago. He trembles, stiffens, foams at the mouth, pees, his eyes glass over, and grows hard as a rock. After several minutes he comes out of it—Jim usually holds him tight—doesn't know where he is, shrieks, then eats a lot, and goes to sleep for a day.) I stayed overnight with Mother & Father a week ago. They're lonely and sad, and Father especially, because he's so alert and cultured, is somewhat bogged down by Mother's continual demands. She simply gets no fun out of anything. She doesn't even cry, nevertheless, but sits for hours going through an old address book, looking up numbers of people long dead. She snaps out of it, knows where she is, but isn't interested in anything (except bodily functions)—and I can quite literally *see* her living in her girlhood. In a way this is bad for me: I identify, and am a terrible hypochondriac. Jim has to live with my endless complaints and high doctor bills (mainly for a urethra condition which hasn't cleared up after two years, and causes me continual discomfort), but I hate to see myself sinking into . . . Oh, shit, forget all this. . . . Next day I went to Curtis: two of my three students had a swell orchestra concert of their own works. I felt proud. Of *myself.* . . . Jim and I have just returned from a weird 5-day vacation—my first in 30 years—in Puerto Rico, which is so poor and lush and cultureless. But those beaches! They brought back all the other gorgeous beaches of my past, at Paestum and Nobadir and Caleta and Lake Michigan. Speaking of the past, it's been 38 years since we first met, at the 1944 Washington Square show where Allela was standing by her paintings and drawing quick studies of passersby. I was 20 and today I'm 59. . . . Last night I had a long talk with Rosalyn Tureck at a party, and we spoke very warmly of you. Ditto with V. Persichetti on the train from Philly last week. . . .

Love and Merry Christmas, now and always, from me & Jim.

Ned

### To Daron Hagen

*5 January 83*

Very dear Daron—

It wasn't until last night that I read your letter, on returning from Nantucket, although Jim Holmes had told me the contents of it, by phone, a few days ago, on *his* return from Nantucket.

I will never forget your mother's face, so pale, yet so vital and intelligent as she gazed across the table in the Barclay bar, the night of your concert. Was that only six weeks ago? Your mother was very proud of you, and I am moved and honored to have known her. And also to have known your father. Please tell him that I have written you, and send my heartfelt condolences.

It is ironic (though I don't know if it's right or wrong) that here I am, 39 years older than you, with my own mother still physically hale, more or less, nor do I know, yet, the severed feeling that must come from the death of a parent.

Don't be too concerned (though your concern is understandable, at this moment) with being inappropriately expressive in your music, or with being honest, or truthful, or any of those other vast concepts. I've never discussed esthetics with any of you, mainly because there's little we can do about it anyway. "Deeply felt" music (like Mahler's) isn't necessarily "better," morally or esthetically, than music written to order, like Bach's. Your experience will obviously have a deep effect on you—but you can't oblige it to have an effect on your music—i.e. a "good" effect. We'll talk more of this when we meet.

When will that be? Perhaps as soon as next Monday, or maybe Wednesday. I've asked Michael Carrigan to contact you, and we'll see.

Meanwhile, you have my affectionate regards.

Warmly,

Ned R.

### To Andrew Porter

*1 February 83*

Dearest Andrew—

Every day I await, always in vain, the announced sequel to our to-beam-or-not-to-beam exchange. But the mails are tardy, especially within the area of our mutual zip code.

I did, however, see your report about the Eastman Philharmonia of January 17th and it made me queasy. I can't prove it, but I feel that two points you raised—the coincidence in theme between the end of *Appalachian Spring* and the start of Piston's *Fourth,* and the unseemliness of a white man's first-person identification with the "we" of a black text—would not have been raised, at least in the words you chose, had I been elsewhere that evening. Not that a critic need ever credit the perspicacity of his companions (though Virgil used to, adding warmth to his wisdom), since great minds run in the same channels. But I would have enjoyed a passing nod in the next paragraph about who is played how much on which broadcasts, since my representation is perhaps no rarer than, say, Kirchner's, and since, at least orally, you often show good will toward my tunes.

Love—

Ned

### To Andrew Porter

*13 February 83*

Andrew,

Thanks for your dear letter in reply to mine which I wish I'd never penned. I concur, of course, with your remarks, and will always love and respect you, even though on certain musical matters we will never see eye to eye (or hear ear to ear). Perhaps it's a question of genes as much as of conditioning.... Can we meet often and soon?

Fondly,

Ned

In reply to your (rhetorical) question, "Is it only Europeans who find that kind of open theme peculiarly and characteristically American?", I would answer that Americans find it American too. Why? Because only Americans build themes on fourths (Hindemith used quartal harmony, of course, but not so much in tunes), and specifically on two rising fourths and a drop of a minor second, as in the Piston and Copland pieces ... not to mention Bernstein and everyone else and even me during my "American period" which lasted three weeks in 1954. It possibly doesn't sound inherently American, it's *come to* sound American. But I do remember Aaron, way back when, saying he had simply *taken*, for the *Lincoln Portrait*, a Kentucky folk-tune and dressed it up. That tune was the fatal fourth motive in question. Could it be argued that American Sound is due to a single gesture, made once, quite consciously, by Copland—who may never have thought of doing so were it not for Virgil, who wouldn't have thought of it but for MacDowell's avoidance of doing so? Or something? Love eternal. N

### To Edmund White

*Nantucket*

*7 May 83*

Dear Edmund—

For most of us mortals it is not given "To see oursels as ithers see us!" and thus, even at its most disconcerting (as when, for example, Eichmann reads about himself in Hannah Arendt), the experience is always flattering. That anyone should care!

Your words on my book and myself in the *Native* describe something I don't always recognize, but I'm warmed by the attention and intrigued by the person portrayed. I can't help but feel that both your style and view-point would have been different were you writing for, say, *The Nation.* But wherever you appear you do remain essentially you—a writer I admire—and I'm touched to be immortalized by your pen.

Your

Ned

### To James Lord

*29 May 1983*

James, my only!

The *Washington Post*'s *Book World* has asked me to do an essay, for their "Rediscoveries" column, on a "neglected" book. For next autumn.

I want to do two books, and compare them. I'm thinking of Sarah Orne Jewett's *The Country of the Pointed Firs* (circa 1880), and your Giacometti Book *About the Several Sittings.* The two works have nothing in common beyond my interest in both. Would you be insulted if I deemed your book neglected, only so as to write about it? (I realize it's a classic, on everyone's coffee table.)

*My* two books have just appeared. I wish *you* would appear. Time flows by, never to be retrieved.

Next week, Nantucket for the summer, and a vast amount of overdue music to write. Nervous.

Send me your news. . . . And give my love to all of Paris.

Fondly ever—

Ned

### To Paul Bowles

*Nantucket*

*15 June 83*

Dear Paul—

Too much time has passed (a year perhaps?) without direct news. Yes, I've seen people who've seen you . . . but I've not "seen" you myself.

This will warn you of yet another book of mine en route to Tangier. It's called *Setting the Tone,* and, among other things, contains certain old essays including, I'm afraid, the one on you. Perhaps the rest of the contents will intrigue you, and, as always, I'd love to hear your comments.

And this will warn you too of yet another friend of mine en route to Tangier. She's called Francine du Plessix Gray, and among other things, she once wrote an article about Jane Bowles. You'll see her in September. She is not ordinary, very high strung, handsome and blonde and underweight, age 49, with a unique and clear sense of words and sentences, and an earnest if sometimes dishonestly slanted urge for *reportage,* especially on religious and political matters. She would like you to find her intelligent.

I'm in Nantucket again, for the whole summer, chained to my desk to finish two huge oratorio-type pieces. One is for 800 (yes, eight hundred) male singers, with brass orchestra; the other—for full chorus SATB and the Pittsburgh orchestra, with a text, or texts, undecided, but probably to be 19th-century prose.

Would you compose more music if someone asked you (paid you) convincingly? People sometimes ask me that. But maybe you *are* writing music.

Fondly forever—

Ned

### To Dolores Fredrickson

*Nantucket*

*4 August 83*

Dear Dolores—

Your letter alerted me to some disagreeable but necessary news. I had no idea that [Georges] Auric was dead. When and where did you learn of it? As you know, he and Nora (who died less than a year ago, after which Georges married the young maid, to whom presumably he left his inheritance) were dear friends of mine during the 1950s. How little we care about the art of music, from country to country, when the death of such an important French composer goes unnoticed in the American press.

Nor did I know of Barbara Schulgasser's identity until you told me. I was offended by her ill-written review of my book. Not that I insist on good notices necessarily; but every one of her points was ill-taken, and her overall tone was snide and petty. What does she have against me? She also made the crucial error—a trap that critics sometimes fall into—of trying to review me in my own style, glib and epigrammatic.

I liked (but did not love) the articles by you about Gorodnitsky and Rodgers. You give a true picture of the former. He seems a bit dogmatic, and his notions about music are standard (he adores the predictable German classics and says not a word about the French). You meanwhile are perhaps a bit over-indulgent. Surely there must be reservations somewhere?

. . . See you next year.

Best always—

Ned

### To David Del Tredici

*Nantucket*

*8 October 83*

Dear David—

I'm so hoping to see you on my birthday the 23rd. It goes without saying that Joel's invited, since it's his birthday too (as it is Maurice Grosser's, Miriam Gideon's, Franz Liszt's, and Johnny Carson's), you may have other plans.

The piece in *Parnassus* is a very pretty chunk of literature in itself. I learned from it, even to changing my mind about certain things. For example, your clear statement that "when a composer borrows from a previous style one tends to hear at first only what's borrowed and not what isn't." But do you really believe that "an exceptional ear" could "hear how the different instruments . . . create that overall shape"? What if the music, as it appears on page 265, were printed—heaven forbid!—in the current style of putting the *horns* above the trumpets, of placing the horns on two instead of four staves, of employing a wider space between the various choirs of instruments, and of using two instead of four clefs for the violas? The music would sound the same but would look quite different. . . . Now that I've spoiled your fun, please know that I love only you.

Ned

### To James Lord

*23 October 83*

Fond James—

In case they cut it, I'm sending this unrevised version before it appears in the *Washington Post Book World*. A cream puff—but I hope not unappetizing to you.

Probably I'll come to Paris for a fortnight in early December, and write it up for *Geo* magazine. *Please be there* and think of things I can quote you about! I'm thrilled. Ought I to stay at the Saint Simon? or are there other more propitious hotels? Let me know.

Today's my 60th birthday. Big party in 2 hours.

Happy birthday—

Love

Ned

## To Andrew Porter

*2 March 84*

Dear Andrew—

During your dozen years in America you have shown toward me, by letter or in person, regular feelings of friendliness and respect, feelings which are certainly reciprocal, although as professionals—you a critic, I a composer—we have no meeting ground. During those same years you have reviewed hundreds of new works and thousands of concerts on many of which I have had pieces (sometimes large premieres) performed. Yet as far as your readers are concerned I may as well not exist.

I will never know your deepest opinion of my work. Still, even if that work repels you, it has nonetheless prevailed and is to be dealt with. I am my music. Insofar as you deny that, your friendly protestations are vain.

Always,

Ned

## To Edmund White

*18 West 70th Street*
*3 March 84*

Mon bel Edmund doré . . .

I'm coming to Paris.

I arrive on April 6 in the morning, and leave a brief fortnight later on the 20th. No doubt I'll stay in one of those nice hotels—l'Université, Lenox, Marrionniers—near St. Germain des Près. I'm being sent by *Vanity Fair* for whom I shall describe my visit, diary style, in some detail. The prospect of being again in this magic city of my youth fills me with almost ecstasy, and at the same time scares me to death. And the prospect of seeing you is among the chief pleasures of anticipation. What a catastrophe if you're to be away!

It is you now who know, far better than I know, the geography and fauna of the city, and I'd like to rely on you somewhat: Who are the Americans? Who's writing what? How do they feel about the nuclear threat? How do they differ from Americans queer-wise and AIDS-wise? Can you think of any concerts or plays we might attend together?

Most of my musical friends are dead. Only the venerable Henri Sauguet survives, and so vital.

David Kalstone provided your address. Could you send me your phone as soon as you read this?

Je t'aime

Ned

## To Daron Hagen

*2 May 84*

Dear Daron—

A note in great haste before vanishing to Nantucket.

I read your whole diary in almost one fell swoop and was quite impressed. Diaries are dangerous, being the most subjective of literary forms (and subjectivity is boring), but yours makes it, and is the real thing. The book's faults are also its virtues (as is always the case with diaries)—so there's little formal criticism I might make. I squirmed a bit here and there, as I do in rereading my own. And I found the remarks about me revealing and instructive. . . . When we are next together we can talk more. Meanwhile, know that I was truly moved by much of it.

Fondly—

Ned

(David Diamond must never see the remarks about him which you attribute to me in Florida. They are not what I feel, and are brutal. Please. . . .)

On the train to NY on Monday I rode with Persichetti. Then yesterday, I saw Lukas Foss for awhile. Both spoke of you. Yaddo is necessary for you now. Perhaps a little less need to get ahead, to be a "professional"; a little more introspection and, indeed, egotism, will do you good. But who knows? One man's meat, etc. . . .

### To Paul Bowles

*Nantucket*
*15 July 84*

Dear Paul—

Since you never—as you always have with my other books—acknowledged receipt of *Setting the Tone,* probably it never arrived in Tangier. Now that it's to be reissued in paperback by Proscenium, I'll try again. It's due out in about a month, and you're of course on the list.

Meanwhile, I have your wonderful collection of songs from Soundings Press, and also *Points in Time*. It's been a joy to go through all those songs again, and to find old favorites that I thought were lost forever—"Noche de Quattro Lunas," "David," and so many others I never knew. There's more Kurt Weill than I'd remembered in them. Alas, the edition is seething with misprints (mostly omitted accidentals) and someone, probably you, should go through it with a fine-toothed comb, since I'm sure the songs will sell. I shall refer them to all the singers I know. . . . *Points in Time* is serious and original and frightening and cool. Someday, if I dedicate a symphony to you, will you write a story that is optimistic and even silly? and a song that is tortured and fatalistic and grand? It's a bet. My life is quiet, half in Nantucket, half New York, and I'm overwhelmed with (I'm pleased about it) musical commissions. I support myself entirely that way. . . . Last April I went to Paris for two weeks. Nostalgic. But also decadent in the realest sense: every single one of the arts has putrified, and people chatter blindly the way they must have just before Nero burned down Rome. . . . Send me your news. It's improbable I'll ever get to Morocco again. I'm sixty now, and traveling holds no allure.

Fondly forever—
Ned

### To Leonard Bernstein

*26 October 84*

Dear Lenny—

I've just finished reading, for the first time, your *Unanswered Question*. The vitality, wit, and originality hold up throughout, and I wasn't bored once. Your biases coincide exactly with mine, and also your tastes for the most part; and even though you give Chomsky too much credit, your basic premise is invigorating.

(Someday I'd like to talk with you about Verdi-&-Stravinsky, and about still other nests which I.S. rifled, almost intact.)

So thanks for the book. It contains a great deal. Tried to phone you recently, hoping you'd put in a good word for Stuart Pope with the London office of B. & H. But it's too late. He's leaving.

When will we ever meet again? *Dans un mois, dans un an?*

I love you

Ned

To Paul Bowles

*19 November 84*

Dear Paul—

Isn't it funny how much we can admire essayists who write on varied subjects, except when they write on what is closest to us! (I think of Susan Sontag, for example, who seems so smart, until she makes remarks about music.) I'm pleased that you seem to like my new book (which is called *Setting the Tone,* not *Setting the Pace*) in general, and sad that I offended you in the article on yourself. Of course you're right: quotations are in order, and I provide none. And yes, my word "willfully" is indeed meaningless. I had thought, however, that I was characterizing your novels—and only a small part of them—and not your short stories which are second to none in America. I have infinite regard for most of your work, and, as one of the few (at least until recently) who know both your prose and your music, I never fail to sing your praises.... Anyway, if ever I write about you again, I'll be more careful.... You mean a lot to me. Words are so much more easily misunderstood than music, I suppose.

Your words, for example, about *Setting the Tone*—"What a busy brain! ... (like) watching a particularly fascinating ant colony"—make me feel that you feel that I bustle about, to no avail, having "experiences" solely in order to put them on paper. Whereas in fact I live mostly in seclusion, composing music, which is my sole way of earning a living. I am paranoid, yes.

New York is filled with sleet. An actress resembling Jane Bowles recently did a one-woman show about JB off-Broadway. Aaron, whose autobiography I assume you've read, is sadly senile, Virgil sharp as a whip. I wonder how you're feeling? Can you discuss why you visited a Swiss hospital? I'm extremely sympathetic. My father just turned ninety, mother 87. Happy thanksgiving.

Faithfully,

Ned

## To Leonard Bernstein

*25 January 1985*

Golden Lenny—

Your love letter—the one about the Oratorio—was a thrill to receive. I've been chained to my desk trying to finish an Organ Concerto, and now it *is* finished, so time is looser. Tried to phone you, so that we could continue our never-to-be-completed (I hope) conversation. Call me back when you can. (I just may be in Nantucket for a long week after Feb. 7.)

Meanwhile, lest we forget, I'll want to talk about:

1) The Oratorio's last page—which you say is feeble.

2) Stravinsky's debt to Verdi's *Requiem,* more than to (as you claim) *Aida*—and other of his plagiarisms.

3) My theory of language and non-vocal music.

Pedantically yours,

Ned

Not until I withdrew the last page from the typewriter did I discover that, because of the insignia below, it looks like Saint Peter crucified upside-down.

## To James Lord

*25 March 85*

Dearest James—

Doubleday wrote me that you wrote them that there's already under-way a book on Marie-Laure. Who's doing it?

Over the years I've been approached at least three times—as I'm sure you have—to do such a thing, and decided against it for various reasons. But naturally I'd like to be in contact with whoever (whomever?) is doing it.

Yours in faithful haste. (I've the flu, but must go upstate for the premiere of my Fiddle Concerto.) Will you never call

your adoring slave

Ned

## To Monroe Wheeler, re. Glenway Wescott

*Nantucket*

*24 May 85*

Dear Monroe—

Could you get a copy of the current *Christopher Street* (the one with an announcement about AIDS on the cover)—it can be found at the "better" newsstands—and give it to Glenway? It contains a little memoir called "What Truman Capote Means to Me" which should interest you both. I'd do it myself, but I haven't Glenway's address here, nor are the better newsstands to be seen in Nantucket. Let me know your reaction.

Today I sliced severely my left forefinger while opening a can of cat food. Otherwise I thrive in the (for the moment) peaceful clime of this island, and am beginning work on a String Symphony. I won't be back in New York until mid-September. Can't we see each other oftener then?

Affection always

Ned

## To Morris Golde

*Nantucket*

*26 July 1985*

Best of Morrises:

Re. solicitation, on your behalf, to contribute to NY Repertory Theater for VT's *Lord Byron* production.

I'm not in a position (few composers are) to contribute financially toward the promotion of a world-famous colleague. It's a philosophical stand. Composers help each other by talking and writing about each other, and by playing each other's music. Obviously, from time to time, they arrange for scholarships and prizes for younger musicians, and sometimes even give money to their students. But it's not their business to invest in each other: that's the business of corporations and performers and Patrons-of-the-Arts. If I feel strongly about this, it's because Virgil himself educated me in such matters, and he'd be the first to understand. Meanwhile, I continually champion Virgil in my writings, speeches, interviews, and often accompany his songs in concert. As for his birthday, I'm doing a little piece for him (as are other composers) which will be included in a festschrift from Boosey & Hawkes by way of *Tempo* magazine. Please understand. (And I do intend to buy an expensive pair of tickets for the December 7th concert!)

Just returned from a too-strenuous stint with Gregg Smith in Saranac, and in a week must go for another fortnight to Santa Fe where we launch my new *Septet*. I've nearly finished a String Symphony for Atlanta, and must now make a long essay about Mussorgsky for *Opera News*. Jim enjoyed talking to you last week on the phone. I think of you daily with tenderness.

Love to Gene.

Ned

## To Angela Lansbury

*14 December 85*

Very dear Angela and Peter—

What a pleasant surprise to get your card. I hate to lose contact. We see you from time to time on television and it's like coming across a long lost cousin (albeit a cousin now knee-deep in murder), but it's not as satisfying as real life.

I'll be in town most of May, in theory, and if you give warning ahead of time, we can plan a meeting. I'm relieved about Dierdre. Italy seems somehow a much better country for her than America. We can talk about this when we meet.

What a wonderful experience, in every way for you, the TV series.

Jim Holmes sends you his best regards for Christmas, and so does Judy Collins with whom I just spoke.

And I send all love to you both. . . .

Ned

## To Edmund White

*Valentine's Day 86*

Fond Edmund—

Yes, Valentine's Day—and I still have the magnetic crimson heart with which you favored me and other guests how many? ten? years ago.

Any day now a copy of *OINK!* should land on your doorstep. It's a Chicago "little mag" containing the lengthy diary entry, dated Paris, April 4–20, 1984, which *Vanity Fair,* as you may recall, commissioned, paid for, but never used. I'll be most interested in your reaction.

I've read *Caracole* with mixed feelings. Every sentence therein deserves to be extracted and framed (like a magnetic crimson heart?) for its accurate grammar combined with novel opulence and dangerous metaphor. But as a whole the book seems an étude, which never comes to life. With all its length and admirable craft, it doesn't breathe and vibrate anywhere near as much as your current brief story in *Christopher Street*. JH too loves your story. You're reviving a literature of Innocence Abroad, popular in the nineties, the twenties, and the fifties. No one's done it in three decades or more.

Is it too soon to ask you to mark June 8th on your calendar? On that date the Atlanta Orchestra, under Robert Shaw, will play my new *String Symphony* at the Châtelet. I doubt if I'll be there (or if I'll ever visit Paris again), and I'd like an American spy to report.

Everything you do interests me — "I adore what you burn, you burn what I adore" — and I'd love to have news first hand. When are you to be in America? Or are you here as I write?

Please: fond wishes to John.

Love

Ned

## To Kenneth Koch

*22 March 86*

Dear Kenneth—

As promised on the phone the other night (and how sorry I am not to have been able to join in the celebration of your witty, sad, intelligent, original, and inspired new book), here's my observation:

When I reached the middle of page 70 and read

> On the edge
> Of the cup,
> Of the street,
> Of reading Mallarmé

I assumed that the title of your book was drawn, indeed, from Mallarmé's *Placet futile* (a sonnet musicalized by both Ravel & Debussy) which begins [my translation]:

> Princess! Envious of the youthful hébé
> rising up on this cup at the touch of your lips

> I spend my ardor, but have only the low rank of abbé
> and shall never appear even naked on the Sèvres.

Somewhere from your past this must have emerged as you penned the poem.

    Love
    Ned

### To David Del Tredici

*28 April 86*

Well, that's quite a piece, dear David.

    Its defining property is size (the way that, say, Varèse's defining property is orchestral color, or Debussy's is harmony). So people can't legitimately complain about its length any more than about a child's being too tall at birth. You, of course, are the child, Alice; you're not the narrator. It's one huge, mad, good-natured tantrum, and I'm glad you've now let Scriabin (via his *Poem of Ecstasy*) into the fray. As I told you, I wasn't bored, and that's saying a lot. The texture is continually absorbing, like a big blotter with a kaleidoscopic ink-blot that never dries. The tunes are spacious and true and contagious (though I could do with some modulation, and with more quiet moments). And the theatricality, finally, is effectively spooky, even frightening. Time will tell whether it's all "successful" (the way time has told about Edward Albee's *Tiny Alice*—who turned out, at least in the play, to be gigantic and all-encompassing). Meanwhile, do you agree that the performance was marvelous? It certainly struck *us* as marvelous.

    Your loving fan
    Ned

### To Edward Albee

*29 April 86*

Dear Edward—

    I'm terribly interested in reading your adaptation of *Lolita*.
    Might this be possible?
    Fondly always,
    Ned

### To Gary Graffman

*May Day Night*
*1986*

Best of Garys—

The mention of Cambodia goes way back. The only real biography of Debussy is, astonishingly, Lockspeiser's prissy mess, first published in 1937, the year that I, age 13, purchased it. On page 138 he writes: "*Pagodes* makes use of the five-note scale . . . borrowed from, or at any rate suggested by, the music of the Javanese and Cambodian dancers heard at the Paris World Exhibition." . . . But I'd take your word against Lockspeiser's any time. (*Lindaraja* turns out to be Spanish, and the ballet *Khamma* turns out to be Egyptian, so my memory betrayed me.)

[Vladimir Ivanovich] Rebikov: Debussy (three years his senior—I thought he was younger) could have known him during his lengthy visit to Madame Von Meck in 1880. Anyway, Grove dictionary states that "his use of whole-tone harmonies earned him a reputation as the finest Russian impressionist . . . ," and, as I told you on the phone, my teacher Felix Borowsky said, in 1940, that he used parallel dominant ninths before Debussy. So there! However, I'm not a historian, and will say anything for effect, so it's good for you to call my bluff.

Meanwhile, I've been looking at photos of Debussy again. He resembles Simone Signoret, with those great sad eyes. . . . The years pass. Looking forward to the 16th.

Love to you both
Ned

### To Gary Graffman

*18 May 86*

Dearest Gary & Naomi—

Thanks for the so edibly exotic menu, and for the canny conversation. Quiet, pleasant, we both were pleased.

But I forgot the most important thing: Have you a picture of the two of you that you'd permit me to include in my new book, *The Nantucket Diary*, which comes out in ten months? (The picture is needed *soon*.) I'd like something special, even odd, like something in Burma, or on top of an elephant, or with big smiles, or sitting at a table covered with food and drink. Not, however, a wedding picture. . . . If so, could you send it to the below address. It will be returned, but not for a year or so.

Love always and looking forward to the autumn.

Ned

### To Daron Hagen

*Nantucket*

*12 August 86*

Dear Daron—

My favorite sequence in your letter is: ". . . yesterday we spotted 20 vultures roosting in 2 nearby trees. The animals here are affectionate. . . ."

Yes, let's make a date for September 20th in New York. Shall we say 4 p.m. chez moi? Meanwhile, please send your new vital statistics, in case I need to contact you, or change the appointment. I received today from B & H the nice bound copy of *Homer*—the same one you presumably received. It shouldn't be too big a job for you. But I'll want you to copy the parts too, a month or so later.

How very wonderful that you're in love. Most of what one hears about these days is suppression, death, disease, and perilous stupidity. But love, almost never. I wish you all the best. . . .

I plan to fly to NYC on September 13.

Keep in touch.

Always

Ned

If what you told me on the phone is true, about the Friedheims—that it's predetermined that John Adams will be the winner "because there's never been a minimalist in first place before," then the whole procedure is illegal. Not only is the voting rigged, but the reason for determining the winner centers on fashion and not on quality.

### To David Diamond

*6 September 86*

Dear David—

I'm glad about the Cantata you're composing with Elie Wiesel. I pray that within the context of such a work you will persuade him to incorporate something about the systematic slaughter of hundreds of thousands of homosexuals under Hitler. Because it's discouraging—terrifying—to learn that the organizers of various holocaust memorials, now being erected both in Germany and in America, consider it indecent that homosexuals should presume to liken their suffering to that of the Jews. (And what about homosexual Jews!) One has only to read the *Advocate* every week to discover how the memory of gay torture and death is being suppressed. You, and you alone perhaps, are the one to revive Hope—as your piece is named.

I never used to believe that art and politics could be convincingly joined: politics is transient, while art is a permanent reflection after the fact. But now I'm not so sure, especially in light of, say, Britten's *War Requiem*. In this age of AIDS and of increasing legalized repression, we, as musicians, must try to do something. . . .

Love—
Ned

### To Daron Hagen

*30 September 86*

Dear Daron—

To call upon Proust, in order to set me straight, is not only an appeal to the highest court but the essence of tact, since, as you know, the word Proust sets me to trembling even more than the word Shakespeare. (He is the most all-encompassing European author of his generation, and—for me—on a par with Henry James and even Simenon.) However, just because Proust says it's so doesn't make it so, and the paragraph you quote is uncharacteristically one-sided. He omits not one but two vantages in telling the reader that even as we judge another person, that person is changing into *another* person.

If indeed the person we perceive contains "only the old impressions which we have already formed of him," by the same token we too—the perceivers—are continually changing. Thus, if I still see you, as I did five years ago, as someone who sometimes says what he feels his listener wants to be true rather than what in fact *is* true, then you too see me as I was five years ago. If I repeat myself verbally, remember that I'm not the same person (according to your—and Proust's—observations) repeating; therefore, the repeating is not repetition at all.

However (and this is the second vantage ignored by Proust in that paragraph, but profoundly demonstrated by him throughout his book), people don't ever change much. They become more of what they always were. A nasty young man doesn't suddenly, in old age, become lovable. A lovable person doesn't turn nasty as the years roll by. True, saints are said to change overnight, their absolute evil turning to absolute good. Well, I've never known a saint, have you? Anyway, we *all* have revelations and break-throughs, but these thrilling flashes don't alter our character. A person without charm cannot buy charm, no matter how rich he is, and a person with charm cannot shed it at will—even when committing murder.

In short, Proust notwithstanding, you're always going to think of me in a teacherly way (as I do with Virgil T.), even as I always see you as a Young Composer, even when you're fifty—if I live that long. . . . And so forth.

Thanks for all the news. My book's due next spring. Enclosed is the recommendation you request.

(*Homer* is going rapidly. I may have to ask you to re-do 2 or 3 pages.)

Fondly always

Ned

## To Reynolds Price

*18 October 86*

My very dearest Reynolds—

The moment I read your letter I hurried out to get *People*. I was hith-erto unaware of your condition, and now I am dismayed and dazzled and (dare I say it?) vaguely envious . . . envious, that is, of your *faith*—for I have little faith—and the ensuing prolificity. I shall think of you daily, and hope that your talent continues to steer you, for decades, to ever greater heights. I've seen good reviews of *Kate Vaiden*, and shall get it soon. Look forward to seeing you in person here next spring, as promised. I live in Nantucket now about a third of the time (with Jim Holmes, whom you met years ago when we were in NC visiting Wallace Fowlie), but will make a point of being in New York when you come.

Touched by your words about the diaries. I wish you would say as much to Jack Shoemaker. He's supposed to do the new volume, *The Nantucket Diary—1973–1985*, this coming spring. (Would you care to write a blurb?)

Please, dear Reynolds, let's stay in touch. I see your cousin Leontyne every once in a while, but it's not the same thing.

Love

Ned

### To Eugene Istomin

Fondest of Eugenes—

Under separate cover my new *Song and Dance* is heading for you. It's an A-B-A (hard-easy-hard) showpiece for piano solo. Both the A's are identical, almost, but with different spacings, so it shouldn't be that difficult to master. Musically the piece is what it is: spicily ugly and flashy, cornily touching and siciliennish, then spikey again. Learn it a little, then tell me what you think. If the contestants [of the William Kapell Competition] played the Perle badly, maybe it's that they were bad pianists. There's no excuse for them not applying themselves to a new piece with the same respect as to a Schumann Toccata, even if they don't care for the piece. Perhaps they should be given the piece 2 or 3 months in advance. It *could* be in print by maybe April 1st.

As for your plan for a little Rorem festival next summer, we can talk of that as the months draw near.

I saw Mrs. Perle yesterday, affable and combative as ever, at a little tea party here whereat Louise Talma and I played tapes of our recent bonbons, followed by a *goûter à dix couverts* consisting of Sacher Torte with masses of chantilly, a homemade raspberry-walnut cake steeped in Grand Marnier, several apple tarts, two dishes of cashews, and lots of blue grapes, plus espresso coffee and/or yellow wine.

Have you yet read Richard Howard's translation of *Past Tense* [Cocteau's diaries]? Smooth as silk.

Love to Martita. Please, let's see each other soon.

Ned

### To Dolores Fredrickson

Dear Dolores—

. . . The *Études* were certainly written with Emanuel Ax in mind. The Fifth in particular exploits his unique gift of being able to spin an elfin web of feathery filigree around a solid tune. Just as much of my orchestral music is conceived vocally (I write what human voices might sing, then remove the voices and give the material to colder instruments), so my piano music is sometimes conceived orchestrally. Here, for example, the left hand should imitate five trombones in close harmony, while the right hand is an

English horn in its freakish high register. The two ingredients interweave, and are occasionally interrupted when a ruby necklace is thrown at them, breaking, and splattering all over the floor. . . . As for the seventh Étude, it resembles my Third Piano Concerto, opening movement, in being strictly for the right hand. In both cases the form is mirror-like—a Rorschach test. An inkblot test. Here, for example, the G-sharp fermata is the note from which, before and behind, the other notes all splay out symmetrically, like a peacock's tale.

I've just finished a piece called *Song and Dance,* which will be inflicted compulsorily on the contestants of the William Kapell competition next summer.

Keep in touch.

Fondly always,

N

To Paul Bowles

*Tuesday, 27 January 87*

Very Dear Paul—

A visit from Edouard Roditi on Sunday, and then a viewing last night on television of the complete "Eight x Eight," reminded me yet again that it's been well over two years since last we corresponded. Which doesn't mean that you're ever too far from my mind.

Edouard suggested you'd been a bit unwell, and I feel sympathetic. I hope that whatever it is, you don't have to leave the country for treatment. . . . Virgil just returned from the hospital—decay in the spinal column, or something like that. He's uncomfortable except when sitting upright. As you must know, he's had a very glorious year, and homages continue but are abating. The abatement, plus Maurice's dying, have injected an unaccustomed melancholy into his daily tone, but he never, never complains. There will be a memorial for Maurice in two weeks: I'm supposed to play four of VT's pieces with a so-so baritone VT himself has supplied. Others will speak. (Not other baritones—other guests.) . . . Aaron is excessively vague but also excessively canny about the vagueness. He's adroit about not wounding close friends of long standing by actually forgetting their names. It's not Alzheimer's disease, but something degenerative all the same. I seldom see him. Vivian Perlis (his biographer) keeps one posted.

I'm the same but older—as are my parents, who cling to life staunchly and seem to have a new kind of zest suddenly. Father's 92, Mother 89, and both find positive reasons for getting up in the morning. I continue to support myself by writing music of every description. And two more books will come out later this year, a diary, and another collection of essays. You'll of course receive copies.

This humdrum news stands in guise of keeping in touch. I doubt if I'll ever come to Africa again . . . or even Europe. And you may not ever want to revisit America. So will you write me from time to time? I do keep up with you through interviews and memoirs here & there (most recently in the *Native*, a "recollection" by one Joel Redon which was unthinkably stupid), but it's not the same thing as your words.

Forever—
Ned

### To Monroe Wheeler, re. Glenway Wescott

*23 II 87*

Very dear Monroe—
My heart is with you today, and every day, forever.
Love
Ned

### To Jack Larson

*26 Feb 87*

Best of Jacks—
David Huntley, a mild-mannered but actually high-powered representative of Boosey & Hawkes and in his mid-thirties, will be in California for a fortnight on business. I presumed to give him your number. Should he not use it, you may see him at Betty Freeman's, where he plans to be for a Boulez colloquium *sans musique*. For a decade I've depended a great deal upon him professionally, but know little of his "life," except that he's consumed with music.

. . . Loved seeing you the other month. Please come back soon. Meanwhile, I may be there next fall. Freeman (whom I've never met) wrote that she'd like me as her guest for a day, so maybe I could work that in with a San Francisco lecture/concert scheduled for, I think, November.

Maurice's memorial was spirited, cultured, warm, and brief. Virgil didn't attend, but afterward, everyone (50 people) went to him at the Chelsea. Tell Jim I love him, as I do you. . . .

Ned

## To John Cage

*9 April 87*

Cher John—

Maybe we're both right about the number of voices for *Socrate*. My vocal score, purchased in Paris in 1949, variously states *"Drame Symphonique avec Voix"* (which could be plural or singular), and *"Partition pour chant et piano."* Grove says "1 or more vv." I've performed it in public twice: first in Buffalo in 1960 with two sopranos & piano, and again in 1968 with [Hugues] Cuenod & piano. But I've heard it in many versions, they all seem to work, but the simpler the better.

I've a fairly big Satie collection—some of it early editions from Satie himself inscribed to and stolen from Valentine Hugo. Treasures. But I don't have *Vexations*, nor can I find it. Someday maybe you'll show it to me. What you say about it (that it's "even better than Socrate") seems thrilling.

How pleasant to see you in the car the other night. It's not every day that I see another musician who knows and cares about my very favorite piece.

Affection always

N

## To Judy Collins

*31 July 87*

Judy Judy Judy—

Herewith I send you, without comment, a tape (plus the lyrics) of five songs by two friends. I do this because I promised them I would, but it's for you to form an opinion.

You once met Tom Steele at my house. He's co-editor, with the lyricist Chuck Ortleb, of *Christopher Street Magazine.* His vocal delivery, though rasping, doesn't quite sabotage the songs. Steele & Ortleb worship you, and would like your opinion. They're young.

I worship you too, but am too old for an opinion, perhaps. Am working on a quintet, a symphony, two books, and a speech to honor Lenny

Bernstein next week at the MacDowell Colony where he receives a gold medal.

Trust your heart.
Love to Louis,
see you in the autumn
Ned

### To Nan Talese, Judy Collins's editor

*20 September 87*

It's no news that Judy Collins has a way with lyrics. But now her prose, too, turns out to be resonant, orderly, touching, and terse. *Trust Your Heart* is a self-portrait of a true artist continually seeking to learn what it means to be a serious musician and a serious female in a resistant world. Its shape is that of a diary with flashbacks, affording a double perspective on a double life—that of an utter professional in the performing milieu, and that of a vulnerable creature who loves, suffers, drinks too much, and comes to terms. Its tone is at once sentimental and businesslike, tactful but frank, sometimes gruesome yet somehow optimistic. And its texture, like the singing voice of the author herself, reflects the no-nonsense loveliness of an icy brook turned pale gold by the sun.

—Ned Rorem

Dearest Nan [Talese]:

You can use any of the above for whatever purposes you choose. I loved reading the book. I didn't keep track of the array of misprints, knowing that proofreaders would doubtless pick them up. But just in case: on page 163, the first two lines, Kazuko Hillyer, who is a woman, is referred to as "He." And on page 168 the composer Haydn's name is twice misspelled as Hayden.

I miss seeing you.

Fond regards, also and always, from JH
Ned

### To John Ashbery

*27 September 87*

Dear John—

If you are upset by anything I've written about you, then I too am upset, for I value our long acquaintance and treasure you as a poet.

It's unfortunate that of the fourteen brief references to you in the new book (most of which are either neutral or admiring) the Kirkus Service should choose, and misquote, the only one that might seem disobliging. I was relating an anecdote which I found amusing, but which obviously misfired. Certainly I didn't mean to put you down, as Kirkus clearly means to put me down.

I'm not trying to excuse myself, only to explain.

Best to you always

Ned

## To Lou Harrison

*28 October 87*

Dearest of Lous and Bills—

What a dazzling, attractive, and intelligent tribute—the Soundings *Reader.* I'm thrilled to have it in my collection of Harrisoniana.

In a fortnight I'm returning briefly to California for the first time in a decade, and perhaps for the last time.

Could you come to the Black Oak Bookstore in Berkeley at 8 o'clock on November 17 (the birthdate of my still vital father, age 93) or to the Herbst Theater in S.F. the following evening for the City Arts & Lecture series?

. . . I'll be at the Stanford Court Hotel on Nob Hill, or else care of North Point Books in Berkeley. . . . (The enclosed advertises my new book by them, which features you, among others.)

Jim Holmes sends love.

As I do.

Ned

## To Russell Platt

*Tuesday*
*10 November 87*

Dear Russell—

Thinking about yesterday, and the question of modulation, it seems to me that your chief problem in getting your (often touching, sometimes beautiful) ideas on paper lies in a difficulty to see the forest for the trees. You become so concerned with a detail of expression—a brief phrase in Whitman, the "split rocks" in Millay—that the *whole* becomes lost. I recognize the difficulty all the more clearly that I have it myself, and so does every composer. Indeed, the whole process of composition—and of *teaching* composition—is the ability to see, or to hear, the entirety before you begin writing; details can be filled in later.

Please, for my sake, do as I suggested with the new choral piece. Keep it all in a ¹²/₈ barcarolle meter. If you must modulate, don't tie yourself in knots, just *do* it, start in another key. When a poem already exists, the skeleton is there and a composer can know where he's going to end even before he begins. Simplicity is the essence.

I always wish we had more time. Ideally, I would rewrite everyone's pieces. Practically, that's madness, and, in a way, condescending. But I must encourage you, as always, to *copy* what you admire. Don't refer to textbooks, go to the source. Witness how Mahler, or Barber, or even Schoenberg, use this or that device for getting here or there; then do likewise.

I believe in you. And I empathize with your allergies. Everything will get better. Believe me.

Ned R.

## FOR STEPHEN HOLDEN, RE. JUDY COLLINS

*21 Nov. 1987*

The texture of remarkable voices is best described by metaphor. There are four main kinds: Salt tears, as with Von Stade or Ella Fitzgerald; cat gut, as with Callas or Bessie Smith; hot chocolate, as with Leontyne Price or Libby Holman; and icy silver, as with Lily Pons or . . . Judy Collins.

High voices, at least in opera, usually represent heroines (with the Queen of the Night a notable exception), while mezzo sopranos are usually villains (with Carmen a notable exception).

In pop music, what sounds high for females is inevitably mezzo: Streisand's or Garland's altos correspond to the unstrained middle section of a "concert" contralto's range. Low female pop singers have a tessitura identical to a baritone: Marlene Dietrich, Juliette Gréco, etc.

Now, although Judy resists the label of pop singer—or, still more of folk singer, she is nevertheless 100% of the first, with an indelible hue of the second.

The difference between a pop song and a so-called art song (or between a Musical Comedy and an Opera) is not one of kind but of quality. A pop song (and this applies even to Gershwin, perhaps America's greatest songwriter) is Variable. It can be sung by any sex in any key at any speed with any instrumental backup, and still retain its integrity. Its text is a lyric, that is, verses designed (sometimes simultaneous with the music, or even superimposed after the music) to be sung. An "art-song" is Invariable. It can be sung only by a specific voice type, solely in the key and at the speed designated by the composer. It never involves improvisation. It is always the setting of a pre-existing text, usually high literature, often by a poet long dead.

Judy Collins has a pop singer's voice, a pop singer's repertory, and a pop singer's limitation—which aren't the same as a classical singer's. (Viz. Education, instincts, training, and societal location. Eileen Farrell, DeGaetani, Te Kanawa, etc.)

Her uniqueness as an interpreter—of her own or anyone's music—lies in the paradoxical timbre of purity-and-toughness. At her best her sound is as unpolluted as a mountain stream, while her delivery can be no-nonsense, even businesslike. Unlike most pop singers, she uses almost no vibrato. (All this is echoed in her prose-writing.) This sort of purity doesn't lend itself, on the face of it, to high drama, because, as I've said, high drama, *evil,* is for vibrating mezzos. But again, the paradox: precisely because of timbre purity, her hardness can be even more pernicious than Lenya's, viz. the "Pirate Jenny" song from *Threepenny.*

As for Judy the composer, she's right in the tradition of the Troubadour, as distinct from the lieder composer. That is, she is her own interpreter. Like all pop songs—indeed, like all songs, period—hers must sink or swim on the trend of the tune. Her harmony is unadventurous, her rhythm is foursquare, her counterpoint is nil, her coloration (i.e. her scoring) is by lackeys. There remains the sovereign ingredient of melody, and Judy's best melodies are memorable.

I'm not certain if, as a musician, Judy knows quite who or what she is. Her classical training (Antonia Brico) lends a cachet to her conversation which is in no way reflected in her own composition or performance. Nor has she a way with shape, in the sense of development, scope, large forms. She is a miniaturist—like most songwriters.

Her songs are American, in that they depict a state of mind or body which is static and "now," as opposed to French songs which are narrative (viz. Piaf), and progress from point A to point Z.

Because I am a walking blue pencil I often give Judy advice, sometimes solicited, sometimes not. The advice inevitably concerns not the music but the words, sometimes accepted, sometimes not.

To Andrew Porter

*9 December 87*

Dearest of Andrews—

Your missive, after our tea party a month ago, was indeed touching with its evocation of amities that retain their warmth despite separations of long miles and years. Now I have your note of last Friday exemplifying Madame de Sévigné's "letters are the wings of friendship."

I read—or read at—*Flaubert's Parrot,* a year or two ago when it came out, without quite getting the point of it, although Julian Barnes is admired everywhere, even in France. Indeed, I saw him on a replay of *Apostrophes* whereon his elegant, if sometimes ungrammatical, French permits him to sneer at Enid Starkie's "atrocious French accent." I've just read, at your suggestion, Chapter Six. (Incidentally, *I* don't hate critics. Some of my best friends, etc. And if critics are by their nature parasites, the best ones are that in the highest sense, like pilot fish or cowbirds which keep their larger brothers comfortable. Composers are parasites too, in that they feed off the past, all of them, without exception, and all the time. Composers, of course, *can* exist independently of critics.) Anyway, Chapter Six is amusing and pithy. One conjures images of what some Nabokovian pedant might make of Kafka's *Amerika* ("Why, it's not a bit like America!"). And even I, when recently enjoying *The Healing Art* by an author of your country (excuse me —your *adopted* country), A. N. Wilson, while impressed by his uncannily good ear for English dialogue, was busy making marginal notes on his inadvertent lapses in American dialogue, e.g. "in hospital" for "in the hospital." Et cetera. (Incidentally, you and I have never finished our conversation, begun a decade ago, about "to beam or not to beam." See pp. 241–42 in *Setting the Tone.*) I do think Barnes is good at distinguishing between truth versus fact. As for my robin, what ought I to do in another edition?

Yes, I'd have liked you to hear "Eleven Studies," it's among my better pieces. But as Jim said the performance was lackluster—and there *is* a recording by Louisville.

Do I still write songs?—that is, pieces based on lyric poems for voice & piano? Well, not much, really. There's irony in that. I used to be called "America's leading song composer" (that's easy: no one else was doing it). I also earn my living almost exclusively as a composer: it's been nearly three decades since I've written an uncommissioned piece. Knock wood. HOW-EVER, what commissions have I had for writing songs in the past thirty years? In 1959, a series (not a cycle) of Roethke poems for Alice Esty, $600. Since then, only cycles, and very few. *Poems of Love and the Rain* for the Ford Foundation in 1962 ($3000), and *The Nantucket Songs* for the Library of Congress in 1979 ($5000 or thereabouts). The only other cycles in this period were composed for individuals: *War Scene* in 1969 for Souzay (no money changed hands). *Women's Voices* for a young soprano, Joyce Mathys, in 1975 ($2000). And *The Calamus Songs* for a young baritone in 1983 ($3000). All my other solo vocal music during this time has been with instruments, either chamber groups or orchestra, and even *Ariel* (for Curtin in 1970) was an unpaid-for labor of love. It hadn't struck me until recently that more than half of my entire huge output is choral, and more than half of *that* is "sacred." (I'm an atheist, although I do believe in poetry.) So . . . do I write songs anymore? Certainly not just for the love of it. Who's there to sing them? There is not a single American singer—in this land of two hundred million souls—who can earn a living as a recitalist, the way dozens did two generations ago, and the way that only an Ameling or Fischer-Dieskau can today. The reasons are probably economic. Our young singers veer toward opera, and when they do sing songs (usually in languages they can't speak, but occasionally even in English), they belt them, and roll their R's in the Italianate style. My most recent songs are, yes, for voice-&-orchestra, based on James Schuyler poems. (Phyllis Bryn-Julson will premiere them in North Dakota in April. Will you come?) I'd thought, perhaps greedily, while composing them, that I'd make a piano-vocal arrangement (the reverse of [John] Harbison's coup) and kill two birds with one stone. But it doesn't work—any more than Ravel's *Schéhérazade* works on the keyboard. No, I don't write straight songs anymore because there's no outlet anymore, either financial or practical, no singers who know how to do them, or where to do them. I *do* assign poems to my pupils at Curtis to be set for voice & piano—the same poem to each, then we compare the results, their esthetic choices, declamation expertise, etc. But I always warn them, sadly, that there's no literature being created for the medium, because there's no longer a demand.

I'm rambling. But it's a sociological question, and no one writes about it (because no one thinks about it) anymore. Will Crutchfield, who does care, simply claims that Song has had its heyday, especially in the USA, and now that heyday, which lasted fifty years, is part of history, and on to something new. But what am I to make of that?

We must meet soon, very soon.
I treasure you. . . .
Ned


## To James Lord

*16 December 87*

Very dear as always James—

Hasn't it been too long? Whole years go by when I hear not a word from friends in Paris. Such news as I get is always oblique (through Americans), and generally sad: that Philippe Erlanger is now no more, for example, or that Edmund White has "tested positive." I continue to suggest you to people doing books about this & that—most recently to someone hoping for something on Jacqueline Picasso—which you know better than I know. Hope you don't mind. . . .

I have a new book just out, a long one, called *The Nantucket Diary,* in which you figure, almost always in relation to Giacometti. What are you now involved with literarywise? Why not tell me about it in person, as well as gossip of France? Will you be here soon?

I have commissions through 1991, mainly on large choral works for which I'm seeking apt texts. No plans at all for coming to Europe.

Years flow by.
Love to Bernard.
And you always.
Ned


## To Lou Harrison

*17 January 1988*

Fond Lou, thrice-blessed (for your talent, for Bill Colvig, and for your platinum curls):

Thanks for so very much for the two concertos which I instantly attended. The slow movement of the second one (the one recorded in Japan) was, to me, so moving that I immediately played it again, lay upon the floor, and gave myself to it. Jarrett plays very very musically, and with an accurate finger dipped in a steel chalice filled with high-priced apricot nectar. (His own music, however, I don't buy.)

You're seventy? That seems so young, in light of my parents now both well into their nineties, and still quite alive though not kicking much. I'll be sixty-five next October. Yes, I'd like you to hear *Winter Pages,* yes.

I'm concerned about your diabetes, and think daily about you, and about Bill. Love to him. And to Madeleine Milhaud, if you see her. Also from Jim.

Ned

## To Kenneth Koch

*23 January 88*

Fond Kenneth—

Within ten days you should receive FINALLY the recording of *Hearing*—the "opera" version for 4 singers and 8 instruments. It was made already six years ago. The performance is disappointing. The soprano is awfully good, but the tenor, who sets the tone ("Oh what a physical effect it has on me . . .") which should be vigorous and enthusiastic, is passive and dull. Also, the tempos throughout are slack: the last movement, especially, drags. Well, anyway. . . . The other pieces, both choral, are beautifully per-formed: *Letters from Paris* on words of Janet Flanner, and *Give All to Love* on words of Emerson.

Do send me your reaction all the same.

Affection, dear poet, to you in this new year. . . .

Ned

## To Andrew Porter

*8 II 88*

Andrew, Andrew—

Surely you are right about *engloutie.* The infinitive, *engloutir,* what's more can have a lewd meaning (it's what the cruel vulva does to the poor *membre virile*), and that could never jell with Debussy's intent. . . . But Ys? Wasn't Ys the site of prehistoric (and thus pre-Christian, and pre-cathe-dralic) Paris? I learned once that the name Paris derived from *pàreil a Ys*— the aspiration of city planners who began to reconstruct the destroyed other town. . . .

Two or three weeks ago you referred to a married couple (I think it was a soprano and her legal spouse) as "wife and man." Doubtless you meant to be quaint as well as feminist, but wouldn't "woman and husband" be less sexist?

I do pray that you got my last missive—the one answering, weeks later, yours about word settings. It was mailed to *The New Yorker,* because I didn't have your home address here in Nantucket. Jim, who arrived today, brought your words about the Debussy. Now, alas, we must both return tomorrow by auto to New York. A sad emergency. So perhaps I'll even see you before your eyes fall upon these verbs. If not, may we meet soon.

Love always

Ned

To GARY GRAFFMAN

*25 March 88*

Fond Gary—

It would be tempting to suggest that, in his Left-Hand Concerto, [Erich] Korngold swiped a trick or two from Ravel, both melodically (the second theme resembles that of Ravel's 2-hand Concerto in G) and virtuosically. But Korngold's piece seems to predate MR's by nearly a decade. Anyway, at its best, it's got a shamelessly satisfying opulence that raises it high. Formally, it's a bit vague maybe, and fustian's rife. But you're right to champion it. . . . The quartet is a less interesting piece, but you perform it nobly (better than the stringsters). As for the Ravel, I was raised on the Cortot-Munch version of 1939; yours is at once more leisurely and more crisp (and certainly more accurate) than Cortot's, and Leinsdorf is jerkier than Munch. What a continually strange piece, so dark and yet so somehow campy. Thanks for the unique tapes which I'll treasure ever. (The piano's a bit remote in the Ravel Concerto.)

And thanks again for the unique dinner party (so dark and yet so somehow campy). Naomi's menu was, as always, nonpareil, and it was a pleasure to socialize again with the Hortenses after so many years. Your slides, as I told you, were gorgeous as well as upsetting. Despite having lived in Morocco for 2½ years (and if you ever go there, please let me know ahead of time), I could *never* as a tourist, envisage Western China, or even Peking. Oddity and hardship and curiosity wane as I grow older. I'm jealous, sort of, of your enterprise.

Will you be at school Wednesday? I will.

Love always—

Ned

To David Diamond

*8 May 88*

Dear David—

My precious mother died four weeks ago. It was a sad, mysterious week that followed: no amount of wisdom or experience can prepare one, and I feel quite changed, suddenly, at *my* age! We had a beautiful memorial a few days later, with all my sister's progeny, and JH, at Friends Meeting House in Philadelphia, with Father patriarchally declaiming from his wheelchair (he's 93, and fairly well off, despite slurred speech from a mild stroke some months ago). Sylvia Goldstein had six trees planted in Israel "in the name of Gladys Rorem," and Rosemary and I may eventually strew Mother's ashes—as she wished—over the Lordly Hudson. I knew you'd like to know.

The enclosed invitation will explain why we can't attend your concert at the Jewish Museum. Jim's been preparing this scrupulously for months, and it won't be over (i.e., the disrobing of the chorus, the dissemination of guests, the post mortem) until way after yours begins. I'm sorry to have to miss so many of your events. Maybe we can have a tape-session, or at least a meal, before summer sets in. We'll probably leave for Nantucket on the 22nd. There's much to discuss.

Lenny's appearance at ASCAP last week was as chaotic as Marilyn Monroe's appearance at the Academy in 1959. All sorts of cultured sexagenarians behaving like adolescents in their eagerness to glimpse the Great Man. He'll conduct my Violin Concerto, with Gidon Kremer and the NY Phil next November, and I'm thrilled.

Love from us both.

Ned

To Edward Albee

*Nantucket*
*3 June 88*

Dear Edward—

Forgot to say, when you called, that Noel Farrand came for a visit a couple weeks ago. He remains elfin, dogmatic, overweight, garrulous, and charming, a Rachmaninoffophile, speaks warmly of you, and lives in Maine where he "gives Flanagan concerts." But doubtless you know all this?

Is Montauk near Bridgehampton? If you're in the former could you come to the latter on August 6th when I have a little quintet called *Bright*

*Music* being given its premiere by the Bridgehampton Chamber Players?
I'll be there for just a day, maybe less, and would love to see you.

Forever
Ned


To Daron Hagen

Lonely Daron—
Well, it's the condition of man. Colette said, "No one asks you to be
happy. Just get your work done." Of course, the current ravages of the
Greenhouse Effect suggest we're all doomed anyway.

I'll be back around 10 Sept. and maybe we can start on the Oratorio,
now called *Goodbye My Fancy*.

Much affection
Ned


To Judy Collins

Dearest Judy—
As soon as I got the memo about Antonia Brico I phoned my childhood friend, Perry O'Neil. She conducted him in Ravel's Concerto for the
Left Hand in their joint debut with the Illinois Symphony (one of Roosevelt's WPA projects) in January of 1941, and I was there. Perry promises to
write Brico immediately. I'll do the same if you want me to, although there's
no zip code with the address you gave, and letters might not arrive. [Brico
was our first woman conductor and a mentor of Judy, who made a documentary about her.]

Since last we spoke both my parents have died: Mother in April, Father
three weeks ago today. My sister Rosemary and I were with Father at the
end. I've never seen a person simply vanish—it was melancholy, strange,
urgent, hopeless, and rather wonderful. They were 90 and 93, and both were
fond of you.

Will we be seeing each other soon? I'm back in New York now for the
winter.

I love you.
(I love Louis too.)
Ned

### To Gary Graffman

*25 October 88*

Gary, Gary, Gary. . . .

Use the enclosed "Letter of Intent" instead of the previous one mailed a week or two ago. I really hope the project can be realized: musical notions are fomenting already in my febrile brain.

How can I tell you how moved I was by Sunday's concert! Every single piece was performed in a manner which, for a composer, exceeds most professional presentations. The students never once questioned (at least in my presence) the value of the experience; I only hope it was one-tenth as exciting for them as it was for me. And you are to be thanked for promoting such a happy celebration. It made my year.

I'll be at school again next Monday. But if our paths don't cross there, they will the following Friday.

Shirley and I loved our quiet meal with you at the Barclay, and we both send our love to Naomi.

Ned

### To Leonard Bernstein

*1 Nov. 88*
*Tuesday*

Dearest Lenny—

At your suggestion I (re)read Leviticus, and found it less frightening than I'd remembered, and more poetic. But I only read The Holiness Code.

Loved seeing you last night. The concerto [NR's Violin Concerto], if it sounds half as effective as your plans, will overwhelm the world. I'm looking *almost* as forward to your Jubilee piece.

Meanwhile, I don't know whether you have this new book. Anyway, you don't have a signed copy, so here it is.

We'll meet again, and soon.

Forever

Ned

"The stranger that dwelleth with you. . . ."

To Paul Bowles

*Thanksgiving Day*
*1988*

Dear Paul—

Mainly this is a note to renew contact—it's been almost a year since last we wrote, and too much time should not go by. Also I want to say a few things: Weidenfeld & Nicolson sent me, "for comment," bound galleys of [Christopher Sawyer-Lauçanno's biography of P.B.] *An Invisible Spectator* which I've now read about half of, and with great interest. Although the style is a trifle careful (I guess it's his first book) and the form a trifle dogged in its chronology, with a superabundance of quotes from pre-existing material, the narrative flows and gives pleasure, at least to me, since I know you and many many others mentioned. BUT—and this is crucial—as is usual with biography, everything rings true *except where I'm concerned*. If I find that the first few mentions of me (especially regarding our first meeting in Taxco) are inexact, I can only conclude that similar mentions of others are inexact, and that thus the whole work is slanted according to the author's whim. Christopher Sawyer-Lauçanno clearly admires you deeply and hopes to be thorough; he sent me a typescript of the pages concerning me (plus the long Mescaline Letter, which reads pretty well) and asked me to make changes. I made changes but they weren't incorporated; perhaps they will be before the May publication. In any case, I have mixed feelings about all biographies, especially of living people. There's just no such thing as The Facts, let alone The Truth.

As you may know, I've been teaching at The Curtis Institute in Philadelphia for the past eight years. This year I've assigned two of my students, Troy Peters (age 19) and Kam Morrill (25), to make dramatic settings of, respectively, Jane Bowles's *A Quarreling Pair* and *In the Summer House*, Act I. Should these settings prove workable and get beyond the student production stage, whom does one apply to for rights? You?

Both my parents died during the past six months and I feel (as does my sister) suddenly vulnerable. Yet I've also just turned 65—an orphan at 65— and the best thing about that is a spate of performances. The most auspicious of these is Lenny B's conducting of my fairly recent Violin Concerto, with Gidon Kremer, for four separate programs this week with the (scandalously underprepared) Philharmonic. I was almost as thrilled by a tape I've just heard of your songs, wonderfully sung, by a baritone named Duesing in Nice. These songs (which don't include the Lorca, although that was announced on the program) are almost all perfect; they took me back over the decades. No one writes songs that good anymore. I've not yet listened to the piano works.

Not having heard from you, I assume that my two most recent books — a diary and a collection of musical essays — didn't reach your shores. Publishers don't give a damn about anything but money, which they know they won't make on me, so they don't send out the books. Though if maybe you *did* receive them, let me know. Else I'll mail them myself.

I don't have Gavin Lambert's address. Tell him I very much enjoyed both his recent TV movies, and that I'd love to hear from him.

Always
Ned


### To Leonard Bernstein

*1 December 88*

Blessed and tragic Lenny —

It's been a strenuous week, fairly close to you on a daily basis, like a marriage, and now we are divorced again until another five years pass. Meanwhile thank you for making my music vibrate. There is only you.

Je t'aime
Ned


### To Gary Graffman

*20 December 88*

Dear Gary —

Progress report:

The piece I'm writing for Évian should be finished in a week or so, and orchestrated shortly thereafter. It's in two parts — a *Fantasy & Polka*. The Fantasy is around four minutes of ruminating profundity, the Polka will be two or three minutes of vulgar frivolity based on the same material. This is longer than you'd bargained for, I know, but I figured that if Rostropovich is conducting, he should have something more than a giddy curtain-raiser. The exact orchestration will be listed when you get the score, in mid-January.

Questions: Will Rostropovich conduct it in Philadelphia, prior to Évian?

Will there be, as you had mentioned, a concert of my chamber music in
Évian? If so, I thought maybe I'd use that as an excuse to return to France
for a brief visit, after five years' absence. Are you going? and are you hiring
a plane?

Tell Vera Bruestle that Loeb's catalogue insert looks o.k. to me. Meanwhile, the four composer applications I've examined thus far have been
laughably inferior. I'm sure better applicants will turn up: I need one more
pupil for next year; and I do think that this season, at least, they can continue to apply after the deadline set by Loeb as January 15th.

So glad to have seen you, with the Lloyds, at my little concert last
Saturday. What a drama!—with the horn player literally at death's door just
minutes before performing. . . . Might David Lloyd be coming to Curtis?
I'll be there next on Jan. 16 for the whole day.

Happiest of Holidays,
and love to Naomi
Ned


To Gary Graffman

*22 January 89*

Gary, Gary, Gary—
On the desk before you lies a score of the new *Fantasy and Polka*.
Whatever it's worth, it should *sound* good. It would mean a lot to me if
Rostropovich could include it in his Philadelphia program, as well as at
Évian. That way I can (presumably) get a tape, and hear it myself. Other-
wise it will get lost. Can Évian be persuaded to let America have the first
hearing—since their fee is otherwise so comparatively low? (Incidentally,
they now owe me that fee.)

This afternoon we drive to Nantucket. My flock comes to New York on
February 8. I'll be next in Philadelphia on the 22nd, for [my student] Kam's
opera, and staying overnight at the Barclay. Can we see each other then?

I've accepted an 18-year-old from Scotland, David Horne, for next year.
He wants to be a double major as a pianist. His own music is expert within
its considerable limitations, and I'll be most curious to hear how he is as a
pianist.

Love
Ned

To Eugene Istomin

*Nantucket*

*27 January 89*

Fond Eugene—

Your record is valuable. Jim concurs. The moment it arrived we placed it on the new CD player, and *Reflets dans l'eau* bloomed forth like an oil of molten amethysts on a surface of silver velvet. Your sound is (always has been) like no one else's, and loses nothing in transfer to disc. (Your emotive breathing is also transferred, but not as noticeably as Schnabel's.) All the Debussy is more rubato and perhaps slower than I'm used to, but it's full of love and care and accuracy. The Schumann too is so personal, and again the *sound* is magic. Especially the first two movements, which are better as music than the last two. . . .

Love to Martita. Peter Gravina's extreme praise on the jacket copy is not misplaced.

Love

Ned

For *The American Academy*
VIRGIL THOMSON
*1896–1989*
*By Ned Rorem*

When I first beheld Virgil Thomson, nearly fifty years ago, he was on a stage for one of those benighted roundtables about Meaning in Music. His fellow panelists, straining for a definition of the art, were about to settle for the Bard's "concord of sweet sounds" when Thomson yelled: "Boy, was he wrong! You might as well call poetry a succession of lovely words, or painting a juxtaposition of pretty colors. Music's definition is: That which musicians do." Which settled the matter. If Shakespeare erred, albeit divinely, Congreve did too, with his "charms to soothe a savage breast." Thomson, like all composers, disdained metaphoric ascriptions of music as mere cushion for the emotions. His businesslike summation was the first professional remark I'd ever heard from a so-called creative artist, and I was soon to hear more, from the horse's mouth, when I quit school at age 19 to work with the master.

I already knew of course that he was born in 1896 in Kansas City, excelled at Harvard, then moved to France in 1920. And that in the next two decades he sent back to America not only trunkloads of sonatas and songs, but quartets and symphonies, a ballet called *Filling Station,* scores for movies of Pare Lorentz, a best-selling book called *The State of Music,* and, above all, a collaboration with Gertrude Stein, *Four Saints in Three Acts,* which was then and perhaps remains the most viable opera by any American. American he utterly was despite, or maybe because of, the removal from his homeland which gave him a new slant toward his roots. For it was he who first legitimized the use of homegrown fodder for urbane palates. He confected his own folk song by filtering the hymns of his youth through a chic Gallic prism. This was the "American Sound" of wide-open prairies and Appalachian springs, soon borrowed and popularized by others.

At the start of World War II, Virgil Thomson returned from Paris to begin his fourteen-year stint as critic for the *New York Herald Tribune.* And the rest, as they say, is . . . well, it's geography. Thomson single-handedly changed, for a time, the tone of serious American composition from the thickish Teutonic stance which had dominated since before MacDowell to the transparent French-ness of those in the Boulanger school.

He was at his peak when we met in 1943. As his in-house copyist, for which I received twenty dollars and two orchestration lessons a week, my daily chores were done on the parlor table within earshot of the next room where—propped in bed, a pad on his lap, an ear to the phone—Virgil ran the world of music. During those first months, by being accountable for his every note, by heeding his ever-lucid but never-repeated dicta on instrumentation, and by eavesdropping on his talk with, say, Leopold Stokowski or Oscar Levant or colleagues at the paper, I gleaned as much, esthetically and practically, about the terrifying golden milieu of my future vocation as in all the previous years.

Virgil the author, as his ten books attest, was the world's most informative and unsentimental witness to other people's music. These qualities were enhanced by his addressing the subject from inside out—from the standpoint of the maker—and by his readability which owed so much to Paris where, in art as in life, brevity is next to godliness. Beside him, other critics were superfluous. They may have shared his perception, even exceeded his scope, but none boasted his knack for cracking square center with that perfect little Fabergé hammer.

Virgil the musician, over and beyond his affable innovation (based not on new complication but, ironically, on age-old simplicity), was our sole composer as convincing in song as in opera. His music cannot be assessed on the same expressive basis as any other music, even Satie's, since his more than any other depends on words. If Virgil never received a bad review (or, except for the Stein operas, a really good review), it's less because reviewers were intimidated by Papa than because they didn't know what to say about this seeming inanity. In fact, the inanity was sophistication at its most poignant. His every phrase is aria-in-a-microscope, built from but two or three intervals. The result differs from folk song only in the ambiguous accompaniment and eccentric literariness. The songs are rarely sung right, but despite their sparseness they do need to be heard to be believed. They are not *Augenmusik,* yet the critic's ear is not often given to listening to them, even in imagination. Thomson's unique urge was to codify simplicity, the way others have been urged to codify complexity.

Virgil the man had concerns, but not anxieties like we morbid others; he didn't agonize about the daily news—which may account for his longevity. Emerging from anesthetic after an operation three years ago, he asked: "Will I live?" When the doctor said yes, Virgil replied, "In that case I'll need my glasses."

His music resembles himself, is impatiently terse, free of padding, sensuous without self-indulgence, not especially warm but often quite dear. It is also very, very witty—if that adjective makes sense when applied to nonvocal works. His art is generous by its very frugality—we recall it accurately forever.

If in texture Virgil Thomson was American as apple pie, in "message" he was French as *tarte tatin,* because he was not a specialist. During the decades of our friendship (sometimes warm, sometimes cool) I never thought of him as less than this century's most articulate musicologist and most persuasive opera maker. Like all artists he was able to do what cannot be done. Through his prose he convincingly evoked the sound of new musical pieces, and through his musical pieces he continues to evoke the visual spectacle of all our pasts.

When I last beheld Virgil Thomson two weeks before he died, he was ensconced as usual in that armchair near the piano, gazing at paintings by dear friends—Stettheimer, Arp, Grosser, Bérard—that had for so long hung on his east wall at the Chelsea. In the dreamy murmur that was now his sole voice (contrasting with the glib staccato that once so intimidated most of us), he announced: "Just sitting here, day after day after day, I realize how beautiful my pictures are." That is how I like to remember him—a general practitioner, in taste as in talent, never blasé, dying as he had lived, among an array of old acquaintances.

## To Eugene Istomin

*6 February 89*

Dear Eugene—

And now, on another note . . .

I'm going to Greece. I hate to travel, having been almost everywhere. But Greece is the only country I've never been to that I long to go to. The Greek Broadcasting Corporation wants me to judge a 2-evening finale of a composers' competition (international composers under forty) at an orchestral program to be conducted by Theodore Antoniou. In exchange, they'll give me a free trip to Athens plus a week in the islands, plus a similar deal for anyone I want to bring. Jim can't go because of his church job, and also Sonny, the dog, can't be left alone. So I've invited Ellen Adler. Do you approve? The last week in May.

Anyway, since you know Greece, will you keep in mind what and who I ought to do and see there? I know *nobody* there—except Princess Irene and Melina Mercouri. (I'm reminded of Virgil returning to Rome after a hiatus of twenty years: "I don't know anyone there anymore, except the French ambassador and the Pope.")

. . . Much love forever.

Ned

## To David Del Tredici

*5 March 89*

Fond David of the platinum slippers—

Phoned you without response to say it was pleasant to glimpse you at Sylvia's seventieth birthday party. I wish we met oftener. But I find (don't you?) that as the years seep by there's less time just to gossip and eat and cruise with old friends (work seems so all-consuming), when cruising and gossiping and eating are perhaps more important, after all, than anything else. Of course, you have a lot of social intercourse now with the Philharmonic probably, while I see people only at Curtis. Apropos of which, Curtis (i.e. Gary Graffman) is anxious to invite three or four composers down for one day each, $500 per visit, to talk to the student composers (and others), and to hear a piece or two of his or her own played by the fledgling performers. You were specifically requested as one of about five others. G.G. will be in touch.

Yaddo meanwhile has been after me, as usual, and wanted a series of *rich people* to send invitations to. I told whoever it was that wrote me that you, the chairman, should contact me. I'll be glad to give you names, but it should be soon, no? Meanwhile, I almost surely won't be in town on April 13. It's too expensive. And Calvin Trilling, like all funny people, bores me. I'll be in Nantucket. But do call me soon.

I love you.

Ned

## To Eugene Istomin

*Nantucket*
*11 April 89*

Ever fond Martita and Eugene—

What a success your noonday party was! Everything about it—not least the underlying care and affection for Shirley Gabis—was flawless and honest. And for me too you were perfect hosts. I love your apartment, and I loved having some all-too-rare time with you.

... Next week L.A. for Cocteau's hundredth birthday and a musical setting of *Anna La Bonne*. Then Chicago for a well-planned concert with the Ferris Chorale. Then New York again until late May. Then no Greece, but Nantucket for the summer. You're both welcome, alone or ensemble, whenever your whim strikes you.

Love always, and always, and also from Jim. . . .

## To Jack Larson

*24 April 89*

Dearest Jack—

How super-swell to see you both last week, and your glamorous friends. Forgot to tell you that a month or so ago a Korean soprano at Juilliard gave a concert of same-poem-different-composer songs on which she juxtaposed David Diamond's settings of your "Do I Love You" verses with mine. Effective. (Especially mine.) Please thank Jim for the peach pie. And tell him to think again about the Nantucket investment. The maker of *The*

*China Syndrome* cannot afford to contribute to the ravaging of a very fragile island. Come and see for yourselves: you're welcome anytime.

Love, and also love

Ned


## To Gary Graffman

Fond Gary & Naomi—

Naturally I'm curious about how my piece went in Evian. Since Rostropovich (not to my surprise) has evinced no interest in the fact of my existence, you're the only ones I can rely on for a report. Even if it went badly,
I'd love a reaction, a program perhaps, and certainly a tape. So would Boosey
& Hawkes.

My new Scotch student, David Horne, is quite interesting. I didn't
meet him during his brief visit a few months ago, but he sent me cassettes
of his performances of Beethoven's First Concerto and of Rachmaninoff's
Paganini. He's a dazzling pianist, with infinite control, glittering accurate
fingers, and intelligent emotionalism (except in the D-Flat Major varia-
tion, the "corny" melodic one, which is overdone). To say he's only eighteen
no longer means anything, since most true pianists have more technique at
that age than they'll ever have, and from then on it's all downhill. (Like the
sexual drive, at least in males, according to Kinsey.) However, his composi-
tions, although brash and involved in effect at the cost of carefulness, are
pretty mature too. He knows how to make a piece *go*. Will he be a double
major? He should have a piano teacher who will give him Bach and Satie
and force him to play simply. Let me know what you think.

We're here for the summer now.

Love always

Ned


## To Rosalyn Tureck

Dearest Rosalyn—

The CD of the *Goldberg* is flawless. I've just played it from start to finish giving it total attention. The sound is extraordinary and your every note
is golden. Yes, of course it's a great work. And I realize now that each vari-

ation is a crucial rung on the kaleidoscopic ladder which is never the same from performance to performance, but which always adds up to an inevitable whole. (This image is reckless, but it means the piece is perfect, unchangeable, in form and content.) Your playing satisfies me utterly. I kept wondering how Bach would take it. Variations 22 and 25 move me deeply. Buckley's notes are amusing. And his piano is fabulous, don't you think? Thanks.

Love
Ned

To Paul Hoover of *New American Writing*
Re. Kenneth Koch

*Nantucket*
*8 July 89*

Dear Paul—

Yes, an essay or homage should be penned about Kenneth Koch's relation to music, and I suppose I'm the one to do it, since, so far as I know, except for Virgil Thomson (whose settings of *Mostly About Love* are among America's major songs), I'm the only composer to have extensively used Kenneth's poetry. But I haven't the time, beyond the following ramblings which you can use as you will.

Poets and painters are sociable, almost tribal, and particularly the so-called New York Group—O'Hara, Ashbery, Schuyler, Koch, Freilicher, Rivers, Frankenthaler, and other protégés of the late John Myers—the English they spoke, and still speak amongst themselves, is a tribal English, in both nuance and accent. Composers, on the other hand, are loners. Occasionally, as with composers who are setters of words like myself, one will pass from his lonerhood into what you term "collaboration" with the painters and poets who have been collaborating with themselves daily for decades. I've done this, for better or worse, with all the above-mentioned, including Kenward Elmslie (a short choral work and, of course, the big opera *Miss Julie*), most copiously with Kenneth Koch.

. . . Interestingly, the one "collaboration" which could be called that never saw the light of day—at least as the opera it was intended to be. That was a commission in 1968 from the Metropolitan Opera Studio. Since heart transplants and student demonstrations were both in the news that season, Kenneth wrote, in 24 hours, a well-wrought libretto incorporating both these themes, called *A Change of Hearts*. This was rejected by the Met Studio on the grounds that young audiences wouldn't get it. (Children, in fact, understand "art" wonderfully, until they grow up.) Instead, I set his famous *Bertha* to music, also rejected, but widely performed elsewhere since.

*Hearing*, a song cycle from 1965, was not a collaboration. Rather, it was a selection of K.K.'s verse, chosen from disparate sources, and sewn together by my music. It was published (as was *Bertha*), by my regular editors, Boosey & Hawkes, with a cover by Jane Freilicher—a bouquet of posies. Many years later, James Holmes made a libretto out of the cycle, by eliminating one of the songs, changing the order of the others, assigning segments of the solo vocal line to four singers who "reply" to each other, and by superimposing a scenario and a suggested décor. This I orchestrated, for nine instruments, in 1973 (?) on a grant from the N.E.A., and in this form it's been recorded by the Gregg Smith Singers.

That's all. And nothing in seventeen years. But Kenneth is wonderful for music: the poetry, though sometimes melancholy, is never depressing or obscure, and is often witty, even laugh-making, in a manner direct enough to be comprehended when intoned. He also has a stronger sense of drama, of theater, than most poets. (He did write another libretto, *Angelica*, about France in the nineteenth century, for Thomson. Never used.)

KK and I, in 1982, were approached by producer Stuart Ostrow to make a "musical" from *I Never Told Anybody*. This came to naught for financial reasons, but it remains a terrific idea.

Always and always. . . .
Ned

### To Lou Harrison

*Nantucket*
*20 August 89*

Dearest of Lous—

Grove Dictionary, for their Opera Edition in 1991, has asked me to do 600 words on you, and 200 on *Young Caeser* (sic). I said yes—unless you're unwilling, in which case I'd understand. But if you're willing, I would need score & tape of the opera.

What's to be done? As it happens, I'm supposed to go to *Chico* for three days in early November. It's possible I'll stop off, before or after, in San

Francisco to visit for 24 hours George & Shirley Perle who will be living there then. And it would be divine to see you there then too.

Then again, I may not stop off. . . . Write me.

The summer—is it possible—is already oozing to a close. In three weeks: back to New York, then to classes at Curtis, as usual. Tons of work, just done, and to do. Both my parents died last year, mysterious and awful, and now my sister Rosemary and I are orphans at sixty-five. Jim continues as the most important person in my life.

Virgil, indomitable, his new book on words just out, not bad, academic, crusty.

To you, love, and to Bill love too.

Ned

# Part Five

# 1990s

*Forever dear Jim:*
**THIS SERPENTINE ETUDE**
NED ROREM
*is unrevised. But then, so is my feeling for you, which has*
*merely augmented since first we met, 23 years ago this month.*

Christmas Eve 1990

*7 February 1990*

Dear Paul—

You look both handsome and wise in that photograph in the white automobile. I'm terribly sorry you're suffering from sciatica. But it will go away. Everyone I know has pains now, but they finally disappear—(the pains do) then others replace them.

Yes, Arthur Gold was a shock. Bobby Fizdale says it was "the best death" he's ever witnessed, as far as humor and lack of complaint are concerned. I'll be seeing Bobby on Saturday and will suggest he write you. Unless he has already.

After your mentioning of my being "angered" by your likening my mind to an ant colony, I re-read all your letters of the past forty years. (They would make a nice little book—should we do something about it—perhaps with some of my answers? North Point Press could be interested.) In the past 15 years there are innumerable references to the ant colony, and to *your* being angered by my review of *Without Stopping*. But these references are sometimes hot and sometimes cold; once you even wrote, after reading elsewhere something nice I'd said about your music, that now you understood, while before you'd thought I was being flippant. Anyway, I myself am now thrilled to have a mind like an ant colony. It could be so much worse.

As for your music, I've been looking again at the old songs (in preparation for an all-American group I'm doing with a soprano in Santa Fe next August), and they hold up so nostalgically well. What condition are they in, so far as being in print? I'm pretty sure that E. C. Schirmer, in Boston (the best of the new small houses), or even Boosey & Hawkes, could be persuaded to publish a group, if you were interested. Are you? The Song Recital, long dead as a genre, is reviving.

Next letter I'll describe Virgil's memorial last November. At Saint John the too too Divine's. He would have loved it.

Ned

*3 March 1990*

Dear Paul—

. . . Just heard from Yaddo. They've asked me to stay there for a few days next summer when I'll be guest of the newish Saratoga Performing Arts

Festival, as pianist & composer in and of *The Auden Poems* for Tenor and Piano-Trio. So I'll be visiting again the long lost but (for me) beloved ghost of Elizabeth Ames. I'll tell you how she is when I find out. [Ames, a dear mentor of NR, was director of Yaddo for five decades.]

Yes, I do have the Sounding Press edition of your songs. It's done with affection and with a certain care, and it looks good and feels good in the hand. But it seethes with misprints, and the mixture of print with hand-written copy looks sloppy—though may be appealing to non-musicians. Also the preamble by Peggy Bate seems windy and redundant. Yet maybe that's the best way for distribution of your songs; and it's wonderful that they've just done the 2-piano concerto. This summer I'll be in Santa Fe, and perhaps I'll meet the Soundings person, or people.

I think I've solved the mystery of why you're recurrently disturbed by my disturbance about being likened, as a thinker, to an ant colony. My disturbance comes from the relationship (at least in my mind) between the busy but perhaps directionless ant colony and your sole reference to me in *Without Stopping:* "I remember Ned Rorem rushing here and there, always in a mist of alcohol. . . ." The difference in our ages (so slight today) was such, in the old days, that I sought your approval, and maybe felt slighted by your dismissal. You were, after all, the first professional composer I ever met. God knows I've learned, after publishing twelve books, that in the eyes of various people, who are less important to me than I to them, I've sinned more from omission than from slander. Anyway. . . .

Your reports of physical suffering are frustrating. I wish there were something I could do beyond sending sympathies on a mere sheet of paper. . . .

Ned

### To David Del Tredici

*9 March 1990*

David of Davids—

Bravo. . . . On its own terms *Steps* is successful. Those terms are energy, and then more energy. The piece, as I said, consists of two minutes of Prelude, followed by a 28-minute ending. The ending doesn't appear to have much shape or contrast, but it does have a core. From the core comes a constant explosion, hot, sometimes campy, always brash. There's a healthy vulgarity too (although your jazzy bits were a touch square compared to, say,

Copland's), and people will chide you for this. But as Picasso quipped—though Cocteau usually gets the credit—What others censor you for, cultivate it, it's you. . . . I wasn't bored (and neither was Jim Holmes), which says everything. And the performance seemed super.

Best to Paul. Let's meet soon.

Love always.

Ned

## To James Purdy

*28 May 90*

Dear James—

The first grown-up (if you want to call him that) that I ever "had sex" with, was Alfred R. . . . in 1938 when I was fourteen going on fifteen. He lived on 57th between Dorchester and Blackstone, and invited many another of my adolescent pals to his lair, where he played Cyril Scott's *Lotus Land* on his out-of-tune Baldwin.

Am I correct that you, and perhaps one or two others, shared his apartment? And were you very blond? But you're exactly my age, and I recall Alfred (where is he now?) as in his late twenties.

Anyway, next year I'm beginning an autobiography for Simon & Schuster, and thus am dredging up the past already. Never fear, I'm not going to mention names. But I *am* interested in re-weaving my addled past into something coherent.

I'm returning to Chicago next Sunday to give a recital, with Arleen Auger, in Orchestra Hall. Then Nantucket and Santa Fe for the rest of the summer. Can we meet—after so many years—in September? Perhaps with Paula Fox, whose new book I've just read with mixed pleasures?

Your fan . . .

Ned

## To Daron Hagen

*Nantucket*
*29 August 90*

Dear Daron—

Yaddo was odd because, while it looks the same as of yore, most of the inmates weren't born when I was first there. Yes, I met several of your friends, and am distressed that the impression I gave them, where you are

concerned, was as your employer. You are for me, first and foremost, a colleague, as well as an ex-pupil (I can't help but think proudly of you that way);
as a copyist you're invaluable, of course, and that's the most active part of
our relationship sometimes. But I assure you, I'll underplay it in the future.

Did you hear my *Sunday Morning?* [Charles] Dutoit was given short
shrift by the Philadelphia Orchestra, so now they'll get what they deserve
in stodgy germanitude. . . . As for Bard, you'll see that Nicholas Maw is a
very nice man (at least I find him so). But I agree with your implication that
[Leon] Botstein is something of an arrogant number. His current much-
publicized Brahms festival strikes me as quite ho-hum. Bard, of all places,
should be having festivals of contemporary music.

If your libretto, as you suggest, is dauntingly voluminous, then cut it.
Virgil T. always claimed that a libretto outline should fit onto one page, and
the whole book onto twenty. Of course he was dealing with Gertrude Stein.
Still, remember that librettos are mere blueprints for plays.

I've orchestrated about 25 pages of *Plows & Swordshares* (Freudian
slip!). Your work is exquisite to see, but sometimes exasperating. You leave
unaccountably small space on certain pages where we talked about large
space. Elsewhere, you presume to re-notate rhythmically the vocal parts in
5/8, so that I must lose time by erasing and changing it back.

Am returning, for Curtis, for a long week on Sept. 9. (New student
named Eric Sessler, guitar, colorful vocal writing, lives in N.Y. Know him?)
Then will be back in NYC to stay, as of the end of the month.

Always
Ned

To Daron Hagen

*Nantucket*
*28 October 90*

Dear Daron—

While sewing buttons on an old coat (it's getting nippy and I've nothing to wear while taking [our dog] Sonny for walks), I listened carefully to
your tape, much of which I'd already known in different contexts.

*Heliotrope*'s sassiness is too close for comfort to [Michael] Torke, with
late 30th dance bands and Bernstein thrown in for good measure. Doesn't
jell. . . .

The 1985 Symphony's first movement simply contains too much information and sounds confused (this is your chief negative trademark) and inexperienced. But the second movement is beautiful: lean and successful and honest, and the most perfect single piece on the whole tape. The third movement again is confused, but with better material than the first. The three movements together have nothing to do with each other: it's a symphony only because you say so.

The Second Symphony (all of which I know already) has the same vices and virtues. And *Common Ground,* whatever its irregularities, is very very nostalgic.

Your influences (and your music is made up of tangible influences— like most people's) are odd—for your age. Lots of LB, and lots of uncensored, or unrefined, piano improv transferred to the orchestra.

You've yet to find your "voice," and yet paradoxically your pieces begin to sound like you. The same could be said for Barber.

I write these remarks without hesitation, simply because you are my favorite ex-pupil, and I never fail to mention you first when talking about— as I always do—the so-called new generation.

How did the Friedheim turn out?

Always—

N.

RE. LEONARD BERNSTEIN
To: BERNSTEIN ESTATE
POSTSCRIPT TO NED ROREM'S 1987
BERNSTEIN CATALOGUE APPRECIATION

*November 1990*

Three years and five days after the above words were written, Leonard Bernstein died in his Manhattan apartment at the age of 72. Next day, flags were lowered throughout the world. But in the dark weeks that followed there were signs of light: memorial concerts were everywhere performed, and in a society that one thought had grown utterly anti-art, Bernstein was given the publicized send-off of a head of state.

Meanwhile, seemingly irrelevant questions were continually posed: how well did you know him? what made him so American? did he smoke himself to death? wasn't he too young to die? what was he really like? Still, no questions are finally irrelevant, and these seem as good as any to inspire a brief remembrance.

I first knew him in 1943; but to "know well" has to do with intensity more than with habit. Everyone in Lenny's vast entourage felt themselves to be, at one time or another, the sole love of his life, and I was no exception. That he conducted my music in a meter that jibed with my very heartbeat, was naturally not unrelated to the love. Years might pass without our meeting, then we'd be inseparable for weeks, during which he would play even as he worked, with a concentration as acute for passion as for Passions.

Why was he so American? He was the sum of all his contradictions, the most significant being that of Jack-of-all-trades (which the French aptly call *un homme orchestre*), surely a European trait, whereas Americans have always been specialists. If he did want desperately to create a self-perpetuating American art, his own music, even the show-biz scores, was a grab bag of every imaginable foreign influence. He was frustrated at forever being "accused" of spreading himself too thin, but the spreading, like the frustration, defined his theatrical nature. Had he concentrated on but one of his gifts, that gift would have shriveled.

Was he too young to die? What is too young? Lenny led four lives in one, so he was not 72, but 288. Was he, as so many have claimed, paying for the rough life he led? As he lived many lives, so he died many deaths. Smoking may have been one cause, but so was overwork, and especially sorrow at a world he so longed to change, but which remained as philistine and foolish as before. Which may ultimately be the brokenhearted reason any artist dies. Or any person.

So what was he really like? Lenny was like everyone else, only more so. But nobody else was like him.

To Paul Bowles

*3 December 90*

Dear Paul

Ruth Ford, having seen and loved the movie of *The Sheltering Sky* some weeks ago, arranged a private screening last night, for about forty people, including me and Jim Holmes. (Jacqueline Onassis was there.) I wonder what the general public will think. As a travelogue it's grandly and expensively gorgeous and revives my years in Morocco four decades ago. (I never ventured farther south than Tinerhir, but the landscape seemed dreamily familiar, albeit filtered through an Italian eye.) And I wonder, too, what you think. For all its filmic virtuosity, it seems to lack your flavor. Debra Winger is always winning and true, but Malkovich and the other man are insufferable. It's overlong with shots of flies on carcasses, pubic hair for no reason, doggedly heterosexual erotic scenes, camels in the desert, but overshort on basic information: who is the doctor administering the hypo? who is the Caucasian whirling through the windy gate? what's in the hypo? what has the ending to do with anything (while in the book it's compact and germane)? I wonder, too, what kind of music *you* would have written. The score here (except for the Moroccan bits) seemed very 1990, as did other anachronisms. . . . (Oh yes, and what were the tattoos on her hand at the end?) I wouldn't dream of offering these reactions if *you* had made the movie, especially since you've not invited them. But I can't help it, and I do care.

When we got home, the phone was ringing to announce Aaron Copland's death . . . which was then all over the television. Well, it was not unexpected. But America weighs less now that Aaron's gone. Young music here today can't begin to replace his unique and human flair. His music is on the radio all day now. Nostalgia.

There was a question a year or so ago of E. C. Schirmer's doing your complete songs, with an introduction by me. When Boosey & Hawkes (my regular publisher) learned of this, they felt wistful. Maybe it's not too late. I've heard nothing further. But of course it's up to you. Whoever (whomever?) gets the songs will be lucky. They're beautiful, most of them.

. . . Aaron died six weeks to the hour after Lenny. The world is fluctuating.

No more paper.

Always

Ned

### To Joel Conarroe

*20 December 90*

Dear Joel—

These are rough times economically for us all. I live almost solely off commission; yet, having recently completed two big works, I've been told by the commissioners that they cannot meet the final payments. Which leaves me stranded. It is ironic therefore, but probably understandable, that the daily mail consists mainly of requests for money—the poor leading the poor. These requests are generally from opera companies, or other "profit" music organizations, or Yaddo, etc.

However I was shocked to receive a solicitation from the Guggenheim Foundation. It is not for artists to raise money for each other, much less through a philanthropic organization founded to help them. No artist, by the very nature of things, is in a position to "pay back" the largesse of his Guggenheim grant, and it is unfeeling to suggest otherwise. The Foundation was founded to aid artists, not to ask them to support each other; that is its sole and profound purpose. If the foundation is faltering, then perhaps it should sink. Or perhaps truly rich people—the Vanderbilts or Whitneys or Tullys or Trumps—should be conscripted. That's how patronage works.

Nevertheless, for the sake of argument, suppose I *could* afford to give you, say, five thousand dollars. Or suppose that your go-between, Dominc Argento, could do so. Then suppose that in a few years we applied for a renewal, and were granted that renewal. Would we then be subsidizing ourselves? In which case, as with the N.E.A., shouldn't we have some say as to who else gets a Guggenheim? Suppose that, say, Norman Podhoretz, or some scientist who deals with torturous animal experiments, receives a grant, paid for in part by my dough. I would be forced to disapprove, and would say so publicly. Whereas heretofore I've never questioned the workings of who gets what in the Guggenheim plans.

I've taken too many words to make my point—which is that it's unfair, even indecent, and certainly contrary to the nature of the Guggenheim Foundation, to send letters like that to people like me.

I say this with personal affection as always for you, and with tender Christmas wishes.

Ned Rorem

To Joel Conarroe

*Nantucket*
*2 January 1991*

Dear Joel—

I very much appreciate your detailed letter. While reading it, however, I realized it wasn't a reply to my letter, and that my letter must have been badly expressed (I have no copy here in Nantucket). It was sloppy of me to have clouded the issue by suggesting that contributors should have a say in policy; or to suggest that composers are not, by definition, able to pay back money bestowed upon them by foundations (although I firmly believe that).

The issue is that if a Guggenheim Fellowship is now a *quid pro quo* deal —like, for example, your alma mater asking you to repay a student loan—it means it's no longer a philanthropic organization but a bureaucracy. Which is fine. But that's not how it all began.

Your letter also, in stating you'd received piles of contributions "from individuals stating how much their Fellowship meant to them," hinted that perhaps I was ungrateful, or at least blasé, about by own Fellowships. In fact, these fellowships saved my life. But it seems to me that the nature of a Guggenheim is to encourage a composer (who has already proved himself) to continue a specific line of work without financial strain. The result of this line of work should more than redeem him. I am neither embarrassed nor guilty when I say that I feel that the music I have written, thanks to my two Guggenheims, is more than enough visible evidence of my gratitude. I don't believe I'm untypical in saying that most of my musical friends, even the world-famous ones, are in no position to also contribute cash.

Let's not continue this correspondence. I'm too fond of you to want to engender rancour, and anyway I hope to see you—if not before—on February 10th chez Joe Machalis. (You'll get an invitation.)

HAPPY NEW YEAR,

Ned

To Gloria Vanderbilt

*20 February 1991*

Very dear Gloria—

At our meeting the other day in Mortimer's, then during the long trek up Lexington and the hour in your house, I felt that we were simply completing a sentence begun a quarter century ago, and starting a new paragraph. I felt no hiatus—absolutely none—did you? You looked exactly the same.

I'll be interested in how you and Hortense [Calisher] get along tomorrow. You've had similar sadnesses in your recent lives, as well as many other things in common.

You said you'd like me to let you know when I'm having something played. On Sunday, March 10 at 2 o'clock, the Beaux Arts Trio is performing my new Trio, called *Spring Music,* on a program in Town Hall. Will you come with me? Afterward we can return to my place and have an early supper with Jim Holmes.

But maybe we'll also meet before that. I hope so.

Always

Ned

## To Gary Graffman

*28 February 91*

Gary of the Garys—

It's quite possible that I'll be able to finish this Concerto (piano reduction) by mid-June. This is ahead of schedule, and may affect your plans. It would be nice to play the piece in early 1992.

For the past two months I've had an afflicted right arm—either arthritis or tendonitis. What can this mean?

Yesterday I did a "master class" of my songs at Juilliard and who should show up but Eric Zivian. Since one of the accompanists did not show up, Eric sight-read two wildly difficult and fast songs as though he'd been practicing for months. How can he do this?

My new Trio will be played by the Beaux Arts in Town Hall on Sunday, March 10, at 2 p.m. We're going with Gloria Vanderbilt. I told her I'd seen a picture of her son, Stan, in the Curtis newsletter, but had thrown it away. Have you another copy?

For composer-guests next year at School, I'd thought of Ellen Zwilich and . . . I have mixed feelings about her music, but she's wonderfully communicative, affable, and has gobs of chamber music. Will you think of asking Phyllis Curtin sometime too, now that she's retired?

Anyway, this is mainly to report on the Concerto. It will almost surely be in 8, but maybe 7, parts.

Love to Naomi and to you.

N.

## To Andrew Porter

*31 March 91*

Dearest Andrew—

In reviewing the tea party after you left yesterday, I wondered if you might have felt we were picking on you for being a critic. Maybe we were, but I regret it.

When I'm a host I sometimes, in my nervousness, try to be clever and outrageous, and in retrospect am filled with embarrassment.

The profession of critic is as decent and needed as any other (certainly as decent and needed as the profession of composer), and you are that profession's noblest exemplar.

With abject respect, I remain—

your slave—

Ned

We're off to Nantucket this aft. I meant it about accompanying me to some concert—*any* concert—while I'm alone between the 13 and 26. Jim will be in Kansas, toward and from which he'll be *driving* (not flying!) with Sonny, and I worry.

## To David Diamond

*Nantucket*
*12 April 91*

Dear David—

What a shock—to learn from you that Robert Veyron-Lacroix had died. He was a dear friend during all the years in France, and one of the few with whom I retained contact. Exactly my age. Now Morris just phoned, to say that Jimmy Schuyler died this morning (diabetes plus a stroke). Exactly my age, too. More and more we're being abandoned on this planet, and the experience is never easy. One can never get used to death. . . . We return tomorrow to New York by car. The following morning, after his services, Jim starts driving to Kansas (with Sonny) to visit his parents, both of whom are unstable, and he plans to stay 2 weeks, then drive back. I'm very much against all this driving, especially since J. is none too stable, physically, himself. But he's stubborn, as you know. This means I'll be alone for two weeks, and anxious to the point of nausea. Well. . . .

I'm 7/8ths finished with the Left-Hand Concerto for Graffman (though not the orchestration), and now by May 1st must write an essay on

American Opera for *Opera News.* Then, for the rest of the summer, the autobiography. . . . The Beaux Arts play the new Trio beautifully, *malgré* your premonitions. I'd like you to hear the tape. And the new quartet's scheduled by the Guarneri for this June.

Your description of the Academy dinner was hilarious.

You ask if I'm "pleased with the Juilliard Rorem CD." But I don't know a thing about it.

Please stay alive, my only David, and call me when you can.

Always,

love

Ned

<br>

### To Andrew Porter

*Sunday noon*

*14 April 91*

Andrew, Andrew,

We returned from Nantucket late last night to find your dear letter, and the two messages on Jim's machine, as well as the melancholy news about Robert Veyron-Lacroix (through whom you and I met forty years ago), and Henri Hell—my two best friends in Paris. It happens, of course, more & more, but I'm shocked every time.

Yes, I probably would like to hear *Byzantium* tomorrow night. But when I phone you a hideous screech (fax?) greets me every time; and when I phone the Brooks, to learn if you have another number, nobody—or rather, a disembody—answers.

So call me again. JH has just left for Kansas, and I feel anxious.

Meanwhile, here's a clutch of tunes just off the press. Most of them are old, some of them are new, all of them are borrowed, one of them is blue.

Je t'attends. . . .

Ned

<br>

### To Stephen Sondheim

*3 May 91*

Dear Stephen—

Thanks so much for your essay on *Theater Lyrics* (parts of which I'd already read elsewhere). It's intelligent, useful, unprecedented, thorough, and good-natured. I shall keep and treasure it.

Two observations (not quibbles):

Page 80: You state that the "i" in "feminine" "is just that much off the 'o' in 'lemon'." In English, unaccented syllables get thrown away (as distinct from unaccented syllables in multisyllabic words in other languages—*citron* in French or *limone* in Italian, for example, where unaccented syllables are pronounced as written). In English, "lemon" could as well be spelled "lemen" or "lemin," since the second syllable is always given short shrift, by upper and lower classes alike. Your witty rhyming of "feminine" with "them in in—" is terrific, but for the ear, is Harnick's rhyming really illegitimate?

Page 81: You state that Hammerstein claimed that "talk" is not a good ending word because it's "not graceful for a singer to hold." Absolutely correct. Another reason, though, has to do with meaning. "Talk" is the reverse of "song."

I loved seeing you the other night. . . . I've been working my way pleasantly through all your recordings. . . . Will you come for a musical tea sometime next month? . . . The essay in *Opera News* is due in July. Our discussion is winnowed to a long paragraph. . . .

Always
Ned

To STEPHEN SONDHEIM

*Nantucket*
*20 May 1991*

Dear Stephen—

Your nice note just reached me here.

I don't recall ever writing a negative reaction to your music. But I admit to having been resistant to it for years (why, I don't know—maybe jealousy), and tell you this now because I have a deep admiration for so much of what you do—its bravery, its soaring meanness, its frequent contagion, its occasional great beauty, and especially its originality in this age of expensive claptrap.

For five days next week, from May 26–31, I'll be back in New York for the last time before September. Could you come over one of these afternoons and let me play my big new oratorio for you (45 minutes), part of which is stolen from *Sunday in the Park*—(but will you recognize it?). I've nothing to do in NY except rehearse my new quartet with the Guarneri, but won't have a date for that until Thursday. Thus, I'll phone your NY number on Friday morning, and hope you'll say yes.

N

### To Edward Albee

*21 May 91*

Blue Edward—

Coincidences no longer surprise me. Shortly after we said goodbye at the Academy yesterday, I went to a small gathering which contained a youngish Texan painter, Robert Batterton, who spoke not unobsessively of you.

Meanwhile, I've written to Stephen Blier, co-founder with Michael Barrett (perhaps you know them?) of the New York Festival of Song, the only outlet in America for contemporary vocal chamber music. I suggested that they devote at least a part of one of their upcoming programs to songs of William Flanagan, and they suggested that possibly you, Edward, might be persuaded to say a few words, especially if settings of your words were used. (But are there any—other than "The Lady of Tearful Regret"?) The NYFOS is the real thing: hard-working, first-rate repertory-minded vocalists, and great pianists, in wonderfully inventive programs.

I'll keep you posted.

Always

Ned

And I hope to read—was it named *The Story of the Baby?*

### To Gloria Vanderbilt

*New York*
*Sunday*
*28 July 91*

I can't tell you, dear friend, how enthralled JH was when I brought back your two extraordinary pictures. We spent some time deciding where they should go. The cat—the whimsical mysterious cat—now holds its own just to the left of Joe Brainard's huge collage in the dining room. *The Peaceable Kingdom* goes to Nantucket. Thank you. And thank you.

Cummings's poem begins:

> Doll's Boy's asleep under a stile
> He sees eight and twenty ladies in a line.
> The first lady says to nine ladies
> You take his lips for his eyes are mine. . . .

Etc.

I set the whole poem to music in 1944.

Woke up for a long time in the middle of the night, and thought a bit about your beliefs in afterlife. It did strike me as . . . curious? touching? when I asked if Wyatt had ever seen your 1976 picture. "Yes, he saw it when the curtains were still red," you said. But *I* never saw it when the curtains were red. Yet Wyatt and I saw the same picture.

Will you write before September comes?

Je t'aime

Ned

## To Gary Graffman

*New York*

*11 October 91*

Cher Gary—

Our Concerto—the full score of it—will weigh in at 209 pages. I've already orchestrated about 90 pages, and it flows smoothly. (A lot of time is saved by Troy Peters' preliminary layout.) It could be completed in about six weeks. But next week I must take a little time off, in Nantucket, for an operation (prostate), and hope that will proceed as smoothly as the orchestration. Think of me, on the 18th.

Meanwhile, in going over the music, I find various minor mistakes in the piano part. Eventually we must compare notes, so that you don't learn the wrong ones. (For example, some of those mounting chords in *Conversation* are more systematic than I've mistakenly notated.)

Ms. Breustle phoned recently about "young composers" and the Chicago Opera residency proposition. Alas! our two most capable applicants would be Shailen and David (Horne), but they're not American citizens. Which leaves them out of many advantages. It's unfair.

Love to Naomi—

Ned

## To Gloria Vanderbilt

*Nantucket*

*29 October 91*

Oh, Gloria—

It all seems like a kind of nightmare: the tubes everywhere, anesthetics, blood, eternal sleeplessness (which continues) and anxiety and pain. But the hospital, nurses, and "service" were ideal. Rosemary and Jim were perfect, brought me home after four days. We had my birthday dinner in the kitchen, me in pajamas, and a cake with giant pink roses. After twelve days I still feel anxious and have cancelled lots of things. But if all goes well I *will* go to Boston on the 18th of November. (Enclosed is a brochure about the "event." If you think you might like to be there, let me know quick.) From there, Waco, Texas, for three days. Then New York, where we'll finally meet again!

I couldn't finish the Nancy Mitford biography since it dealt so graphically with her illness, so I've begun Patrick White's pretty interesting *The Vivisector*. And I orchestrate the Concerto. Take cat naps. Drink quarts of water. And complain.

Feeling nineteen, suddenly I realize I'm old, like my father was, and priorities are all switched around. You hate this kind of talk, I know, and I envy your ability (perhaps women have it more than men, because of their childbearing, and despite post-partum depression) to *objectify* yourself from physical strife.

It's the kind of letter to be written and not sent. Still, I'm thinking of you, and thinking out loud.

For the next five days I'll be alone here. Jim has his crucial job in the city —but I shy away from the idea of New York . . . so I'll read and recuperate. Eugenie [Vorhees] lent me Julian Green's beautiful little book, so sad, and a local woman—a Mrs. Marilyn Whitney—sent me two dozen roses from her garden, the last of the season—très Fantin-Latour, edible almost, pink like the roses on a birthday cake, sea green, lemony, snow white, lavender. . . . The gale-force winds continue and the furnace roars. Polly King sent a sweet note . . .

I love you, always you, yes. . . .

Ned


To Andrew Porter

*Nantucket*
*8 November 91*

Dear Andrew
It was thoughtful of you to have faxed John Pope-H[ennessey] about my prostatic anxieties. He immediately sent me a letter which put me more at ease, telling me what to expect. The "procedure" (as they say in medical

parlance) occurred three weeks ago today in the perfect hospital here, with a urologist from Hyannis. I stayed four days in the hospital, then convalesced at home with my wonderful sister, Rosemary, and Jim with whom I feted my 68th in red flannel pajamas. Tell John. I'm better now. (Thanks.)

Better enough to wonder if your citing of Cyril Connolly's wonderful phrase—"ten minutes' extra thought on the choice of a word . . . may make in the lyric a difference of a thousand years"—is really applicable to a piece of music that's been in the works for 35 years. If Boulez can't make up his mind in all this time, maybe he should abandon the piece, for he's no longer the same man who began it decades ago. Like poets who revise their early poems years later—always for the worse—for their Collected Poems. Viz. Auden.

Jim was upset by the rest of your current article and wrote you a long letter. Then threw it away. But I kept it and may show it to you when next we meet.

When will that be? Boston next week for new piece. Then Waco, Texas, for a brief stint (all this travel in my "condition"), then finally New York again after so long. Which is when I'll phone you.

Did I ask if you've read *Gerontius* by James Hamilton-Patterson. I can imagine you liking it.

Always
Ned

### To Gloria Vanderbilt

*15 December 91*

Dearest Gloria—

At your bidding I read Timothy Ferris's thing in today's *NYT* magazine. It didn't exactly cheer me up, but it did italicize the melancholy mood I've entertained for several weeks. Somebody once told me (was it Father?) that even with the most hideous death, as when being burned at the stake, the split second before crossing the line is protracted indefinitely into an endless field of silver jonquils over which we float in golden light. But how can one know? The difference between being almost dead and really dead is vast. No one has ever come back from the dead; to say that Lazarus was medically dead is merely to stretch a medical point. . . . I keep meaning to ask you: Were you raised in any Church?

Tonight I played a new CD of Chanticleer, an unaccompanied men's chorus, singing a large piece of mine called *Pilgrim Strangers*. It's the best performance I've ever had of anything ever (on Whitman's words), one which I'd like to be remembered by.

You mentioned Philadelphia. What exactly did Naomi Graffman invite you there for? To visit the Stokowski collection at Curtis? Anyway, I plan to be there next on Monday, February 3, for a concert of my students. And again on Wednesday, April 15, for an all-Rorem vocal concert. On both nights I'd do about four hours teaching, and probably spend the night, after the concert. If you were to come too we could return the same evening. If the last train is at 10:00, which is cutting things short, maybe Jim could rent a car and drive us. A regular Amtrak takes 90 minutes. The Metroliner takes an hour. . . . But we'll see each other often before we decide? . . .

Merry Christmas, my only one.

Always, and always . . .

Ned


To Gloria Vanderbilt

*20 December 91*

Dearest—

Forgot to mention:

On March 4, a Wednesday evening, the Guarneri is performing the New York premiere of my Third String Quartet in Alice Tully Hall. Could you join me, plus Alice Tully herself and Jim, for an easy meal here early, and then go to the nearby concert? I'd be honored.

Thanks for the lecture by Dr. Slaby. It is caring and original. My own feeling about the so-called creative personality, however, is this: An artist, if he's able to work freely and be appreciated for that work, is the best adjusted of all humans. That he is neurotic and drunk or suicidal is a myth. An artist, after all, is the only person, in our philistine society, who knows what he wants to do and how to do it. If he does it well, he has little time to get into trouble, and usually his ego prevents his suicide. For every name listed by Slaby (and many are not even what he calls creators, but rather performers —Janis Joplin, Jimi Hendrix, Js. Morrison) there are hundreds who led dull and productive lives, starting with Bach. Even Oscar Wilde.

Yet suicide is valuable to contemplate. Camus said suicide is the basic philosophical question: Is life worth living? But I feel more strongly: If life's not worth living, is it worth dying? Dying's a pretty lively business.

Postscript: Miss Tully (do you know her?) is deeply wise and quite witty. But she's not at all young. She may back out at the last minute. Please say you'll come, however. We'll meet and talk often beforehand. Or will we? Polly's coming over tomorrow.

Love. And then again, love.

Love for CHRISTMAS

Ned

### To Paul Bowles

*22 January 92*

Dear Paul—

If, when the time comes, I nominated James Purdy to the American Academy & Institute of Arts & Letters, would you second the nomination? When a musician nominates someone in literature, it can only be seconded by two others in literature. (You of course are in literature, although you should also be in music.) I'd thought Joyce Carol Oates might also second him.

I think of you so often as time rolls inexorably by. Since October I've not had one but *two* prostate operations. Non-malignant, but no fun either. *Si vieillesse savait!* as Beckett so charmingly wrote.

Are you all right? And Gavin?

Ned

### To Paul Bowles

*18 February 92*

Dear Paul—

Thanks for seconding James Purdy. Maybe I'll ask Reynolds Price also (Joyce Carol Oates refused, on the grounds that he once gave her a bad review, and therefore "might not be pleased" to have her recommend him), because two seconders are required.

My *interventions chirurgicales* were a prostate operation, or TURP (transurethral prostectomy) in October in Nantucket, botched, and another in New York in December, successful. But now I'm bent over and in dire pain from maybe either post-herpetic neuralgia, or Lyme disease. I see no one. Nevertheless, I'm supposed to go in three days to U.C.L.A. for a week. Probably, I shall, because money. Etc.

How exciting about the upcoming book of letters. Which ones to me are they using? Did I tell you I'm writing an autobiography—*Knowing When to Stop*—for Simon & Schuster? It's due next fall, but I've only done 100 pages because of musical commitments, and illness.

It's too bad the E. C. Schirmer deal fell through. Boosey & Hawkes is still interested in a volume of your songs, and I'll try to push it. They're my sole publishers, and are willing to take chances. (Songs, even by Schubert, don't sell, certainly not in separate copies. But a volume might break even.)

William Schuman died last Saturday after hip surgery. He was 81, and had been ailing for quite some time with a mysterious disease passed on from his mother.

Of the Old Bunch, David Diamond survives intact, and has had a revival: his music's being played and recorded all over the place, thanks mainly to his mentor, Gerard Schwarz.

Several months ago, Peter Owen asked me to write a 500-word souvenir of you. Which I did.

Always,
Ned

## To Judy Collins

*21 February 92*

Dear dear Judy and Louis—

Your little note contained a gleam of hope, for me as well as for you. The past four months have been physically gloomy (not one but *two* prostate operations, an undiagnosible and continuing neuralgia, and now a broken toe), resulting in no work and lots of depression.

Nevertheless, tomorrow Jim and I are going for a week to California where I have a series of classes and a concert at U.C.L.A. Back on the 29th.

Gloria V. tells me you saw each other. I love her as I love you. Maybe we can all get together—many of her problems she faces with the principles of AA (although she's not an alcoholic). On March 4 I'm taking her to hear the Guarneri do my new Quartet in Alice Tully Hall. Could you be there?

Anyway, we'll phone each other soon after that and make a date. Keep me in your prayers.

Love. And more than love.
Ned

## To Jack Larson

*1 March 92*

Golden Jim and Silver Jack—

Because we left UCLA at 5 a.m. on Friday we couldn't call to say good-bye.

What a pleasure to see you so copiously again—and how we did appreciate your hospitality! Already now it seems so long ago.

Wednesday before the concert Don Bachardy joined us at the Hamlet Gardens. (What are we to make of his friend?)

California is Lethe somewhat, compared to the ice in the east—and the furnace is off today. Thanks for putting up with my complaints.

Jim Holmes was perfect, of course, and was intrigued with the west.

Please stay in regular touch.

Love, and more than love . . .

Ned

## To Gloria Vanderbilt

*6 March 92*

Dearest Gloria—

Doesn't it always happen? No sooner do we talk of Elizabeth Bishop than I open the current *Village Voice* to find this (not very good) article . . . In the 1950s I set several of her poems to music. You shall hear them. She remains monumental. . . . I don't remember your sending May Swenson's poems. When?

I've told the American Academy & Institute of Arts & Letters that we'll be coming on April 7. It should be oddly educational. Shall I ask that we sit with Hortense Calisher? Hortense's daughter killed herself many years ago after years of depression and incarceration. Perhaps it's not my place to mention this, except for the discussions we've been having. I talked with Judy C. yesterday. She loves you. But what a Greek Tragedy hovers above you all—*us* all—mysterious, meaningless.

. . . Your persimmon coat is a masterpiece.

We shall talk soon.

Soon.

More than love—

Ned

To Gloria Vanderbilt

*Friday afternoon*
*20 Mar. 92*

Dearest Gloria—

A word, before I limp off to the therapist (the rapist) for a second massage.

Jack Mitchell, the photographer, was pleased with the notion of our double-portrait. I prefer the abstract impersonal décor of his studio to the parlors of either of our houses. We agreed on Tuesday afternoon, April 7. At 2 o'clock he'll do a study of me for my publisher. At three he'll do us both, plus a study of you. And at 4:30 we can take a cab to the Academy. (Details later.) He wants me in a dark turtleneck, and asked what you might wear. . . . I envision, for the double-portrait, something affectionate—sitting on the floor, maybe—and something strange, on different planes, like Stein & Toklas in Cartier-Bresson's picture. But then, I'm not the photographer.

Back from the-rapist. It's late evening. Tired. Asked JH if I were a pragmatist. He said, Well, no, but that I'm calculating. Is that the same thing? Shouldn't one be?

The days go by. . . .

I'll phone you in a day or two or three.

Yes, I love you more than anyone.

Always
N

To Reynolds Price

*21 March 92*

Very dear Reynolds—

The poems in *The Use of Fire* are troubling and true. I don't always "understand" them (is one ever supposed to understand poetry, as distinct from responding to it), but they mostly speak to my condition. They are strong and original—like your eyes in the photo on the back cover: the left eye is merry, the right one sad. . . . The poems aren't singable, at least for me now. They don't seem to require music. No, that's not so. I've only read the first half; the second half, some of them, might. . . .

Love always
Ned

## To Paul Bowles

*29 March 92*

Dear Paul—

Botched is perhaps not the word, "incomplete" would better describe my first prostate operation last October. I had decided to have it in the peace of Nantucket (performed by a single urologist who makes tri-weekly visits from Hyannis) rather than in the anonymous pit of a Manhattan hospital. But he (the doctor) removed too little, and six weeks later I became again "retentive." (Original symptoms had been urethral burning for a decade, plus less and less freedom in peeing.) There was no malignancy at all, and my prostate was not really enlarged. Anyway, I had it again in NY Hospital on December 30th. Similar procedure, i.e. a TURP, which isn't a word, as you say, but an abbreviation. It means Trans-urethral-prostectomy: removing (most of) the prostate with a sort of scraper through the urethral tract, rather than with an incision. I had been forewarned that, although orgasm would be the same as ever, it would not be accompanied by ejaculation; rather, the semen is referred to the kidneys and excreted when you pee. Of course, I didn't experiment for at least five weeks, not wanting to have a spasm or a rush of blood or some other trauma. Now, although the sex drive is hardly what it used to be 30 years ago, I have no problem with complete erection, or with orgasm. . . . I wonder if your operation could have been of a different kind, and also if your doctor(s) gave you no post-procedural advice.

I'd love to know how you're approaching *Hippolytus*. I did music for an off-Broadway production of Leighton Rollins's translation of that play in 1948, with Muriel Smith as Phèdre. There were at least two songs, I recall.

In California three weeks ago we saw Gavin Lambert, still cool and wise, but very Hollywoodian despite all that.

My present pains, three herniated discs, are unrelated to the prostate, *unless* my position on the operating table was such that, while anesthetized, I was wrenched out of shape.

Always

Ned

To Andrew Porter

*Nantucket*

*27 April 92*

Andrew of the Andrews—

Jim brought your letter, along with a batch of less welcome mail, here to Nantucket where I'll spend another six days trying to finish one piece and start another. I appreciate, understand, and agree with your long words about Thomas Mann. And yes, I would like to write an opera on *Mario and the Magician*—at least I would have liked to. But somehow I now fear it's too famous a story, especially since all those other settings exist, or are about to exist.

Now at your gentle nudging, I've just reread *Tonio Kroger*, which I read first at Tonio's age of fourteen, when he loved Hans, along with, and so many times, all the other *Stories of Three Decades*. How familiar it seemed after all these years, almost banal, as if in the intervening half-century I hadn't been putting to intellectual practice all of Tonio's very smart conclusions. But would it make an opera—even, as you say, a "scenic song-cycle"? I too love "hints, half-grasped notions, shifting, exciting shafts of light." But is it wrong, or is it willful and chic, to feel the opera should, at least for me, be more "American"?

The reality of doing an opera now is fuzzy. I couldn't dream of it without a solid commission. My relations with Christopher Keene [then director of the New York City Opera] are cool, but they could possibly be rekindled.

I read your libretto for Bright Sheng *[The Song of Majnun]*, and admire its economy, its—your—knack for getting straight to the point without moving ten tons of scenery, thereby moving the heart, if you will. There's one terrible line ("and the mad man . . . will be a sad man"), one false analogy ("bitter as rosewater"—rosewater's sweet), and one dubious assumption, that a medieval mideastern girl, even from the best family, can read & write. Or am I being literal-minded—as Tonio Kroger longed to be?

If you've nothing better to do, come hear my new String Quartet, by the Guarneri, on May 9th, at the Met Museum. Also I want to play you, if I can organize a tea-party before you leave, the big *Swords and Plowshares*. . . . Most especially, it would be fun to talk about librettos. (Not that you were suggesting a collaboration betwixt us. Though it's not an illogical notion. George and Shirley [Perle] did see *Majnun* last month in Chicago, and admired it, and your pithy book.)

Have been listening to lots of music for its own sake, which I so seldom do anymore, when alone. Dutilleux's two symphonies, over and over, which owe so much to Honegger's two, and are inferior to. . . . Many orchestral works of the magical Debussy as conducted by one Geoffrey Simon (do you know of him?) with the Philharmonic, quite lustrous. But the result is at once too opulent and too prim, and half the pieces are for piano, orchestrated by either Percy Grainger (amusingly), Caplet (appropriately), or someone called Gleichman (disgustingly). Listened again with an open mind, several times, to Elliott C.'s Violin Concerto, which still seems sprawling, incoherent, charmless, and without value. It reminds me of nothing so much as a seriously constipated person trying in vain for thirty minutes to shit.

Thanks for the review of the Simenon biography, which the *TLS* also raves about this week. Sort of. Simenon in the 1950s wrote a novel, very like *Tonio Kroger,* called *Le Petit Saint*—a portrait of the artist as a young man. So did Patrick White in *The Vivisector,* which I read last month. (Too long.) Perhaps these books could be joined into a libretto—the White and Simenon are about painters. Yet, can one make art about an artist? When Auden did it with *Elegy for Young Lovers,* he at least brought down the curtain before the "art" was delivered. And there was melodrama there.

I love you
Ned


To Andrew Porter

*Sunday*
*17 May 92*

Always always Andrew—

Because in an hour we drive off to Nantucket I can't respond thoughtfully to your generous last letter. We will discuss it, and our possible collaboration, *à vive voix* at the bittersweet occasion of the Brook's farewell party for you.

Meanwhile, one feels queasy about Griffiths [Paul Griffiths, who was replacing Andrew Porter as *The New Yorker's* music critic]. I know really nothing about him. But a year ago, when I wrote a lengthy review of the

Britten diaries for *Lambda,* a classy gay rag in Washington, I was provided with previous reviews, and now remember that I said this—toward the end of my article:

"... But Paul Griffiths, London's chief music critic, reviewing the book at length in the *Times Literary Supplement,* filled most of his space with psychoanalytic speculation. '... what he sought in a lover was, in part, a mother (some of the letters to Pears sound more childish than those he was writing at the age of nine).' 'Britten himself reveals so little ... he was very far from being a writer ... lack of interest in verbal expression.... The occasional letter by Pears comes as a beam of sunlight, his writing being so much more relaxed and competent.' '... cautiousness about what was being revealed, left the music lamed.'

"On this last point Griffiths rashly propounds the origin for the so-called Creative Process. Can anyone know what is 'revealed' in music? or if 'cautiousness' figures in the revelation? or, if it does, can it indeed leave the music 'lamed'? What is music's meaning? Do we compose about what we feel now, or about what we know about what we feel now? I can write happy music when sad, sad music when happy, and so can any professional.

"Griffiths concludes with the idle game of might-have-been (idle, because it's always about another person—the one who 'might have been'): 'What might have happened if Britten had succeeded in his plan to study with Berg? [Or] if there had been no interruption—perhaps the escape— of the period in America? But most tantalizing of all: ... if he had maintained the alertness and curiosity ... of his music in the 1930s?' Griffiths laments that were it not for 'the lost possibility of a father figure' Britten might have revolutionized British music in the 1940s and 1950s the way Olivier Messiaen, 'who also around 1940 was caught in a forbidden love (in his case because he was a married Catholic),' changed the music of France. Farfetched analogy, and the speculation is vain, because Britten *did* revolutionize British music. (Not that greatness has anything to do with revolution, or even originality, so much as excellence and personal expressivity.) Britten, what's more, is the only composer ever to devote a whole opera to 'forbidden love' when he musicalized *Death in Venice....* Et cetera."

Does *The New Yorker* need the sophomoric Freudianisms of a Griffiths when it could have the ...? But the world is small.

Je t'aime

Ned

To Paul Bowles

*29 May 92*

Dear Paul—

Your *Picnic Cantata* is really a good piece, not least because its energy does not flag from start to finish. So much fast music! and always engrossing. Such excellent vocal writing (both solos and ensembles): and always beguiling. The harmony moves, the counterpoint, what there is of it, seems apt, and the percussion sounds integral, not decorative. The piano writing is scintillating, and the piece builds and climaxes, then descends, lasting just the right amount of time. What more can I say? The singers, none of them young, were collectively good and had their roles from memory. The drummer was exact and snappy, with a black ponytail and red tie. The pianists were responsible. Real music. Bravo.

Nobody knows the details about Roditi. The *Times* two days ago said he died in Paris, May 10, from an accident received in Spain. Various friends had vague reports that, in fact, he died in Spain of a heart attack at the home of "a rich man." Do you know more? I had thought, hoped, he would last forever.

Always—

Ned

To Gary Graffman

*30 May 92*

Dear Gary & Naomi—

(Have tried countless times, in vain, to reach you by phone at your various numbers.)

Last Thursday Eric Sessler and David Horne (the latter with his hair dyed bright orange) came for their lessons and we tossed around the notion of great composers. They're not thrilled with David Amram (they feel they'll be seeing him anyway in their Shakespeare class), but *would* like Stephen Sondheim. But *I* don't want Sondheim (he won't come anyway— I asked him a year ago) unless there's a class in Musical Comedy, which there isn't. They would be interested in Dutilleux, but that seems dubious. Also Oliver Knussen, who now I think lives in New York, and that's much more likely. Also Leon Kirchner. Finally, Elliott Carter's a notion.

I do strongly feel that if a composer visits, some strong effort should be made to present at least one major chamber work of his/hers, even if it requires a great deal of rehearsal. Otherwise, why have them? In the case of Diamond and Corigliano, I was a bit embarrassed, even though it was not I who officially invited them. If they're worth inviting, they're worth practicing on. No? Yes.

About Gloria. She has gone into hiding for a month, seeing no one, and asked that I write, not phone. So I sent her a letter two weeks ago about being on a ticket-selling board (in name only, mostly) for the Previn concert, and hope she'll say yes.

Organists? Have you heard Weaver yet? There are many other possibilities.... After June 7 we'll be mostly in Nantucket.

With love, and more than love ...

Ned

To Gloria Vanderbilt

*Nantucket*

*28 June 92*

Belle cherie—

You remember Mimi Beman, the proprietor of the second bookstore we visited, the one on Main Street? Well, even as we chatted with her, her brother, age 38, committed suicide (liquor, carbon monoxide) on another part of the island. If only we....

Anyway, she phoned Friday to say that Carol Matthau's book had come in. Yesterday I picked it up, and read it immediately.... Is she a writer? During the first half, her tale seemed mostly one of frothy sorority gossip that doesn't dig deep (she knows only wildly famous people, but doesn't explain their fame—their character, their panache, their art, their necessary exceptional-ness), and her narcissism is that of a ten-year-old. But a certain breathless charm is there, and a likeability that can't be faked. I'm a slow reader yet I gulped the book in one sitting. So yes, she's a writer.... The second half is far richer. She quit the Auntie Mame role and became an observant explicator. Her style is certainly not elegant nor even especially "professional" formally, but her portraits of Saroyan, and especially of Walter Matthau, also Agee, are unique and "telling." She is a very kind person, and most important, she is respectful of creative artists. I was touched by her fidelity to you. And by her description of growing old at the end. (Was her Tunisian illness ever diagnosed? She just drops it in midstream.) It's an extremely *female* book, whatever that means. I can't imagine a man, any kind of man, as having penned it.

I loved your being here. Will you return often, for longer and sunnier visits? I'd like you and Jim to know each other better.

Finished the English Horn Concerto finally, a large piece, and you can hear it with the Philharmonic in about a year. Now the autobiography! Suddenly, as always, I'm confronted by a blank page.

Je t'aime
Ned

## To Gore Vidal

*Nantucket*
*6 September 92*

Dear Gore—

Your phone call out of the blue of Italy last January was welcome, though I was lying on my back throughout and trying to sound alive. I wish I had your stoicism "As I now move . . . toward the door marked Exit."

I've read both your books (and so has Jim Holmes, my friend of 25 years, who labors as organist in—coincidentally—the Church of Saint Timothy on 84th Street). Or should I say, your *book:* Parts One and Two. You seem to be saying the same thing, but with a different form, in both. *Screening History,* diffuse, nevertheless holds the interest from start to finish, and would make life seem hopeless, except for the important fact that you managed to *write* it (also that you offer a sort of solution towards the end). *Live from Golgotha* could be your bid to become America's Salman Rushdie were it not for the fact that Rushdie doesn't write satire, and that your possible foes will never read the book. I enjoy everything you do, always, you know that, and wish we could talk about it more sometime. (Am I allowed to point out that there are small errors in grammar and in French in both books, which the publishers might correct before the next editions?)

Having finished a great mass of music, I'm now writing an autobiography, not out of vanity but for the money. It's not interesting. Have you any notion when we first set eyes on each other?

I'm always either in Nantucket or in New York. And you? I don't really have your Italian address here, not anymore, and wonder if you'll ever see this page. If you do, give Howard Austen my very best regards.

Who did the uncredited cover of Golgotha?
Love from your old fan. . . .
Ned

To Leontyne Price

(for *Opera News*)

*15 Sept. 92*

Leontyne Price is the only superstar soprano of her generation to express as much concern for the music of her time as for the standards of the past. Is there one major American composer she has not performed? She wraps her tongue around her native language, and with a moist voice of fire and velvet, she shows us that a song is a song—not an aria in miniature.

Among the dozen of my songs that Leontyne has intoned over the decades, each one was honed and tailored by her as much for text as for tune, with a result that for me was total satisfaction.

Her instrument is her own, yet much of her art she owes to our mutual friend, Florence Kimball, who imparted stance and appearance along with vocal technique, and to her expert pianist, David Garvey, whose sense of repertory is impeccable. Her rendition of my song, "Ferry Me Across the Water," in Carnegie Hall eleven winters ago was the most rewarding performance I've ever had of anything by anyone anywhere. That final high G-sharp, plucked from the air like a firefly, became a non-vibrating silver thread suspended not just over the final chords, but over the years and into the room where I write these words today.

Sometimes I wonder, on hearing those luscious notes pour forth: Is that sound there within her, like the web within the spider, when she is not spinning it out? But one may as well ask if the composer's work is in him when he's not working.

Anyway, dear precious Leontyne, you are my favorite singer, and I send you these words with love forever.

Ned Rorem

To Gary Graffman

*2 December 92*

Forever dear Gary & Naomi—
What a thrill to hear our Concerto last Saturday, and of course to share the savorous meal after.

The piece seems to hold nicely together from start to finish, and you play it with fiendish mastery.

My only concern now is about things that don't yet exist: balances. You will, won't you, be able to try it with the orchestra before André gets at it? And to make a tape? A tape would be of infinite import for me, to judge waits and measures.

Two suggestions:

The speed of the second movement seemed too close to that of the first movement. Maybe it (the 2nd mvt.) could be a trace faster, friskier. And maybe too a slightly longer pause.

Certain syncopated accents weren't accented enough. . . .

Otherwise, and especially in the "reflective" portions, your sound is that of expensive whipped cream dished forth with an ivory ladle.

Love, and more
Ned

### To Angela Lansbury

*Nantucket*
*28 December 92*

Dear Angela—

We saw *Mrs. 'Arris* last night. What scope! with this on the other side of *Manchurian Candidate,* and the raft of contrasting roles in between. What sense of detail! with your mastery of detail from close-up to back row, and the myriad nuances in between. And what panache! with your ability to deal with other players, singly and in ensemble, with generosity and style in between. What fun to be an actor! to be literally inhabited by another soul for awhile, without being accused of madness. I'd prevail on our acquaintance for a cameo in one of your films, except that I have absolutely no talent.

The years whirl past. I'll be seventy in ten months. I won't dread it, but it *is* a kind of thrilling burden. It would be a pleasure to see you again. I'm almost always either here or in New York, and you & Peter are always welcome. (Occasionally I come to California.) In any case, let's think of each other.

. . . And best affection always to you and to Peter—
Ned
Happy New Year

### To André Previn

*Nantucket*

*4 January 93*

Happy New Year, very dear André—

Where e'er I walk I see notices of your triumphs, and am still anxious to hear a tape of the results of your Battle battle. Curmudgeons I admire, and who are hard to please (i.e. George Perle), declare it to be a superior work.

Speaking of which: the score of my Left Hand Concerto has approximately one hundred errors in it, mostly small, a few big. All of the corrections have now been entered into the parts; only your score remains virgin.

I do plan to be in Philadelphia on the evening of February 2. Before that, I'll be here in Nantucket until January 15, then New York for two weeks (except for the 27–29). I'd love to go over the score with you, not to mention just seeing you for the pleasure. Could you come for lunch or tea or something? (Maybe, though not necessarily, we could talk about the Trio too.) . . .

Always—

Ned

### To Stephen Sondheim

*29 March 93*

Dearest of Stephens—

Thanks for the *Sunless* cycle [Mussorgsky]. What an extraordinary performance! It's uncredited. We were trying to figure out if (a) the recording were from perhaps the 1930s, and (b) if the singer, who is clearly over the hill but marvelously intelligent and inside the music, were really Russian, or perhaps German or maybe Bulgarian.

Miss Harolyn Blackwell is an agile soprano with a very pretty sound. I do recall the song from *Sweeney Todd*.

Don't worry about the Barber/Menotti mix-up. You are you. (*The Medium*, incidentally, dates from 1946.)

Good wishes for your opening next Thursday. The preview was a flawless pleasure. Think of me the next night, but please don't come, even if you're free. I'd rather you came to more professional demonstrations next fall.

JH likes you. And Peter [Jones] too.
Always—
Ned


### To Kenneth Koch

*8 April 93*

Dearest Kenneth—

*The Red Robins* has style, strength, originality, and even some Shake-spearian beauty—though it's YOU from start to finish. Some of it's sing-able, too, maybe. As it stands, however, it's longer than *Parsifal;* an opera libretto shouldn't be more than twenty pages long. We'll do something sometime, but something new.

What fun to see all the other night.

You're almost my favorite poet.

Ned


### To James Lord

*Nantucket*
*31 May 93*

Dearest James—

Your new book is perfection. Jonathan Galassi [of Farrar, Straus and Giroux] sent me an advance copy, and I digested it pretty much in one swallow. . . .

Nothing is tougher than a memoir, since almost by definition there is no climax. But you solved even this by your two letters at the end, which serve as a catharsis and a wrapping up (whether or not one agrees with whether you should have sent them). . . . I envy you your craft and talent, and your ability to be interested in others enough to make *them* interesting. I'm currently writing a memoir which, because I'm more (at least out-wardly) self-involved than you, involves more what others think of me than what I think of them. It covers my life up until 1951, when the published diaries begin. But I could never hope to rival you. You're a real writer.

. . . Will we ever meet again? Most of the summer I'm here, except for July in Aspen where I'm a guest star. Please always keep in touch. I'll be back in New York to stay by mid-September.

Love as always, and also to Bernard.

Ned

## To James Purdy

*Nantucket*
*3 June 93*

Dear Genius—

As it turns out I *did* receive the blue-covered "Collected Poems" a year or two ago—at the Academy I'd thought you were talking about a more recent book.

I've just re-read it, and find your bittersweet lyricism and affectionate despair as active and persuasive as ever. You're like nobody else.

Jim and I are off to Aspen, in a car with the dog, Sonny, in a few weeks. Then back home. Then New York again in the autumn.

Let's stay in touch forever—

Love

Ned

## To Jack Larson

*Nantucket*
*7 June 93*

Dear dear Jack—

What a shock.

Joe called me a few hours ago from Long Island, and I still can't believe it. None of us ever will, especially you.

What can I say, except that Jim was loved by so many and is irreplaceable. . . .

The weather today is resplendent, warm and sparkling: the fact that Jim is not here to share it seems insupportable.

I love you, and am here for you at all times. In a week or so I'll phone.

Jim Holmes sends his heartfelt condolences. The very sun seems so transient.

Always. And always.

Ned

## To André Previn

*26 September 93*

Very dear André—

For months I've owed you a letter—in response to your saying you might do my Trio in London. That's a thrill, and I hope you'll make a tape for me.

The Left-Hand Concerto is finally slated for appearance on New World Records. It will be paired with Eleven Studies for Eleven Players, written in 1959.

Did I ever tell you how divinely right your conducting of the Concerto was (is)? I feel honored that you, and Gary, and that terrific orchestra were able to emulate my metabolism so intimately.

I've still not heard your Toni Morrison piece. You couldn't bring it to this concert (see enclosed) of humble madrigals on October 23? There's a party afterward at Joe Machlis's.

The years accumulate like sludge. Or rather, since that's not an apt simile, they fly by like a snowstorm. Come help me be a grown-up at seventy. Or is growing up the last thing we should aspire to do?

Always,

Ned

## To Gore Vidal

*26 October 93*

Dear Gore—

Your letter arrived just as I turned 21,550 days old. (Am I the first of "us" to enter the eighth decade?) Thus, I'm less jealous than wistful at your being a movie star. Anyway, though I long to be one myself, I just can't act. I did see you in *Bob Roberts* and thought you were convincing playing yourself. I can't even play myself.

I'm impressed—and a bit confused—at what you say about director Alek K[eshishian]. I did see the Madonna documentary *[Truth or Dare]* which had its very good points, though much too long, and not really a documentary since we saw nothing about "real" backstage life, like rehearsals and orchestra functioning, etc., though it's a thrill to see her reading *The Paris Diary* in her dressing room. Now I've nowhere to go but down.

The main solace in being seventy is that one's music gets played, which can't happen quite to writers. I've also finished a memoir (a *memoir*, not a diary) of my first 27 years, which is only 750 pages long, and is called *Knowing When to Stop*. Due out in a year.

Whatever became of *your* biography, the Walter Clemons one? It's time.

No, Frank O'Hara wasn't a "stuffed culture vulture under a glass bell," though the biographer, Brad Gooch (who never knew him, but is himself very cute, if you like the type, which I don't), may have made Frank sound that way. He was, as a person, one of a kind: wide-scoped, and generous and indefatigable and actually rather cold, with a warm exterior; as a poet, he authored three very good poems, and three thousand spin-offs of those three.

I just read in galleys Paul B's book of letters. I opened the book with a sigh, because, as he quotes you as having said (to me, I quoted it somewhere), "He tells you what he had for breakfast." But in fact the *accumulation* shows him as caring and involved and clever and analytic when discussing literature—with, for instance, James Leo Herlihy, now alas gone, he too. Letters to you also. Though *whom* PB writes to seems less important, less differentiated, than *what* he writes. The *destinateurs* could all be switched around with no harm to the sequence.

When might you come to America? Doubtless I'll never be in Italy again, but I'd truly love to see you.

All best to Howard,

Always and always

Ned

To Judy Collins

*26 October 93*

Dearest Judy—

Lisa Kirchner sent me a tape. She sounds like you—crystal clear, warm & cool, slick and arching, "musical" and pleasant—but with little of her own. She's flawlessly professional, but without that added touch of individuality—of madness, if you like—that makes a memorable artist, a Judy. . . . Well, I'll find something to tell her.

I miss you, and was glad for your call.

Do, yes, plan on January 27 world premiere of my English Horn Concerto at the Philharmonic. (The only problem is that I must be there at 6:30 for a pre-concert discussion on stage.) Would you prefer an all-Rorem song-concert the previous Sunday afternoon at five, at Greenwich music school on Barrow Street, after which we could go dine somewhere, with Jim and Louis? It would be more intimate maybe? Or anyway, just a get-together, for perhaps a meeting?

Like you, I'm in & out of town these next several weeks. But unlike you, I feel daunted by far-future plans. Since I'm seventy now, be indulgent. The years swoop by. . . .

Ned

[I wrote this the day after Judy called me (I was taking a nap), sang "Happy Birthday," and I didn't recognize her voice. I explained, "You sounded so beautiful I couldn't believe it was you."]

To Edmund White

*Nantucket*
*20 Nov. 93*

Dear Edmund—

I was thrilled by your call from Seattle, and frustrated that our love-affair must consist of mere tri-annual phone chats. After we hung up I felt like a shit for having found only one thing to say about your new book: that, on examining the index in a bookstore, I saw three misspellings. (Is that how you spell mispellings?) So I rushed out the next morning and bought *Genet*. And though I've given it only a few hours of non-chronological perusal—I'll write you again when I've read it straight through—it seems indeed to be an *oeuvre considérable*.

For me it's evocative not least because I was there so much of the time: during the appearance of the last novel and of all the plays; of *Un Chant d'amour* which I saw a dozen times (François Richenbach, who lived across the square from Marie-Laure, would screen it regularly for visiting queers); of the various contretemps with the courts. Also Carco's *Jésus-la-Caille* was mounted as a play in 1951 (starring Philippe Lemaire, who then married—and divorced—Juliette Gréco), and Dudognon's novels, *L'homme orchestre* and *Jean-Paul*, were published—all this so close in subject to Genet that I assumed everyone in France was writing about underworld homosexuality. Julian Green disapproved (do you know him?), but Paul Goodman, America's Genet, had already primed me. (We must talk about PG someday.) And though I never met Genet, or perhaps *because* I never met him, I was, and remain convinced of his . . . his *vastness*. (I did *see* him once. He was walking west on Blvd. St. Germain with Jean Denoël, and talking in a high-pitched, rather queeny voice, which belied his butch aspect which resembles to a T New York's current police commissioner [Ray] Kelly with his ski-jump nose. He was complaining, loudly, lest observers not hear, about how Sartre's book had castrated him.)

When I've finished your book I hope I'll know more about what he actually preferred in bed, and whether it was smoking that did him in. (Jim has quit, with the aid of Prozac, and is suffering frightful withdrawal, still after two months.)

... Fairly recently, for the Cocteau centenary, I set to music his *Anna la Bonne*. Do you know it? It pre-dates *Les bonnes* by a decade, but both, of course, stem from the murders in the 1920s of the Papin sisters. (Apropos Cocteau, was it I who told you that he would *tutoyer* both taxi drivers and countesses, and whole rooms-full of people?)

Your book is a model biography. There's not a dumb phrase in it, and you like your model without fawning. You can put words together, and you've researched massively. Far be it from me to ask another artist why he chooses such and such a subject; Genet is something you had to do. (Did he, by the way, know you were working on him? Or was he already gone?) But sometimes I miss *your* voice. You do use occasional frenchisms—e.g. "he *confided* the manuscript to Jouhandeau"—which lend a flavor to your style. But I miss the hilarious White-isms—e.g. in the erotic (to me) post-fellation scene in your novel: ". . . he considered all this to be pleasure, as Herod thought Salome's dance was fun until he heard what she wanted as a reward." (One pictures the old Jewish king rubbing his hands and exclaiming "such fun!")—which are uniquely and cannily your own.

Yes, Genet was a genius, a word I never use. But why don't I like him? Not because he was a hypocrite about avoiding publicity while being as self-promoting as any star. Rather, because had he known me he would have looked through me: I would have had no effect. *Par contre*, I don't like many people upon whom I do have an effect. No, it must be that his very biography is so linked with his "creation" (as, say, Rimbaud's is not, or Baudelaire's, or Jane Austen's) that, when he throws sand in the reader's eyes, the very sand *is* the work. Yes, he was Paul Goodman. But I loved Paul.

This letter is scrambled. Forgive. I turned seventy-three weeks ago. The sole good thing is that a composer, as distinct from a performer, can use that as a peg for having festivals. My music seems to be getting played all over (except in France) this year, and that's one reason for persevering. Another reason is Jim who is brighter and handsomer than ever, and anguishing too, but hard-working. A third reason is you.

Love to Hubert.

Always

Ned

### To Judy Collins

*Nantucket*
*22 November 93*

Dear Louis & Judy—

Nothing could have brightened my day more than that heap of Godiva chocolates. Thank you. And thanks again.

So I'm sitting here in Nantucket, trying to finish a choral piece, having just finished a huge memoir, and am about to start a string-quartet.

Jim, who stopped smoking two months ago, is still suffering deep withdrawal traumas but stays stable with the help of Prozac and Nicorette gum.

Cold weather begins. The sky is cruel and gold, the cats remain inside, and Sonny too.

I love no one more than you.

Soon we'll meet again. Soon.

Happy chocolate.

Ned

### To Angela Lansbury

*15 December 93*

Dear Angela and Peter—

Pleased, as always, to get your warm card. The years swoop by and it's important to keep in touch.

I've just been commissioned to compose a piece for the Los Angeles Chamber Symphony (with the stipulation that it be dedicated to the memory of Jim Bridges—the director, whom surely you must have known), so maybe I'll see you out there eventually, if not in Cork or New York.

You asked a year ago about Judy Collins. Her son, Clark, killed himself a while ago, and she is understandably undone. She's in group counseling, and working harder than ever, but the tragedy dominates her existence. Clark was her only child.

I've finished another book—a memoir of my first 27 years, which will be published next fall.

This note has an elegiac tone. But so, probably does everything from now on. . . .

Always, with affection, also from Jim Holmes (who has given up smoking after 40 years)

Merry Christmas

Ned

### To Kenneth Koch

Hearty old Kenneth of the onyx spit-curls:
Welcome back to America!
Herewith—a new CD culled from recordings of a decade-and-a-half ago.
You'll see that the instrumental version (by Jim Holmes) of "Hearing" as a
duet is included, as well as the single song, "Hearing," as a solo.
The years amass.
 Love
 Ned


### To Judy Collins

*29 January 1994*

Dearest Judy and Louis
 The lavender tie is more than a tie. It is a sonorous strip of love, like the
protracted plaint of an English Horn, flowing from your hands through my
neck into Avery Fisher Hall and then out into the reaches of the universe
forevermore. Thank you.
 And thank you for your sustaining presence on Thursday. I could never
have lived through it without you.
 Thanks also, Judy, for the Zabar's production, and you, Louis, for the
protective taxis during the worst weather of the decade.
 I wish we all could meet oftener. But just knowing you're there is a permanent pleasure.
 Ned


### To Judy Collins

*1 May 94*

> a book for her intellect . . .
> a concert, for her emotional soul . . .
> a bonbon for her insatiable taste buds . . .
> And an ocean of love for Judy

From Ned
[*Gerontius* by Hamilton-Paterson, CD of Leonard Bernstein concert,
Godiva chocolates, and $60 of flowers from JH]

## To Edmund White

*7 May 94*

Dearest Dearest Ed—

Hubert was a handsome, tactful, charming, intelligent, and very special person—as you know far better than I.

My heart bleeds for you with love and understanding.

Always,

Ned

## To Gloria Vanderbilt

*Nantucket*
*May 1994*
*Friday the 13th*

Dear fellow galley-slave—

Now that I've seen it, I understand your reticence about James Lord's portrait of Marie-Laure de Noailles. His writing is somewhat dry-eyed, and she comes off as something of a monster. However, he's a pretty good writer, especially as a non-fiction portraitist, and his version of Marie-Laure in many ways—at least from his vantage, is true and honest. And Marie-Laure *did* have her monstrous side, as many bigger-than-life artists have. But she was other things too: witty, vastly cultured, original, generous, multi-talented (in painting and in writing), one of a kind. She was profoundly helpful, not to say influential, where I was concerned, and after my mother she was the most important "older" woman in my life. Don't dismiss her wholly (or James either). If only you could have known each other!

I've finished the galleys. Thousands of changes! And you? It makes one nervous, as well as thrilled, as the pub date looms, doesn't it?

Back next week for a few days. Then Chicago and Toledo. Then New York again, and then Nantucket.

Sometime during the first week of June could we meet? On the 4th, the Philharmonic's playing the new English Horn Concerto again, prior to taking it on tour to Asia. . . . On the 7th I'm being "honored" (along with Comden & Green, Hirschfeld, Tommy Tune, and Scorsese) by Marymount, in New York's Palace Hotel. Could I take you to any of that? Or will you take me to see the Sondheim or Albee plays?

Last night I took, for insomnia, three aspirin, one valium, and one hal-
cyon. Today: SHEER BLUR. But I see clear enough to know I love you.
Forever—
Ned

To James Lord

*1 June 94*

Dear Little James—

Back in Nantucket now, I've finally been able to read your piece on
Marie-Laure. As you know, I've just written an extended reminiscence of
her too, and my first reaction is how close, in substance if not in style, are
our two viewpoints. Of course, although I did see her extensively in the fall
of 1969 (two months before you sent me the terrible cablegram), I wasn't in
on the seeming disintegration of the previous six or seven years.

. . . Your portrait is well-worded and well-shaped. God knows what
unalerted Americans will think of it all; she was one of a kind, and our
country is ever more drearily rigid.

Questions. Is it true that Laure [Marie-Laure's daughter] died of cancer, rather than of strangulation on a chicken bone? . . . Is it true that
"Oscar's prices have steadily risen"? . . . Is it true that Laure "covered" for the
sleeping Vicomtesse when the Gestapo arrived [at] Pl. des Etats-Unis?
(ML's version, at least to me, was that they'd come to arrest Peggy Guggenheim [!], and had gotten the names mixed up.)

Do you really feel that [Maurice] Gendron was "a musician of second-
rate importance" and that the war had "not caused them much inconve-
nience"? I found Maurice to be a first-rate musician in general, and a gorgeous cellist in particular; but with the *recul du temps* and my comparative
innocence, it's hard to judge today. Marie-Laure did tell me that she and
Maurice were interned together in a camp in northern Italy (Maurice
claimed to be half-Jewish); that she was called merely Noailles and had to
peel potatoes; and that she was finally released, by appealing to the Latin
sensibilities of her captors, when she sang the tenor-aria from *Tosca* with
tears streaming down her face. . . . The correct spelling of her first chauf-
feur's name is Bacchat—Fernand Bacchat; he had an affair with Theodore
Keogh simultaneous with ML's affair with Tom Keogh.

I very much liked your picture of Arletty. For me, the two of you make
an incongruous duo. And why not! You didn't mention that among her

other triumphs was Cocteau's playlet, *L'École des veuves*. (I think that's the title.)

The photo of you and Toklas was taken during intermission of an all-Rorem concert, June 1957, at the American Embassy. The seat on her left was previously occupied by Eddie Waterman.

I look forward to your other chapters. And to your other biographies....
Love to Bernard. Stay always in touch.
Ned

To David Diamond

*Nantucket*
*18 June 1994*

Very dear David—

Thanks for the permission to use your letter in the new book, which will be available (Simon & Schuster) in about two months. You can't imagine the fuss that lawyers now make over permissions these days; it's like England's libel laws, much more stringent than ten years ago. Be aware of this when your book is being prepared for print: Every minor allusion to anyone still living seems libelous; and any letter used, even one from someone long-dead, must be cleared by the estate. (Julius Katchen's widow coldly vetoed any quotes from his correspondence, and Nancy Mitford's estate charged 444 pounds for use of two minor missives to me in the mid-fifties.)

I mention all this, because the mail twixt you and me dates back half-a-century. Reading through what I've retained, it's quite lively. If you've kept any of my early letters, let me state here formally that you have my permission to use them for whatever purposes you may wish eventually. Could you write me a similar statement? Someday one or the other of us might wish to make a little book of both sides of our correspondence—a device which has seldom been tried—and this "formality" would simplify matters. I do get requests from small presses for ideas like this. So, probably, do you.

Jim's father died. He's taken it hard, not so much because of the loss itself (which was a blessing after great suffering), but as a rite of passage. He also works too much, smokes too much, and pressures himself. But remains handsome and smart and infinitely loveable.

Having just finished three biggish pieces (a choral tetralogy for "The Singing Sergeants"; an 8-movement suite for voice, guitar, cello, & clarinet; a suite of monologues with piano for Claire Bloom), I'm about to embark on a fourth string quartet. How daunting! You're an old hand at it, but for me it's like trying to enter the Pentagon without a key. . . .

Write.

Love

Ned

To Judy Collins

Dearest Judy—

What a pleasure it was to record our little Christmas Carol two weeks ago. You sounded and looked as well as I've ever heard or seen you: accurate and clear, bright-eyed and kempt. Let's do a whole group one day.

I miss seeing you more often. Do you find that with the passing years it's less easy to see all one's friends and still get work done? A conundrum.

I've just finished a spoken narrative with piano for Claire Bloom, in three sections, on words of Jean Rhys, Colette, and Elizabeth Hardwick. (Might you do this sort of thing sometime?) Now I'm about to start a new String Quartet, probably in eight movements, each movement depicting, in sound, an early Picasso.

Nantucket continues cool despite the heat-waves in Manhattan. I'll be in Manhattan for four days starting July 20. Could we go to a meeting? In any case: eternal love. Also, and always, to Louis.

Ned

To Gloria Vanderbilt

Very dear Gloria—

. . . How thrilling—your final galleys. Naturally, I'm anxious to read your book, but will wait for the printed copy (when it's too late for irritating suggestions). My own uncorrected galleys are already, to my horror, circulating, filled with errors, among potential reviewers. *Vogue* will do an advanced page, as will many less visible literary mags. I'm scared. It's so personal and intimate and nobody's business. Yet maybe all so-called art is an expression of "nobody's business" that magically becomes everybody's business by virtue of stating what we did not know we knew.

Musically, I've just finished a melodrama, *Three Women,* for spoken voice and piano which Claire Bloom will do at the Y in January, then take on tour. . . . Now I'm beginning a String Quartet for the Emerson. After that, nothing for the rest of my life.

I'm not phoning, because of your letter of some weeks ago, and because I can't deal with answering machines. But I wish you'd call whenever you feel like it. Meanwhile, I'll be in the city for five days between July 19 and 24. Would you like to "do something" on the evening of the 19th: dine, maybe, and/or see Sondheim's thing? On the 20th I'm seeing John Gruen and Jane Wilson (master photographer, him, and major painter, her). Will you join us? OR: On the 21st, I've invited my associate editor, plus composer, David Del Tredici, out. Will you join us? The 22nd, I'm seeing, all alone, *Angels in America.* The 24 and 25: no plans. It's wrong to let too much time pass.

Have you read Lincoln Kirstein's memoir? Odd, crude, readable, necessary, but not especially lovable.

I cherish your many pictures which I live with every day. . . .

Love—

Ned

## To Daron Hagen

*Nantucket*

*8 July 94*

Always dear Daron—

Although I don't believe in marriage per se, except for tax purposes, I do feel that two people who engage in a mutual commitment, and who invest year after year in that commitment, do produce something that's singularly theirs. Short of being physically repelled by each other, it's too bad for them to throw the investment overboard. I should talk. Still, concessions and accommodations have to be made every day. You & Donna seem nice together. Keep working. (But I understand your *cri du coeur.*)

Nor do I think that to produce a decent work of music one needs to be "inspired." You're a composer. Ergo, you compose. It's your craft. Naturally you hope the result will *sound* inspired, but that's beyond your control. I'll be interested to hear the new fiddle concerto. . . .

As for doctorates, are they so important? I suppose it depends on what you want to do. . . . I never got a doctorate (well, yes, I have some *honorary* doctorates, but they're unearned); it's only good if you want to teach. Besides, your reputation at this point goes far beyond such petty academic exigencies.

You're prolific as always. Me, not. Lazy. . . . The new book, *Knowing When to Stop*, should be in stores end of August.

Idaho sounds icky. . . . On the 25th I'm going to Yaddo for 18 days. . . . Stay always in touch. Jim sends affection.

Ned

### To Rosalyn Tureck

*Nantucket*
*16 July 94*

Fond Rosalyn—

Thanks so much for the CD and the essay.

What deep pleasure to have the house filled with the sound of your Bach again. (I already have the Goldberg.) Every piece is an old friend, and your versions are as close as possible to the ideal versions I hear in my head when I play. That is the ultimate compliment. . . .

I perused the "authentic" essay. Your notions are strong, and your quotes are apt. Years ago, at your request, I sent you a long and carefully reasoned letter about how I might feel about hearing my own music on "future instruments." I felt . . . well, wistful, that you chose to quote Carter and Schuman instead.

. . . Brava, as ever, for your valiant research and comforting performances.

Don't leave America. But if you do, I'll understand . . .

Ned

### To Jack Larson

*Nantucket*
*27 August 94*

Jack, Jack—

If I've taken so long to answer your affectionate letter it's because (a) I've been under the weather again for a few weeks (a summery pneumonia, not grave, and I test negative to everything), and (b) the Chamber Symphony has been dithering. But Boosey & Hawkes says that contracts are now signed, and everything's set.

I won't be able to get to the piece for 2 or 3 months. But I feel that, given the terms, it should be a straight symphonic work, perhaps a suite in many movements, rather than something sung which would be more expensive and would preclude many performances. Whatever materializes, it will be called "More Than a Day." We'll talk more about it in person. And that will be soon, I trust, because:

I'll be in Los Angeles for 36 hours next month, to plug the new book ... en route to San Francisco. . . .

The only people I know, besides you, are Gavin, Don Bachardy, and Angela Lansbury. I'll be in a hotel. Could you come to at least one of the "events" so that I won't be stuck there friendless, in an empty store? Can we arrange a meal with Betty Freeman? Who knows when I'll ever get to California again.

Jim sends you his love. He's this minute building, with concrete and oaken beams, an area to park the new blue truck in.

I love you.

Ned


To Edmund White

*NYC*
*9 October 94*

Dearest Edmund—

I did appreciate your call from Paris to Nantucket several weeks ago, and even more your letter about my new book. On this second matter I now take pen to paper, to voice that most abject of all authors' laments: Why has the book sunk without a trace? The gay press has been pretty good across the land, and a few local papers (front cover of *Washington Post Book World,* for instance). But the *Times,* who should have featured it on the cover, has been inviolably mum, both daily & Sunday. Are you in a position to propose yourself as a reviewer (should you even want to do so) to anyone over here? (Sandy McClatchy had, at the last moment, to drop his review for *The New Republic.*) I'm embarrassed even to send this letter. But you know how I feel.

I've just been through my file of your letters, for I've kept everything you've sent, since 1977, except, alas, your review of *Setting the Tone* ages ago in the *Native.* Also some of my answers. Mutual admiration society. Very nice. Then this morning your gorgeously published collection of essays landed on the doorstep. This will be my bedtime reading for the next week. I've had time only to absorb one article, the one on Truman Capote, which is an exemplary and ever-so-readable portrait.

When shall we meet again? I have a premiere (on words of James Merrill et alia) on October 30th. Then *Miss Julie*'s being done, probably in a good production, here in December, three times. Might you be around?

And might you one day want to write a libretto—something mean and strong about love and seduction and about the almost ruination and redemption of one man by another, with lots to sing about, including a murder? Why not? I'd like to do one more opera before I die, but it needs to be commissioned. Generously.

I love you.

Ned

### To Claus von Bülow

*Nantucket*

*14 November 94*

Fond Claus—

What a pleasure to get your letter!

And yes, we must get together: too few of us remain from the old days at Hyères. As the past evaporates while the future shrinks, I for one value all links.

Are you going to do a book too? You write well (re. Js. Lord: "... some biographers inadvertently give a picture of themselves while endeavoring to portray their subject"), and would, I suppose, have a lot to say.

Will I ever return to Europe? Probably not. And London, although my music publisher, Boosey & Hawkes, is centered there, doesn't tempt me, at least professionally. I hate to travel ever more. Mainly I stay fixed in New York, or retreat here to Nantucket (with Jim Holmes, my friend of already 27 years) and work.

Please, let's at least have tea next time you're here, and let me know a week ahead of time.

I miss you.

Always

Ned

To Jack Larson

*Nantucket*
*17 November 94*

Dear Jack—

Just thinking out loud.

Even if I use all seven *Do I Love You*'s plus the other 3-stanza poem, it's still not a huge text. I must figure out a way to stretch the piece into seventeen minutes.

You've heard by now that the singer will be the very young countertenor, Brian Asawa, who's a hot property and the best of his kind. I've never met him, but was pleased when the orchestra asked my approval. Very pleased. His odd sound might be the ideal medium.

. . . It's not too soon to think about recording. . . . Records are more important than anything, even if they bring the orchestra to New York, which they doubtless won't.

Jim Holmes has Crohn's Disease. He suffers, and is anxious. Tomorrow we drive back to New York. Saturday, depending on JH, and on the southern hurricane, I'll go to the book fair in Miami for 36 hours.

Do I love you? More than a hurricane.

Ned

To Reynolds Price

*26 February 95*

Very dear Reynolds—

I've been rereading both *A Palpable God* and *The Honest Account of a Memorable Life*, and making my three (male) pupils, all young, do the same, with the hope that they'll find libretto material therein. For me, unChristian though I be, some of my most "honest" settings have been on socalled sacred texts; and though I don't believe in God, I do believe in Belief —and in the zeal that has sometimes caused great poetry to be.

Jim Holmes has cancer. A lymphoma of the stomach. After some more tests this week, he'll probably begin chemotherapy soon. Naturally this condition occupies us 24 hours a day, during which he suffers a lot, but believes intensely (more than I do) in the power of positive thinking.

Somehow I wanted you to know . . . for we had talked a bit about it at the Academy some months ago.

Love always

N

### To Stephen Sondheim

*1 March 95*

Dear Stephen—

Meryl [Secrest] told me about the fire. What a catastrophe! Above all, my condolences about your dog.

I've missed you. But Jim Holmes is seriously ill, which precludes much socializing. . . . The whole world seems blanketed in sadness.

Affection always—

Ned

### To Kenneth Koch

*March 1995*

Very dear Kenneth—

Even as you are Poetry, so I am Music.

We have already been married twice, and will—I hope—be wed again many times.

There is nothing I love more than the fact of you.

Ned

### To Andrew Porter

*24 March 95*

Very dear Andrew—

The years whiz by ever faster, and with each one, perspective shifts. I think of you so often, always affectionately. America (England too?) is growing so philistine in every way that the recollection of your caring elegance at *The New Yorker* is just that—a recollection. Ignorance reigns. Yet I continue to write my pieces, and so do all our friends . . . the ones that remain.

Jim Holmes has a serious cancer. Lymphoma in the stomach. He has grown quite thin. We'll have a clearer prognosis after his second chemo treatment next week. The atmosphere is mostly sad, at least for me, though he is persevering in his work and uncomplaining despite awful pain. We've been together almost 28 years. He's only 55.

I've no plans to come to England, or indeed anywhere, for travel no longer delights. But how I would love to visit with you again, if ever you're here. Or at least to have a word. Are you stable? thriving?

Always

Ned

To Judy Collins's editor

*To Tom Miller*
*Pocket Books*
*Re. Judy Collins's* Shameless
*21 April 95*

Judy sparkles as a Renaissance woman in an age of dull specialists. For nearly four decades everyone has known her as the indefatigable vocalist of popular music. But she is a lyricist too, and a composer, a poet, a movie actress, a stage actress, a painter, and a memoirist. Now she turns to fiction —with a vengeance.

*Shameless* is a carnal whodunit, with lots of plot, character study, unearthly fantasy, and earthy sex. The plot revolves around artistic jet setters in moments of high stress. The character study devolves from a vastly successful cast interacting in the business and pleasure of Manhattan's pop intelligentsia. The fantasy, italicized between chapters, blooms through flashbacks and troubling dreams. And the sex is ubiquitous and graphic. For the author is not a tease. Judy comes across.

—Ned Rorem

To Judy Collins
Re. Her novel *Shameless*

*Good Friday*
*1995*

Why Judy—

I was truly shocked by the salacious, the lewd, indeed the *shameless* tone of your prose—from my innocent friend of all these years. But after page 23 you snared me with the plot. In one swell foop I finished it, and now I send you this congratulation.

It's clearly a movie, as I suppose you realize, and I hope you'll let me play one of the more villainous roles. Brava!

Sunday if Jim's up to it we're off for a quick week in Nantucket, before he comes back to more chemotherapy. . . .

Love to you and to Louis
Ned

To James Purdy

*23 April 95*

Dear "Creative Genius"—

Although I'd already seen the terrific review in the *TLS* (it's about time!), I was touched that you sent it to me. . . . I'd love to see you. But when and where?

Jim Holmes has cancer. It's serious. All my plans now revolve around his well-being. The whole universe seems more irreparably melancholy than ever.

Ned

To James Lord

*May Day 1995*

Fair James of the pale amber bangs—

Because I'm sorting correspondence for my so-called archives, I last night went through the Lord file and read it all straight through. I've kept everything you've written me since 1954 (and I to you, all typed, since 1960), and it makes good reading. You can't imagine how many long-hand missives you sent: the whole makes quite a nice little book, with a developing plot.

. . . Jim Holmes has a lymphoma of the stomach. Please tell Ed White, who knows JH, but to whom I hesitate to announce the news. . . . The hideous chemotherapy is nevertheless promising, and we're hoping it'll all be part of the past. He's only 56.

As always I miss you. And as always, in our letters, I beseech you to come visit. Send me news, any news, of Bernard, and of Marcel Schneider, and of any of *la bande* who may still prevail. . . .

With more than love,
Ned

To David Diamond

*Nantucket*
*27 May 95*

Dear David—

I should have acknowledged the [André] Brincourt book ages ago. But Jim is not at all well, and his well-being is my chief concern. The chemo treatments are poisonous, and he subsists on strong pain-killers. Some days are better than others, and he loves to work on the house here. But he hasn't the stamina of yore. Also I've had flu, and feel depleted.

André's book is really terribly French, don't you think?: logical, unsentimental, intelligent, economical, apotheosizing figures who are entrenched in Parisian culture but quite unknown beyond the borders. Also his *language* is French—in the sense of being not only tidy but irreversible: complicatedly simple, even mannered—at least to my mind. It's not easy reading. Thanks for thinking of sending it to me. It brings back a way of being that is nearly lost, and in a city that I'll doubtless never see again.

... I've just finished a gloomy memorial for James Bridges, for countertenor (Brian Asawa) and chamber orchestra. Also a quartet, my Fourth, for the Emerson, based on Picasso pix. (Shades of your Klee.) Now am trying to write a piece for two pianos.

You appear to be energetic and prolific. I hope that in eight years I'll have one-eighth of your vitality.

Stay always in touch.

Love

Ned

## To Edmund White

*Nantucket*
*16 June 1995*

Very dear Edmund—

You don't mind, do you? I've nominated you for membership in the American Academy, using the following citation:

"His subject is responsibility as achieved or eschewed through various modes of hedonism. This he has accomplished in nearly 4,000 prose pages broaching all literary mediums: autobiography, biography (Genet), travelogues, essays, interviews, the diary, novels (three of them), and a collection of criticism. Yet, as with all good authors, it's not what White writes, but how. His 'how' is dangerously purple; but the risk is itself the message, at once luscious and stark, reckless and sure, tragic and comforting."

This was somewhat queerer until Jim Holmes told me to cool it—the academy is, if not homophobic, at least stuffy. Which is why my two seconders are irreproachably solid citizens: John Updike and Joyce Carol Oates. (The latter wrote: "... I'll be delighted to second the Edmund White nomination. The academy has become rather vague to me—I haven't attended a 'ceremony' in years. Why anyone would want to join is a mystery; yet not to be invited is, I suppose, a disappointment. Such is our moral vanity!") *I LOVE being a member.*

JH has had five of his six chemo treatments. They're devastating. A wistful foreboding permeates the household. I think of you without Chris, without John, without Hubert. . . . And mediocrity lives on throughout the globe.

. . . I'm working on music (2-piano variations, and choruses) and two books (a collection of essays, and another diary). . . .

Love
Ned

## To Lou Harrison

*Nantucket*
*25 June 95*

It's been, dearest Lou and Bill, too long.

Last September while in San Francisco so briefly I'd hoped we might see each other. Again, I'll be in California next November for a new piece with the L.A. Chamber Orchestra. But it all depends on Jim Holmes's health.

He has cancer, and I wanted to tell you. A lymphoma of the stomach, plus Crohn's disease, very painful, and he's only 56. The 6th, and hopefully last, of his chemotherapies takes place next Friday. Will you say a prayer?

I miss you dearest Lou, and the ever-receding past. Even if we never meet again, you're vitally present always. I know you're working, as I am.

Be fruitful and multiply.

Love

## To Edmund White

*24 Sept. 95*

Dear Little Edmund

Your prose is so far beyond my own, in style and form and panache, that I'm not even jealous. I've just finished *Skinned Alive;* it's your best, and least forced, book. It flows and is honest. It touches and is breezy, both. And you yourself come off as nice, patient, and a good listener. (The reverse of me: I'm ever more cranky in growing older. 72 next month.) I especially liked "An Oracle." But every one of them evoked time and place and gave me the blues, in a joyous sort of way. . . .

As for the story in the recent *New Yorker,* all America loved it. I too. It's like an un-identical twin of the narrative on pps. 92–96 of *Knowing When to Stop.*

Would you consider writing a libretto for me? When will you be in America?

Jim Holmes is not well. Every new day makes its own stern rules. You, of all people, know those rules. My life is governed now by his. France is not on my agenda, nor even nearby cities where I have new pieces being played, unless JH can come too. . . . But it would be such a pleasure to see you.

Paul Bowles has been here for several days, the hermit with the hype of Madonna. The two concerts were badly performed but very expensive and jam-packed with the well-off hippies from the Sixties.

[Anthony] Tommasini's biography of Virgil Thomson, which apparently is being sent to you, is on target, but perhaps not quite what Virgil would have had in mind.

As for the Academy, the votes are not for several months. . . .

Much love to James Lord. Even more to you.

Ned

## To Daron Hagen

*5 Nov. 95*

Dear Daron—

Your brass suite (or concerto, as you whimsically chose to name it) is skillful to the eye and effective to the ear, from the Bernsteinianly-titled *Sennets and Tuckets,* through the variations on "Believe Me If All Those Endearing Young Charms," to the Torke-esque Invention and (my favorite) the Romanza, which evokes Ava Gardner in some lewd 1940s crime film. I make these comparisons involuntarily; they're in no sense negative. Except that most of the movements are twice too long (and easily shortened), the piece is enviably professional, knowledgeable about brass, and sometimes touching. The harmon-mute effects are, at least on my machine, enough to make the music invisible; and the change from B-flat to C trumpets (belied by the markings at the end of II and the start of III) is a bit confusing. The performance seems fair-to-good. I don't really like brass ensembles, including my own, but yours is as good as they come.

What do you think of the Britten biog.? I reviewed it for the *Washington Post* about two years ago (the review will be in new book) and admired it, though I stressed that only a straight writer, such as Carpenter, could be so obsessed with finding pederasty in every last note the poor composer penned.

JH went today to Nantucket for a few days. I had a world premiere last night in Los Angeles (countertenor & orchestra) but didn't go. The days are getting shorter ... but always long enough to contain my affection for you & Donna.

Ned

## To James Lord

*12 January 96*

Dear James—

No, I hadn't heard about Claude Lebon, and am dumbfounded. Was he ill? Depressed? How did he do it—with pills? ... Ah, what a crucial segment of my past! ... [Claude Lebon (see pages 24–43) committed suicide in Paris in 1995.]

Elysium Press sent me your brief memoir. Beautiful edition. Of course one longs to read the whole book eventually. ...

So I count on your springtime visit.

Love

Ned

## To Edmund White

*19 January 96*

Dear Fellow-Immortal—

The Academy absolutely forbade me to send this to you before they make their public announcement. But I'm not to be trusted—and thought it would make you pleased.

Let us know when you'll be around again.

Love ever

Ned

(enclosed: His election announcement)

## To James Lord

*1 February 96*

Sweet James—

Yes, I read Gore Vidal's memoir. In general I'm a fan (and have read probably two-thirds of his large output), agreeing with his politics and literary slant, while sometimes uneasy with his arch above-it-all stance. But *Palimpsest* I found both dull and dishonest. Dull, because he stresses again his lineage to prove his superiority; and dishonest, because he'll invent—or at least rearrange—a situation in order to put someone else down and him up. Considering he's always taken others to task (Truman Capote et al.) for fabrication, plus mistakes in French, he now errs as heavily as they do. *Bref,* the book made me uncomfortable.

Am I to conclude that you in turn were made uncomfortable by *my* memoir (since you've not mentioned it), or have you simply not read it? I would like your reaction. Edmund can lend it to you, or we can wait for our reunion in the spring. Be sure to let me know well in advance, because more and more we're in Nantucket: Jim Holmes's health is a constant concern and we live day to day.

Please give Bernard my fondest, and thank him for the sad details about Claude.

Love

Ned

### To Reynolds Price

*9 February 96*

Dear Reynolds—

After we spoke by phone, I realized I hadn't told you that I'd read *The Promise of Rest*. Is it because we divorce flesh-&-blood authors from their books? Certainly I was engrossed by the novel from start to finish, but (this was 2 or 3 months ago) I didn't particularly think of *you* while reading it. I thought of *it*. . . . I do remember that I got out Milton again after finishing your first noble chapter, and was bored to distraction. Hutch's admiration for Milton is more strongly put than is Milton himself.

Anyway, we'll see you and Adam on March 1st at the Residence, as agreed. Jim has his ups & downs. Today he's down. But he's very very anxious to see Chapel Hill again, where he spent so many crucial college years. . . . I'm all right. Old and tired, but all right.

Do you want to write a libretto? Think about it before we meet. . . .

Love

Ned

To James Purdy

*28 February 96*

Dear James—

How warming to read those intelligent and praiseworthy praises of your work in the French press. Especially I reacted to your quote about the Mediterranean: "Nothing human is foreign to me" versus Americans': "All that is human is foreign to me." Our land becomes ever more foreign to *me*. But where can we go?

Jim Holmes next week will have more "tests." Meanwhile, we're driving for a few days to Durham, NC, to visit Duke's music department, and also Reynolds Price. Do you admire him?

I admire you.

Always

Ned


To Edmund White

*12 March 1996*

Dear Old Edmund—

Pleasant to get your letter, and to learn (wistfully) that you were in America and have now returned. Yes, of course I'll "sit" for one of your portraits. I just sat for a group photograph of five (it was to be six, but John Corigliano, when he saw the layout of necklaces and feather boas we were to don, left the studio, never to return) gay composers for an "Out" CD. Corigliano was right. David Del Tredici, meanwhile, insisted on wearing long diamond earrings and swathes of pearls about his neck, humorlessly insisting I was reactionary and homophobic. He of course encourages homophobia by ghettoizing his musical sisters in a manner he can't truly believe in. Unless he has gone—as is possible, with his dear friends dying, and his career on hold—off the deep end.

What is *The Farewell Symphony*, a novel? Whenever I pick up anything, you are in it—at the height of your productivity. . . . What a thrill about Michael [Carroll] in your life. Reassuringly, many other friends are finding love these days, in our Buchanian mire.

Three of my small operas have come out on CD. I shall be-gift them to you when next we meet. When will that be? I also have a book of essays coming out chez S&S in July. Called *Other Entertainment*. (The title is from the IRS, who didn't know how to classify a composer-author, except in this category.)

Jim Holmes's health is somewhat stabilized. He sends you his fondest, and I my love.

Ned


## To Eugene Istomin

*Nantucket*
*12 April 96*

Fond Eugene—

I think of you daily, with the affection of 53 years, especially when, seated at the keys, I evoke your evocation of *The Lady from Shanghai* during the picnic scene when the soundtrack quietly begins to play that insidious tango that everyone knows but no one can name.

Because I won't be in Washington, could you keep your eye out for reviews of *Lions* which (I think) the National Symphony is doing on the 22 and 23 of April. And especially for the local premiere of my Fourth Quartet (a long affair based on Picasso pictures) which the Emerson Quartet is to play on Saturday the 27th. . . .

The years slide by, sometimes sadly, but a certain energy prevails. We're in Nantucket today. It's raining, with crocus and daffodils finally rearing their ugly heads, and the air is fresh. Tomorrow: back to New York by truck. Jim's health is, as they say, *stabilized* for the moment. Every day makes its own rules.

And *your* health? And Martita's? Couldn't you, O couldn't you, come for tea one day not too far off? I'd love to talk to you.

Always
Ned


## To Gore Vidal

*23 April 96*

Dear Gore—

In June, John Corigliano and his friend, Mark Adamo, will be touring Italy, and they long to meet you, if only for a cup of tea. John (mid-fifties and handsome) is, as you may know, the composer, with librettist Bill Hoffman, of the opera *The Ghosts of Versailles*, which the Met commissioned, premiered, and revived with success these past years. Mark (early thirties) is also a composer, and a prose-writer about music. I've given them your addresses, in Ravello and Rome; they'll write, and you can respond as you see fit.

I did read your memoir, with a certain awe and admiration, and otherwise mixed feelings. We can maybe talk about it when next we meet, if ever. . . .

Jim Holmes, my friend of nearly thirty years, has had a wretched bout with cancer. We stay pretty much put—he's directing his church choir in adventuresome programs, I trying to compose a magnum opus called *Art of the Song*. No social life.

Please write occasionally, dear Gore. Or phone.

Affection always, also to Howard.

Ned

## To Gore Vidal

*Tuesday*
*7 May 96*

Dear Gore—

You'll be thrilled to learn that I took John Simon as my date to the premiere of my new String Quartet in Tully Hall on Sunday. He'd wanted to peruse the galleys of my new book which contains the forty-page interview I did with him for the *NY Native* eleven years ago on the occasion of his loudly announcing, during an intermission, that all homosexual playwrights should die of AIDS. He brought me the December issue of *The New Criterion*, which contains his review of your memoir. Then yesterday in *Time*, which I perused at the doctor's office (I have diverticulitis) I saw Charlton Heston's righteous indignation, so late in the game, about your notorious *Ben Hur* comment. (Instead of saying he was outraged, why didn't he say he was amused?) Poor boy, I did music for a play he was in in 1948. He was sweet and friendly. Twenty years later I met him again—at the White House, as it happens—and he turned his back. Anyway, in today's *Times*, along with a review of my quartet, is the enclosed by Russell Baker. I don't know how many friends send you clippings, so I'll do so here. . . . Your health sounds dramatic. Is it colitis? I have little advice, but lots of compassion. . . . I've only read *about* the Mann diaries, including his remarks on you. But haven't *read* them. . . . John Corigliano will write you directly. His —*their*—sojourn is scheduled for June, just when you say you won't be there. . . .

Love always
Ned

To Andrew Porter

*27 May 1996*

Always dear Andrew—

It's been a year since last we whispered to one another across the waves . . . Jim has grown fat, thank God, and looks beautiful with his gray crew cut. We still live each day as it comes, but the cancer seems behind him now. . . . I'm fat too, and gray haired, but still gorgeous and smug and anxious. . . . Jacob Druckman died yesterday. We were never close, but with each leaf that falls from the greater family tree one feels more strongly the urge to cleave (is that the word?) to those friends who remain. I wonder that the earth is wide enough to house the increasingly vast array of tombstones. . . . We think of you daily, always with affection. I'll never come abroad again, but do like to muse on the past. Did I send you the memoir, *Knowing When to Stop*? . . . Also, the NY Philharmonic is touring the British Isles with my English Horn Concerto this summer. They play it at Royal Albert Hall on Aug. 20. If you can't go, could you anyway send a clipping? The piece is well-played, though not as exciting as the Left-Hand Concerto which predates it by a half-year. . . . How are you? Is your job in any sense rewarding? Your health? Your loves? . . .

Love always, also from JH
Ned

To Daron Hagen

*1 June 96*

Dear Daron—

Jim, I know, has written you under separate cover. I concur with all he says. Separation is traumatic, but it isn't death or disease; indeed, it can sometimes be the reverse: relief and health. It's also remedial—if you change your minds, you can reinstate yourselves, and turn back the clock. Whatever you decide, in the next twelve months, it will be the right thing.

Wistfully I notice that (since I seem to be subscribed to Bard's concert brochures) the Emerson Quartet is playing at Bard, but *not* my Fourth Quartet. Since programs are selected by the so-called presenters from those submitted by the performers, and since I assume that Botstein is the presenter, I can only conclude that Botstein vetoed my new piece in favor of the very standard fare that *is* being played. Since the student body at Bard would, by definition, be interested in a new American piece, I must also conclude that Botstein vetoed my piece either because of the grudge he still presumably holds against me for my remark in *Harper's* decades ago, or because he simply doesn't care for my music. If the latter case is true, so be it. If the former case, however, is true, it does seem a bit childish. I'm 72 now, and would like the quartet to be heard by as many young people as possible before it sinks into oblivion. I also have great respect for Leon Botstein, and for what he's done for Bard both musically, financially, and intellectually, as well as for his work on the *Musical Quarterly*. Bring him to tea sometime, if you're both in New York at the same time. You're free to show him this letter—for I have no, and have never had, hard feelings.

We leave tomorrow for Nantucket.

Affection

Ned

## To Edmund White

*1 June 96*

Fond Edmund—

As always happens, when one sees an old friend after years, under forced circumstances (but what circumstances are not forced?), I felt frustrated at the Academy the other day by all that was left unsaid, especially when I learned that Sandy McClatchy saw you under more social circumstances a day or two later. Well, anyway. It was agreeable to observe your healthy look, to welcome you to the asylum of the Golden Few, and to meet your friend, who is cute, but whom I scarcely spoke to.

A small film crew of three, run by a Mr. Jim Dowell, is making an ongoing documentary about me. So far they've shot around eight hours (rehearsals, soliloquies, singers singing and me playing) and want to do more interviews with friends. Would you "sit" for him, either in New York or in Paris, depending on where you'll be for the next many months? He'll be in touch with you. It's for, hopefully, a 55-minute slot on PBS.

Let me know where you'll be when. We leave tomorrow for the whole summer in Nantucket (except for July 7–11 in NYC).

With more than merely love—

Ned

To Paul Bowles

*Nantucket*
*8 June 96*

Dear Paul—

Just checking in. Gavin Lambert phoned to say you're having problems with your leg. My profound sympathies. So many acquaintances are having leg problems that it seems an epidemic; but if it's any consolation, most of them recover, thanks to massage, hot baths, and walking. Of course, I don't know the details of your ailment. . . . Gavin also says he's doing the preface to a little book of our letters. Are you as astonished as I, that such a book could exist? After all, since 1961 when I was last in Morocco, we haven't seen each other for more than around four hours. Before that, in 1949–51 when I lived in Fez, we saw each other for maybe twelve hours. Most of our fraternizing (as Virgil used to say) was from 1941 in Mexico until the end of that decade, perhaps 27 hours. Which comes to a total of 43 hours over a period of 55 years. Well, maybe that's why there are letters. I retain no copies of mine to you from before around 1970, but have nearly eighty from you, beginning 1949. (Earlier ones are lost, since I had no sense of archival immortality before the age of 35!) Anyway, they read and flow quite nicely. Which is why David Deiss wants to print them with his Elysium Press. I've met him twice: under forty, black hair, very concerned with literature, somewhat hermetic in New England. The Press is elegant, beautiful paper, rarefied editions of Cocteau, James Lord, etc. . . . Are you writing on your own? music or books or stories? . . . I've read the galleys of Tommasini's biography of Virgil, about 700 pages. It might not be quite what Virgil had in mind, but it's awfully good: frank, caring, respectful of VT's music and prose while documenting his mean streak and closety love life. But it's warm, analytical, and very readable, especially about VT's earliest days. . . . I'm in Nantucket for most of the summer, a bit at loose ends. Jim Holmes has had his ups and downs with cancer, which makes one live each day at a time. Which one does anyway, more and more, after the age of seventy, or even forty....

Dear Paul. Yes ...

Ned

### To Daron Hagen

*3 July 96*

My heart bleeds for you, it really does, dear Daron, during this period of tribulations ... with Botstein, Donna, your grandmother, and the Las Vegas veto. In all of this Paul Sperry really seems like a mensch: he's one of a kind, especially in this era of dwindling brains and culture.

I don't know how to pacify you: things don't necessarily get "better"; indeed, after fifty they get "worse," in the sense that, added to every other slap in the face, the specter of death—one's own and one's friends—lurks ever more real.... Health is crucial. And getting work done, then hearing it played, preferably well.

I'm sad about your grandmother. The Bard situation seems unfair, at least from your side. Carolann P. was a trauma for me and I hope never to work with her again. As for Donna, that's really too bad. But nothing is ever wasted.

... Jim's health remains unsteady. Every new day makes its own rules.

Stay always in touch, and let us know if there's anything we can do. I'll start at Curtis again, and Manhattan, during second week of September. See you then, if not sooner.

Always

Ned

### To Stephen Sondheim

*Nantucket*
*19 August 96*

Dear Stephen—

I'm unhappy at your displeasure at the two references in the new book. But since the article is therein reprinted verbatim from the *Opera News* version in 1991 (remember when I came to "interview" you?) and since you never openly objected to that version, I supposed all was okay. I can see how you might feel misinterpreted by p. 222 (though I think it makes you out as both sweet and smart.... As for [remarks about Leonard Bernstein and musical and film score orchestration], it could be argued (since I'm well aware that composers for musicals and films never do their own scoring— that, indeed, it's practically illegal), my phrase means that Lenny *knows how* to orchestrate and often does so, while you aren't interested in doing so. But perhaps it's grammatical. Or semantic or something.

Anyway, in the current (August) issue of *Opera News* I've again used your name in the first paragraph of a long essay on so-called "Art Song." Will you find that I've used the name in vain?

Summer's coming to an end. Jim has his ups and downs. The world seems sad as well as silly. I do hope that Peter is thriving, as well as you. Your music is almost daily in my mind.

Always
Ned

## To Gore Vidal

*19 August 96*

Very dear Gore—

I was concerned about the report on your health when last you wrote. I empathize more than you might suspect.

Please know that you are always warmly in my thoughts, that I miss you, and that I'm glad to keep up with all you do through your vivid writings and occasional (but ever welcome) letters.

Ever—
Ned

(Spent a long evening in New York last week with [Franco] Zeffirelli— the first time we'd met in three decades—because the *NYT* asked me to interview him apropos of his upcoming *Carmen* at the Met. He says you're neighbors. What do you think of him?)

## To Gore Vidal

*14 Sept 96*

Fond Gore—

Thanks for your pithy portrait of Franco Z. *My* portrait of him was in last Sunday's *Times*. (Do you get it in Italy?)

The enclosed review will amuse you.

As for Paul B[owles], his letters and mine (about 60 on each side), between 1943 and 1996, are being printed by Elysium Press. Imagine! So we're in contact. He was in NY a year ago for a huge fête in his honor. But he was, and is, in pain. He wants to die in Tangier. But seems intellectually alert—not sad or self-pitying, like me.

Love, from your unpolished emulator
Ned


## To Edmund White

*4 November 96*

Fond Edmund—

In what repute stands Eric-Emanuel Schmitt, author of the play *Variations énigmatiques,* in Paris? He was on *Bouillon de Culture* (broadcast Sundays in NY) last night, and I found him cute as a bug. Tell him. . . .

And in what repute is Renaud Machart, music critic for *Le Monde*? He interviewed me for five hours last month, for a series of broadcasts (mainly of my music) on Radio France in early 1997, and he seemed very well informed—especially for a Frenchman on American music.

Went to a reading of our James Lord at A Different Light. He was profoundly indifferent, even hostile, to his audience, as though the whole thing bored him to tears. . . . (I made a faux pas, when I said I longed to spend an hour with him—it's been fourteen years since last we met. He replied, correctly, "What do you mean? I saw you at your place, here in New York, just a year or two ago." I'm not gateux. It's just that *where* one sees one's friends is somehow more crucial than *when*.)

Time flows by. Jim ails and eats badly. I'm tired, insomniac, and just turned 73. Be a good boy. You are a born writer.

Love—
Ned


## To Edward Albee

*Nantucket*
*19 December 96*

Dear Edward—

Last Saturday, flipping the dials, I fell upon your recent discourse in Chicago. You seemed intelligent, caring, well-prepared, professional without coldness, and also good-looking. I agreed with everything (almost) that you said. (The business about the end of the monkey's tail being the start of art could use, perhaps, a bit of polishing.) And I was impressed with how you spoke, so concernedly, about the crucial need for, along with the terrible vanishing of art in our society, without relating this to yourself so much as to the near-hopelessly dumbed-down world.

I didn't see *Three Tall Women*. A year or so ago I had tickets (from Miss Seldes), but a last-minute crisis prevented using them. I *did* read the play and was, as usual, touched by your unalterable "musical" language, as by the characteristic melancholy.

So I'm writing to say thanks for your gifts. Thanks too for seeing the filmmakers recently for their little documentary. I spent a couple of hours some time ago with Mel Gussow, but have quite forgotten how we talked.

It would be nice to meet again, after so very very long, and maybe play some music. But such meetings aren't, at least for me, as off-the-cuff as they were in the old days. I'm back and forth between here and New York. And you, I think, travel a lot. But if I call you toward the beginning of the new year, will you consider coming uptown?

Still, if we never meet again, know that I always think fondly of you and your theater.

Ned

## To Lou Harrison

*Nantucket*
*Christmas Night 96*

Fond Lou and Bill—

Warm greetings for the season, and for tomorrow and the next three centuries.

I've been perusing again with pleasure *Young Caesar*. The libretto is mostly very good, isn't it? Who is Robert Gordon? He has a way with words, written and uttered.

Jim and I live from day to day. He suffers some, and dreads, understandably, more chemotherapy. Will next year be any gentler?

Even if we never meet again, know that I love you always.

Ned

## To Morris Golde

*Nantucket*
*26 December 96*

Dearest Morris—

Driving out here yesterday, after Jim's Christmas service, we veered over to the Grand Concourse. And I was actually reminded of how, 52 years ago, we came there for your mother's gefilte fish and your father's little songs; and how today the neighborhood, though still physically grandiose, is radically changed in its ethnic composition.

Anyway, have a tolerable holiday season. We'll be back in the first week of 1997. Meanwhile, I've read Joe Machlis's new novel. Very heterosexual, and full of standard repertory (Brahms, Wieniawski, Vivaldi) with no hint of contemporary Americana. But well-crafted and slightly raunchy.

Love forever—
Ned

## To Morris Golde

*12 II 97*
*Ash Wednesday*

Dear Morris of the glittering triceps:

It would mean everything to me were you to attend the all-Rorem program at little Weill Hall on March 26. They won't give out free tickets, because the place is so small. But Jerry Hadley will chant *The Auden Poems*, and I'll play with the Moscow Trio, and Ellen Zwilich will be hostess in slacks and a bow tie.

Have just finished correcting galleys of *Dear Paul, Dear Ned*, fifty years of correspondence between Bowles and me, in which you're mentioned often. It will be published in a small edition, 150 pages on silk paper, this Spring, Elysium Press.

Jim, who is just fairly well, sends you his love, as do I.
Ned

## To Jack Larson

*18 II 97*

Fond Jack—

When we spoke Saturday I was harboring the flu which has now burst forth with fever, aches, insomnia, and coughing beyond endurance. And Jim's in Nantucket, until tomorrow, which is maybe for the best, since all I'd do is complain if he were here. But your "condition" is more serious, and I wasn't able to commiserate (is that the word?) too well, being wrapped up in myself. . . . I just listened to *More Than a Day* for the first time in a year. Its performance is better than I recalled. Asawa is really quite good, and the orchestra is too—except in the dramatic penultimate movement which is too fast and too casual. The words (with the melodies) moved me very much. . . .

What do you think of the Isherwood diary? It's certainly the work of a writer, without itself being "writing." (Sort of the opposite of me, in my career as author.) Authority he has, but not, unlike his novels, polish and selection.

I'll get a neighbor to mail this, since I haven't the stamina to go out.

Fond Jack, your health means everything to us.

Love

Ned

### To Reynolds Price

*23 March 97*

Fond Reynolds—

It's been over a year since our last intercourse, at that restaurant in Chapel Hill. Now in this morning's *Times* I was all a-twitter (as was everyone else) by your piece on James Dickey, and especially by your witty mention of "us" in relation to him. (You'd already once told me that he said that if he were queer, the two men he would most want to consort with are you and me.) You sound spry and filled with life. If you've anything new to send me, I'll do likewise for you, plus CDs if you like them.

Jim Holmes still shifts between high and low, and takes dozens of pills daily. I wish I had his indefatigable will to live. Maybe I do. But, among other things, we're being threatened with *eviction* after nearly thirty years in this big rent-controlled apt. The experience is demoralizing and undeserved, nor is it certain that our lawyer will resolve it favorably, although I'm legally in the right. Please, *please* pray for us.

Meanwhile, I'm concentrating—during endless insomnia—on a massive project called *Art of the Song*, 36 songs for four voices and piano, to be performed without intermission.

I love you. So does Jim.

Always

Ned

To James Hamilton-Paterson
c/o his publisher in London

*1 May 1997*

Dear James Hamilton-Paterson—

You are a wonderful writer. Every word is in place, every idea is original, and all the words and ideas conspire to make a prose that is necessary and urgent. You make the reader know what he did not know he knew, and you do so magically.

You are perhaps not as well known in the United States as (at least I feel) you should be. I have nominated you for honorary foreign membership to the American Academy of Arts & Letters. Since I as a musician am nominating someone for the literary department, I'm required to find two seconders among the authors. These will be John Updike and William Maxwell.

Theoretically nominees are not meant to be told what I'm telling you, because of the likely event that they won't make it. Also, you may be completely indifferent to the whole idea. But it gives me, at least, a moment to chat with you.

I'm a composer (and writer, mainly of diaries and essays), seventy-three, raised in Chicago, weaned in Paris, and have lived in New York and Nantucket for the past four decades. Do you ever come to America? Will you ever receive these paragraphs?

Warmly

Ned Rorem


To Reynolds Price

*2 May 97*

Gold Reynolds—

I bought your *Collected Poems* at Barnes & Noble, where the book is prominently on display, and have been browsing therein. The poems are true poems, and filled with old friends. I can't know yet if any of them are "singable" (at least on my terms), but they are certainly readable, and I'm proud, as always, of you.

The weeks continue in all ways dark.

Jim sends his love, as do I

Always

Ned

Gossip. Mary Cantwell, a very good author, and a longtime acquaintance with a pleasantly sour style, sat next to me at a small party last Monday. "I don't want to spoil your fun," she confided, "but James Dickey *did* once go to bed with a man, despite what Reynolds Price claims." It turns out that she, Mary, had an affair with JD about 25 years ago. JD, as always, drank too much, and "spoiled" Mary's life in certain ways. And of course he told her all sorts of stories that may or may not have been true. Also he took her to the Academy one evening, where she found everyone pretentious and full of rivalry.... To see the world through another's eyes!

### To James Hamilton-Paterson

*Nantucket*

*2 June 97*

Dear James—

(For that is what I shall call you henceforth, and we'll probably never meet. Also it's the name—Jim Holmes—of my companion of nearly thirty years, also a musician.)

How pleasant to get your letter.... As for putting your name forward [at the American Academy], it'll probably take several tries in the coming years for the rockbound American Academy, the literary members of which all have their own pets. Anyway, Richard Howard has agreed, along with Updike, to second you. He's our leading translator from the French. (Maxwell's out of the picture.)

It was about five years ago that Richard Dyer, the music critic for the *Boston Globe*, gave me *Gerontius*. I've never read anything like it; and, for an American, to use Elgar as hero, seemed workably eccentric. Not a word out of place, and every word needed....

You say: "I am not on the Internet. Even less am I married." That can't mean.... But no! Perish the thought! In fact, you're a touch sarcastic about two queer shipboard passengers in *Gerontius* (though in *The Music* you're more indulgent). As for my own books, naturally I'd like you to like them, but even more, my music (have you a CD player?). The first book, *The Paris Diary*, made something of a stir in 1965, not because I was a flag-waver for gayety, just too lazy to pretend to be otherwise. *Other Entertainment*, the last, and 14th book, is a collection of previously printed essays. It's still in print, as is *Knowing When to Stop*, a memoir of my first 29 years. I'll send some of this to you, as soon as I learn how.

Meanwhile, you live in Arezzo. So does Bill Weaver. Do you know him? He's Umberto Eco's translator, and quite smart, about my age, maybe a year or two older.

... Too tired to continue.... More later....

Always

Ned


To James Salter

*Friday the 13th*

*June 97*

Fond James—

This will be short(ish), because I'm not sure of your address (no return on the envelope), and because I've only just grazed your book.

Thanks for the proofs of *Recollection* (in the singular: good title). I've just read the last chapter, and find your portrait of our beloved Robert [Phelps] to be special, caring, and skillful. Everything rings true—except the remarks about me. I've found out, first-hand, that the moment one publishes a memoir—or diary—readers will say what I've just said. Because there is no all-encompassing truth, there is only a writer's truth, and even that is *fact* rather than philosophy. Anyway. I have no notion of what "He was busy changing lipstick" means, either as a general quip or as a personal remark.... Gloria proposed to me, not me to her.... Etc....

Leafing through the rest of your pages (which I'll scrutinize carefully soon), it's heady to come across old friends—Julian Beck, Ethel Reiner, Arnold Weissberger, Peter Glenville, and especially Harold Brodkey the insufferable (we were lovers for six weird months, 1962–63). Also your "take" on Paris was so distant from my own, with a milieu exclusively American despite the *indigènes* who dwelt on every street....

My paragraph on your writing in *The Nantucket Diary* sums, I think, you up. Even your dogged heterosexuality is as much a part of your style as of your content. Do you know the remarkable prose of James Hamilton-Paterson, English, 55, living in Italy & Manila? Or of Edmund White?

Anyway, let's see each other when you can....

Love

Ned

To James Hamilton-Paterson

*Nantucket*

*27 June 97*

Dear Friend—

Walking back from the post office, where I picked up and read your welcome letter, I stopped by one of our two quaint bookstores and had them send you *The Nantucket Diary* and *Knowing When to Stop*. (It should take around ten days.) Bear in mind two things: (1) I'm a composer who also writes, not a writer who also composes; (2) I'd rather you know my music than my prose (I think), although the two are as opposite as possible—at least so far as any "artist" can judge himself, which isn't far.

Then, walking back from the bookstore, where I signed the two books, I realized that in one I may have made a mistake in Italian. I wrote TO JAMES, IL MIGLIOR FABBRO, and probably misspelled "miglior." As you know, that's what T. S. Eliot used as a dedication to Pound (though grammatically he could have meant that he, Eliot, was the better craftsman). Anyway, as soon as one risks pretentiousness, one is punished by one's own hand.

*Knowing When to Stop* (the title is explained on page 25, and means that only a true "fabbro" knows when his work is finished—that an amateur goes always on too long) is a memoir of my first 28 years, 1923–1951. Though written only two years ago, it serves as a prelude to the published (out of print) diaries, that begin in 1951. . . . *The Nantucket Diary* goes from 1975 to 1985.

As for CDs, I have dozens, but doubt that they're available in Italy. "Songs of Sadness," however, isn't (yet) recorded. Eventually I'll send you some.

I'll respond to your warm letter in some detail soon. At the moment I'm overwhelmed. Jim Holmes, my "partner" of the past three decades, aged 58, is quite ill. We've also been fighting eviction in New York. My mind's too fuzzy for logical letter-writing, and what you've written requires . . . mmm. . . .

What do you think of Paul Theroux? He's coming to Nantucket next month and wants to get together. He's a real writer, if long-winded, and voyages to exotic climes, like you. (And like I did in Morocco, but probably never again.) . . .

Always fondly,

Ned

## To Edmund White

*Nantucket*
*July 1 97*

Dearest Edmund—

When Jim brought the *Yale Review* back from the post office he had already read your essay therein, and "prepared" me by saying it was "good, especially the last paragraph." Indeed, I was happy to read it. If I squirmed a bit here and there, it's because my early diaries now also make me squirm (I've had to re-peruse them lately, they're to be reissued by Da Capo), just as Howard Moss's wonderful take-off made me cringe. . . . What most interested me was your reaction to me in person. Unlike me, there is no malice in your bones; you often hit square center without wounding. I've lived with myself for so long that it's hard to be objective. Except about my music. Because music has no subject, ever. I love your writing, and am moved that you care about me. . . .

We long to see your new book. Jim's been up and down in health. Me too. But we're—especially him—persevering. I've nearly finished a HUGE cycle of 36 songs for four singers and piano named *Evidence of Things Not Seen*. A full evening. Twenty-four different writers, including Monette, Doty, Julian Green, Colette, and Wordsworth. Premiere in the little Weill Hall next January 22. Will you be here?

Dearest Edmund—don't ever lose touch.

Always
Ned

## To Russell Platt

*8 July 97*

Dear Russell—

Your odd new Quartet, *Present Night,* is successful, and sometimes moving, never less than professional, and, yes, ugly (though, of course, not ugly *enough!*). I especially like the slow parts, the Nightingale movement which seems to dig deep, and the song-like "Beautiful Dreamer" ending. And I'm envious of your gift for writing truly fast music, which palpitates purposefully like a motor. So bravo. You are prolific.

The performance is acceptable.

Bravo too on your literary career. If you want to review the Bowles/Rorem letters, I'm sure they'll give you a copy.

I'm finishing a huge cycle for the New York Festival of Song. *Huge—* a whole evening.

How is your private life? Details.

All warm wishes to Alexander. And especially to you.

Ned

## To Cynthia Ozick

*Nantucket*

*22 July 97*

Always dear Cynthia—

If I say that *The Puttermesser Papers* is an odd book indeed, it's meant as a compliment. If the shape at first seems loose and random, it gradually pulls itself together to become tight as a marionette's strings. Likewise the content: she ends up (so horribly) all of a piece.

Your book was all the more jolting in that I'd just finished four WASP male authors (2 gay, 2 straight) bestrewing their non-religious but Puritan whimsies: James Salter, Paul Theroux, Ed White, and James Hamilton-Paterson. Do you know them? They're each almost perfect, in ascending order as listed.

I sense that in many important ways you & I look still in opposite directions—my deepest Quakerism makes me forever an unrepentant pacifist, for instance—but in the most important way, through the lens of art (dare I use the word) we see eye to eye.

Love

Ned

Three decades ago Norman Podhoretz, nothing if not a Jewish authority, at least then, claimed that *fudge* was a goy thing—that chocolate for American Jews was presented in another fashion. True or false?

## To Cynthia Ozick

*10 August 97*

*(my parents' 77th anniversary)*

Fond Cynthia—

Your enumerating, apropos of Fudge, the Seven Deadly Sins recalls Dorian Gray and the Seven Deadly Virtues. I forget what they were, but do know that we Americans are made to feel guilty about anything that is pleasurable. Meanwhile, that woman who died in France last week at the age of 123, credited her longevity to a daily dose of chocolate. Therefore, not out of cruelty but out of compassion, I will send you tomorrow a humble box of the fudge for which Nantucket is semi-famous.

To have it suggested that I am "in the horrid company of neo-Nazis, KuKluxers," or that I am even vaguely a Holocaust denier, alarms me. I'm old enough to remember going through Germany with my family in 1936, on a train, and finding the atmosphere weird. I was twelve. My sister and I were "warned" by my Mother and Father not to make fun of the militaristic prevailing mood . . . that the Nazis were not given to humor. We were heading toward Norway via Denmark; the crossing of the frontier was like emerging from—not hell, but some strange darkness into light. Nine years later, when the first newsreels of the concentration camps were shown all over New York, I was among the millions who recoiled. I am, by definition (as a Quaker, though not, alas, as an artist—many great artists are monsters) against any form of persecution; and the *organized* persecution in Germany of the Jews, gypsies, homosexuals with their pink triangles, Poles, Jehovah's Witnesses, vagrants, is more than I can bear. . . . Thus if my remarks about Anne Frank come off as anti-Semitic—and you're not the first to say so—then obviously I've misrepresented myself in the name of glibness. I don't doubt for a minute that Anne Frank penned her famous diary; my heart bleeds at the thought of her last years; and I'm glad that the world has been made aware, through her diary, of a certain aspect of that tragic time. My sole objection is to the crass commercialism made of her book: the fights between Hellman and Levin (both of whom I knew), the back-stabbing in the name of compassion. I admit that I know Anne's diary only through the play and the movie. I've never read the book itself. (Is there, by the way, an "original" of the book, or a facsimile thereof?) My objection to the famous final line, about Anne's believing in the basic goodness of man (which *I* don't believe), has nothing to do with the truth of the utterance, but rather with the adoption of the utterance as literature.

My apologies to you, and to everyone else I may have offended, by my apparently callous remarks.

Yes, I admire your writing. What I admire not least is its theatricality. Have you ever written a libretto? That is—written for the stage with sung music in mind, perhaps an adaptation of one of your fictions? Would you like to? Maybe someday, before it's too late, we might consider doing an opera together, if we can get a joint commission with a respectable deadline and a definite performance. Will you think it over?

Meanwhile: On January 22 will take place, in New York, the premiere of a huge piece, a full evening, called *Evidence of Things Not Seen,* 36 songs for four voices and piano. The title, a definition of Faith, is from William Penn, by way of *Hebrews,* II:1.

I'll be back in the city after mid-September. Will you and your husband come for a meal one day?

Always

Ned

To James Hamilton-Paterson

*14 August 97*

Fond James—

I'm distraught that the books haven't arrived, after nearly two months. Yes, everyone says the Italian mails are hopeless (an acquaintance recently moved permanently from Rome to Amsterdam, so as to receive letters), but one still wonders where all those pages are. Should I try again? As with the correspondence of Barrett and Browning (even though I started it, let me be Barrett!), I'd like you to know the various sides of me.

Meanwhile I'm terribly flattered that you were able to find those CDs, and that you responded to certain movements within them. Yes, clarity is what I too strive for. Indeed, in the opening of the memoir you'll eventually receive, is a two-page description of the difference between the two, and only two, esthetics on earth: French & German. French is clarity, German is obfuscation. Though maybe you're more German than I, judging from a hint or two you've dropped. I hadn't realized you're a composer too. Would you send me some music? The Valse Triste, for instance? (Can the waltz actually be a form, as you suggest, or merely a rhythmic device?) Or is it as complicated sending packages out of Italy as into?

William Burroughs is dead. The only thing depressing about that is the vast amount of publicity, at least in the U.S.A. He was a sophomoric old geezer with no substance. Meanwhile, I've tried reading Faulkner again, as I do (yawn) every ten years or so. Now it's *The Hamlet.* There are certain "masterpieces" I allow, without loving, like, say, Beethoven's Ninth. Others which I just don't buy, like Faulkner (of whom Burroughs is an offshoot). He's dated, of course, like everything else once it exists. But boringly so. Too much description, which was stylish in the thirties. Nothing elliptical. In the second paragraph he uses the word "now" eight times, surely not for echo but from oversight. Then on page 7 he uses the word "one" seven times. Is this for style? or from a leaden ear? . . . I mention this to you, who are a master craftsman, in style and content both.

The eviction business was resolved, in our favor, after four dark months. . . . Jim Holmes is stabilized, as they say, and works hard, very hard. I'm trying to write a Double Concerto for Cello & Fiddle (it will be done in Scotland, incidentally, in October 98), and a large affair for organ solo. Got any ideas?

Even if you hate them, let me know when the books arrive. And stay forever in touch.

Always
Ned

## To James Hamilton-Paterson

*Nantucket*
*15 Sept. 97*

Dear James—

A quick reply to your long and good letter. What a relief to know that the books finally arrived.

. . . I'm embarrassed that any remarks I may have made about Elgar might be taken personally. Your *Gerontius* is a masterpiece. Although it's not still fresh in my mind, I recall it as something an American couldn't have written, simply because Elgar doesn't signify to us what he does to you; nor do we have a composer who, in the mid-1920s, was apotheosized as he was. Oh, perhaps Gershwin. Elgar's greatness is not the question; rather it's the perception of his greatness. As for English music in general, as perceived by an American, or at least by me, I'll write you an essay on that sometime soon.

The organ piece is underway. I've written vast amounts for that instrument, including a concerto and two huge suites, and three "Organbooks," not because I'm partial to it (I'm not), but because Jim Holmes is an organist, and because organists in general (who often commission me) are more disposed than other instrumentalists to so-called modern music.

. . . Did you know I lived in Italy in 1954–55? When *The Paris Diary* is reissued in March, I'll send you it, and what it relates about how I learned Italian in bed. . . .

More soon.
With affection.
Ned

To David Del Tredici

*6 October 97*

David, my hero—

The Boosey & Hawkes newsletter indicates, as well as can be deduced, that you've used the same [Paul] Monette text as I: namely the first of his *Elegies,* "Here. . . ." In 1989, I set it, for men's chorus and piano 4-hands. It's about seven minutes, title *Love Alone,* and published by B&H (recorded too). I'd be interested in your opinion, and in hearing your version. (Monette and I corresponded, but met only once. A very nice, intelligent, attractive man.)

What is your feeling about the Academy's "Ives Living" award, of nearly $350,000 to a "deserving" but needy composer over forty? I'm against it, at least as the rules now stand. But if I nominate Barbara Kolb, will you support me? Or are you on bad terms with her? She fills the bill—being jobless, and a real composer, getting on, and a pain in the neck.

I miss you, and the years are flowing by. . . .

Yours

N

To Edmund White

*3 Nov. 97*

Dear Ed—

Finally I've finished *The Unfinished Symphony.* Each word is well chosen, the sentences flow, and the paragraphs have natural composition. The subject matter is overwhelmingly nostalgic (although my gaiety started a generation before yours and was just as gaudy) and workably personal. I was thrilled to see my name, undisguised, used twice as, I guess, an anchor to locate time & place. . . . Your book is still being reviewed everywhere (the publishers have been expert), and most of the critiques are good. You are for me one of America's three writers. (The names of the others on request!)

How sorry I am that we didn't see each other more last month. There is no longer anybody in Paris for me but you. Nobody. Next time you come, can we meet more at length? not least for the following reason:

Joe LeSueur says you're doing a piece on Joe Brainard. I had a "thing" with Brainard in the early sixties, before Kenward took up with him. As a result, I have a sheaf of warm letters, drawings, poems, etc. that I treasure— about three dozen sheets. He also did the odd and beautiful cover for the publication of the 1954 *Four Dialogues* by me and Frank O'Hara; and a cover, never published, for *Miss Julie,* which I'll show you, as well as four huge pictures (painting-collages) which are among his most satisfyingly original. . . . It's not that I want to horn in on your project (although I do), but for the sake of completion, it might prove worthwhile.

And your health? I'm so tired, now at 74, that I just drag about. Insomnia, and hemorrhoids. But what's that compared to Jim Holmes, who is valiant beyond all imagining, and the love of my life. Raw intelligence. Cooked, too.

Affection forever

Ned

### To Gary Schmidgall
### Re. *Walt Whitman: A Gay Life,* Dutton 1997

*3 November 97*

Dear Gary—

Thanks for having your big Whitman book sent. So far I've only leafed through it, but it's quickly clear that the book has style and rhythm: you know how to choose words, write sentences, compose paragraphs, and shuffle chapters. When I've devoured it from cover to cover I'll write again.

Meanwhile, there's nothing I hate more than to receive letters about my books to set me straight: All I want is, as Frank O'Hara said, "undying love." But I am a walking blue pencil, and that fact is stronger than tact.

You've told us a great deal about what music meant to Whitman, but almost nothing about what Whitman has meant to music. In this you are in the glorious company of the good biographers of Dickinson, Stevens, Auden, etc. who, like most intellectuals, are simply not concerned with music. But you *are* concerned.

More than any poet except King David, Whitman has been musicalized. And it's international. Think of Kurt Weill. And the huge oratorio on "Lilacs" by Hindemith in 1946. Long before that, what about the large pieces of Vaughan Williams, Delius, Holst. And in America the sizeable settings by Sessions, Persichetti, Luening, Lees, Ward, Bacon, Dello Joio, Kleinsinger, etc. (all of them straight, by the way). In 1972 the Wannamaker catalog listed over 200 separate composers who had dealt with the poet. Since then, in the post-Stonewall period, there have surely been twice that many young musicians who have been "helped" by him.

Myself, in the past fifty years, have made at least three hours out of

Whitman's verse & prose with my musical setting. Enclosed is a list of those works, most of them published, some of them recorded.

Forgive these words. Nothing is easier than to criticize a book for what it does not contain. But I believe in you, and just wanted to show off a bit.

Always

Ned

## To James Hamilton-Paterson

*12 November 97*

Dear faraway friend—

You did not make it through the finals at the American Academy. I'm profoundly embarrassed vis-à-vis you, and deeply repelled for them. My nomination, coming from a musician member, was a shot in the dark among the literature crowd who all have their own axes to grind. O well, next year, maybe. Meanwhile, were it not for the stuffy Academy, we wouldn't know each other. (It's just that your books aren't circulated enough over here.)

Somebody just gave me a new edition of what's called "The Bell Boy," which I'd already read five years ago. It begins, I notice, with an echo of Vachel Lindsay's *Chinese Nightingale,* with the allusion to a "turquoise" dawn.

Should I send you any more books or music? Are we ourselves complete—people like you and me—or do we exist only through our work? I'd love to have anything of yours, anything. I'm in New York now, but the Nantucket address is best.

On October 23 I turned 74, at which moment I finished a huge cycle, 36 songs for four voices and piano, called *Evidence of Things Not Seen,* which will have a premiere here on Jan. 22.

. . . Dull letter. Please stay always in touch. I need you.

Forever

Ned

## To Edward Albee

*5 Dec. 97*

Merry Christmas, dear Edward—

Since next year Bill [Flanagan] would have been 75 (as I will be too), would this be enough reason to organize some sort of musical memorial? If so, you & I are the obvious ones to do so.

But little concerts are far more complicated than they were yesterday, and certainly more expensive, while singers who willingly sing in English (and who donate their services) are, alas, ever rarer.

"The New York Festival of Song" is the obvious first choice. On Jan. 22, they're doing a huge new cycle of mine in the little Weill Hall (where Bill and I gave those American concerts in 1959–60). Certainly I can put the bug in their ear. But Bill isn't as much of a "fact" as he once was, and the NYFOS has its own flock of favorites. Nor do I really personally know many young singers anymore.

Anyway, let me know what your instincts are....

Ned

To Trish Todd, c/o Simon & Schuster
Re. Kenneth Koch's new book

*7 December 97*

A person in love is torn between needing to keep his enthusiasm secret and wanting to share it with the world. Kenneth Koch in his new book strikes the ideal compromise.

How generous he is with his patient intelligence, and how original with his crucial perception!

Like all real artists, he shows us what we did not know we knew.

He is that rare phenomenon, the poet who can write prose—prose that is necessary and lucid.

With *Wishes, Lies, and Dreams* he taught children to express themselves in poetry. With *I Never Told Anybody* he did the same for inmates of a nursing home. Now, with *Making Your Own Days* (what a great title) he closes the circle by telling the world in general what it means to read and write poems. In so doing, he offers a new and healthy dimension to the life of virtually everyone.

You may use any or all of these disconnected sentences for whatever purpose you wish. Do send me a finished book when it comes out.

Cordially
Ned Rorem

## To Andrew Porter, in Arezzo, Italy

*16 December 97*
*(JH's and my 30th anniversary)*

Dearest Andrew—

. . . We subscribe to the [London] *Times Literary Supplement,* and so see your fairly regular columns. It's a pleasure (usually) to read your non-hyperthyroid appreciations, after the unthinkable *New Yorker* vulgarity today.

The reason I'm writing . . . is this:

I profoundly feel that James Hamilton-Paterson is one of the three most able non-American English-speaking authors of this generation (he's 55). Surely you know *Gerontius?* And other smaller books, like the stories in *The Music.* Lately he & I have been corresponding, like Barrett & Browning of yore (I'm Barrett), and our letters are warm and deep. But now, since he didn't get the American Academy nomination, for which I proposed him as an honorary foreign member, our intercourse has ebbed. We'll probably never meet. . . . Anyway, he lives across the hill from you, except when he's in the Philippines. Is there a means by which, in the next year, you might strike up an acquaintance, and then write me about it?

But perhaps Jim and I will accept your invitation, and come to Italy ourselves.

Forever
Ned

## To Eugene Istomin

*23 March 98*

Fond Eugene—

Since you are half Russian and half French, it seemed an oversight not to have asked if you'd read the recent memoir by one Andrei Makine, *Memories of a Russian Childhood.* I'd like your opinion—and will withhold my own until we can compare notes. The very chosen literati compare him to Proust. Hmmm.

I'll probably arrive [in Washington] on the Metroliner, April 18, and go straight to the Capital Suites Hotel, at 3 o'clock, to meet my sister and two of her offspring. Will stay well into Sunday, since the piece is to be recorded at the Library that day.

It's called *Evidence of Things Not Seen.* . . . I'm most anxious for you to know the texts; it's an extremely intellectual work, and whatever the music's worth, the unrelated texts (related, however, through the score) are high class, as they move from birth to death.

I meant what I said about looking for a publisher, by the way, a publisher of *prose*—I feel bereft in a no-nothing age.

Love
Ned


To James Hamilton-Paterson

*Nantucket*
*10 June 98*

Fond James—

My turn to apologize for this late letter. Though our specialized correspondence is not as urgent as that of, say, two business partners or two lovers, I do believe in staying in touch—believe it in a way you're still too young to grasp. For no matter how smart a young person, or how dull a septuagenarian, the former can't appreciate the whir of Time's winged chariot. Whenever I finish anything, be it a Double Concerto of which I completed the 207-page orchestra score yesterday, or a letter to you, I say, Whew, that's out of the way before I die! (The Concerto, by the way, is for cello & violin, and will be premiered in Indianapolis, then a week later, in October, in Scotland.) Also, the daily observance of Jim Holmes's incredible valiance in the face of weird odds, keeps mortality ever in the forefront. Now that summer's sort of here, we leave New York every Sunday afternoon, after JH's church job, and come here for six days a week. Which means that I attend the Episcopal Mass regularly, but with a sort of repugnance. Quaker by upbringing (my parents converted for reasons of pacifism, not for "God"), I'm an atheist by conviction, and either giggle or vomit at the false fuss of the eucharist and the accusations by the priest of being a sinner. Are you a believer? . . . JH, by the way, is a marvelous organist and choir director. Half my large musical output is for chorus, and half of that by turn is so-called sacred music. For though I don't believe in God, I do believe in Belief, and in much of the art that's been created in the name of the Lord—King David, Bach, Michelangelo, etc. What a paragraph! . . .

Someone showed me a review in the February issue of London's *Literary Review* of your *Three Miles Down*. . . . The review seemed grudging and contradictory. Three beautiful and thoughtful sentences are quoted:

"There is no blueprint, no model, no plan for how the Earth should be. Since Homo sapiens is just another species, everything he does is natural. However it all turns out fine, because that, too, will only be temporary."

To which Andrew Lycett remarks, "If that sounds trite, Hamilton-Paterson carries it off." But that which is trite is that which, by definition, cannot be carried off.

Poulenc. Rather wistfully you admit to what you call "revulsion," feeling that he was "essentially a dilettante, that held [himself] above commit-tal." Well, perhaps it's a matter of simple taste. Poulenc, whom I knew quite well (and whose *music* I've written about extensively) was nothing if not committed, as a Roman Catholic, and as a master of his craft. The nose-thumbing manner of most of Les Six (not Honegger) was simply a 1920s reaction to their forebears. I'd like you to like him, but maybe you don't hear what I hear. How can anyone know what anyone hears—or sees, or feels—let alone how they necessarily *react* to these reactions. I can't, by nature, react to the high seriousness of Bruckner, say, or sometimes Mahler. I don't deny their greatness, but it's a greatness that I don't need—that doesn't "speak to my condition," as Quakers say. That said, do listen to Poulenc's *Stabat Mater*, to his *Gloria*, to the huge opera *Dialogues des Carmélites*, espe-cially the final act. Nothing frivolous there. Nothing.

My full-evening cycle, *Evidence of Things Not Seen*, was premiered in New York last January, then in Washington. It had the best reviews I've ever culled. (Is culled the word?) Which makes me feel wanted. And my Fourth String Quartet has just been recorded on Deutsche Grammophon by the Emerson Quartet (along with a quartet by Edgar Meyer). Will you listen to it? It's based on eight Picasso pictures, sort of.

Some time ago I had a new reprint of my earliest diaries sent to you from Da Capo Press. Very narcissistic.

. . . This letter is loose. But I do, dear James, feel close to you. Even vaguely erotic. Do write when the spirit moves you. On June 24 we're driving to Denver in a rented car, mainly because of the dog, a Bichon named Sonny. Gone for two weeks. Then the address is again Nantucket.

Stay busy.

With great warmth.

Ned

## To Mitchell Ivers, Re. Judy Collins

*Nantucket*

*8 July 98*

Dear Mitchell Ivers—

Thanks for the advance manuscript of Judy Collins's *Singing Lessons* (good title). I'd like to have a finished copy, when available. Meanwhile, you may use the following for whatever purposes you wish:

Judy's book is a macrocosm reflecting the content and contrast of her best songs: poignancy and determination, balance and folly, anxiety and resolution.

Impelled by horrific tragedy, her memoir, swerving artfully between poetry and prose, depicts how a survivor learns to live in the shadow of a question which will never be answered.

Cordially—

Ned Rorem

## To Edward Albee

*10 July 98*

Dear Ralph—[NR's camp name for him in the 1950s]

Thanks for having had sent the play about the baby, which I read with interest. Not least in the interest is how with a playwright (or any prose writer), but not with a composer, one can trace a biographical thread throughout his life. Yes, a composer can be all of a piece and create high-class works in youth as in age—viz. Ravel or Chopin—or be unequal, or have "periods," like Stravinsky or Copland or Beethoven. But we don't know his secret anxieties as we do with, well, you. As with your plays of forty years ago, the new one remains obsessed with your origins, and with questions of identity that will never be answered.

Other reactions will remain mute until next we meet. Meanwhile, do use the *second* ending: it should be wistfully horrific in the best theatrical sense.

Love

Scarlet [his camp name for NR in the '50s]

(I use only one T in my name now, as befits the simplicity of age.)

## To Gunther Schuller

*Nantucket*

*10 July 98*

Dear Gunther—

What a nice idea—to have sent me your book. . . . Did I ever write you about the previous book, *Musings,* about which I had strong reactions? Anyway, I've only just leafed through the new one, and find it very much you. . . . When I've finished, I'll write you again. Meanwhile:

I'm one of the few composers in the world who is not a closeted conductor. I have directed my own works from time to time, but it was agony, and I never got the bug. Nor have I an exact conviction as to the tempo of anything I've composed. It depends on the time of day, how old the piece is, how old *I* am, who's conducting, and especially the venue. What sounds right in this reverberating hall sounds wrong in that dry hall. (Fauré, when asked how fast a certain song should go, answered, "If the singer is bad, then very fast.") If you look at composer-conductors of our day, like, say, Stravinsky or Copland, their tempi vary with the years. And have you ever heard the tapes of Debussy and Ravel playing their own pieces? They're like 19th-century pianists trapped in 20th-century composers' bodies. Debussy plays *freely,* like Chopin, but sloppily. Ravel ruins the icy exactitude of his *Sonatine* by always anticipating the right hand with the left hand, Paderewsky-style. And Messiaen! what's on the page and what emerges under his fingers are sometimes quite unrelated.

How flexible are you vis-à-vis organ music? Surely the massive instrument of Notre Dame versus the modest ones of a Midwestern church impose different attitudes. Or singers? Surely a baritone singing the same song as a soprano, is allowed latitude in speed, even in the same key, because his voice possesses fewer (or is it more) overtones.

These words are not meant to be scolding; they mean to say that there are as many "right" ways of singing a song as there are good singers. I'm thrilled that you, a colleague in this ever-more vulgar world, are still concerned by crucial values while others are mostly singing in the wilderness. . . .

Love

Ned

To Judy Collins

*Nantucket*

*10 July 98*

Dearest Judy—

Late last month Jim & I drove (drove!!) to Denver where we stayed five days at the Marriott for the American Guild of Organists Convention at which I was a shining star. Your picture was in the hotel *TV Guide*, but alas, the ET station was unavailable. So we drove back to New York where the galleys of your new book awaited. I read about Denver therein, and sent a blurb to your editor. The memoir, though long, *works*—and that's saying plenty. The binding force is, of course, excruciating, but there are other forces too, and unique characters, starting with your father. We'll talk more about it soon I hope.

Because you'll be here on the 11th of August, will Louis be with you? Can you come to lunch, both of you, that day? Or the next? It would be just us, or at most one other mortal. Let me know soon.

Love forever—

Ned

To James Hamilton-Paterson

*New York*

*9 Sept. 98*

Caro Amico—

Tomorrow I begin teaching at Yale, as visiting Professor of Composition, for the coming scholastic year. Which means I'll go there (New Haven's a bit less than two hours from New York) in a car they'll send, stay overnight, see six private students, and conduct a seminar. On alternate weeks they'll come to New York, where I'll give them quiche and apples. Twelve times a semester. I'm doing it for the money, and am already sick from exhaustion, plus terrible incurable insomnia. Meanwhile, Jim Holmes commutes between NY and Nantucket, and he works awfully hard, but is not doing well physically. Life is pictured as through a scrim: everything seems dark and sad—the lampshade even, the trees, the birds at night, the indescribable heat, which, thank god, seems to be over now. Have you ever taught? Do you even believe in it? I don't especially.

Yesterday I mailed you a small book called *Settling the Score*, strictly on music, from ten years ago. (I can no longer get a book published, so philistine has America become.) Also a CD of the Fourth Quartet. But you may already be gone from Italy, and not back until the end of the year.

In six weeks I'll turn 75. The only good thing about that is various celebratory musical performances, here & there, including the new Double Concerto in Scotland as a premiere. But Jim's well-being is all that counts for me, and melancholy imbues the globe.

. . . You mention Orton in Tangier. A few years ago I reviewed his *Diary* for a gay mag in California. His rough-and-tumble style rather appealed to me, who am an effete snob, but who knows what he was like in person. How did you find him?

Then a year ago a small expensive press in Vermont published an expensive book called *Dear Paul Dear Ned,* letters between Bowles and me beginning in 1949. Maybe for your birthday I'll send a copy.

What a lousy narcissistic letter. I feel unfocused, but also the need, on this dark evening, to talk. Where are you, then, for the next four months? Time is flying.

Forever

Ned

Andrew Porter, a marvelous music critic, lives nearby to you 4 weeks out of the year. He's a friend of Muriel Spark, about 71, and smart.

To Lou Harrison

*First day of fall 1998*

Very dearest Lou—

Yesterday I bought *Composing a World* at the Juilliard bookstore, which displays a great stack of copies, and have only just dipped into it, mainly the lascivious sections. What do you think? It seems a great honor, and well laid out. Also, thorough in its way—though the attached CD will probably speak much louder than words. Congratulations—and will you extend those to the authors?

Meanwhile, the chapter on gaiety seems touristy and specious. Perhaps it's because I've never suffered from it (as apparently you did). Phrases like "Is it likely that such a powerful element as sexuality (especially when one's sexuality is outside the mainstream) would be irrelevant to one's life work," seem simple minded. I feel much more "outside the mainstream" as a composer in this vulgar world, than as a gay person. (And most gay persons today are part of that vulgar world.) Well, anyway, I'll be 75 in three weeks, and the only nice thing about that is having performances. . . .

Jim is not entirely well, and his condition will last forever; but I pray he'll outlive me. He's in Nantucket as I pen these verbs (I'm in New York), and will pick me up at Yale, where I'm now teaching for the money, on his way back here. . . . He'd send his love too if he knew I were writing. . . . And I send mine to Bill.

Always
Ned


## To André Previn

*11 October 98*

Dear André—

First of all, congratulations on *Streetcar.* I've read about it everywhere, and the shreds of the music that were broadcast recently sounded apt and felt. We're all looking forward to the TV rendition. . . . In 1958, and again in 1962, I wrote the scores for two of Tennessee's plays—*Suddenly Last Summer* and *The Milk Train.* Which means I saw him every day for weeks, during rehearsals. Never—not once—did he utter an intelligent remark about the music (except "make it softer"), nor did he know or care anything about any music, except for corrida fanfares and Glenn Miller. What he may have thought of your version, or indeed Lee Hoiby's *Summer & Smoke,* is finally irrelevant . . .

Looking forward to our "conversation" at the YMHA next April.
Always
Ned


## To Cynthia Ozick

*12 October 98*

Dear Cynthia—

While talking to my dear old friend Ellen Adler, I mentioned that in your vivid story called "Actors" you had a character evoke her grandfather, Jacob Adler. And Ellen said, "You know, Stella (her mother), who never spoke of anyone but herself, during her last years would grow teary-eyed at the mention of Cynthia Ozick, and gave Ozick's books away as gifts to friends and students."

We'll meet soon again.

Always

Ned

## To Eugene Istomin

*15 Nov 98*

Dear Eugene—

I can't tell you how moved I was by your call from Paris yesterday.

It's a melancholy time for me these months, and I feel very close to your nostalgia, as you—as we *all*—dip into a never-to-be-retrieved past, yet a past which paradoxically is always present.

Je t'aime

Ned

## To Judy Collins

*Christmas Eve 98*

Judy, Louis—

Until the last moment I'd planned to come to your party last night.

Then Jim had to go again to Emergency NYU hospital

Very sad.

I love you.

N.

## To Reynolds Price

*18 January 99*

Dearest Reynolds—

Jim died ten days ago in the very early morning, after a long and painful agony. Nothing seems to mean much anymore.

He took comfort from your books, and example, and friendship, as do I.

I wanted you to know.

Love—

Ned

### To James Purdy

*1 Feb. 99*

Very dear James—

Jim Holmes died three weeks ago.

Nothing seems very important anymore.

But an all-Rorem program had been planned for the 92nd Street "Y" a year ago. I'd like it to be a sort of memorial for Jim . . . who liked and admired you, as do I.

If you might come, let me know.

Always

Ned


### To James Lord

*7 Feb. 99*

Dearest James—

Your phone call was much appreciated. I'm still in a mournful limbo, which will probably last forever. But a touch of light flickers over there, far off, and maybe I'll sell the house in Nantucket, and try to write an angry song-cycle.

Anyway, you perhaps know I'm "teaching" at Yale as visiting professor for this scholastic year. Vincent Giroud, of Beinecke Library, for whom I spoke on Poulenc last week, speaks warmly of you. At the noisy supper afterward, there was a great deal of talk about Francis de Croissay (whose real name, it seems, was something else). All this came as a surprise to me. Marie-Laure's half-brother is the only Croissay I know of. Please explain the lineage.

I'll never come to Paris again. But maybe I will.

Always

Ned


### To Judy Collins

*7 II 99*

Dearest of all Judies—

How can I say what a help your visit was yesterday. Not only the cornucopia of comestibles, but your optimistic and intelligent conversation. The egotism of grief has made me closed off these days, and I later felt I didn't sympathize enough with your acupuncture problems. Please know that I always love you.

Do send those texts we spoke of; I very much need them, at least for consideration, in the big cycle I'm planning.

See you on the 18th at the 92nd Street Y. I'll leave *four* tickets (not two) at the box office in your name.

Love forever to Louis—

Always

Ned

### To James Hamilton-Paterson

*7 Feb. 99*

Very dear James—

How pleasant to get your letter; too much time in silence is dangerous. But I can't answer it now.

Jim Holmes died on January 7th. It was a long and terrible siege, in & out of the hospital, pain and anxiety, though at least he died at home. He was only 59, and we had lived together for almost 32 years.

Nothing seems to matter anymore, not even Great Art. I'll never be the same, time heals, etc. (nothing but clichés come to mind). Friends are urgent —yet even they seem undifferentiated.

Please understand.

I do want, eventually, to compose a wide song-cycle, perhaps 25 songs on different authors, about anger and resignation. If you have any sugges-tions, verse or prose, let me know.

Love always,

Ned

### To James Hamilton-Paterson

*12 March 99*

Dear dear friend—

Thanks for the three books, which in fact arrived around the same time as your letter a few weeks ago. Since Jim has disappeared (but has he? has he?) I find concentration difficult, though I managed to read the last three "stories" in *The Music*—the ones I'd not read when I gave my copy, years ago, to Wm. Maxwell, who never returned it—and found them masterful and flawless and original and very "musical." I've only dipped into the

Marcos volume, likewise *Three Miles Down,* but will finish them in due course. I still push your writing to everyone, adding that there's not a word out of place. (Oddly, however, you repeat the adverb "this"—is it an adverb? —sixteen times between pages 18–21 of *Three Miles.*)

I do think about sex, however, obsessively, not having had any, at least with another mortal, for years. I dream of burying my face in the steaming crotch of some virile seafarer; I even examined with a magnifying glass the small photo of your legs facing page 121. Do people mail letters like this? I'm not myself . . . nor will I ever be again, feeling more like a pre-adolescent than a septuagenarian. . . . Thanks for the suggestion of the Hardy poetry. Indeed, twelve years ago I did set "The Darkling Thrush"; now, thanks to you, I probably will use one of those 1912 "mourning" poems, if I can find one that's not, as we say, gender specific.

Dear James, how are you? Do *you* have a love life? What do you think about with your organized brain? Maybe I'll go back to Morocco (where I lived for two years 1949–52) at the end of May. Why don't you come too? But no, we mustn't meet. . . . I'm pulling myself together, and value our correspondence.

Please understand—the disarray of this note. I still weep, but less than ten weeks ago, and grasp very little about the sense of dying.

Always
Ned

## To David Diamond

*25 March 99*

Dearest David—

Your "Elegy" for Jim is beautiful and moving, and I shall tell him so tonight, when I whisper into his ashes which are in a jar beside my bed.

Love
Ned

## To André Previn

*26 March 99*

Very dear André

What great news: that you will revive the Third Symphony. It's an effective piece, you're a great conductor, and that combination was brewed in heaven.

(My "life-partner," Jim Holmes, after 32 years together, died in January. Your letter is the first indication of a light at the top of the stairs.)

On the afternoon of April 25th, as you know, we're supposed to talk together intelligently at the Y, prior to (or, if you prefer, during) your concert of chamber music.

Probably we should get together beforehand, at least to plot the course. Or would you prefer to play it by ear?

Always—

Ned

## To Stephen Sondheim

*1 April 99*

Dear Steve—

The YMHA has asked if I would continue next season doing what I've done this season: hosting living composers, by talking and presenting their works. In December it was Corigliano, in February it was me (you were there), and this month on the 25th it will be Previn.

For 1999–2000 we're planning three programs: (1) string quartets by Foss, Rochberg, Laderman, and Perle; (2) song cycles by youngish composers of America; and (3) you, if you'd be interested.

Would you, in fact, want to talk with me, before an audience, about what you've surely talked about a million times before: the difference between a "musical" and an opera, how to write a song, which comes first, etc.? And would it be possible to present, with a few singers and piano (or maybe a few instruments) a program of your songs?

We could either do a whole program of you, or possibly a shared program with Marc Blitzstein.

I hope you'll say yes, and that you'll let us know soon.

Forever—

Ned

## For the Academy
## On Julian Green

*13 April 1999*

Artists are always being questioned about their influences. They know the answer, of course, since nothing comes from nothing. But they hesitate. After all, they've made a career covering their tracks: indeed, the act of covering tracks is the very act of creation. What I shall now reveal, therefore, is something of an admission.

The news of Julian Green's death at 98 reached me last July, just prior to performance in Nantucket of a song by me on words by him. Fifty years earlier, when living in Morocco, I had read my first work of Green, a novel called *Moira,* and was stunned—like meeting my double in a trance. Narrated in compact Gallic language, the story treated an American disorder: sexual guilt of, and murder by, a horny inarticulate red-haired youth in a Southern university. New world Puritan frustration via the mother tongue of Mallarmé. Green spoke American in French, the reverse of, say, Janet Flanner who spoke French in American. We had an exchange of letters, and when I returned to Paris that fall we met. The meeting quickly veered toward a violent intimacy which lasted about ten months, during which I saw Paris through his eyes and the world through his pages.

Green's first novel, *Mont-Cinère,* came out in 1926 and changed the tone of French literature. The subject was family greed in our southern United States, the language was lean and somber. Similar juxtapositions occurred in this American's twenty-odd fictions over a period of sixty years, all but one composed in French. In 1951, when we met, he had also become, along with Gide, Europe's principal master of the diary, a format which, if no more "true" or "confessional" than novels or autobiography, is by its nature more immediate. So I took up my own diary again, influenced, in manner if not in matter, by his. By extension the influence must have touched my music too, though no one can explain quite how, at least not in words (for if the arts could express each other, we'd only need one art). In this same year was republished a brief memoir called *L'Autre sommeil.* Green was in his twenties when it first appeared, but it speaks of his own death with a sadness that seemed . . . well . . . musical. I translated and made songs from three paragraphs. This is the music sung again last summer.

Green eventually wrote several modestly successful plays, one of which, *Sud,* was turned into an opera by Kenton Coe. In 1979 he was the first person of American parentage to be elected to the Académie Française.

Julian Green was not a Thinker, much less a philosopher. If he had a riveting gift for plot, even in such an open-ended structure as the diary, the gift came as a stream of consciousness. "If I have anything to say," he wrote, "I'm hardly aware of it. If I do bring a message, then I'm like a messenger who is unable to read and whose message is incomprehensible to himself;

or rather, like a stenographer who cannot reread his work because he only knows how to write."

But he *was*, in a sense, a messenger. Like many a holy convert he was more Catholic than the pope, his prose is permeated with a sort of hopeless hope that the world will be saved. Those perpetual obsessions with sin and the true way, with prayer and dream, with shop talk (Jesus talk) among clerical friends! If in his *Journal* Julian Green continues, through his specific belief in God, to miss more general points at every corner, in his fiction this very "miss" provides the Julianesque tonality, the singular Greenery. Surely if one-track-mindedness empties the spirit of humor, it does fill the mind with an explosive physicality which remains the *sine qua non* of all large souls. (Humor is not physical but intellectual, and multiple-track-minded.)

Such skepticism was apparent to Julian who deplored my atheism, promiscuity, and what he termed "dangerous frequentations," not to mention an age difference of 25 years. He gave me his books, photographs, insight into a rarefied milieu, a plaster cast of Chopin's hand (which, to his horror, I used as a bookend), and, above all, confidences about his closeted yearning requited by his tactile love for a statue of Apollo. His stifled emotions, the very grist of his early novels, grew less repressed in the later years. "I don't care what anyone writes about me when I'm gone," he often said. And he often said too—quoting Pascal quoting God—"You wouldn't seek me if you hadn't already found me."

Which brings us back to influence. Is it cause or effect? Are we drawn to a work because of what we glimpse of ourselves already there, or do we discover only what we bring? Was my personal feeling—which was less than love and more than love—for Julian the man impelled by the unbearably wistful expertise of Julian the artist? Or was the unbearable wistfulness already in me, minus the expertise?

Today the expanse of time since first we met seems slight, yet surely I have at least a musical voice that has nothing to do with Julian Green. Though by another turn of the screw, I wouldn't be me if it weren't for him.

### To Judy Collins

*2 May 99*

Dearest Judy—

You'll understand when I explain that I'm still not up to big parties. I loved seeing you, and Louis, and the one or two others I knew, but couldn't keep it up. So Susan Crile and her friend and I snuck off and had coffee at the corner.

The piece called "Sixty Notes for Judy" is very soft (it would have been lost in performance perhaps). Each note lasts a second, so your whole life is encapsulated in a single minute. While playing it for myself yesterday the music seemed suddenly sad: with each second, a year vanishes forever, and then the whole piece fades away after the final notes.

Well, anyway, let's hope you have at least sixty more notes in you.

Both Ann Thorne and Gloria Vanderbilt send you fond birthday greetings.

Love now and forever—
Ned

### To James Hamilton-Paterson

*3 May 99*

Very dear James—

First, a vignette, with sociological symmetry, though not much point:

Thirty-five years ago, a Boston friend phoned to say he was in New York, and had just been picked up by a rough Italian, but it didn't work out: the Italian preferred other manners. So my friend gave him my name, and the Italian—Tony Lombardi—called. We hit it off, my body filled with his pungent maleness (etc.), and the "affair" lasted about two weeks. But he was boring, as well as sexy. I like to be the wife in bed, but the husband at table *(Le bourreau au salon et la victime au lit)*. So we drifted apart, since he couldn't take my domineering passivity.

Flash forward to a month ago. My old and dear friend, Gloria Vanderbilt, invited me to a dinner party for Nancy Reagan. I agreed, mainly so I could talk about it later, for I decry Mrs. Reagan much as you must Mrs. Marcos. As for what we—who have nothing in common—might talk about, I wasn't sure. But Gloria, who said I was to be at the head of the table, with N.R. (same initials as mine) at my right, assured me that she could make conversation.... I was the last to arrive. The doorman asked my name, then showed me the elevator, and presumably announced my arrival by intercom. At the door I was greeted by a liveried servant who murmured, "Mr. Rorem, I presume. Remember me? Tony Lombardi." Tony was one of four male servants who, during the evening, would pass drinks, soup, ice cream. Thus, as I conversed with Nancy about movies of yore, Tony would ladle out a meal. . . . I was the first to leave. We made a whispered date, but it didn't work out. (As for Nancy, more later, but she's perfectly presentable, if limited literarily.)

This kind of Proustian encounter—Charlus & Jupien—hardly fills a void. Mostly I feel suicidal, and grasp for straws. But what straws? I look good, at 5 feet ten, 170 pounds, but am 906 months old. If I take after my parents, there may be twenty years left. To do what in?

. . . Jim died of AIDS-related liver dysfunction, a long and painful affair. We didn't tell anyone, but now it makes little difference. I'm HIV negative. And lonely—although I know "everyone." I feel the need for young people around, as much for emergencies as for company. My niece, for example, is perfect. She and I and my sister Rosemary, a couple of friends, buried his ashes in the garden of Nantucket a month ago, and planted poppy seeds thereon. As to what I'll do with the Nantucket property, which was so much his invention, I'm not sure. It's a real distance from New York, and I don't drive.

Do you drive? Don't you think that, after all, we should meet? Would we be disconcerted by, for instance, our various accents? or by our physicalities? But we're not stupid? Look up Nantucket on your map, and decide whether you'd want to visit there for maybe a week this summer. . . .

What a dull, self-centered letter. But I don't keep a diary any longer, and even when I did I seldom discussed sex—mainly because (at 17 and 37 and even 57) I *did* it instead. . . .

I love you . . .
Ned

### To André Previn

*4 May 99*

Dear André—

Thanks for the CD of *Streetcar*.

It's really an awfully good piece. Littell has done wonders in both paring and making singable the original play, without really sacrificing the tone of Tennessee. Fleming is extraordinary, in both beauty and diction. And the orchestra is, in a way, the star, in both highlighting and sometimes upstaging the actors, and in being so complex without being fussy or obliterating.

As for the music, I cried at the end. Partly because when it was televised a few months ago, it was the last thing that my dear friend and partner of 32

years, Jim Holmes, saw and heard. (He died on January 7.) And partly because it is often truly beautiful. A highlight for me is "He was a boy . . .", for
the poignance, and for the French folklike nudging of the high strings. . . .

Meanwhile, I'll tell Claire Bloom, whom I'm seeing on Thursday, about
the high compliments you pay her in the program notes.

Warmly forever—

Ned


## To Edward Albee

*4 May 99*

Dear Edward—

A Mr. Joe McPhillips, who seems to run an English school in Tangier,
phoned me from that city this morning. He wanted my permission to use
the first and last movements of my 12-movement quintet, *Winter Pages,* to
open and close his upcoming production of *The Zoo Story,* to be acted by a
pair of young anglophile Moroccans. . . . So you and I are finally to be joined
in artistic wedlock.

. . . Simon & Schuster sent me galleys of the [Mel] Gussow book [a
biography of Albee] which seems readable and thorough. What's your
reaction? Of course, there are as many legitimate biographies as there are
biographers: everything is Rashomon.

I wish we met oftener. Do you want to write an opera?

Forever—

Ned


## To Edmund White

*7 May 99*

Dear Edmund and Michael—

. . . We were pleased to be with you last night, Claire [Bloom] and I, and
thought the meal, as well as the guests, were super. I try to keep, as the saying goes, busy; then slump back into mild depression when alone. Now I'm
off to Philadelphia and my sister for two days, and will give the commencement address at Curtis (identical to the one I gave there in 1982—because
nothing's changed since then). Then back to NY, and Nantucket off & on
for the summer. Will you come for a visit?

Love

Ned

## To Angela Lansbury

*26 May 99*

Very dear Angela—

Did I ever acknowledge your good note about Jim last January? It meant a lot to me. The world seems numb since then, even futile. But I have work to do (another book, another piece of music) and will continue.

John Kander lives next door for the past thirty years. Last night he told me about *The Visit,* and said you are the most professional, as well as the most civilized and nicest, actor he's ever known. He's right. (I saw Lunt and Fontanne in *The Visit* 41 years ago—a rather softened translation, but still powerful, and thought of making an opera. You're ideal for the role.)

When you're in New York (or even perhaps Nantucket this summer) please call.

Love, now and always, to Peter, and to Dierdre.

Ned

## To Edmund White

*24 June 99*

Fond Edmund

Called several times but no answer. Just wanted to say hello. And goodbye. For the next many weeks I'll be in Nantucket. Hate to lose contact as the years wane.

Have been reading both [David] Leavitt *(Arkansas)* and [Michael] Cunningham *(A Home at the End of the World).* What are we supposed to make of them? Leavitt has originality and chutzpah and sometimes is quite moving, with a good ear for conversation. Cunningham's "fine writing" does pall, and he does go on about pop music; but he too has an ear, and I suppose he "says" something.

Are you, I hope, saying something? I'm sterile for the moment. Nothing seems to make much difference.

. . . Love to you always, and always to Michael also . . .

Ned

## To André Previn

Fond André—

Here as requested, a little essay on Boulez from twenty years ago.

The master once declared, "Any composer today who has not felt the necessity of the serial process, is dispensable." To which I add: Omit the word "not," and I agree.

But the serial killers are less of a threat than they used to be.

Always

Ned

## To Edward Albee

Dear Edward—

. . . I saw the two *Times* reviews of Gussow's book. The Sunday one was empty, but the daily one seemed well-taken and informative. It's quite a good—or at least useful—biography.

Jack Mitchell invited me to be on the committee for the Atlantic Center for the Arts, and I accepted, on the condition that I not go to Florida. Traveling, traveling anywhere, is daunting now.

By any chance have you kept the wild tapes you made in the early fifties, interviewing me & Bill about our indiscretions, with your very sober voice at four in the morning, and us giggling and seamy? I'd love to rehear them.

I'm more or less back from Nantucket now. Maybe we should see each other before too long.

Forever—

Ned

## To James Hamilton-Paterson

Dear James—

I don't blame you for not responding to my pretentious letter of six months ago. But Time's winged chariot swoops near, and I hate to lose track.

It's possible I'll be in Italy in May or June. Will you be there?

Always

Ned

## To James Hamilton-Paterson

*2 December 99*

Caro Amico—

Yesterday I asked Boosey & Hawkes to mail you a CD and publication (beautifully reproduced, for this day and age) of my huge new cycle for four singers and piano, called *Evidence of Things Not Seen*. It lasts ninety minutes. If ever you decide to listen, will you promise to follow with the texts? For whatever the music may be worth, I flatter myself that the juxtaposition of unlikely prose & poetry is rare and workable. Your opinion means much....

Since Jim died, eleven months ago, I've been in a state of insomniac depletion, cranky and old, but am trying (sort of) to think that life has some value, some meaning.

Probably I'll come to France next July, to "teach" at the Schola Cantorum for a bit. It's been seventeen years since.... I'd planned to go to Tangier, but now that Paul Bowles has vanished ... etc....

I still have three of your books to vanquish, and look forward finally to doing so, now that concentration is returning.

Dear James, keep me regularly in touch. Who knows where this will find you—in Italy, or the Philippines, or under the ocean perhaps nearby.

Always

Ned

# Part Six

# 2000 to 2004

## To James Lord

Fond friend—

What are we to make of John Richardson's new book on Douglas [Cooper] (whom I always liked)? His previous books on Picasso were admirable, but this one seemed . . . niggardly. Send me his address if you know it; I did enjoy certain pages because, like you, I knew so many of the minor players. . . .

When I think of Dora [Maar]'s beautiful portrait of me—which Claude Lebon left in a taxi, never to be retrieved—my breath stops.

. . . You won't believe it, but I've been elected *President* of the American Academy of Arts & Letters. And I accepted the 3-year term (no salary), still thinking of my self as a tipsy 20-year-old.

The world seems pointless since Jim died, just one year ago. Nothing will ever be the same.

Except you.

Love

Ned

## To James Hamilton-Paterson

*22 Jan. 2000*

Dear James—

Your welcome letter suggested that the score of *Evidence* was not accompanied by a recording. So I've asked Boosey & Hawkes to send you the CD.

The enclosed picture is how I look today, at 76, grizzled and resigned. The young lady is Susan Graham, a marvelous mezzo who's just recorded 32 of my songs, as well as *Rosenkavalier* (Octavian), and yes, I love Strauss at his Gallic best. Such an odd combination of bourgeois innocence and Greek-style evil.

I've just been elected *President* of the American Academy of Arts & Letters!! When Louis Auchincloss asked if I'd accept the nomination I thought he was kidding. It's the job for a responsible adult, while I'm still a child. But then, every artist is half-child, half-grown-up, and when the grown-up takes over he stops being an artist. So maybe I'm as qualified as any of the other 250 child-members. (Maybe this will help in your becoming an honorary foreign member.)

Work well on the new novel. That's all there is.

Ned

## To Edmund White

*8 Feb. 2000*

My own beloved Edmund—

Your introduction [to NR's new diary, *Lies*] brought tears to my eyes. Not just because of the occasions it revived, but also it didn't sound dutiful. I'm very, very honored. In today's Science pages of the *Times* it is proved that, yes, we *are* alone in the universe. In which case I'm glad that you and I are on this earth at the same time. . . .

Tell Michael we look forward to him in Nantucket from 19 to 23. Couldn't you come too? Remember JH's memorial on April 13. . . . It will be amateurish and familial.

Je t'aime

Ned

## To Lou Harrison

*6 March 2000*

Dearest Lou—

My heart and soul are with you now and forever.

Infinite sympathies from your old friend

Ned

## To James Hamilton-Paterson

*11 March 00*

Fond James—

Thanks for the *Granta* of many weeks ago. Your récit recalled Isabel Eberstat's French writings about North Africa a hundred and forty years ago. Do you know her (unique) catalogue? Your piece was skillful and compelling as usual. In the same issue was a little memoir, by Keith Fleming, of Edmund White. Have you any feelings for White? He wrote the intro to my new Diary, *Lies,* which will be published by Counterpoint next fall. You're in it. I think. And have you any feelings for Coetzee? His hopeless South African resignation I find seductive.

... I'm not going to Paris in July after all. I reneged on the contract—can't face the travel, hotel rooms, students who take and take, and the nausea of nostalgia. Because I'm still having a sort of mild breakdown, a depression, from which nothing looks attractive, even work. Plus insomnia which is nearly violent.

Affection forever

Ned

FOR JUDY COLLINS

AN APPRECIATION

DELIVERED AT THE PLAYERS CLUB

*16 Gramercy Park*

*2 April 2000*

Her initials are those of Joan Crawford, John Cheever, and Jesus Christ, combining glamour, intellect, and a high moral tone. Such is Judy Collins, who claims the added gift of instant likeability.

We had never met when, at a party for a mutual friend, I rang her bell. She opened the door, gave me a long look from out those violet eyes, then covered me with kisses. That was 100 seasons ago.

In the intervening years the spontaneity has never stopped even when we're miles apart. Because, corny though it sounds, we continually share. I gave her the first taste of an anonymous but powerful group which has saved many a body and soul; also a wreath of songs which she sings from time to time. She gave me the sound of her voice made of—of what?—of unalloyed silver.

So I greet you tonight, dear Judy, on the verge of this crucial milestone, with affection, admiration, and a waterfall of arpeggios.

I love you.

Ned

TO JAMES HAMILTON-PATERSON

*22 IV 00*

Very dear—

A brief note, because I'm still weary and sad, and because I'm trapped in the city. Yesterday there were no flights to Nantucket because of bad weather which continues. Maybe tomorrow.

Ten years ago I had an operation for the prostate (two operations, actually) called a TURP, or transurethral prostectomy. The reason was years of NSU, then urinary difficulties. In retrospect it may have been caused by hysteria. Anyway, the prostate was non-malignant, and half-removed. Result, ejaculations, which are the same as ever, go into the bladder and are excreted through the urine.

You are not alone. Everyone I know seems to have problems down there. Any responsible urologist says that one or two orgasms a week are de rigueur. You do have my sympathies. But avoid too much medical solutions.

Not reading. Just Rupert Thompson's well-penned but specious *Book of Revelation*. And not composing. No commissions. But Susan Graham's new CD of 32 of my songs is very pretty. Can you get it?

Forgive this letter. I want to stay in touch, even if boringly.

Forever

Ned

## To James Lord

*Nantucket*

*17 July* 00

Swarthy James of the cranberry triceps —

It's been 31 years since I received your cable about Marie-Laure's death. Who now, besides us, knew her then? Marcel Schneider? Tony Pawson (is he still around)? Tell Bernard that if he really plans a biography, I'd be glad to help.

Ed White's book has been very well received. He wrote a long preface to *my* new book, *Lies*, due in November. Meanwhile, I'm composing a solid cycle for baritone, as a sort of angry epitaph for Jim Holmes.

Love affairs and endless life are past illusions.

I miss you. Send *any* news.

Ned

## To James Hamilton-Paterson

*Yaddo*

*15 August* 00

O Fond James —

Your call to Nantucket a few weeks ago caught me, so to speak, with my hair uncombed. I was depressed (still am) and unprepared. But you sounded great, and as you should. Since then I've come here for the month. It's an "artists' colony" where, at peak periods, 35 artists of various persuasions reside and work intensely, well-fed and well-lodged, each with his own studio. I am the oldest (forty years ago, when I first came here, I was the youngest), and everyone's respectful, though I still feel myself to be sixteen. Am finishing a group of twenty-one angry songs to be called, probably, *Another Sleep,* after one of the texts by Julian Green. Others are by Milton and Sappho, Thom Gunn and Ashbery, Borges and Cavafy. Etc. . . .

A new book, *Lies,* comes out in November, when I'll send you a copy. (In the index, corrected yesterday, are listed eight entries for you.) Meanwhile, I go to New York to get classes started on September 1, then Nantucket again, if all goes well. My niece, Mary, usually drives me back and forth in a rented car.

I think of you daily, despite this self-involved letter.

Forever

Ned

## To Jack Larson

*Sunday*
*1 Oct. 00*

Fond Jack—

Here's a little write-up from a gay rag in Boston. Tony Tommasini says there've been *many* write-ups (where?) and that *his* will appear "soon" (when?).

Am reading Gavin's book, which is original and vaguely disturbing.

I still don't feel especially alive. Not depressed so much as pointless.

But think of you every day.

Love

Ned

## For Eugene Istomin,
### Spoken at Isaac Stern's Birthday Party

*Nov. 26, 2000*

I'm not a great pianist, but I *am* a good mimic. When people say, "Ned, how well you play!" I answer: "I can't really play at all, I'm just doing an imitation of Eugene Istomin."

The imitation began 57 years ago when, as a student composer at Curtis, I roomed just above Gessel's Florist Shop, and just below the Istomin family. During those months of 1943, I absorbed through the ceiling every nuance of Eugene's *Waldstein* and his Brahms B-Flat. The French repertory would come later. He also claimed to have been no less influenced by, say, Serkin, than by Heifetz; Eugene longed to produce on a keyboard the nuanced portamento of a violin. Similarly, still today, when I write a song, be it on the poetry of Ashbery or the prose of Freud, the vocal line is always nudged less by the manner of another composer than by childhood pop singers like, say, Billie Holiday or, who knows, even Eugene's own mother, Feera, who so beautifully sang Russian folk tunes to her son's able accompaniment.

Two of the songs from back then will be performed now by soprano Laquitta Mitchell. They represent a tale of two cities. "The Lordly Hudson," on verses of Paul Goodman (whom we all knew and loved) is an enthusiasm for our native Manhattan. Eugene used to play it with the amateur crooner John Myers. "Early in the Morning," on a poem of Robert Hillyer, is about being young, and in love, and in Paris, composed when I was in Paris, young, and in love.

### To James Hamilton-Paterson

*7 Jan. 2001*

Dearest James—

Not having heard from you for some months, should I fear you did not receive *Lies*? In which case another copy will be sent soon.

I've been feeling lousy: *shingles!* plus depression, and what's known over here as "stress." Yet for the past ten weeks I've been having what's known over here as an "affair"—the first in 30 years. He's half my age and twice my size. Details later. Maybe.

Snow. Snow. Very cold.

Am writing a quartet called *Episodes* for Clarinet, Piano, Violin, Cello. 8 movements.

Thinking of going to Paris for 2 weeks in late May, scared as I am of travel and insomnia.

Too weary to write more than a Happy New Year. But will you write to me?

Love
Ned

## To James Hamilton-Paterson

*6 Feb. 01*

Oh James—

What a hideous embarrassment—to have consistently misspelled your name! We *are* our names; to have them altered is an insult to our identities. And what a stupid irony—that I misspelled yours in the midst of praise. Well, it's Paterson, like William Carlos Williams's book. (Have I just misspelled mispelled?) What does the hyphenated double name mean? To American ears it's quite British.

Thanks for your touching and as-always precious letter. This answer will be short, because I'm tired, an increasingly chronic state. . . . I'll be anxious to hear about Siberia. How long will you have been there before you write me again?

Edmund White, whom I saw last night, would be pleased to get your new book. He teaches at Princeton these days, but lives with a newish lover in New York. . . .

I too have a new lover, since 4 months ago. He's 39, six-feet-five-inches tall, and is a political social worker and publicist for liberal causes. How long will it last? When he's my age I'll be 114 years old. The sex is almost inebriating, since I've been without it so long. Should I describe it?

That the book *Lies* should have so affected you means everything. It's been reviewed here and there, but not in the *NY Times*. Is it because the music critic, Tony Tommasini, threatened to sue, because of an inadvertent pair of references in the index? The indexer, whom I never met, decided that every reference to "Tony" was to Tommasini, who's a music critic on the *Times*. So the book was recalled—8000 copies!—for correction, which killed the inertia. I'll probably never write prose again. But I'm trying to finish a Quartet (2 strings, piano, clarinet) before starting a Flute Concerto.

Oh James.

More soon.

Love

Ned

## To Judy Collins

*6 March 01*

Dearest Judy—

It was a pleasure to dine with you both last week and Jim Gavin was thrilled.

Forgot to say that the little piece I wrote for your birthday, 2 years ago, "Sixty Notes for Judy," I've arranged for Oboe and Piano. As such it's included in a new suite of Nine Pieces (for Oboe & Piano) and has already been played several times. . . . So you're again immortalized, this time through the nasal whine of a woodwind.

Complete love to Louis

Ned

### To James Hamilton-Paterson

*2 April 01*

Very dear James—

My heart is with you—for the physical and mental anxieties of these past weeks. Your gall bladder. Your mother. . . . Nothing will ever be the same. . . . Now you're in Italy, and may have found my last letter. . . . Thanks for the program. As it happens, I recently finished a big cycle, *Another Sleep* (did I already tell you?). . . .

Insomnia continues to plague. On 22 May, my friend Mark and I will fly to London for five days, thence to France where I've not set foot for 18 years. Everyone there now is dead. Might you be there?

Edmund White says he's more than pleased with the galleys of your new book. We'll all be seeing each other tomorrow and he'll have more to say.

Forgive this plodding letter (I'm weary). But my thoughts of you are borne on wings of song.

Ned

### To James Lord

*18 April 01*

Oh James,

I loved your letter and the data about Marie-Laure's exhibition. Tried to reach you by phone. Left message.

My boyfriend (Mark Taylor) and I are going to London/Paris/London between May 22 and June 10th. Will you be there? Will anyone else? It's been eighteen years. . . .

We'll probably stay in a 2-week rental in the 4th or 7th arrondissement. I'll let you know soon. . . .

Your health is ever on my mind.
I love you, and love to Bernard.
Forever
Ned


### To James Hamilton-Paterson

*20 May 01*

Dear Friend—

Because your book only just arrived, and I leave tomorrow for London
& Paris, I can't really crack it until returning on June 11. But the epigraph
startled me. Did you know that Harold Brodkey was my lover for six difficult months in 1962? (See also references in *Lies*.)

I pray you're better, morally and physically. I'm continually weary, and
anxious, but trying to finish a little string quartet, and correcting proofs of
a "Reader" that comes out in the fall. And yes, in the fall, we'll meet. Tell me
exactly when.

I love you.
Ned


### To Claus von Bülow

*16 June 01*

Fond Claus—

It was an important pleasure to see you last Sunday—probably the last
person I'll ever see in London, since I'll never return. You looked and acted
great.

Don't worry about the photos, or about my "writings"; I won't make a
move without consulting you.

Thanks for *your* writings—and the mention of Balthus's funeral. (I just
reached the section on you in Fox Weber's biography!)

Stay always in touch.
Love
Ned

## To James Lord

*First day of summer*
*2001*

Fond James—

Ed White, Francine Gray, and I have conjointly nominated you for the Academy, with a good citation.

I loved seeing you in France, and looking so well.

Going to Nantucket now for most of the rest of the summer.

Am feeling sad.

I love you.

Ned

## To Claus von Bülow

*2 July 01*

Fond Claus—

Your phone call was "relayed" to me here. I won't be going back to New York (except briefly to get a colonoscopy) until September. I'd be eternally grateful if you could send *The World of Interiors* to me here in Nantucket.

Have you looked at Caroline Blackwood's biography?

Mark & I have broken up. Very sad. I'm 77 and lonely. But I'm supposed to be composing a Flute Concerto for the Philadelphia Orchestra. And an NR "Reader" comes out this fall.

Stay always in touch, dear Claus.

Love

Ned

## To Gore Vidal

*Nantucket*
*26 July 2001*

Fond Gore—

If I were to nominate your neighbor, James Hamilton-Paterson, for honorary foreign membership to the American Academy, would you second the nomination? (As a musician-member I'm allowed to nominate a literary type, provided I get two literary members to second the type—I'm thinking of Ed White or Francine Gray, besides you.) But maybe you're not interested in the workings of the Academy.

I do wish we could have one of our once-in-a-decade meetings, you &

I; the years are piling up. I went back to Paris last month, after eighteen years, and found it empty of memories, not to mention of culture, "creativity," or even language. I'll tell you why during our meeting. But when will that be? I've no intention of traveling ever again. Next week I'm off to Yaddo for a month, to force myself to compose a Flute Concerto. Then New York for a while, then back to Nantucket.

I admire everything you do, despite minor quibbles, and miss you too. Don't ever stop.

Will you give my very best to Howard?

Stay in touch always.

Always

Ned

### To James Hamilton-Paterson

*Nantucket*

*31 July 01*

Fond James—

Unlike politics, say, or friendship, strong works of art don't change us— don't make us "better people"; they make us more what we already are, they show us what we did not know we knew. If that's the case, then your new book, at its own pace, and with your almost perfect tongue, made me recognize myself anew. I especially like your asides on Love, and on Time. . . . I'm still not sure what you prefer to "do" in bed . . . but I do know that death haunts you as much as it does me. And if I divide the universe into two, and just two, categories, French and German, then you divide it between tea and coffee. I'm coffee, by the way, but seldom drink it anymore: insomnia is destroying me, along with diverticulitis and diverse diseases of the imagination. . . . I'm nominating you again for the Academy, using Gore Vidal (do you know him? He's your neighbor) and Ed White as seconds. . . . Tomorrow I'm off to Yaddo . . . where I'll try to get the Flute Concerto off the ground. Then back to the city around September 1st. . . . When are you coming to America? It wouldn't hurt for us to meet at last. I think of you with a kind of love.

Forever

Ned

To James Lord

Oh, fond James—

I think of you every day.

Ed W. and Michael were pleased to see you recently. . . . If ever you
return to Hyères, could you take some pictures for me? *Il ne reste que nous,
comme témoins*—and maybe Claus Bülow, whom Mark & I visited in
London. (I'm still broken by the break with Mark.)

Could Bernard send me any news, sad or happy, about Jean Leuvrais?

Next week, back in New York, where I'll await your visit.

Always

Ned

For Morris Golde's memorial

Sometimes I tell people that I've been married nine times, but never
divorced. If that's the case, my first spouse was Morris Golde. After one
passionate year our love-that-was-more-than-mere-friendship evolved
into a friendship-that-was-more-than-mere-love, and remained so for six
decades.

It began in 1943 when I was attending Curtis in Philadelphia, far from
my native Chicago. I used to come up to New York every few weeks to hear
concerts and cruise bars. In one of the latter, the Old Colony on 8th Street
—toward 3 on a July morning—I met Morris, and we lurched back to his
place on the top floor of where he lived until the end, at 123 West 11th. Like
most 19-year-olds I was wildly sophisticated and wildly naïve. I was drawn
to Morris's tough Bronx accent which belied his vast culture. Working by
day at the Michael Press, which he founded with his brother, and where the
young Barbra Streisand was at the switchboard, by night he read Kafka
(whom I'd never heard of) and listened to Beethoven, whose quartets I'd
only just come to know. Indeed, with all that butch swagger, he was the
most cultivated man I knew, his closest friends included the tenor William
Horne, harpsichordist Ralph Kirkpatrick, and pianist Hortense Monath
who founded the New Friends of Music.

The unique angle of Morris's love for art and artists was that, not being
an artist himself, his magnanimity bore no trace of competitive envy. His

press printed free brochures for his professional friends. He was generous with time and—perhaps more important—with money. And for me he was helpful in strictly practical ways with my problems as a young composer. He had answers. If it weren't for him, I wouldn't be me.

Lauren Flanigan and I will perform two songs of mine which somehow seem apt for Morris Golde's memory. "What If Some Little Pain," words of Spencer, was composed in 1949, and concerns Death as a welcome release from Life. "Early in the Morning," on a poem of Robert Hillyer, was composed in 1954, and is about being young, in Paris, and in love.

N.R.

### To David Del Tredici

*18 Nov. 01*

Is, dear David, the piano part of your new song at all derived from the *Siegfried Idyll*? I set the same Millay sonnet sixty years ago. Our minds overlap. (Take me over your lap.) Fond wishes to Ray.

Forever

Ned

### To Gloria Vanderbilt

*30 Nov. 2001*

Dear Gloria—

It was all so long ago. . . . And now, out of the blue, you revive it, and suggest I'm a liar. I don't have a copy of Salter's book here, but I do have a copy of the letter I sent to him on 13 June 97. Here is the second paragraph:

> Thanks for the proofs of *Recollection* (in the singular: good title). I've just read the last chapter, and your portrait of our beloved Robert [Phelps] seems special, caring, and skillful. Everything rings true—except the remarks about me. I've found out, firsthand, that the moment one publishes a memoir—or diary— readers will say what I've just said. Because there is no all-encompassing single truth, there is only a writer's truth, and even that is *fact* rather than philosophy. Etc.

If you've not read my recent journal, called *Lies*, I'll send you a copy. (There's a picture of you in it.) Its premise, among others, is that which I've more or less written to Salter, but expounded over 300 pages. . . . I don't clearly recall what Salter said in *Burning the Days*, except that he was quoting Robert Phelps who was (mis)quoting me, about you.

I don't believe in the weak phrase, "I'm sorry," since it explains nothing; nor can I apologize for what someone else says, about their *perception* of what I've said through a third person's memory. But I can say that I regret that you've been hurt by what you perceive to be my fault.

I do know that in life as in art I'm abrasive and ironic. But as I grow older, I value my friends more and more, and among them you are on the top of the list.

Letters are dangerous: they can exacerbate as much as they can explain. Still, I'll mail this anyway. And always with love.

Ned

### To Gore Vidal

*Nantucket*
*25 July 02*

Dear Gore—

*Perpetual War for Perpetual Peace* is a crucial, brave, and scary book. Raised a Quaker (philosophically, not religiously), my parents taught me that there is no alternative to peace. They would have been so happy with your book.

I've been invited by the American Academy in Rome to spend six weeks there next year, from April 15 to June 30. I've not seen Italy since 1970. I do pray that you'll be there—or at Ravello. I'll be with my niece, Mary. Will you write?

All very best to Howard.

Fondly
Ned

### To James Hamilton-Paterson

*29 July 02*

Ah James—

A year since we last communicated.

Is your health stable? Do write, however briefly, soon.

During all August I'll be incommunicado at Yaddo, trying to write a Cello Concerto for Geringas, due in seven weeks, and I've not yet begun.

Intense heat. Fatigue.

I love you—

N

(I'll be in Rome, as guest of the American Academy, for 6 weeks starting April 15, 2003. Probably my niece will accompany me. Shall we drive over to see you?)

## To the Associates of the Arts Commission
### Re. Bobby Short

*18 Nov. 2002*

My name is Ned Rorem, and I've been asked to talk about Bobby Short. We are both musicians. But he is a jazz performer and good at ad-libbing, while I am a classical composer who cannot improvise. So I'll read my speech. Since Brevity is next to Godliness, I'll stick to the four minutes allowed.

How well do you know him?, people often ask, as though there were a precise answer. "To know well" has to do with intensity, not with frequency. In the decade of our acquaintance, Bobby Short and I have spent no more than eight hours together, of which four were in the midst of a crowd. Yet he has that gift—and it's a gift, not a quality that can be bought or learned —of making you feel, when you're with him, that you're the sole person in the world who matters. The gift extends to his audience, each member of whom feels that Bobby's singing to them alone. Thus I can state that I know Bobby better than dozens of people I've seen daily all my life.

We went to different schools together. Close to the same age, we knew many of the same people in Chicago during the 30s and 40s and in Paris during the 50s and 60s. Yes, our paths often crossed, but never when we were walking on them. We didn't actually meet until 1992, at a party celebrating Bobby's fifty years of friendship with Jean Bach.

Here's a brief résumé of his career up to then. Born in the late twenties in Danville, Illinois, Bobby Short taught himself piano as a kid, and was soon referred to as "the miniature Fats Waller." Since age twelve he has exclusively practiced the same trade, at first in Chicago, eventually in New York. In 1954 he made his first recording, and met the English *diseuse,* Mabel Mercer, whose repertory, and practice of remaining seated while singing, became a mannerism of Bobby. In 1969 the two of them recorded a highly successful joint concert, and that same year Bobby began his longstanding engagement at the Café Carlyle. Short soon became the most popular performer of American and British theater songs in a café setting. Not a technically polished singer, his style is generally termed "sophisticated," and is characterized by a wide range of vocal inflection and accomplished, jazz-like piano accompaniment.

Let me praise his diction. The first rule in classical singing (and, I might add, in acting) is not feeling, nor even intelligence, but clarity of speech. The composer, after all, has supplied the meaning through the very rise & fall of his notes: just sing what's on the page, please, and the interpretation will be inherent. In Jazz, however, it being semi-improvisatory, more freedom is permitted. But compared to today's pop-singing wherein elocution, tune, harmony, beauty of voice, variety, and nuance, have vanished, Bobby Short is a paragon of cleanliness.

Let me praise his repertory. Again, compared with today's pop-singing of simplistic screams and no identifiable composer, Bobby Short almost single-handedly glorifies the lyrics and tunes of the thirties—Porter, Gershwin, Ellington, Bessie Smith, Kurt Weill—who are on a par with Monteverdi, Schubert, and Debussy.

Let me praise his pianism. He doesn't read music. Which may account for his spontaneity, despite playing the same repertory night after night. I'm reminded of André Breton, founder of surrealism in France, who, when asked why he never learned English while in America, answered: "So as not to tarnish my French."

Bobby and I represent seemingly opposite musical roles: mine all strict classical, invariable, in large forms; his all free popular, variable, in small forms. But with the passing of time, aren't we closer than we seem, especially in what we aim to express, namely, immediacy through words as those words are heightened through melody? And we both have insomnia.

In his oft-closing song Bobby Short echoes what everyone here feels, by using the iambic pentameter of Ira Gershwin, which could be the first line of a Shakespeare sonnet:

> "It's very clear our love is here to stay"

His honor tonight by the Art Commission is well deserved, for having erected a statue of Duke Ellington. Because Bobby Short himself is as much a part of New York as the Statue of Liberty.

—Ned Rorem

To Robert J. Harth,
Artistic Director, Carnegie Hall

*30 Nov. 02*

Dear Mr. Harth—

Last night at Carnegie Hall I shared a program as guest artist of Judy Collins. I had my own dressing room, supplied with roses and fruit, and other amenities. The program went beautifully and I felt wonderful—until the post-concert session on the fourth floor.

Several friends of Ms. Collins and mine began to take pictures. Two members of your staff (an Afro-American woman and a white man, both of early middle-age) interrupted us so rudely that we were quite shaken. When I explained that I didn't know the rule, they said that "the world is made of rules," and "if you can't follow the rules, you should leave." Then they proceeded to evict us, and when I said I wanted to stop by the dressing room they forbade that, on the grounds that the doors were locked. I felt I was in a fascist dictatorship; the evening which began so beautifully, finished on a grotesque, even frightening note.

Basic manners on their part would have precluded this scene, witnessed by several of my "fans." And I thought you should be made aware of this.

Sincerely,
Ned Rorem

To Angela Lansbury

*1 Feb. 03*

Heartfelt condolences, dearest Angela.
Peter was a perfect man.
Forever
Ned

At a memorial for Charles-Henri Ford

*St. Mark's Church, Second Ave. at 10th St.*

*8 Feb. 2003*

When Charles-Henri Ford vanished four months ago at the age of 97, it seemed clear that there is no right time to die; the longer friends live, the longer we feel they'll continue to live. Then whiff! another leaf falls from the family tree, and suddenly our world weighs less.

I've known both Charles-Henri and Ruth for nearly sixty years, both as

friends and colleagues. I composed the score for one of Ruth's theater portrayals, and collaborated with her brother on a musical puppet show in the
mid-1940s.

Last night I shuffled through a half-century of correspondence with
Charles-Henri, dozens and dozens of letters and cards and drawings. How
could I have forgotten our myriad projects for operas, his verbal portraits,
plans for sung filmscripts, descriptions of Pavlik's fading health, plus Q & A
lists for the revival of *Blues Magazine?* Our final professional intercourse
was his cover for my final diary called *Lies*—here—a photograph against a
painting. . . .

To Joel Fotinos,
Judy Collins's editor at J. P. Tarcher
Re. Her book *Sanity and Grace:
A Journey of Suicide, Survival, and Strength*

*26 May 03*

Dear Joel Fotinos—

You may use any or all of the following for whatever purposes you
choose.

Albert Camus claims that suicide is philosophy's primary question:
before we decide what life "means," we must decide whether life is worth
living. Judy Collins claims that there is another consideration: that of suicide survivors. They may be either the recovered victims, or the dead victim's loved ones.

In her intelligent and painful study, Judy examines every aspect of suicide. She does so comprehensively, from the vantage of one whose only son
killed himself, and of one who herself is filled with tendencies. The references beyond herself are exhaustively researched and will sound a chord in
every reader, because every reader has—to some extent—heard the self-
destructive call.

Judy's book did not change me so much as reveal me to myself.
Ned Rorem

## For his birthday: Andrew Porter

*June 2003*

Dear Andrew—

If it weren't for you I wouldn't be me. Admittedly every instant of our lives seethes with "events"—a speck of dust, a face on the subway, a distant car horn—that alter us forever. (I am not the same person who began these words a moment ago.) But some events are more altering than others.

When we met, through Robert Veyron-Lacroix fifty years ago in France, there occurred a sudden rapport which has continued till now, reconfirmed through our dozens of letters. On my side the rapport lay perhaps in equal doses of attraction, admiration, annoyance. The attraction came through narcissism: We seemed like intercontinental twins, physically and intellectually. The admiration was for your writing: except for maybe sex, your every thought was about music, and that thought was transferred to paper with necessity and clarity; indeed, except for Virgil Thomson, you were the twentieth century's chief music commentator. The annoyance stemmed from your *parti gris*. Of course, every human critic must be biased as well as generous. If Virgil, for example, favored all things French and shunned Bruckner and Brahms, you have been generous to all things contemporary while stressing certain languages which to me are repugnant. The repugnance does come from envy, though you have been professionally very nice to me. Disagreement is a crux of friendship.

So Happy Birthday, dear faraway friend. Will you continue forever to make me more of what I already am?

Ned Rorem

## To Claus von Bülow

*27 June 03*

Fond Claus—

The clipping about Marie-Laure's house was not only depressing in itself, but as an indication of increasingly dumbed-down world.

I'll never come to Europe again, so I hope you'll come over here. Because we're the only ones left.

Ever

Ned

(I'll be eighty in five months. The only good thing about that is celebratory performances. The BBC is doing something big, probably on my birthday, October 23. Could you send me anything you see? . . . Are you fine? I'm fair; insomnia and sadness mainly.)

*20 July 03*

Dear Claus—

Your reviews are expert, caring, literate, and well-informed. We'll talk more about them when next we meet. But when? I'll never come abroad again. Rome, where I was at the Academy for five weeks in May, was loud and ugly, and I had to be operated on for hemorrhoids. All my friends there are dead, as are those in Paris. Also insomnia precludes travel. I do see John Richardson occasionally.

So we must stay always in touch: we're all that's left.

Forever

Ned

*31 August 03*

Dearest Eugene—

Every day I think of you.

And yesterday too, and the day before.

Do you remember, sixty years ago this summer, with Shirley, we composed *à trios* a wonderful poem based on the alphabet:

> <u>A</u>nnie
> <u>b</u>athed
> <u>c</u>oquettishly
> <u>d</u>ousing
> <u>e</u>ach
> <u>f</u>oul
> <u>g</u>em

etc. and ending:

> <u>w</u>ildly
> <u>x</u>-creting

yellow
zlish.

Everything I learned about piano-playing is from you. I have to accompany some songs soon; but instead of practicing, I'll just do an imitation of you.

We'll remain in constant touch.

Love to Martita

Ned

To Edmund White

*Nantucket*
*15 Sept. 03*

Dearest Edmund—

The [Irma] Kolassi CD carried me back to a frame of mind I'd nearly forgotten. She was a very French singer, wasn't she, in that her voice wasn't especially lovely, but her diction and intelligence were a prime concern. Jacques Leguerny I knew a little bit (he seemed the poor man's Sauguet), and was so moved to hear again his perfect setting of the Ronsard words, "*Ma douce jouvence est passée . . .*" And the picture of [Reynaldo] Hahn: he's always seemed sexy, don't you agree? As for my little opportunistic drawing, I'm still up to the same tricks. Thanks so much for sending it all.

I liked our evening together a few weeks ago, talking about what no other two Americans anywhere would talk about: [Robert] Desnos, [Raymond] Radiguet, etc. (I'm now reading *L'Enfer* of [Henri] Barbusse.)

Bette Davis designed needlework for a cushion saying "Old Age Isn't for Sissies." That rings ever truer.

Love to you, and to Michael.

N

To James Hamilton-Paterson

*Nantucket*
*20 Sept. 03*

Fond James—

As of this writing I'm not yet eighty; that condition, which happens to others but not to oneself, will occur on October 23. I've been depressed, physically and mentally (insomnia and hypochondria) for years. But better to be depressed and admired than depressed and ignored, and the coming months will hear a lot of my music. All this in response to your letter which my Manhattan neighbor, Barbara [Grecki], read to me over the phone. But I'll be back in New York by the time you see this.

How I wish you'd be here for some of the celebrations, including the opera *Miss Julie* in Philadelphia on Nov. 7.

But why don't we settle for a meeting on, say, Nov. 13, a Thursday, chez moi at six o'clock. We'll go to dine somewhere. If this doesn't fit, tell me when, I'm pretty free.

Since last we wrote I was in Rome for six weeks, and had to have emergency surgery for hemorrhoids from which I'm still not recovered.

How interesting it will be to meet finally.

Phone when you arrive (after ten a.m.) and we'll arrange our rendezvous precisely.

Looking forward

Ned

## To Martita Istomin

10 Oct. 03

Dearest Martita—

Heartfelt condolences.

Forever,

Ned

## To Edward Albee

28 Oct. 03

Dear Edward—

Your words last night meant everything to me

and my heart is with you

now as always

Ned

## To Romulus Linney

29 October 03

Fond Romulus—

Only you could have thought of such a unique gift: Debussy playing his own music. The program notes are fairly lucid and useful: too bad the translator translates "*esquisse*" as "exquisite" rather than as "sketch." The playing I've always thought is vaguely misrepresentative of how that music should go; Debussy like Ravel was a twentieth-century composer trapped in a nineteenth-century pianist's body. . . . But hearing it again today is like eavesdropping on a long-dead friend.

Much affection—

Ned

### To Edward Albee

*2 Nov. 03*

Fond Edward—

Yesterday, in Northern Pennsylvania, I spent several hours with Dana Gioia who, as you know, is the high-powered new head of the National Endowment for the Arts. He in his high-school years was an avid fan of Bill's music. He claims that he is in a position to publish a recording of Flanagan songs, plus a booklet of Flanagan articles (reviews and letters), if you and I could pull such a thing together.

Well, I've got a lot of my own similar work to do. But I do have a great deal of Bill's published songs (though not his recordings). As for his letters, they may be in the Library of Congress. I've forgotten where his parents lived (Detroit? Rochester?).

Anyway, if you're interested, maybe we can contact Gioia.

Again, thank you for your warm words at my musical birthday. And my very very best to Jonathan.

Ned

### To American Academy of Arts & Letters
### For Lou Harrison

*13 Nov. 03*

In 1944, age twenty, I earned my living as Virgil Thomson's copyist. I labored daily at his dining room table, while he ran the world of music over the telephone in the nearby study.

One morning out of the blue there sat another person at my worktable. Tall and bigboned but somehow fragile, like Orson Welles on a tulip stem, effusive but shyish, obsessed with how music looked on the page, this was Lou Harrison. A California composer six years my senior, he had worked with Schoenberg and with Henry Cowell with whom he had founded New

Music Edition for publishing what was then deemed experimental work. Now he was uprooted for the first time, about to begin a stint as a stringer at the *Tribune* and meanwhile helping Virgil with extra copy work. More skilled than I (Lou's hand-drawn musical and prose artifacts are world famous), with a practical sense of performance broader than mine (he had formed his own percussion orchestra with John Cage in San Francisco), and with a grasp of intercultural workings that surely exceeded my grasp, Lou became Virgil's valuable colleague. Indeed, Virgil may have let me slide out of sight were it not for his devotion to my cause; nor was Lou interested in replacing me. As it was, we got along famously: Lou as a person was a total original, as a composer a total eclectic. His social style was Californian, easygoing, even Oriental, but with more than a twinge of daftness which led later to a turn in the loony bin, and a predilection for Negro males. His music style was anything that was asked for; Lou felt that one ought to be capable of all, and had earned a living from choreographers (twenty-five dollars a minute was his fee) of every persuasion, composing fandangos for José Limón, folkish diatonicisms for Jean Erdman, Webernian mood pieces for Charles Weidman. Lou taught me the whole bag of tricks of the so-called twelve-tone system in about an hour, and I applied them for about a week. Finally, however, his eclecticism was original. Lou Harrison sixty years ago was concocting raga-type ostinatos identical with those today of Glass or Reich, with the notable difference that while all three men prepare canvases that are nonpareil, only Harrison super-imposes a drawing—a melody—upon the canvas which gives it a reason for being.

Weekends we would gather at Lou's on Bleecker Street, where he lived with his black clergyman, and while swilling quart after quart of Schaefer beer, talk of his idols, Ives, Ruggles, and Varèse, artists he pitted against Copland, whom he disdained. Lou adopted me, was helpful in many ways, for he had his foot in every door. It was he (I *think* it was he) who gave me entrée to certain organizations that performed me, like the International Society for Contemporary Music. Etc.

---

There is no right time to die. All death is unexpected. The older our friends become, the more we feel they'll always be there. A child's death is really no more tragic than an old person's. As for our own death, Freud claimed it is unimaginable, "and when we try to imagine it we perceive that we really survive as spectators. . . . In the unconscious every one of us is convinced of his own immortality."

But for artists, immortality is a given. Thus Lou Harrison will continue living, not just in the minds of we brief mortals who knew him, but forever in our recordings and concert halls.

—Ned Rorem

### To Edward Albee

*19 Dec. 03*

Fond Edward—

*Counting the Ways,* which we saw last night, is filled with charm, economy, personality, and just the right length after the somber Beckett. Marian [Seldes] is flawless, fairly understated (for her) and with good diction (unlike [Brian] Murray). Maybe the music between scenes could be shorter and/or more varied. Nowhere in the program does it tell when the play was penned. Late '70s?

Merry Christmas to you, and to Jonathan, who looked very good at your party.

Always
N

### To Angela Lansbury

*5 Feb. 04*

Dearest Angela—

Thank you for alerting me to *The Blackwater Lightship,* which I watched last night. It was effective, and personally quite painful (I lost my Jim to AIDS just five years ago). All three of you women were skillful, alone and together, and the men were well cast. The peaceful shots of Ireland contrasted with the sorrowful illness. And you yourself were perfection, as always.

I'm proud that we are friends.
Ned

# Epilogue

I've just reread these letters from start to finish. Unlike those few other brave souls who may have done likewise, I've re-reread them often. Of the forty-nine recipients, many are now gone, and by the time these words see print, still more may be gone, including me. In the preface I wondered: if the forty-nine had been another forty-nine, would the result have shown another Ned? To some extent we invent our friends just as we invent ourselves. And as I move toward (what for others is) the Final Exit, perhaps I've also invented the Universe and even Death. Of course, when anyone dies—a Ptolemy, a farmer, even a firefly—their perception of the universe dies with them.

Here in Nantucket, as I write this, we are snowed in, the power is off, the sun is gone. Yesterday Susan Sontag died, which means we all can die. Today in Indonesia a tidal wave has, in a matter of hours, destroyed a civilization. Tomorrow, I hope, despite hopeless fatigue, to continue on the opera of *Our Town,* and to finish it before . . . Well, yes, I've an urge to "leave something." And though an opera is not my actual flesh, it could not prevail above ground except for me.

Three people close to me are not included here, since usually we don't send letters to those we see daily. Mary is my dear and intelligent niece without whom, since Jim died, I couldn't function in any practical way. Barbara is a neighbor in New York, a constant support and source of shared values. And there is my beloved sister, Rosemary. To these women I dedicate this collection:
Mary Marshall. Barbara Grecki. Rosemary Rorem Marshall.

Is this Epilogue a letter to myself? Should it then be signed
With bemusement? With relief? Or With Love?

*Ned*

# Index